Death
in
Salem

Death in Salem

ELEANOR KUHNS

MINOTAUR BOOKS
NEW YORK

DEATH IN SALEM. Copyright © 2015 by Eleanor Kuhns. All rights reserved. Printed in the United States of America. For information, address St. Martin's Press, 175 Fifth Avenue, New York, N.Y. 10010.

www.minotaurbooks.com

Designed by Steven Seighman

The Library of Congress Cataloging-in-Publication Data is available upon request.

ISBN 978-1-250-06702-9 (hardcover)
ISBN 978-1-4668-7494-7 (e-book)

Minotaur books may be purchased for educational, business, or promotional use. For information on bulk purchases, please contact the Macmillan Corporate and Premium Sales Department at 1-800-221-7945, extension 5442, or write to special markets@macmillan.com.

First Edition: June 2015

10 9 8 7 6 5 4 3 2 1

*Dedicated to Papa Wolven, who first inspired
my interest in sailing and ships.*

Acknowledgments

I am grateful to my friends Will Delman and Jess Smith, Salem residents, who gave me several leads for researching Salem's past.

Chapter One

Rees had planned to drive straight down to Salem's harbor to look for a shop. Although he wove enough to keep his wife and children clothed and some extra besides to sell, he could not duplicate the colors or the patterns imported from India by this great sailing center. And he certainly could not weave muslin so fine it was almost transparent or beautiful Chinese silks; he especially wanted to purchase a quantity of the latter for his wife. But on the way to the harbor he was stopped by a funeral procession heading northeast on Essex Street. Rees pulled up next to a farmer with a wagon full of hay and jumped down from his seat. Bessie, his fourth mare of the same name, was more skittish than the earlier three horses and was already beginning to dance and shy. Rees clutched her bridle and crooned wordlessly to settle her.

"You a weaver?" The hay farmer standing next to Rees threw a glance at the canvas-covered loom in the wagon bed. Rees nodded.

"Not much call for weavers in Salem."

"I know. I came south from the District of Maine; most of the farmwives in Maine and northwest of here will never manage to travel into Salem." Rees had left his family to embark on this weaving trip two weeks ago. They needed the money, that was true—but if he were honest, Rees would admit he had also needed to escape the chaos of his suddenly enlarged brood.

A frantic plea for help from their old friend Mouse this past winter had sent Rees and Lydia rushing to New York. Mouse had been accused of a murder, and after solving it, Rees and his wife had adopted the murder victim's five young orphans. Neither Rees nor his wife had been able to abandon them to the cruel indifference of the town selectmen in Dover Springs, where they'd lived. These children had brought happiness into Rees's life but also constant noise and upset. And Rees's fifteen-year-old son, David, resented the addition of the new children to the family so much he had moved to the weaver's cottage and spoke to his father only when absolutely necessary.

Then there was Caroline. Rees groaned at the thought. Caroline's demands had become relentless. She blamed him for striking her husband, a blow that left Sam touched in the head and unable to work. Now she thought her brother should support her family. Although Rees *did* feel responsible and he was willing to assist her, he would not allow her to move in with him and his family. Not again, not after the terrible way she'd treated David the last time she'd been charged with caring for him.

Rees pushed away that unwelcome guilt. "I thought I would stop and purchase some imported cloth for my family. Calicoes and such."

"Here comes the Boothe family," said the farmer.

Rees inspected the matched set of four black horses pulling the carriage slowly down the street. Black plumes and rosettes decorated the bridles and ebony bunting was swagged around the vehicle's windows and door. Because of the heat this bright June day, the shade was not drawn, and Rees had a clear view of a man sitting with his head bowed and a sobbing girl in the seat across from him.

"Jacob Boothe and his daughter, Margaret. And the rest of the family beside them," murmured the farmer.

"They seem to be important."

"Indeed, yes," the farmer replied. "Jacob Boothe is one of our most successful merchants. He is a good man, fair to all. It's his wife, Anstiss, who died. Poor lady, barely forty, or so I'm told. She leaves four children. And Jacob is prostrate. He doesn't deserve this. But God does as He wills . . ." The farmer turned his gaze upon Rees. "You know, if you're in town anyway, you should attend the averil. It'll be at the Boothe home as soon as the poor lady is put to rest at Burying Point. Plenty of good food and drink." Rees shook his head; he didn't want to stop in Salem longer than he had to.

"You could follow me over," the farmer said in a persuasive voice.

Rees prepared to refuse the invitation, but before he could push out the words, he thought he saw someone he knew: the undertaker swinging his silver baton as he strode before the wagon with the coffin—surely that tall, long-limbed man with the jerky movements was Rees's old friend Twig. "Twig," Rees shouted. "Twig!" During the War for Independence, Twig, more formally known as Stephen Eaton, had saved Rees's life by tackling a Redcoat just as he was about to run Rees through with a bayonet. Twig and Rees had remained comrades throughout the War. Twig's head swiveled as he searched the crowd. When he spotted Rees, he used his baton to wave and gesture forward. Then he moved past. "Thank you," Rees said, turning to the farmer. "I will be happy to follow you."

The farmer nodded and pointed to the carriage following the coffin. "That's the Coville family; Anstiss's mother and brothers. Big whaling family." Although the Covilles rode in a carriage, it was not as big as the Boothe's and the horses that drew it were a mismatched lot: a white mare next to an ordinary chestnut and two brown geldings. Mrs. Coville's face was buried in a handkerchief and all Rees could see of her was her black silk bonnet. Even from the side of the road, he could hear the guttural cries of the young man sitting across from her.

"Anstiss's brother Dickie," said the farmer. "By all accounts, he was much attached to his sister."

"What a shame," Rees said. Even now, as an adult, he could remember how devastated the death of his infant brother had left him and his mother.

"Yes. Anstiss was a great beauty in her day. But she's been ill for a long time."

The last of the procession rumbled past, and all the onlookers rushed to their own conveyances. Rees scrambled up on his wagon seat and fell into the line of traffic, right behind the farmer, as he drove further into Salem town and toward the averil at the Boothe home.

"You stole her from us!" The scream broke into Rees's conversation and he turned to look. A young man with the lanky unfinished look of someone in his mid-teens staggered across the floor; it was Dickie Coville. "You took Anstiss away from us and now she's dead," the boy shouted. The buzz of conversation faded as everyone turned to stare. "You!" His wavering forefinger pointed at Margaret Boothe, standing with her father. "It's your fault she's dead."

"Now, Dickie," Mr. Boothe said as he stepped toward the weeping boy. "All of us grieve for Anstiss." Moisture glittered in his eyes but he willed it away. "I miss her so much."

Rees admired the man's control in the hour after his wife's funeral. He knew how he would feel if Lydia died. Just the thought of it left a gaping emptiness in his belly and brought moisture to his eyes. He quickly wiped away his tears. Twig turned and threw his old comrade a questioning glance.

Before Jacob Boothe reached Dickie, two men, Dickie's brothers by the resemblance between them all, rushed forward to the boy. The taller and older of the two extended his hand to Jacob Boothe.

"I am glad to see you here, Adam," Jacob said, grasping the proffered hand. "And Edward." He turned to the other man, who had grabbed Dickie and was dragging him to the inside door.

"Please forgive Dickie," Adam Coville said. "He misses Anstiss terribly, and I fear he has already partaken of your very fine Madeira."

"Of course I forgive him," Jacob said. "We all loved Anstiss."

"Yes." Adam's face contorted as though he were fighting his emotion. He mastered himself and said in a voice that trembled only slightly, "Dickie has always been high-strung and prone to nervous fits. You know that." As Adam spoke, Edward thrust Dickie into his mother's arms. Under her black bonnet, her face was swollen and flushed with weeping.

Boothe pumped Adam's hand and with his other hand clapped his brother-in-law upon the shoulder. "It is an emotional day for all of us." Coville flinched.

"Yes, yes it is," he said in a hoarse voice. He dropped Boothe's hand abruptly. "We'll take Dickie home now. You understand. When he gets at the drink . . ." His voice trailed off.

"Of course. I hope we meet again under happier circumstances." Mr. Boothe reached out as though to embrace his brother-in-law again, but Adam shied away. With a bow, he hastened across the floor to rejoin his family in the inside hall. They disappeared toward the back. After a few seconds, people returned their attention to their companions or, especially in the case of the poorer sort, to the excellent repast set out for them. Boothe had not stinted upon either food or drink. Twig helped himself to more rum. Now that the excitement—and the possibility of a fight—was over, he'd lost interest in anything but the flagon in his hand and maybe a brief conversation with an old friend. But Rees, seeing tension between Mr. Boothe and his daughter, did not remove his eyes from them.

"Peggy," Mr. Coville said, reaching out for her as though he were pleading. She glared at him, tears of grief pooling in eyes still red and swollen from weeping. "No," she said in a low, furious voice as anger twisted her features. "No." She turned away from him, a shudder shivering through her, and fled into the inner hall and up the broad central stair.

Jacob Boothe's hand dropped and his head sank to his chest. Inhaling a breath so deep that Rees could hear it even from several yards' distance, Boothe pasted a smile upon his face, raised his head again, and assumed the mantle of a host. A wave of pity for the man swept over Rees.

Mr. Boothe looked around the room and then, perhaps finding something appealing in Rees's expression, approached.

He shook hands with Twig and said to Rees, "Having enough to eat and drink, I hope?" Close up, he looked every bit of his fifty years. His sandy hair was shot with gray and pouches of loose flesh hung under his eyes. But the creases fanning out from the corners of his eyes were laugh lines, and Rees thought in happier times the merchant had enjoyed his life. "I haven't seen you before."

Rees was astonished that Boothe, even in the midst of his grief, was able to express interest in a stranger. "Yes," Rees said, "I—um—came to buy some imported cloth, you know, some of that fine Indian cotton and maybe silk, and then I saw Twig . . ." Realizing he was stammering, Rees shut his mouth.

"Well, you won't find better than Mrs. Baldwin's Emporium, corner of Essex and Walnut streets," Mr. Boothe said, clapping Rees upon the shoulder as though they were old friends. "She's a lovely lady, a widow, you know, and her prices are fair. Tell her I sent you. She'll treat you well."

He moved on, speaking as easily to the poorest sailor as to the most affluent butcher. "He seems a fine gentleman," Rees said.

"He is," Twig agreed in a heartfelt tone. "He is well regarded by everyone." He was still as tall and angular as Rees remembered from their first meeting twenty years ago, and although a few white strands glittered in his hair he looked much the same. "So, what brings you to Salem, Will?"

"Weaving trip," Rees said. "I was north and west of here." He purposely kept his response short, reluctant to share the whole truth. Since he had injured his brother-in-law Sam, Rees had been the butt of jokes, insinuations, and outright accusations in his hometown of Dugard, Maine. Weaving commissions had dropped off, so cash was scarce. And since many men were now fearful of facing Rees directly, it was David who bore the brunt of the gossip. He often returned from town with bowed shoulders and a white line around his mouth. Rees sighed. He'd hoped all of that would die down with the arrival of good weather and farming chores, but it hadn't. If anything, it had gotten worse. So Rees had been glad to leave town for a while on this weaving trip, and earn some extra income while he was at it.

"We have no need of weavers. Ships dock here with cotton from Bombay and silk from Cathay." Twig's comment broke into Rees's thoughts.

"I thought I would purchase something for my wife."

"Ah. And you have a son, I believe?"

"Yes. David." David, who was furious with his father, especially since Rees and Lydia had returned home with several adopted children. Since David had moved out to the weaver's cottage, Rees only saw him when they were both engaged in doing chores. Their relationship was as bad as it had ever been. Rees brushed away the despair that swept over him and continued speaking. "He's the oldest. Three other boys, two girls, and baby on the way. You?"

"Not married," Twig said, but his expression was so furtive Rees wondered what secret Twig was hiding.

"But what?" Rees asked. Twig leaned in and whispered.

"I will be soon." And then, as though fearing he had said too much, Twig turned and started away. Rees grasped his sleeve.

"Wait." Now he remembered how Twig was. The manners that were pounded into most people during childhood had passed him by. "You can't leave it like that."

"Secret," he said, and folded his lips closed, his gloved hand polishing the silver ball at the end of his undertaker's baton. Since he looked ready to scurry away, Rees cast around for another topic of conversation.

"And what exactly did Mrs. Boothe die of?"

"Oh, natural causes. She's been ill for as long as I've been in Salem and that's fifteen years. Jacob Boothe was a catch for Anstiss; he was already successful and pulling in wealth with both hands. The Covilles aren't poor, you understand. But Mr. Boothe seems intent on giving King Derby and merchants like him a run for their money." He jerked his head like a startled rabbit. "They're probably in the dining room right now."

"I see." Of course, Jacob Boothe had set up a separate room for close friends and family. But he was not ignoring the poorer sort. Once again Boothe's generosity impressed Rees. "Do you enjoy being an undertaker, Twig?"

"Indeed, I do. It pays well. People keep dying. I don't mind the dead. Quiet. No trouble at all. I've got to go." He turned and hurried away, rapidly cutting through the door to the inside hall and disappearing around a corner.

Well, that was Twig. Never doing what was expected. As a soldier he'd been more likely to fling himself face down on the ground at the first sound of gunshots than to return fire. But

sometimes he would hurl himself at the enemy with reckless brav-
ery, as he had when he'd saved Rees's life.

Rees eyed the tradesmen and the poor folk around him. He
did not quite dare pursue Twig into the second room where those
of Boothe's social class congregated, and anyway, perhaps Twig's
startling departure was for the best. It was time to leave.

He'd planned to quit Salem soon after noon and be well away by
nightfall. But when he descended the front steps into the brilliant
June sun he saw that it was already several hours past noon. And he
still hadn't bought anything for Lydia and the children. Rees jin-
gled the coins in his pocket. He was already so late he saw no point
in hurrying now. Grabbing a sailor who was climbing the steps—
people continued to enter the Boothe home for the averil—Rees
solicited directions to Mrs. Baldwin's Emporium. Then he collected
his horse and wagon from the stable yard behind the Boothe's
house and drove into the street. From the corner of his eye he saw
two more sailors, one of them black, disappear into the house.

Chapter Two

With the excitement of the funeral and following averil, the shop—in fact, most of the shops along the road—was empty of customers. Rees was able to browse at his leisure, under the eye of Mrs. Baldwin, of course, who busied herself straightening merchandise. A short woman and plump, she wore her gray hair scraped back into a bun. A white wave sprang from her forehead, struggling to curl in defiance of her efforts to discipline it. Rees thought she was no older than forty, despite the gray hair and the lines furrowing her forehead. And she did not intrude as he examined all the different fabrics, dizzying in their colors and patterns.

A variety of calicoes beckoned, the cloth inexpensive enough for several yards of two or three patterns. He suspected most had been printed in England. In an effort to protect their own industry, the wool merchants of almost one hundred years ago had forced through a number of laws forbidding the importation of printed calico from India into either England or the colonies. Rees wasn't sure the industry in India had recovered, even though America was now a separate country and could import what they chose—although they had to outrun the British ships to do it. The British had not accepted their former colonies as a separate country yet. The trade to India and Cathay by American captains was very recent—not even fifteen years old.

Rees fingered a number of the calicoes he found most appealing and decided to purchase several bolts more than he needed for his family. The women on many of the far-flung farms in the northeast where he sold his own cloth would have little opportunity to see, let alone buy, such fabrics, and he could make a good profit.

Then he turned his attention to the expensive cottons and silks. Rees fingered the sheer lawn enviously, wondering about the delicate threads. How many dents, the slots per inch, would a reed require? He did not think his large hands could manage such tiny filaments. The silk was even finer and more delicate, the threads gossamer. He could barely conceive of threading a loom with such thin strands.

The embroidered scarlet with its silken luster drew his eye, but he knew better than to purchase that bright color. Although Lydia had left the Shakers a few years previously, and had surrendered her square linen cap upon her marriage, she still adhered to simplicity of dress. Perhaps a blue? Mrs. Baldwin appeared at Rees's elbow. When he asked the price, her answer sent Rees's eyebrows shooting to his hairline. Silk was too dear for his purse; he couldn't afford enough yards for a gown. Perhaps she could make a shawl? Or rework one of her older dresses with the new silk? After several moments of cogitation, he selected a pale blue embroidered with flowers. Even the few yards cost a significant portion of the coins in his purse, but he would not see Lydia poorly dressed in front of Dugard society.

Rees wondered how a widow like Mrs. Baldwin had obtained the necessary brass to buy and outfit such a shop.

"Are you here for Mrs. Boothe's funeral?" Mrs. Baldwin asked as she figured the tally.

"I did not come to Salem specifically for it," Rees said, "but I did attend the averil. Mr. Boothe has a fine home."

"He does indeed. Earned by his own sweat, too. He began on one of the merchant ships as a cabin boy, and look where he is now. Such a tragedy about his wife . . . he is a good man."

"He referred me to you," Rees said. "Do you know him?"

Mrs. Baldwin nodded her head. "I've met him. He is active in a small group of captains and supercargoes that extend help to widows and orphans of seamen. When my Ezra died . . . well, I didn't know how I would support myself and my son. I didn't want charity," she said, lifting her chin with defiant pride. "But he made sure the committee lent me the money to start the shop. Oh, that first year was hard, but I paid back every farthing. A good man is Jacob Boothe, and one who deserves only the best."

Rees carried his purchases to the wagon and stowed them under the lashings that held the loom down. He'd lingered in Mrs. Baldwin's shop longer than he expected and now afternoon was bleeding into early evening. The salty tang in the air seemed more intense than ever. Rees examined the sky in concern. He wouldn't make it very far before dark and would have to spend the night by the road. Not that he'd mind, he'd done it many times before, but he expected he would be close to the city this time. Salem was only slightly smaller than Boston and he didn't relish trying to sleep next to the clatter of Salem's busy roads. After a moment's thought, he returned to the shop to ask Mrs. Baldwin if she knew where he could rent a room. Her initial surprise transformed into a careful inspection.

"Well, since Mr. Boothe sent you to me, I daresay you will be all right. I have a room to rent. Upstairs. Would you care to see it?"

"I would," Rees said. She motioned him to the back of the shop and through a door into a hall. These were her living quarters. Rees saw her kitchen and main room through one opening and a small garden and stable yard through the other. Stairs led to the upper levels. She preceded him up to the second floor.

Two doors, now closed, led off the hall to rooms above the shop, one bedchamber for Mrs. Baldwin, the other for her son. She directed Rees to a room he thought was situated over the kitchen and at the back of the house. Rees preferred that to a room at the front of the house, where iron-shod horses and wheels would fill the air with noise. Although small, the room was very clean. And Mrs. Baldwin offered him the use of the barn at back for Bessie and his wagon. Rees brought up his canvas valise and settled in for the night. From the windows that overlooked the yard, if he turned his head to the right, he could see the masts in the harbor. Mrs. Baldwin's Emporium could not be more than a street or two west of the docks.

About six, her son came home, and soon after the sounds of quarreling penetrated Rees's room.

"I found a berth on a whaling ship. And it's time for me to leave home," the boy said, his voice rising.

The sound of Mrs. Baldwin weeping was audible. "Please, Billy. I already lost your father to the sea. Please, stay home."

"No." Billy refused in an angry and resentful tone that was so like David, Rees almost looked around for his son.

David had never completely forgiven Rees for abandoning him to his Aunt Caroline and Uncle Sam. After Rees's first wife—David's mother—had died, Rees had embarked on a series of weaving trips to earn the money necessary to support them, and had entrusted David into Caroline and Sam's care. But they had treated David more like a servant than a son, and David still hadn't forgiven his father for not taking him along. Although their relationship had improved when Rees and David had moved back to the farm together, the adoption of the orphans had now set it back once again. David's feelings of abandonment had resurfaced. Rees had tried to explain several times that the adoption did not mean he loved David any less but the boy always responded in such a nasty and aggrieved voice that Rees had wanted to strike him. Fortunately, David's anger centered upon his father; he maintained a cool politeness with Lydia and ignored the children.

And Caroline, well, she believed she should own the family farm. Like Rees, she'd grown up there, and once he'd allowed her and her family to move in, Caroline thought it should be hers. Especially after Rees's fight with Sam that had led to the injury that now prevented Sam from finding work. And with at least half the people in Dugard blaming Rees for it . . . He sighed. If it weren't for Lydia and the children waiting for him at home, he would be tempted to keep traveling south. He missed them all—he even remembered the constant noise with some nostalgia.

A slamming door marked the end of the argument between Mrs. Baldwin and her son, and when Rees looked out his window he saw the youth storming to the stables. He disappeared into the shadows within. Rees would wager that most of the mothers in Salem experienced the loss of both husbands and sons to their watery mistress. He had never felt any desire to set sail or even work on the small vessels that plied the coast of Maine. A traveler he might be, but he preferred his travels on dry land.

And what had the Baldwin family's final decision been? Would the boy go or stay home? Well, it wasn't Rees's problem to solve. Yawning, he took off his shoes and washed his face in the basin provided. Best go to bed. Early tomorrow he would start for home and his family. He could hardly wait to see them.

Chapter Three

He was awake before dawn. After breakfasting at the nearest tavern, Rees collected his horse and wagon from the stable and set off for home. Rapidly leaving the seaport behind him, he struck northwest. Other wagons, as well as horses and buggies, also traveled this road, although most of the traffic went east, toward the ocean. Farm wagons laden with rolled hay cocks, straw, and harvested produce trundled by, all filled up although the farms were kept small and struggling by the stony soil. Rees wondered how the farmers managed to wrest anything from this poor land. No wonder they'd also turned their hands to fishing. Rees would have to tell David about this hard farming—if his son would ever speak to him again.

By midmorning Rees was well away from the coast and angling north. Within a few days, he would cross the border into the District of Maine, and a day or so after that, if nothing unusual happened, he could expect to arrive home.

Intent upon his thoughts, he heard but did not consciously notice the hoofbeats thudding up the road behind him until he heard the shouting. "Rees. Will Rees. Stop." Rees glanced over his shoulder and saw the horseman, his face covered by a scarf, galloping toward him. Swerving to the road's shoulder, Rees pulled Bessie to a stop and turned around.

The rider loosened the cloth tied about his face, revealing himself as Twig. "I've been riding after you for hours," he gasped. Rees stared at the other man. Both he and his mount were covered with dust and sweat.

"What happened?" he asked.

Twig stared, his face a mask of agony. "Mr. Boothe has been murdered."

"Mr. Boothe? Mr. Jacob Boothe?"

"Yes."

"Oh, no," Rees said involuntarily. Despite Boothe's recent bereavement and the obvious quarrel with his daughter, he had made time to be kind to a stranger.

"Who would want to murder such a good man?" Rees asked. Twig's expression went through a variety of contortions.

Rees stared at his friend in dawning horror. "Surely no one believes you . . ." But wouldn't Twig be in jail if he were a suspect?

"No, not me. My . . . my woman. She's a servant in the Boothe household. She attended Mrs. Boothe, oh, for the last nineteen or so years. The deputy sheriff arrested my Xenobia when Mr. Boothe's body was discovered."

Rees said nothing. Like the deputy, he would wonder about Mrs. Boothe's servant also; no one could hate a person quite as much as someone who had to see that person every day. And Rees remembered Peggy Boothe's reaction to her father at the averil—perhaps that did suggest some form of ill treatment. But asking Twig if he was sure his lover had not murdered Mr. Boothe, especially in light of his extreme distress, seemed unnecessarily cruel. "How was Mr. Boothe killed? Was he shot?"

"I don't know. I don't know anything." Twig's voice rose. "Xenobia got word to me that she was in jail . . ." He broke down into the rough, unrestrained sobs of a child. "I remembered you found a murderer in the War," he gulped. "And I'll pay you. I have some money put by. Help me. Please."

If Twig had reminded Rees he owed his old companion his life, Rees might have said yes, but he would have resented it. He was keenly aware, however, that he *did* owe Twig his life, and the fact that the other man did not attempt to call in the marker made Rees feel even more beholden. And then there was Jacob Boothe, a kind man who had not deserved to die so soon.

"Don't worry," Rees said, knowing he sounded silly; Twig couldn't help but worry."Of course I'll help you. We'll sort it out. The deputy may already realize he's made a mistake. Why, he might have released her by now."

Rees was not certain of anything of the kind; the deputy might be one of those who did not worry about the truth and chose the easiest solution. But Twig's sobs began to lessen.

"Let's see what the situation is," Rees said, urging Bessie into motion and guiding her in an arc across the road. "I'll follow you back to Salem."

"Hurry, hurry," Twig shouted. "God knows what's happening to Xenobia right now."

"Nothing, yet," Rees said, glancing at Twig's mare. She was tired and blowing hard. "Walk a ways, give your mount a rest."

"They might be preparing to hang her," Twig cried in alarm. "Can't your nag travel any faster?"

"Meet me at Mrs. Baldwin's Emporium in two hours," Rees said. The words were barely out of his mouth before Twig whipped his horse into motion and disappeared east in a gale of dust. Sighing, Rees snapped his whip over Bessie's flanks. She broke into a canter back toward Salem.

———

By the time Rees reached Mrs. Baldwin's store, closer to three hours later than two, Twig's feet had already worn a discernible path through the dust. "Come on, come on, come on," he cried as soon as he saw Rees approaching. A bright blue cloth square was now tied about his neck. Rees looked at it curiously; he had seen other men wearing something similar at yesterday's averil and was puzzled by the strange fashion. "She's in jail. We must hurry," Twig said insistently.

Rees held up a hand. "If she's in jail now, a few more moments will make little difference. Allow me to speak with Mrs. Baldwin and determine if her extra room is still available. And if I can put Bessie and my wagon in her stable." Twig grabbed Rees's arm in response. Rees shook him off. "Please, Twig," he said in a stern voice. Twig backed away.

Rees tied up Bessie and told Twig to watch his wagon while he stepped inside the store. Mrs. Baldwin's eyes widened when she saw Rees, and she came forward with a smile. Yes, Rees's room was still available. Yes, he was free to put his horse and wagon in the stable. He settled Bessie in the stall with the wagon beside it, but hesitated before taking his loom and recent purchases to his room. He hoped he'd be able to leave soon, maybe even tomorrow. Not only was he eager to see Lydia again but he was beginning to worry about her. How was she managing with those children? He hoped David was keeping up with the farm; that heavy work would be too much for his pregnant wife. After several moments of indecision, Rees finally took everything to his room. Then he rejoined Twig outside and they set a rapid pace through the streets to the jail.

The jail was several blocks south of the docks, so distant that it took Rees and Twig almost twenty minutes to reach it. Constructed of stones pulled from the rocky soil, the cell was large enough for several prisoners to be crammed in together. Rees wondered if this was the jail that had housed the accused witches one hundred years ago. A young woman, quite tall and garbed in a black cloak, stood outside with her face pressed to the bars. She glanced at them, said something reassuring to the prisoner inside, and hastened away. Rees had a confused impression of an angular face and fair hair under a straw bonnet. She looked familiar.

"That's Peggy Boothe," Twig said in surprise. Now Rees knew where he'd seen the young woman before: at the averil after her mother's funeral. She was the girl who'd been so angry with her father. "What is she doing here?" He pushed Rees up to the barred door. "Obie," he cried through the bars. "I've brought help as I promised." Rees wondered how much time Twig had spent at the jail since this woman's incarceration.

The stink of vomit and urine, the odor of prisons everywhere, eddied into the lane. Rees stepped back a pace and eyed the woman on the other side. She was small and slender, a black woman, so-called although her skin was no darker than a warm brown. She was plainly dressed in black calico and had wound a black shawl, recently dyed by its streaked appearance, about her shoulders. Rees directed a penetrating stare at his friend. Marrying a servant was of no great importance, but marrying a black slave was quite another issue. Was it even legal in Massachusetts? Maine had laws prohibiting such a marriage. No wonder Twig wanted this connection kept private.

She examined Rees, asking in a lilting voice, "What can he do? Miss Peggy has promised to speak to Deputy Sheriff Swett."

"You know I have no confidence in Swett," Twig interrupted her. "If only Sheriff Ropes had not passed away. Now, he would sort this." Glancing at Rees, Twig explained, "Mr. Swett is an appointee. The deputy sheriff expected to succeed Mr. Ropes is currently away with the militia." Turning back to Xenobia, Twig continued. "Rees has had experience and I promise you he'll find

Mr. Boothe's killer. And free you from this prison." Xenobia shot another look at Rees, frowning in doubt.

"If you are innocent of murder," Rees said. He already entertained some doubts as to whether a small woman could overpower a gentleman as tall and strong as Jacob Boothe.

"Of course I didn't kill him. What would I be doing in the tunnels?"

"Tunnels?" Rees asked.

"Besides, he was good to me, Mr. Boothe was," Zenobia continued without pausing. "He was a good man."

Rees sighed. "Yes. I met him only once but he seemed an honest and affable gentleman. His death is regrettable."

"It is tragic," Xenobia said, the soft lilt of her speech not quite masking her tart reply. "Who would want to kill him? Everyone liked him."

Rees did not make the obvious retort; someone had clearly hated Mr. Boothe enough to murder him. "How was he killed?"

"I don't know, no one told me." She paused, hesitated briefly, and added, "But he's laid out at the house. Maybe Miss Peggy knows."

"I'll speak with her," Rees promised. He moved away, offering Twig some privacy as he murmured loving pledges to the jail's inmate.

Finally, reluctantly, Twig separated himself and joined Rees. "Can you help her?"

"Perhaps. I need to see the body first." He looked at his friend. "And speak to Miss Boothe. Miss Peggy may be able to use her family's influence to achieve Xenobia's release. If she believes Xenobia is innocent."

"She does. I'm certain of it." Twig, his mouth trembling, turned to Rees. "We must hurry." He started away, lengthening his stride until Rees, even with his long legs, had to hurry to keep up.

They soon reached the Boothe family's fine mansion. At least three stories high and painted white, the house was notable for the four pillars at the entrance. Several buggies and a wagon were drawn up outside. Rees and Twig climbed the front stairs and entered the house; there was so much commotion that no one stood at the door to stop them. They passed through the front foyer and the beautifully carved wooden doors to the interior hall. Rees, who had not been this far inside the house before, looked around curiously. A fine rug in shades of blue and red ran the length of the hall, and various exotic objects—a porcelain Chinese bowl, stone and wooden carvings of strange creatures, and a chair upholstered in bright blue brocade—revealed the completion of successful voyages to the Orient.

When a man, who carried himself with the consequence of an upper servant, approached them, Twig promptly asked for Miss Margaret Boothe. The servant hesitated, clearly in a quandary. Leaving Twig to resolve that, Rees followed the dirty trail on the floor to a room at the back, just before the grand staircase rose to the second floor. The desk identified it as the housekeeper's office, although the small room also held a large table, now bearing Mr. Boothe's body, and a number of chairs pushed to the paneled walls.

Only one man attended the canvas-shrouded corpse. He was dressed in breeches and a black linen jacket; the doctor probably, Rees thought. The gentleman turned and said, "You shouldn't be in here." Doctor certainly, from his educated diction.

"This isn't idle curiosity," Rees said as he approached the body. "I have been retained by Miss Boothe to look into her father's murder." At least he hoped that was the case—otherwise he was barging into a place where he had no business. "How was Mr. Boothe murdered?"

The doctor hesitated and then said, "He was stabbed." Before he could say anything further, Rees flipped back the canvas. Jacob Boothe's bloodless face stared up at the ceiling. Rees felt a spasm of sorrow. Violent death was never acceptable but Rees felt worse knowing that Jacob Boothe had been an agreeable gentleman. Someone had closed his eyes; Rees was thankful for that. He hated seeing the empty, staring gaze of the dead. Pushing away his emotion, Rees carefully re-covered Boothe's gray face. "It's not pretty," the doctor began. He stopped talking when Rees bent over the body to examine the wound himself. The pungent metallic odor of drying blood overlay but did not disguise the hint of decay. Corruption would occur rapidly in this June heat.

Boothe's coat had been unbuttoned and opened, revealing a neat gray waistcoat and a crisp white shirt underneath. But the left side of his chest was so sodden with blood Rees could see nothing of the injury. Taking his own pocketknife, he rapidly cut through the wet waistcoat and linen shirt beneath.

"Now, see here," the doctor remonstrated. Rees ignored him as he bent over the wound. The blade that had made it must have been several inches wide. Although the weapon had not struck the heart, the sharp point had gone deep. Rees wondered how deep.

"Help me turn him over," he said to the doctor, trying to flip the well-nourished body. The doctor hesitated but curiosity got the better of him and he joined Rees in nudging the body over. A gold guinea, two shillings and a large key fell out of Boothe's pockets onto the table and into the blood that had pooled underneath the wound. The back of the linen jacket was saturated. "The blade went all the way through," Rees murmured in astonishment. "Hold him, please." While the doctor steadied the body, Rees used his knife again to slit first the jacket, and then the waistcoat and shirt, up the back. Both men regarded the exit wound, a long bloody gash fringed with flesh, in silence.

"Whatever the weapon was," Rees muttered, "it was wicked

sharp. Not a knife either. More of a sword?" His voice rose as though asking a question.

"He bled to death," the doctor said, his voice shaking. "Dear God. And it wouldn't have taken long."

"But what was he stabbed with?" Rees asked. "Saber? Sword? Not an ordinary knife, surely."

"No. The cut is too extensive. I'm not sure," the doctor muttered, leaning forward to peer at the wound. "The blade was both long and sharp. Squarish. And whoever wielded the weapon must have been strong. Piercing a human body in this manner would not be easy."

"What the Hell are you doing in here?" a strange voice demanded.

Chapter Four

Rees jumped and spun around. Two young men stood just inside the door. The eldest, in his mid-twenties by the look of him, and with a close enough resemblance to the man on the table to identify him as a relative, stepped inside. His hair was not quite as dark as his father's, and he shared Peggy's long-limbed build and angular features. His face was dusky with anger.

"I'm sorry, William," the doctor began.

The younger man, a shorter, fairer version of his brother, paused in the hall. He looked at his father and his face went white. "I'm going to be sick," he announced, gagging.

"Get Mattie out of here," William shouted over his shoulder. Two servants grasped the young man under his armpits and hauled him away.

"I'm Will Rees," Rees said as he and the doctor carefully lowered the body to the table beneath. "Xenobia asked me to speak to your sister, Margaret."

"Did she now?" William's voice trembled.

"Be calm, William." The young woman Rees had seen at the jail strode rapidly into the room, accompanied by Twig. She wore a ruffled black gown that, although obviously mourning weeds, still managed to appear feminine. It was totally unsuited to her and she kept plucking at the ruffles as though she wanted to rip them away. "That idiot Swett arrested Xenobia. Mr. Eaton assures me Mr. Rees can help."

"But Peggy, this stranger." The elder brother gestured to Rees in disdain. "How can he possibly help?"

"No woman, and few men, would have the strength to cause this wound. Or the skill," Rees said with certainty. "I venture to say the good doctor will agree with me; Xenobia could not have done this." The doctor nodded.

"That is so. Xenobia, who I have had occasion to meet several times, is a small woman."

For the first time Peggy noticed her father lying upon the table. Her eyes widened and filled with tears. The doctor hastily re-covered the body with the canvas as William, shooting Rees a glare, put his arm around his sister and made as if to urge her from the room. Peggy angrily shrugged off her brother's arm.

"Don't baby me, William. I can manage. We must see that Xenobia is freed from jail without delay."

"Perhaps we should continue this conversation elsewhere," William said, turning toward the door, but not before Rees saw William's eyes glitter with moisture. He took out a white handkerchief and wiped his eyes. Straightening his shoulders, he motioned everyone to the hall outside.

"Very well. In the morning room," Peggy said, dashing away her tears with an impatient hand. William nodded and frowned pointedly at Rees and the doctor.

Rees looked at his bloody hands in dismay and made some attempt to scrub them clean upon the canvas. The doctor, whose hands were untouched by blood, gestured to a basin of water and a cloth that had been set aside for his use. Rees quickly availed himself of the water, scouring his hands until the water turned reddish-brown.

He then followed the doctor and the Boothes out of the small housekeeper's office and into another room across the hall. A large fireplace dominated the opposite wall and over the mantel hung a portrait of a young woman with fair hair. Although the artist had painted her in a stiff pose against a red drape, he'd possessed enough skill to catch the roguish glint in her eyes. Her lips were curved in a sweet smile.

"My mother," Peggy said unnecessarily, her voice beginning to tremble. Rees nodded and looked around. Decorated almost exclusively with items brought from the East, this chamber boasted walls hung in embroidered silk, a black lacquer table, and several beautiful porcelain bowls. There was even a strange blue statue with four arms. Rees stared at it for several seconds before turning his gaze to the spindly furniture. Imported from England but still in the Eastern style, it did not seem sturdy enough to hold Rees's weight. At more than six feet, he towered over everyone else in the room save Twig, who Rees outweighed by at least fifty pounds. As the aptly named Twig sat down, Rees propped himself up against the wall. William turned a frown upon the upstart but Twig did not notice. Rees marked William's expression; here was a young man very conscious of his own importance.

Miss Peggy dropped onto a bench as though her legs had collapsed beneath her, but the face she turned to her brother was fierce with purpose. "I could not believe Xenobia guilty of Father's murder, William, and now we know that she was not. You must speak to the deputy sheriff without delay so she can come home."

"Home?" he asked, lifting an eyebrow at her. "She was responsible for caring for Mother. With Mother's death, Xenobia has no further function here."

Peggy's mouth tightened with annoyance. "She can look after me then," she said. "I won't permit you to sell her. Unless you sell her to me. Then I shall promptly free her and employ her myself. Really William, she is part of the family."

William's expression darkened. "Must I remind you that I am the head of this family now? Father allowed you too much latitude, but I will not make that mistake."

"Perhaps not," Peggy said, exhibiting no anxiety at all. "But perhaps the contempt of our neighbors will sway you. We already bear the burden of gossip for owning a slave." Leaning forward, she added emphatically, "You know how many of them despise us for that. If you sell her or turn her off you must realize we will all bear the brunt of disapprobation." Rees nodded at the girl approvingly. He wished his wife Lydia was here now; he thought she would admire the fiery Peggy Boothe greatly. But William's scowl was thunderous.

"Very well," he said after a moment's silence. "I will do nothing. For now. Yes, Peggy," he held up a hand to forestall her speech, "I will instruct the sheriff to free Xenobia and she may return home. For the time being. No doubt we shall require an extra pair of hands now that we have lost . . ." Abruptly his voice hoarsened and he turned aside. No one spoke. Tears filled Peggy's eyes and dripped down her cheeks. She wiped her eyes with her fingers until Twig offered her his handkerchief. She nodded her thanks and pressed the grubby square of cloth into her eyes. Rees found Twig's behavior surprising. First, because he had a handkerchief and second, because he was willing to offer it to someone else.

William's shoulders tensed and twitched with the struggle to govern his emotion. When he turned around, his face was red but he'd recovered control of his voice. "Where's Betsy?"

"Still abed." Peggy frowned, adding in disapproval, "I expect she will not emerge until Mr. Morris arrives to comfort her."

"*If* he arrives," William said. He sighed, his shoulders slumping, and Rees glimpsed the pressure under which this young man labored. "He's one of the Crowninshield cousins after all. He might feel his consequence is too high to wed a woman whose father was murdered. Especially after the death of her mother under somewhat questionable . . ." Recollecting his audience he glanced at Rees, and seeing he was listening with great attention, William jerked abruptly to a stop.

"Russell Morris would never break our betrothal, not for something like that," a light voice said from the door. Peggy turned and, upon seeing her sister, rose to her feet.

"No doubt you're correct, Bets," she said, stretching out a hand. "I know he loves you." But a worried line insinuated itself between her fair brows. Rees guessed that Peggy, and William too, feared the scandal would break both the betrothal and their sister's heart. And Rees thought they might be right. That was the way of the world.

Rees focused his attention upon Elisabeth Boothe. She was as fair as her sister but more strongly resembled the portrait of their mother. Betsy's features had escaped the sharp nose and chin Peggy and William shared. Large blue eyes and a trembling mouth gave her the appearance of softness, and as Rees watched Betsy, tears welled in her eyes and began running down her cheeks.

"My wedding has already had to be postponed," she whispered. On her, the black gown, identical to Peggy's, was flattering. She looked both beautiful and delicate. Even Rees, who was more attracted to Peggy's fire, felt the desire to protect this fragile young woman from harm. He could imagine the effect she would have upon younger, unmarried men.

"Don't cry, Bets," William said. "Don't worry."

Peggy, however, looked at her sister with some impatience. "Of course, Father had to postpone the wedding," she said. "It would be most indecorous to go forward with it immediately after the death of your Mother. And now, with Father's death . . ." Her voice trailed off as Betsy began to weep.

"Don't be cross with me, Peggy," Betsy said.

Peggy exchanged a glance with William and said bracingly, "Now Bets, I'm absolutely certain your Russell Morris will wait until you're out of mourning."

"I don't have time for these female dramatics," William said. "I want to catch the sheriff and free Xenobia today. Finish this task before it steals any more of my time."

Rees turned to Twig, who nodded slightly. "We too, will take our leave," he said. "In fact, if you don't mind, Mr. Boothe, I'll join you in your search for the sheriff."

"Why, Mr. Eaton," Betsy Boothe said, looking at Twig, "I apologize for my poor manners. I didn't see you there." She smiled up at him and Rees could see the undertaker melting, bending toward her, like a candle to a flame. "And who is this?" She directed her full attention at Rees and he felt its warmth. She must have had a wide choice among the single men in Salem for her future husband.

"Will Rees," he said. "I am a friend of Tw—Mr. Eaton's."

"I am delighted to make your acquaintance," she murmured, extending her hand. Rees bowed over it, but not before he caught the expression upon Peggy's face. She looked as though she'd just bitten into a lemon.

"And I, yours," Rees said automatically.

"Thank you for your assistance, Mr. Rees," Peggy said, breaking into the exchange. "Mr. Eaton promised me you would unknot this tangle and he wasn't mistaken." She heaved a sigh. "Poor Xenobia can now return home."

"Indeed," Rees agreed. He hesitated. It was not his place to say anything, but he felt he owed it to Jacob Boothe. "The question is, though, I mean, if Xenobia is an innocent party, then who murdered your father?"

Betsy emitted a loud wail and fled from the room.

For a moment no one else spoke, frozen into a rigid tableau. "There is that, I suppose," William said, his face white with shock. Rees suspected the young man had not thought beyond Xenobia.

"Can you . . . I mean, will you?" Peggy looked at Rees, her hands clasped beseechingly. "You immediately proved Xenobia's innocence and Mr. Eaton says you have both experience and skill."

"Peggy, really," her brother said. "He proved nothing, he merely drew our attention to an improbability. There are others in town who might study this for us. Mr. Rees is a stranger and I'm quite certain he has work of his own to attend to."

"Exactly," Peggy interrupted, turning to stare at her brother. "He doesn't live in Salem and will leave when his investigation is done. In other words, he won't be dining out among our neighbors on tales of our tragedies."

"Although I'm certain everyone knows of the quarrels between you and Father," William said, drawing himself up in outrage, "I have no regrettable secrets."

"No, of course not," Peggy said. "But with a Salem man living in our back pockets, well, I daresay you won't mind if every detail of your courtship is bruited about with little regard for truth." William went pale. "Besides," Peggy continued with a nod, "Mr. Rees is not quite a stranger. He and Mr. Eaton have known one another for more than twenty years. And you've known Mr. Eaton almost as long, William." She paused and Rees, who was surprised by her insistence, thought she'd made her case. But she spoke again, adding one final shot. "If you're unwilling to employ Mr. Rees, I will."

"With what?" William snapped. "I'm now the Head of this Household." Rees heard the capital letters.

"I have funds of my own," Peggy said, fixing a stubborn glare upon her brother. "Or are you planning to claim you have control of those as well?" Although she did not say it, Rees knew she would fight her brother over every penny and never yield.

"You betray an unfortunate combative streak that is most unfeminine," William said. "I shall never marry you off."

Oh yes, Lydia would like fierce Peggy. Rees chuckled quietly to himself, although he felt a twinge of sympathy for William. Peggy would be a difficult sister to manage.

"Pooh," Peggy said inelegantly. "You know the deputy sheriff cannot handle a matter of this delicacy. So, what will it be, William?"

Gathering the rags of his dignity about him, William turned to Rees. "Very well. If you think you can solve this mystery, I offer you employment. What is your fee?"

"I haven't yet agreed to take on this commission," Rees said. He hesitated, thinking. He was eager to return home to Lydia, but there was the money to consider. And Jacob Boothe needed someone to fight for him. Rees rapidly added sums. He knew how much he might earn weaving on the journey home and added a bit more for the expenses of staying with Mrs. Baldwin and his meals. "$15.00 for two weeks," he said. "And we can renegotiate the price at the end of the time if I haven't discovered the murderer's identity. And in hard cash, too," he added. "Not that paper money."

William's brows rose at the sum. He turned to Peggy. "I expect you will have something to say if I don't agree," he said. "You are the most willful sister a man could have."

A faint chime of recognition sounded in Rees's head and he wondered if he sounded as arrogant speaking to his sister. Certainly Caroline would say so, and as Rees thought about it he had to admit he probably did. Peggy flapped her hand to brush away William's complaint. "Well, William?"

"Oh, very well," William said to Rees. "I agree to your terms. And now I must look for Deputy Sheriff Swett so Xenobia can be home by supper." Clapping his hat upon his head, William fled. Rees bowed over Peggy's hand, promised to speak with her within another day or two, and followed Twig from the room.

Chapter Five

❧

Rees and Twig trailed William Boothe east, toward the docks. Rees was surprised by the direction; he'd expected William to head toward the jail. But Twig explained it: William expected to find Deputy Sheriff Swett in one of the taverns that lined the waterfront. William swung down the lane at a rapid pace, keeping a few steps ahead of the other two to deny any association between them. Finally reaching a tavern identified by a large anchor, William stepped through the door. As he walked through the room, several men, some garbed in clothing as fine as his, others in the rougher dress of sailors, made their way to him to offer their condolences. The floor was slick with expectorated tobacco.

Rees stepped forward, intending to follow, but Twig grasped his arm and pulled him back. Rees looked at Twig in annoyance. "Not my ordinary," Twig muttered. So they stopped by the door and watched. Rees wished he could hear what was being said, especially after William paused at one table. Most of the men scattered, leaving only one—a gentleman beautifully dressed in a scarlet jacket with a froth of lace at his neck—at the table. Most of the men in this tavern wore plain linen jackets and brightly colored handkerchiefs about their necks just as Twig did. The deputy sheriff looked like some fancy peacock in a flock of common birds. Rees couldn't help contrasting this elegantly dressed fop to his ragged constable friend at home. William sat down beside him and began talking in low, vehement tones. Deputy Swett rose to his feet with alacrity. Now Rees deeply regretted not shaking off Twig's hand and following William inside so he could hear the conversation.

Deputy Sheriff Swett was shorter than Rees by at least a foot. Swett's breeches boasted polished silver buckles at the knees and he carried a white handkerchief in one hand, an affectation that made Rees immediately dismiss the deputy as effeminate. Sparing neither Twig nor Rees a glance as he strode through the door, Swett left with William and they began tramping back to the jail. Rees and Twig fell into step behind them.

Although the walk was not a strenuous one, Swett was panting by the time they reached the jail. He coughed into his linen handkerchief and quickly deposited it into an inside jacket pocket—but not before Rees saw the bloody smudges Swett took such pains to hide. Swett found another clean handkerchief and with that he carefully wiped the dust from his black, buckled shoes. As he did so, he said to Rees, "Mr. Boothe here tells me you're certain that Negress did not murder her master."

"She could not have," Rees said. He spoke politely, knowing now that this popinjay was ill. "Mr. Boothe was stabbed with such force the point of the instrument went through his back. She would not have had the strength. The doctor will attest the same." He did not say that if the deputy had looked at the body, he too would have seen how much strength must have been required.

"So, since you seem to know so much, whom do you believe murdered him?" Swett sneered.

"I don't know," Rees said. "Yet." And then, interpreting the deputy's expression, he added. "I was miles away and could not have done this, even if I wished to harm Mr. Boothe, a man I met only once and who was kind to me."

"That's true," Twig said. "I had to fetch him."

"This foul deed was accomplished either last night or very early this morning," the deputy said, baring his brown teeth. "I believe you were still in Salem then."

"Some work will be required to reveal my father's murderer," William said, frowning at the deputy. "We can't simply choose someone because he is a stranger."

"Who cares about a Negress anyway," Swett muttered.

"My sister," William said.

"Miss Peggy," said Twig at the same moment.

"And, if Xenobia is innocent," Rees said in a cold voice, for he could not respect a man who took no pride in his work, "the murderer is roaming abroad, free to kill again."

"I doubt that he will," the deputy said, glaring at Rees. "It should be obvious to a man of the meanest intelligence that the murderer lay in wait specifically for Mr. Boothe."

"For what purpose?" William said, turning an icy stare upon Swett. "My father was liked and respected."

"Robbery, of course," Swett replied.

"Of course." William eagerly accepted that explanation. "It must be some thief or scoundrel from the docks."

"But Mr. Boothe wasn't robbed," Rees said, recalling the coins falling from Boothe's pockets as he was turned over. "He still had money."

"Frightened away by someone, no doubt," William declared, his voice rising, "before he could steal anything."

"And that sailor," the deputy said, "has probably already taken a berth on a merchantman or a whaling ship. We won't see his return for several months, if not years."

"But we know none of that," Rees objected, looking at William in sympathy. Families rarely wanted to believe they knew the murderer. "Your father may have argued with someone recently.

You might not know of it. Unless . . . are you privy to all of his affairs?" The sour pucker of William's mouth was answer enough. Rees turned to the deputy. "Mr. Boothe was only just murdered. The sailor, if sailor it was, might still be in Salem. How many vessels have sailed since yesterday? One or two? And were any of the captains or crewmen questioned?"

The deputy pressed his lips together and stared at Rees.

"If you have evidence against my mother's maid," William said to the sheriff, "please produce it now. Otherwise, I shall assume you simply took her into custody as an easy solution and I shall apply to one of my father's friends, a magistrate; Mr. Lowell."

The deputy sheriff turned without a word and unlocked the jail door.

Xenobia did not step out immediately but cautiously examined the men waiting outside. Then she noticed Twig and emerged in a rush. "So much past sorrow and fear in here," she said with a glance over her shoulder. Rees eyed her in concern; she was teary-eyed and rubbed her arms as though cold to the bone.

"Let me take you home, Xenobia," William said, inspecting her as well. Rees felt his mouth twist. William had only just realized what jail time meant to this woman. "I know my sister is much concerned and will want to make sure you are unharmed." Xenobia nodded and, with a fleeting glance at Twig, she followed William. Twig stared after them, looking as though he wanted to follow.

"Is there anything else?" the deputy asked coldly.

"Thank you for your help, but no," Rees said, drawing Twig away. As they started off in the direction William and Xenobia had taken, the jail door clanged shut behind them. "What is Swett suffering from? Consumption?"

"The Curse," Twig said. As Rees turned to look at his companion in perplexity, Twig added, "Giles Corey was pressed to death during the witch trials and before he died he cursed the town and the sheriff." He shuddered. "And every sheriff since then has died from some dreadful disease. Swett's is consumption."

Rees said nothing. He didn't believe in curses or witches either, for that matter, but Twig clearly did.

"I should go to Xenobia," Twig said. "She would have been scared, spending the night in the jail where the accused witches were kept."

"Don't go yet," Rees said, wondering if Xenobia too believed in the occult. "Peggy will ensure she is well cared for. And I have questions for you. Where can we go?"

Twig's expression went sullen and he did not reply.

"If I'm to determine who killed Mr. Boothe," Rees said sharply, "I need to know the circumstances surrounding the discovery of the body. I'll need to question Xenobia as well, but I thought I would spare her any more distress today. However, if you decline to help me, I will question her first." Usually he also spoke with local law enforcement, but he could see Swett lacked any interest in justice.

"No." The word exploded from Twig. "I'll answer your questions." He looked around. "We're near the docks. We can walk to the Witch's Cauldron. That's a sailor's haunt and rather rough. Or we can go to the tavern I frequent, the Moon and Stars."

"Let's walk there then," Rees said. "We'll both be more comfortable on familiar ground." He turned but realized he didn't know how to reach that tavern. With a faint smile, Twig stepped around Rees and began walking rapidly northwest. "Wait," Rees called after him. He'd thought to begin addressing the questions bubbling inside of him as they walked, but the pace Twig set made conversation impossible. With a muttered curse, Rees hurried after his friend.

The proprietress in the Moon and Stars recognized Twig and quickly directed him to a table at the back. She stood at the front, keeping a fierce eye upon everyone in her establishment. No one was spitting tobacco, although a few gentlemen smoked the newly fashionable cigars. It was so dark Rees couldn't see well and banged his leg smartly on either the table or a chair, but the gloom suited him right now. He sat down and leaned forward to shout over the noise of conversation around them.

"Where was Mr. Boothe discovered?"

"In the tunnel, not ten feet from his door."

"Tell me about the tunnels," Rees commanded, recalling Xenobia's comment.

"There are tunnels under Salem," Twig said.

"We'll be here all day if you aren't more helpful," Rees said in annoyance. Twig shrugged. "Are they used for smuggling?" Rees asked. The merchant ships arriving from the East were stuffed with cargo.

"Maybe. They probably were before the War and right after. During the time of the privateers. But now the ships are required to stop two and a half miles out for the customs inspector. He rows out to view the cargo." Twig paused. "I'm sure some captains find a way to avoid the tax. But the tunnels, which lead to the docks, also lead to the counting houses. The wealthy merchants, like the Derbys and the Crowninshields," he added resentfully, "use them to transport the most valuable items between their cellars and warehouses. They don't want the lesser folk such as myself to see just how rich they are."

Rees suspected it was more to prevent robbery but didn't argue. "And Mr. Boothe was discovered in the tunnel underneath his house?"

Twig nodded.

"But he wasn't robbed." Rees stopped. He didn't know that;

maybe the pocket watch and few coins weren't worth stealing, not if Boothe had been carrying jewelry or gold. "Did he have bodyguards? Or a pistol?"

"I don't know about a gun. But no one travels with his servants when he's planning on visiting his mistress."

"He had a mistress?" Rees asked. And why should he be so surprised; mistresses weren't uncommon.

"So I heard," Twig said.

"The tunnels go to her door?"

"She lives close to the docks."

Rees nodded. He'd wager both William and Matthew knew about the mistress, but, of course, they hadn't told Rees. "Who is she? Do you know her name?"

"I don't," Twig said indifferently. "I never heard it, not that I know of. But Xenobia might."

"Of course, Mr. Boothe would want to keep her name close to his vest; he was married until just a few days ago," Rees said, more to himself than to his friend. Twig shrugged, his eyes focusing upon the street outside. "Did you ever meet Mrs. Boothe?"

"Of course," Twig said, dragging his gaze back to Rees with an effort. "Once or twice. But not to speak to. Anyway, she seemed a quiet woman." After a pause, he added, "Xenobia wept when she died."

"Two deaths in a few days," Rees mused. "Is there anyone with a particular animosity toward the Boothe family?"

"Mrs. Boothe was ill a long time," Twig said.

"Still, it's a lot of tragedy for one family," Rees pointed out. Twig flapped his hand dismissively. Rees remembered then that his old friend had always seemed somewhat divorced from the feelings of others. When they'd served together in the War for Independence, Twig could always be relied upon to hold down a wounded soldier for treatment, unmoved by either blood or screaming. Rees suspected Twig's profession suited him; the dead did not expect comfort.

"I must go to Xenobia," Twig said now, rising to his feet.

"I'll have to speak to her," Rees warned. "She may know more about that family than anyone else."

"Don't you upset her," Twig said, turning back and leaning over the table. "I won't allow that."

"If I don't identify Mr. Boothe's murderer, Xenobia will continue as a suspect," Rees said without flinching. "I know *that* will upset her. Besides, she surely wishes to see her Master's killer caught."

Twig hesitated. "I'll ask her," he said at last. "I'll let you know." He turned and left the tavern, his tall lanky body moving disjointedly, but nonetheless quickly, through the door.

Rees watched his friend disappear into the crowded street outside and then, deciding he was hungry, shouted for the serving girl.

By the time he returned to the Widow Baldwin's, the afternoon was drawing to a close. Rees went to check on Bessie and found Billy Baldwin currying her. The marks of recent tears were visible around his eyes but caring for the horse had calmed him.

After thanking Billy for grooming Bessie, Rees said, "I understand you're planning to go to sea." The boy nodded.

"I want to. My mother . . ." He tossed his head. "I don't want to spend my life working in the ropewalk and so I told her, I'll make my fortune at sea." Rees found himself in the peculiar position of seeing this conversation as both a parent trying to protect a child and a son eager to break away from the loving arms of his doting mama.

"Do you want to be a whaling man?" Rees asked.

"No, I want to ship out on a merchant vessel. I'd like to become one of the Derby boys. Mr. Derby signs on greenhanders like me. Boys from good families. Ship out, learn the ropes, and someday I might own my own vessel."

"But?"

"The whaling ship is looking for sailors." Billy sighed in frustration. "But my mother begged me to stay home. I've already missed so many chances." He stroked the comb over Bessie's flank several times before bursting again into speech. "I'm a man. It's time I leave home."

"Your mother would surely miss you," Rees said, his tone gentle. Billy's face crumpled and for a moment he fought tears.

"I can't stay here forever," he said at last, gruffly. "I'm not a boy anymore. Time to make my fortune. And keeping a shop isn't for me."

Rees looked at the lad, who couldn't be more than fourteen, just David's age, and shuddered at the thought of his son going whaling. "Know anything about sailing?" he asked, understanding that arguing would only set Billy in his purpose.

"Some," Billy said, armed with boyish bravado. "Been on the docks all my life. I'll learn the knack right quick."

"Well, at least on a whaler you'd be home sooner, months maybe instead of years. But I've heard it's hard, brutish work."

"Yes. Truth is, I don't really want to sail on a whaler," the boy confided. "I just want some experience. I'd make more money on a merchantman. Besides," he added with a shudder, "I've heard that when they bring the whale aboard the decks run with blood. Not that I'm squeamish."

But he was. "That wouldn't be my choice either," Rees agreed. "How long would you be gone, on a merchantman?"

"Six months to a year," Billy said. "Probably more. With luck,

I'd bring home enough money to invest in another ship. There's big money to be made, Mr. Rees. On pepper and other spices, silk and cottons, opium from Turkey as well as India." His eyes sparkled with excitement.

Rees nodded in understanding. It wasn't just the lad's desire to seek his fortune then, but also the spirit of adventure that moved him. Rees wondered how Billy would feel when he returned—if he returned, for this was a dangerous business. He might be ready to settle down and run the shop then, and be glad of it.

"Wouldn't it be better to wait until you can secure a position on a merchant ship?" Rees asked. "You don't want to miss your chance while you're out to sea on a whaler. Especially if that's not what you want."

"I just don't want to be trapped in Salem my whole life," Billy said. Rees hid a smile. To someone thirty-six, almost thirty-seven years old, fourteen seemed unbearably young.

"Was Mr. Boothe successful? As a merchant?"

"The Mr. Boothe that was just found killed?" Billy asked. "Indeed he was. The merchant vessel *Hindoo Queen* is his ship—well, I guess it belongs to William Boothe now. Some say another few good cargoes and Boothe would be in competition with the Derbys and the Crowninshields. And he started as a cabin boy. A sailor who worked his way up to mate and then supercargo and then captain, with bigger shares in each voyage, until finally he retired from the sea and sent other men out on ships he owned."

"Supercargo? I'm not a sailor, so . . ."

"A supercargo goes along on board to look after the business interests of the owner."

"I see." Rees thought that job had to be easier than deckhand. "Was Mr. Boothe already such competition for Mr. Derby or Mr. Crowninshield that they might have elected to remove him?"

Billy laughed. "No, they were all friendly. Besides, plenty of riches in the East. That's what Mr. Briggs, my master, always says. William Boothe went out on one or two of the ships as the super-cargo," Billy continued. "Then he went right into the counting house. They say he has a head for figures."

"And what of Mr. Boothe's wife?" Rees asked. "Was she a member of one of the sailing families?"

Billy nodded. "That she is. Was. Well, whaling. Her brothers run a few whalers, I believe. And I wouldn't be surprised if the Covilles invested in Mr. Boothe's first venture. For cargo and such."

"You seem to know quite a bit," Rees said.

Billy nodded. "I've worked at the ropewalk for a few years now and as I walk back and forth, back and forth, I listen to all the talk. Helps pass the time."

Rees nodded. "Well, I wish you good fortune, Billy. It's a dangerous profession you want to follow." Turning, he made his way to the house's back door.

Mrs. Baldwin came through it as Rees approached. Her eyes, under the white cap, were red. But although she looked across to her son, combing Bessie's rough coat as if his life depended upon it, she said only, "Time for supper, Billy."

The memory of Lydia, with David and the orphans they'd adopted in New York clustered around her, lingering in the farm-house door to wave farewell suddenly popped into Rees's mind. The plight of women: always watching their menfolk vanish over the horizon with no guarantee of their return. He suddenly missed his wife with a physical ache. He wished he could hear her voice, and laughed ruefully, imagining her tart comments on this situation. And the children, oh he missed them far more than he had expected. He'd been glad to leave home and live in quiet for a spell. But now he saw the image of Judah's little head with those big ears, and Nancy's flyaway blond hair that wouldn't stay in a braid, and Joseph's toothy grin—Rees realized all at once how difficult it would be to leave his family for long spells. It had been many years, since before Dolly's death, since he had felt such a strong pull home.

Chapter Six

An hour later, Mrs. Baldwin plodded upstairs to tell Rees he had company. Since he knew few people in Salem, and only one of them well, he was unsurprised to find Twig waiting for him outside the door. The undertaker gestured to Rees and said in a low voice, as though this was a secret, "Xenobia's at my house. She'll talk to you now."

Mrs. Baldwin had retreated into the kitchen at the back of the building and so could not hear them, but Rees made no comment as he followed his friend through the yard and into the warren of narrow streets. In the gloom, and with Twig loping ahead, Rees feared he would never again be able to find his way to his friend's house.

Built at the corner where two streets met, it was small and distant from the docks. Rees thought it was close to the Commons, near the much finer Boothe home, but he wasn't really certain. However, the house boasted a tiny front yard, a back patch with a vegetable garden, and a shed or some other structure near the rear fence. The front door opened into a small hall. As Twig hared off to the left, Rees glanced into the right-hand chamber. Save for a fireplace, unlit, the room was entirely empty. The space they walked through on the left contained a bench, a desk, and a bed that, surprisingly, was made up with clean linens and a bright summer quilt. But Twig hurried forward, into the back room that proved to be the kitchen.

Xenobia straightened up from stirring the fire. "Are you hungry, Mr. Rees? I have some soup here." Rees allowed as how he could eat a bowlful. She swung the pot to the hearth and ladled out a large portion. A chunk of fresh baked bread followed and Rees sat down upon the bench by the rough wooden table. "Miss Peggy begs you to attend upon her tomorrow," Xenobia said. "Now that her brother has retained you to investigate her father's death, she wishes to offer you any assistance you may require." She sounded as though she was quoting something Peggy had said to her.

Rees nodded and, fully grasping the relationship between Twig and this woman from the West Indies, gestured her to a seat across the table. "Please, sit, so that we may talk more comfortably," he said.

She hesitated, eyeing Rees warily. "I am but a slave, Mr. Rees."

"In this house you are the mistress," he said. "Or am I incorrect in that supposition?"

"No," Twig said. "When I've saved enough money I'll purchase her freedom and we will marry. I expect you to treat her with the respect due my wife."

"Of course," Rees said, patting the air in lieu of Twig's back. "Please, Mistress." Rees turned to Xenobia. "Sit beside Twig."

"Twig?" She looked at the man beside her in surprise.

"It was a nickname we adopted during the War," Rees said. "He was as tall as he is now and even more slender then."

"I see. Well, ask your questions then, Mr. Rees. But I don't know what I can tell you. I didn't kill Mr. Boothe and I don't know about the tunnels."

"But you know the family and that's what I am curious about." Xenobia did not reply. "Two deaths within, what, four days?" Still the woman said nothing, her face impassive. Rees wondered if she was hiding something or was just too frightened to react. "How long have you worked for the Boothes?" he asked, trying to put her at ease.

"Almost nineteen years," she said. "Since just before Miss Peggy was born."

"You were hired as her nurse?" Rees asked.

"Yes. It was a difficult pregnancy. And a difficult birth." Pause. This time Rees waited to see if she would add anything further. "Miss Anstiss was an older mother then," Xenobia finally added.

"That explains the connection between you and Peggy then," Rees said. "You raised her." Xenobia nodded. "And how did you come to serve as Mrs. Boothe's maid?"

"She never completely recovered from Peggy's birth," Xenobia said. "Her health was poor ever after. I . . . nursed her." Rees wondered what Xenobia had intended to say. "Lately her health worsened," she continued. "Mr. Boothe sent her to their country farm last summer."

I'll bet he did, Rees thought, recalling Mr. Boothe's alleged mistress.

"But Miss Anstiss fared poorly there too and had to be brought home again."

"How was the relationship between Mr. Boothe and his wife?" Rees asked. Xenobia looked startled and hesitated. Rees could see she was considering the question and kept silent.

"Well enough. I think he genuinely loved her. When I first came into the household, he denied her nothing. But he was a healthy man, active and lively, and over the years he lost patience with his wife's illness."

"He lost patience?" Rees repeated.

Xenobia tensed. "Yes. He urged her to leave her bed. To go outside of her room. Join the family at meals. But, of course, she could not. She was too sick."

"I daresay you've heard about Mr. Boothe's mistress," Rees said.

"Yes," Xenobia said after a short hesitation. "But who knows if it is true? Anyway, I wouldn't blame him. He had great energy, and Anstiss was ill a long time."

Rees nodded in understanding. "Of course. Were there money problems that you knew of? Did Mr. Boothe have creditors whom he could not pay?"

Xenobia laughed, relaxing completely for the first time. "No sir. Everything Mr. Boothe touched turned to gold. He was talking about relocating his family to Chestnut Street." Seeing that Rees did not understand, she added, "That is where the Derbys live. And Mr. Elias Derby is the wealthiest man in the city."

"Although, if Mr. Crowninshield goes forward with his plans to fill in the Commons and build more houses, Mr. Boothe's dwelling will be in a desirable area, too," Twig put in.

"And would he, do you think?" Rees kept his attention upon Xenobia. "Would Mr. Boothe have removed his family to Chestnut Street?"

"Maybe." Xenobia bit her lip. "Maybe not. Miss Betsy, who performed the role of hostess in the absence of her mother, is getting married."

"Miss Peggy?" asked Twig. "Couldn't she do it?"

"Hmmm." Xenobia smiled as though her imagination presented a funny scene. "I don't think so. I can't see her taking tea with the other women and gossiping. Miss Peggy has no patience and even her sister's feminine airs irritate her. Mr. Boothe needs a wife who can be a gracious hostess."

"And do you know the name and address of the woman he was seeing?" Rees asked. "Would she do?"

"I don't know. And why would you want her direction? She

couldn't have murdered Mr. Boothe, for the exact reason you judged me innocent," Xenobia said. "She is a weak woman."

Rees's estimation of her intelligence rose. "Maybe Mr. Boothe told her something. Or maybe another suitor, a jealous one who wanted to claim the lady for his own, wanted Mr. Boothe out of the way." When Xenobia did not speak, Rees leaned forward. "I know you are loyal, Xenobia, and I promise to be discreet. But, if I'm to identify Mr. Boothe's killer, I need to know everything."

"I don't know where she lives. I don't even know for certain if there was a mistress." She sighed. "Anstiss always believed he had one, but that may have been jealousy talking."

"Could he have been on his way to see this woman when he was murdered?"

"Perhaps. But we don't know. He frequently went out in the evenings. The tunnels also lead to the counting houses and the warehouses on the docks."

"And there are several brothels there," Twig said. Xenobia turned a glance upon him that could curdle milk.

"I will not judge," Rees said. Xenobia raised her eyes to him.

"You must understand. Mr. Boothe was a man of sterling moral character, but he was, after all, a man. Anyway, it's more likely," she added quickly, "that he was involved in some private business dealings."

"Smuggling you mean?" Rees said. Xenobia sniffed, offended.

"Of course not. He would never do that."

Rees did not argue but his silence was heavy with doubt. The furtive nature of Mr. Boothe's departures certainly suggested something secret and possibly illegal.

"Is smuggling common here in Salem?" Rees asked, assuming it must be. What port town did not boast its smugglers?

"I don't know. Many of the grand houses have tunnels that

lead to the docks. You must ask William. I don't know much about them." Rees glanced at Twig.

"The tunnels are for the wealthy," Twig said, adding with passion, "but I am certain Jacob Boothe was not a smuggler. I've heard only praise for his honesty. Besides, there's plenty of money in Salem. No need to smuggle. And it would be difficult anyway. The ships wait outside of the harbor for Mr. Oliver, the customs agent."

"Still worth looking into," Rees said. "Along with the possibility of a mistress." He stared hard at Xenobia and she looked away from him.

"I did hear the name Georgianne mentioned once or twice," she admitted reluctantly.

"Do you know a last name?"

"No. I only heard Master William ask his father to put her aside. But William," she added, darting a glance at Rees, "will be even more unwilling to confide in you than I am."

"Still, I'll need to question him. And I must speak to this Georgianne." Rees mopped his bowl clean with a heel of bread and continued. "Tell me something of the children," he said. He had begun to form his own opinions but Xenobia knew them far better and was, he already knew, a perceptive woman.

"Well, you've met three of the four and have no doubt made your own judgments."

"Hmmm." Rees recognized her reluctance to speak about her owners. "I noticed friction between Peggy and her father at the averil. Almost a quarrel. What was it about?"

A grimace passed across Xenobia's face too rapidly for Rees to interpret, although his first impression was that she was frightened. But she dismissed his question with a chuckle. "You must understand, Mr. Rees. Peggy worked as her father's secretary. Not a feminine thing to do, not at all. When William came home,

Mr. Boothe began turning over all those responsibilities to his son. Peggy is angry." Xenobia shook her head. "She doesn't want to behave as a young lady should."

Rees nodded. No wonder there was friction between Peggy and her brother. "And William will inherit, of course, as the older son. Is he anxious to acquire his father's property?" Rees asked. Xenobia frowned, needled out of her stoic calm.

"None of those children would ever hurt their father," she said angrily. "He was a good man. He gave them everything they wanted. Why Matthew . . ." she stopped abruptly, biting her lip.

"And what about Matthew?" Rees asked. "He's the only one of Mr. Boothe's children I haven't met." When Xenobia did not speak, Rees continued. "I suppose he's spoiled. The youngest child for several years, Matthew was no doubt the apple of both parents' eyes. Peggy's arrival must have put his nose out of joint."

Xenobia looked at Rees, her gaze direct. "Yes, you're right. To this day he treats her as though she were a poor country cousin, little better than a servant. He's accustomed to a life of idleness. And now that he's involved in amateur theatricals . . ." She stopped abruptly. Rees had also heard the disapproval in her voice.

"The younger son, spoiled and jealous; Matthew is the wastrel of the family." He made it a statement, and as Xenobia did not protest, he assumed it was true. "So how did Peggy acquire the position as her father's secretary? Shouldn't that responsibility have been placed in Matthew's hands? Why was he permitted to avoid working?"

"Since Miss Anstiss was too ill to pay attention to Peggy, she turned quite naturally to her father. Matthew never showed any interest in his father's business, while Peggy was constantly at her father's heels. Jacob's little shadow. She ran errands for him and gradually took over his correspondence. Mr. Boothe often said Peggy's brain was wasted on a female."

"I'd expect Matthew to protest," Rees said. Xenobia shook her head.

"I told you, he has no interest in business. None. Although he envied the bond between Peggy and their father, Matthew never wanted to work in the counting house. Or go to sea either, for that matter. Too busy spending his time drinking and gambling. And once he went to Harvard and wasn't home, no one even considered involving him."

"But he's home now," Rees said. He could not imagine his own father allowing such irresponsibility.

"Only until the fall. Besides, now he's too busy acting in plays with his cousin." Her tone put acting somewhere next to consorting with the Devil. She stopped abruptly, her hand flying up to cover her mouth. "My unruly tongue," she mumbled.

"No fear," Rees assured her, rising to his feet. "I promise, I won't divulge your confidences to anyone. And now I'll take my leave; it's late."

"Will you visit Miss Peggy tomorrow?" Xenobia asked, turning anxiously to look at him. "She'll be waiting for you."

"Of course." Rees inclined his head in farewell and followed Twig back through the empty house to the dark lane beyond. Matthew, Rees thought, merited further attention.

Chapter Seven

The loud thud of a closing door woke Rees and he sat up quite suddenly in bed. That must be Simon going out to meet David to help milk the cows—but no. For a few seconds Rees didn't remember where he was. He'd been dreaming of Lydia and, when he turned to the space next to him, he almost expected to see her lying beside him. But that side was empty, and disappointment swept over him. For all he'd wanted quiet, he missed the noisy arising of the children, the laughter and the thumping of their feet hitting the stairs as they went down to breakfast. Rubbing his hands across his face, he rolled out of bed and went to the window.

The sky was beginning to lighten. Someone whistled sweetly in the yard outside and Rees saw Billy. He was just exiting through the garden gate to the stable yard beyond. "Billy," Rees called. Billy looked up at him. "Can you show me the way to the docks?"

"Sure. It's easy. You just take this street . . ." He seemed prepared to shout complicated directions from the yard through the window.

"Wait," Rees said. "I'll be right down." He hastily put on his breeches and shoes. When he ran his hand over his face his whiskers scratched roughly against his palm; tomorrow he would have to shave. He knew he must look shaggy and unkempt.

Although he heard Mrs. Baldwin in the kitchen, Rees crept

quietly down the stairs and through the back door. He joined Billy in the yard and together they went through the door into the street outside.

Salem was already waking up. Although some of the houses displayed no light, the lanes were filled with men on their way to jobs on the docks. Some were sailors and carried bags. But others seemed ordinary workingmen: the sail and rope makers, the shopkeepers who furnished the ships' stores and a host of laborers who loaded and unloaded the ships. Others were exotics. Rees turned to stare at a pair of men walking away from the docks. One was short and dark, but not black. He was garbed in a white cap and a long white tunic over white trousers. His companion was even more striking: tall, almost as tall as Rees, this man wore a bright blue costume with flaring breeches and a wide-sleeved blouse. A large wrapped hat with a jewel in the center covered his head and he sported a curved sword at his waist. Although the man's hair was not visible, his mustache and the beard that tumbled down his chest were gray. Rees watched them until they turned down a street and disappeared behind the buildings.

When he turned back, Billy was laughing at him. "Those men," Billy said, "are from India. Where the merchant ships go to pick up cotton and gems and spices."

"My God!" Rees said in an astonished voice.

"I would see other even more amazing sights if I worked on a merchant vessel," Billy said, throwing a wistful glance at Rees. "The world is a wonderful place, Mr. Rees."

Bereft of speech, Rees could only nod.

They turned a couple of corners but always headed east. As the lane wound past one of the houses, a sprawling edifice with weather-beaten gray shingles, a young girl peered out the window. She could not have been more than twelve or thirteen, just a few years older than Jerusha, Rees's adopted daughter, but fatigue painted shadows under her blue eyes. Her fine light brown hair had come loose from its plait and hung wispily around the pale oval of her face. She rested her chin upon one hand and stared dreamily at the movement below. When she saw Billy she smiled, and he looked up at her with a wide grin. Now Rees knew why they had taken a route with so many twists and turns.

"Annie." The sharp voice carried clearly through the open window. "Annie. Where are you, girl?"

The girl glanced over her shoulder and then, without answering, turned back to her study of the boy below.

"Annie. There's work to be done." The sharp-tongued woman summoning the girl must have entered the room; her voice was louder and Annie turned reluctantly, frowning, and disappeared from the window.

Rees forgot the little maid as he stepped for the first time upon Salem dock. All of this sea town smelled of salt, but here the tang, mixed with the rotting stink of the outgoing tide, was overpowering. Gulls screamed overhead and flocks of them rested on every surface; they were almost tame, dropping down to the wooden dock to hunt for scraps. Although accustomed to gulls—he was from the District of Maine, after all—Rees had never seen such brazen birds. The flocks were more like packs of some small carnivore, relentless and demanding, and reluctant to move except at the threat of some attacking boot.

He had come out somewhere near the middle of the docks. Warehouses and businesses lined the dock on either side of him, and wharves of all different lengths stretched greedily into the harbor. One was so long, a mile or more, that the end was lost in the glare of the rising sun.

"I've got to hurry," Billy said. Rees had almost forgotten him. "I expect I'll see you tonight." With a little wave, Billy turned and began sprinting up the dock, heading north by Rees's reckoning.

Rees began his leisurely stroll, following Billy. He made a few excursions down the wharves that stretched like wooden fingers into the harbor. Like the docks, they were crowded with shops, counting houses, and warehouses. The produce of the world was piled here: cotton and sugar, barrels of molasses from the West Indies, raisins and lemons from Spain, and silks and chests of tea from China. Everyone was busy, except him. Even the ship's store was full of customers; men choosing candles and barrels of hard-tack, biscuits and other foodstuffs fit for long voyages. At the extreme northern end of the docks, near the tannery, was the ropewalk where Billy Baldwin was employed. It occupied a wharf's length of its own. When Rees peered inside, he saw Billy and other boys pulling the braided twine back and forth and retwisting it to make many yards of thick rope cables. A cooper next door was busily fashioning barrels for molasses and rum.

Rees turned around and retraced his steps past the piers for the whaling ships. They set sail from the northern end of the docks. Because these vessels did not require such deep water, the wharves here were shorter. The boards and the dirt leading to the ware-houses were black with oil. Sailors of all colors—African black, the coppery color of Indians, and white men burned brown—jostled one another.

Finally, as he walked south, Rees came upon the Boothe wharf. It was shorter than several of the others, and he wondered if the length of the wharf bore some relation to the status of the family. Three vessels were docked alongside. One, the Boothe's *Hindoo Queen*, was preparing to leave.

Rees joined the crowd watching as the ship prepared to set sail. A party atmosphere prevailed. Children ran around screaming in excitement. Street vendors sold pies and fruit and Rees suspected there were more than a few pickpockets working the crowd. He smiled, imagining Lydia's excitement at witnessing the lively play before her. She had lived many years as a Shaker, a plain and simple life without these small joys. Since their marriage she had been busy with all the chores of life on the farm and now, with all the children, was busier still. Rees's smile faded. He wished he could have brought her with him, to enjoy this vivid scene.

It took more than an hour for the ship to leave its mooring and slowly sail out upon the tide, its square white sails catching the wind. The American flag snapped jauntily in the breeze. Rees remained until the *Hindoo Queen* became a black silhouette against the glare of the early morning sun. He wanted to remember everything so he could describe it to Lydia. It would be second best to her seeing it for herself, but would have to do. Then he found a tavern by the waterfront, where most of the customers were sailors with cotton bandannas around their throats and tattoos were common. Although a woman might frequent the Moon and Stars in the company of a gentleman escort, women would not be welcome in this establishment. It was little more than a grogshop.

Feeling rather out of place, Rees found an empty seat and ordered breakfast. The slangy conversations that swirled around him were as incomprehensible to him as Greek. While he waited for his food, he stared at the scenes playing out on every side as though they were some entertainment put on for his benefit. A man with skin as black as a kitchen kettle and scarified dots across his forehead sat at a nearby table. A few stools away Rees spotted a man with something—was that a bone?—thrust through his nose. But when his plate of bacon, fish, and cornbread arrived, along with his coffee, he reminded himself he had work to do and reluctantly turned his attention to it. He made a mental list of tasks. First, see the tunnels, specifically where Mr. Boothe was found. Who had found him? That was a question he should have asked before. Second, talk to Twig again. And third, speak to Matthew Boothe and probably to Miss Peggy as well. He scraped his plate clean and although he could have eaten a piece of pie he decided not to spend any more time here. Throwing three pennies down beside his plate, Rees left the tavern and started back to Mrs. Baldwin's.

He retraced his steps north past the wharves, to the lane he'd walked down to reach this busy harbor. When he reached the house where he and Billy had seen Annie at the window, a tall man whose skin was burned dark by the hotter, brighter sun in foreign climes was sweeping the front steps. He too wore a head covering, but instead of tunic and trousers, he was dressed in a long gown. He looked at Rees suspiciously when he slowed to stare at this man in a dress. The crisp citrusy scent of boxwood mingled with the sweeter fragrance of the roses growing by the fence.

"Mustafa." The young maid—Annie—opened the door and called out. "Come quickly, Miss Mary needs you."

With a final glare at Rees, Mustafa turned and followed Annie inside. Through the door, Rees saw a rich carpet and a chandelier. Several women in wrappers glided by the opening before Mustafa slammed it shut. Rees realized with a start that this house was one of the Salem brothels. He did not like to think of young Annie inside, witnessing God knew what, and exposed to all manner of behaviors. If that were Jerusha inside, Rees would storm the front door and snatch her away. But, reluctantly, he accepted the fact he could do nothing for Annie, and he continued on.

By returning to Mrs. Baldwin's Emporium, Rees was able to orient himself and find his way northwest to the Boothe house. He realized as he plodded along Essex that he could have cut through one of the cross streets instead of walking south and then north again. The Boothe house, like many other fine houses built by the merchants, lay near the Commons but within easy reach of the harbor.

The servant who answered the door eyed Rees's worn clothing askance and reluctantly invited him inside. "Miss Peggy is expecting you," he said, his tone gruff with disapproval.

"Masters William and Matthew as well?" Rees asked.

"Mr. Boothe," the servant said, emphasizing the honorific so as to put Rees in his place, "is in the morning room with Miss Peggy."

"Matthew is still abed then," Rees said. The servant did not deign to reply. He bowed Rees into the morning room and retreated. Peggy, her black weeds a smudge against the blue brocade upholstery, sat before a sewing table of fine Chinese lacquer, the open top revealing a harbor scene in gold inlay. Although most of the ships were many-masted American merchants, some of the golden pictures were of single-sailed exotic ships with pointed prows that suggested a harbor on the other side of the world.

William turned from his position by the window and regarded Rees in an unfriendly silence. Like Peggy, William wore black; only his linen and stockings were white, but he wore his somber clothing with the comfort of a familiar uniform. William, Rees was beginning to realize, was a throwback to the Puritan dawn of this city. He held a cigar in one hand and smoke wreathed his head.

"Oh, Mr. Rees," Miss Peggy cried. "Thank you for bringing Xenobia back to us." She slanted a challenging glance at her brother. William frowned.

"And how is Xenobia this morning?" Rees asked, pretending he had not seen her last night.

Peggy smiled. "Still shaken by her sojourn in the jail but recovering."

"She has too much imagination," William said. "Imagining she heard the cries of the women held there during the witch trials . . . ridiculous."

"Anyone would be distressed after a night in jail," Peggy said.

"What do you want?" William asked Rees, just short of being rude. He clearly did not know of his sister's invitation.

"Why, to speak with you and your sisters and brother. I have additional questions."

"Why aren't you out searching for the sailor who killed my father instead of torturing us?" William interrupted. "We are a house in mourning."

"And I wish to see the tunnels," Rees continued as if William had not spoken. "Tell me, do you know where your father was heading when he was attacked?"

"Nowhere in particular," William said. "If you suspect my father of smuggling, I assure you, you couldn't be more wrong. He was known in this city for his probity and would never countenance an illegal activity."

Rees stared at William in surprise. He had not mentioned smuggling, and defending Jacob Boothe against such a charge seemed suspiciously premature.

"What my brother says is true," Peggy agreed. Tears flooded her eyes but by an effort of will she kept them from falling. "But of course, my father used the tunnels for other purposes."

"Was he planning a visit to Georgianne?" Rees said, keeping his gaze fixed upon William. The other man's face reddened.

"I don't know what you're talking about," he said stiffly. "And even to suggest . . . and in my sister's presence." Rees turned his gaze toward Peggy. He would not be surprised if she already knew about her father's interest.

"You're going to be late to your meeting," Peggy said now, her voice low and calming. William glanced from her to Rees.

"As you see, I have no time to speak with you now," William said. "If you wish, you may return tonight, around seven." His tone was so antagonistic Rees wondered if, should he accept that reluctant invitation, William would even come home.

With a final frown directed at Rees, William left the room.

"Please sit down, Mr. Rees," Peggy said. "My neck is developing a pain from staring up at you."

Rees cautiously lowered himself onto one of the delicate-appearing chairs.

"I'll show you the tunnels," Peggy said briskly. "I assure you, however, as my brother said, my father would never engage in smuggling." She smiled. "Xenobia told me of your suggestion. But he was probably planning a visit to his mistress. She does not dwell very near the docks. Father simply used the tunnel to escape the house, no doubt exiting at his counting house." Rees stared at her, surprised and, yes, a little shocked by her calm acceptance of her father's illicit connection.

"I am not surprised you know," he said, "but you discuss her so, so . . ." He couldn't think of an appropriate word. Gently bred young women were not supposed to reveal their knowledge of such things, especially so matter-of-factly.

"Oh please, Mr. Rees," she said. "I did not expect you to be as condescending as my brother. Frankly, he can be so maddening. Do you have sisters?"

"Yes," Rees said. "Two sisters."

"Well, I hope you don't treat them as though they are empty-headed ninnies."

"I think Caroline would say I do," Rees said. And, he admitted to himself, he probably did. Oh, not so much with Phoebe. She was only two years younger than Rees and had a much more easy-going personality than their sister. But Caroline was the baby and spoiled, at least in Rees's opinion. He'd gotten in the habit of lording it over her. Shamed by that realization, he promised himself he would do better in the future.

"Oh dear. I expected more from your good sense. Of course my father had a mistress. William, well, he expects his sisters to strive for a certain level of behavior. I have no patience for it. And, since he has spent almost a year in Baltimore, he has forgotten my many flaws." She offered Rees an impish grin. "He's become a dry stick, wouldn't you agree?"

"Baltimore?" Rees refused to express an opinion on William, although he agreed with Peggy's assessment.

"Mr. Joshua Humphreys is the acknowledged master of shipbuilding. And since Congress is now demonstrating some interest in re-establishing the Navy, my father sent William to Baltimore to learn from the best. Personally, I think Salem's own Enos Briggs would have been as excellent a teacher."

Rees nodded in understanding. At the close of the War for Independence, Congress had disbanded the Navy because of the expense. But now, with Britain continuing to capture American ships and impress American seamen into the British Navy, the increasing hostilities with France, and the pirates from the Barbary Coast who attacked American merchantmen, Congress was rethinking their over-hasty decision. "And this Georgianne? Do you know her full name and her direction?"

A frown marred Peggy's white brow. "Her last name is Foster. I don't know exactly where she lives, although I believe it is close to Turner Street. Or was it Beckett? No matter," she said with a shake of her head. "I learned of my father's connection recently." She smiled again, but Rees thought he detected hurt underneath her flippant worldly manner. "He seemed genuinely attached and I wondered if he might marry her, when my mother passed on." Her blunt assessment once again disconcerted Rees, and he felt his mouth twitch.

"I hope you don't think me callous. You must understand, Mr. Rees, that my mother was ill for many years. Recently she became quite frail. And at only forty-two. Yet none of us were surprised." She stopped abruptly. Rees recalled his sighting of Jacob Boothe after the funeral and nodded in understanding. Boothe had been in his fifties and, although his fair hair glittered with silver, he had been robust.

"And how did you feel about this connection?" Rees asked, leaning forward. Peggy gazed down at her hands. He watched her expression shift and shift again. She wanted to lie, he could see that, but her innate honesty wouldn't allow it.

"I would rather he waited until he was a widower," she said at last, meeting his eyes. "My mother had so little joy in her life. The constant pain . . ." Her mouth twisted and tears again filled her eyes. "She suffered so. And she knew about Miss Foster."

"Did anyone else know about Georgianne Foster?" asked Rees. "Your sister? Your brother Matthew? I assume William didn't learn of it until he returned home?" Peggy nodded.

"Yes. We all knew except William. Someone mentioned it. William was furious. He felt my father's behavior dishonored my mother."

"And they fought about it," Rees said, recalling Xenobia's report. Peggy nodded reluctantly.

"But William would never harm Father," she said quickly. "Never." Rees reserved judgment. William certainly had a temper and he was a tall, strong young man, well able to attack another man with a sword.

"How did Betsy and Matthew react when they learned about Georgianne?"

"You should probably ask them."

"I will. And they'll probably lie to me. But that won't matter. I'll find the truth." He paused, and when she folded her lips together defiantly he added, "By your reaction, I would guess neither of your siblings was happy about the relationship."

"I think we should . . ."

"Oh Peggy, I heard voices." Betsy Boothe paused in the

doorway. Rees entertained the cynical notion that she knew how well her black gown suited her and hesitated in the doorway for dramatic effect. "Oh, it's you. I mean, how nice to see you, Mr. Rees. I thought, I hoped, it might be my fiancé. I'm expecting him." She floated into the room and perched upon a chair near her sister, the multi-armed blue statuette at her elbow. The foreignness of the object pointed up Betsy's fair American beauty. "We are both so distraught over the postponement of our nuptials and now, with the tragic loss of my father, well, I don't know when my wedding will take place." Peggy put out a hand to halt the flow of words from her sister's mouth.

"Mr. Rees has a question for you," she murmured. "About Father's mistress."

"Mistress?" Betsy uttered a light laugh. "Oh, I don't know anything about that. Surely my father would never . . ."

"Georgianne Foster," Rees said, cutting her off without a qualm. "I know you knew of her."

"Not really," she demurred. "Father kept most of his dealings from me. I only heard a rumor about a woman and of course I paid no attention. I didn't believe it for one thing, and for another I never listen to gossip. But if it were true, I do wish he had been more discreet. Mr. Morris is a stickler about such things and he . . ."

"Did your father ever mention Miss Foster to you?" Rees interrupted.

Betsy's eyes widened. "Of course not. He would never discuss such things with me. And I wouldn't want to know. Besides, my father would never humiliate my mother in such a way." Rees noticed Peggy's eyebrows rise as she rolled her eyes. "Especially when she was so ill. The love between my parents was a great love, Mr. Rees, a love I hope to attain in my own marriage. Surely you must agree with me. Are you married?"

"I am," he said, imagining how Lydia would react to Betsy. His wife had little patience for the fluttery lilies of the field.

"Mr. Rees has come to see the tunnel," Peggy interrupted. "I promised to show him where Father died. Do you care to join us?"

Big tears filled Betsy's blue eyes. "Of course not. How can you bear to see where . . . ?" She shuddered delicately. "I would never sleep again. Every time I closed my eyes I would imagine Father, lying there, so cold and still. And in that nasty, dirty place."

"You'll feel better when you've eaten your breakfast," Peggy said, offering her sister a brisk pat upon the shoulder. Rising to her feet, she said to Rees, "Are you ready? Follow me."

Rees rose as well and followed Peggy from the room. She collected her cloak and lit a lantern before preceding him downstairs, through the kitchen, and into the basement. As they passed through the cellar, she lit several lanterns placed at strategic intervals. Rees could see fairly well and looked around curiously. The cellar was being used as an arm of the warehouses: boxes and twine-tied bales, casks and barrels, and small elaborate chests identified with exotic markings were crowded together on boards. On top of one stack sat an open tea chest brimming with jewelry. Gold and silver trinkets caught the candlelight and threw it back in dancing flashes. "I'm sorry about this," Peggy said with a wave of her hand, as Rees squeezed his large body through the narrow path. "William moved some of the most recently arrived cargo here. He had to examine it himself."

"This isn't all of it?" Rees asked, staring around in disbelief.

"Not even a quarter. William moved what he deemed the most valuable. He has this disturbing notion we are being robbed. Ridiculous! Anyway," she added with a quick glance over her shoulder, "I hope this will soon return to the warehouse where it belongs."

Peggy led Rees through a second room, just as full as the first, and to a small nondescript door set into the stone wall at the back. She unlocked the door and pushed it open.

Although Rees had expected total darkness, some illumination entered the tunnel through a square of glass blocks in the ceiling. The light that came through bore a faint greenish cast, as though the skylight above had been set in a garden. Peggy held the lantern high so Rees could look around, revealing a rough chamber constructed of stones and packed dirt. The air smelled of damp and soil and, very faintly, of the sea. "How long have these tunnels been here?" Rees asked, his words returning with an indistinct echo.

"They were built by wealthy families like the Derbys. William brought much of the treasure you saw in the cellar through the tunnels."

"Do they all intersect?" Rees asked, imagining a web of tunnels that ran underground. Peggy shook her head.

"Some do, some don't. A man has to travel these tunnels many years to learn all of the twists. And now Mr. Derby—Elias Haskett Junior, that is—plans to extend them further." Peggy stepped forward, her face a pale ghostly oval above her dark clothing. But she did not go far, pausing about twenty feet away. In the dim lantern light, Rees could just barely make out the junction of another tunnel ahead, marked with wooden columns.

"My father lay here when we found him," Peggy said, gesturing to a spot on the floor close to the wall.

"Lantern, please," Rees said, extending his hand. Peggy put the lamp into his hand and backed into the darkness. Rees heard the catches and soft cries of suppressed weeping. Betsy might claim a delicate sensibility, but it was Peggy who felt her father's death most keenly.

Rees knelt upon the ground. Blood, a pool of it, marked Mr. Boothe's final position. Not as much blood as Rees might have expected; Mr. Boothe's clothing had absorbed some and the dirt between the stones had taken the rest. But the man had lain here for some time, his blood pouring from him. Rees hoped Boothe had quickly lost consciousness and not realized what was happening to him. Lying alone, in the dark, was a terrible way to die.

"If someone fired a gun down here," Rees said, "would those above hear it?"

"Probably," Peggy said from the darkness, her voice roughened with tears. "Sometimes I can hear my brother." She stopped short, biting off her words. "No one would use a gun unless forced; there might be a danger of collapse. Why?"

"Your father was stabbed," Rees said in an absent tone. "I was wondering why. I mean, instead of being shot. But I suppose everyone knows the tunnels might collapse."

"Perhaps," Peggy said. Her voice, coming through the gloom, sounded uncertain.

"And where do these tunnels lead?" Rees asked. "To the docks, yes? Where else?"

"To the warehouses and the counting houses. Some of the tunnels are already abandoned, but I would suppose that sometimes a family might build a new one. I don't really know. Women don't often come down here."

"But your brothers do," Rees said, rising to his feet.

"Well, sometimes. The tunnels are a labyrinth, not easy to learn," Peggy said. "William uses only the one that leads from the warehouse to home. He's forgotten the other ways."

"So Matthew is the one you hear down here, isn't he?" When she didn't respond, he added in a stern voice, "I know you wish to protect him but please, do me the courtesy of telling the truth."

"He would never kill Father," Peggy said, stepping forward into the light. "You must understand, he is a young man. He . . . enjoys life."

"He frequents the brothels on the docks and gambles," Rees interpreted.

"He also attends play rehearsals," she said. "There's a groups that meets." As Rees stared down at the dark pool at his feet, he wondered if Mr. Boothe senior also enjoyed the services offered at the docks. Had he stopped in at the brothels? Was he also a gambler? Rees had seen no signs of such a vice; money appeared plentiful. But some men were skilled at hiding their afflictions.

"Let's return to the house," Peggy said, drawing her cloak more tightly around her. "I'm cold."

"Very well," Rees said. He held the lantern high for one final look around. In the dim light he spotted a strange shadow on the wall. It was an indentation in the stony soil. He examined it closely, running his hands over it. It felt as though the sharp point of something, a sword perhaps, had pierced the wall. When he held up his hand, the fingers were smudged. He suspected it was dried blood. The image of Jacob Boothe, pinned against the wall by some weapon, made Rees shudder.

"Please, Mr. Rees," Peggy said. "Let's go." Rees nodded and stepped away from the wall.

"Yes," he said, "it is chilly down here." But although the cool damp air was seeping through his jacket, he was not shivering because of the cold. He thrust his trembling hands into his jacket pockets, and as Peggy swept past him he followed her to the wooden door set so incongruously into the stone wall. "Who found Mr. Boothe?" he asked as he bent his head to pass into the cellar. After the gloom of the tunnels, the basement inside seemed warm and welcoming.

"I did," she said. "He hadn't come in for breakfast, you see, and he wasn't anywhere in the house." A sniffle interrupted her speech. Rees looked around at the boxes and bales, the striking statuary, and the glitter of jewels and precious metals.

"Maybe robbery *was* the motive," he muttered. "This cellar is full of treasure."

"Did you say robbery, Mr. Rees?" Peggy said as she brushed past him to lock the door.

"It's something Deputy Swett mentioned." Rees reconsidered the possibility. "Is this door always kept locked?"

"Usually." She paused and when she continued she sounded regretful. "It always will be now. Since my father's m–murder," she stumbled over the word, "everyone is frightened."

Rees nodded in understanding. "Who had keys?"

"My father. This is his key." Peggy turned to look at Rees. "But almost no one other than family travels that tunnel we were just in. That's why William brought the valuables home through the tunnel; so no one would see them and steal them."

"If your father had the only key," Rees said, "then how did you open this door to find him?"

"Oh." Peggy looked startled. "There is another key. It hangs outside his office." She held the lantern up and peered into Rees's face. Although pale, she'd regained her composure. "It is still there, Mr. Rees. I saw it this morning. I assure you, no one is breaking into the house from the tunnels. Common sailors don't use them. William is imagining a problem where none exists. And my father was not murdered for a handful of guineas and a pocket watch." She reached out and clasped Rees's hands. "You'll find the man who murdered my father, won't you Mr. Rees?" Rees nodded. But, although he did not argue with her, he thought robbery might be an excellent motive for murder. Especially if the thief was a member of Jacob Boothe's family.

Chapter Eight

As soon as they reached the top of the stairs they heard Betsy's voice, interspersed with deeper male tones, floating out from the breakfast room. "That's Matthew," Peggy told Rees as she removed her cloak. They crossed the hall to the breakfast room. Betsy was regaling her brother with some long-winded story involving her dressmaker. She stopped abruptly when her sister and Rees stepped through the door.

Rees nodded at her, but his attention focused upon the one member of the Boothe family he had not yet met. Rees recalled seeing Matthew outside the housekeeper's room where Jacob Boothe's body lay, but since the boy had gotten ill and quickly fled, Rees had only a confused impression of fair hair.

Matthew rose slowly to his feet and turned to face Rees. A young man of about twenty-one, he resembled his sisters, sharing their blue eyes and light hair and Peggy's sharp nose. But his chin lacked the definition of Peggy's and betrayed a weakness of character. Matthew sought to disguise his chin with a sparse beard and even sparser mustache. He smelled powerfully of stale wine, and his black breeches and coat looked as though he'd slept in them.

"So, what have we here?" the young man said, regarding Rees derisively down that long pointed nose.

"He's looking into Father's death," Peggy said. "At my request."

Matthew glared at his sister. With last night's Madeira still coursing in his veins, he was belligerent and quarrelsome.

"I know what he's doing," he snapped. "Prying into our lives."

Peggy laughed. "Please Mattie, behave. Mr. Rees is trying to help us. Save your bellicosity for your lowborn friends." Rees thought her attitude of amused disdain toward her brother was more like that of an older sister than a younger, and he wasn't surprised when Matthew took offense.

"And who gave you the authority to employ him," Matthew argued, scowling at Peggy.

"It was your brother William who hired me," Rees said. Matthew turned to Rees, taking a few threatening steps forward as though he might attempt a punch. But even though Rees was fifteen or so years older, he also overtopped the younger man by seven or eight inches and at least seventy-five pounds. Matthew thought better of it and retreated.

"You don't care who murdered your father?" Rees asked, pitching his voice very low and quiet.

Matthew looked startled. "Course I do," he said, dropping into his chair with sullen discourtesy. "But why are you bothering *us*?"

"I'm talking to everyone who knew your father," Rees said. Was it grief inspiring this rudeness in Matthew, or guilt? "I assume you all knew him best and might be able to point the way to his killer."

Matthew's eyebrows lifted and then, very slowly, he nodded. "I see. You should speak to my uncles then. They never liked my father. Especially Dickie. I heard what happened at the funeral." Rees turned his eyes toward Peggy. If pressed, he would have identified her as the person Dickie had been accusing at the funeral.

"Everyone was grieving, Mattie," Betsy said. "Especially Dickie. You know how attached he is—was—to Mother. I think you read too much into his drunken ravings."

"It was only Dickie," Peggy said, moving around Rees. "Really, Mattie, you know better than anyone how high-strung he is. The two of you used to quarrel all the time. Adam and Edward were quite apologetic at the averil. Has Edward said anything to you at your play rehearsals?"

"We are too busy to discuss family business," Matthew replied curtly.

"I wish you hadn't told me about Dickie's little scene as soon as you came inside," Betsy said to her sister. "Mr. Morris gave me such a look. I was so mortified. Sometimes you are as thoughtless as Dickie about speaking out of turn. Of course I hastened to tell Mr. Morris that we rarely see that branch of the family. I didn't want him to assume . . ."

"There's something wrong with that boy," Xenobia said from the door, startling everyone. Rees wondered how long she had been standing there. She stepped confidently into the room. Here, among the Boothe family, Xenobia seemed more comfortable than she'd been when first meeting Rees.

"You frightened me, Obie," Betsy said, widening her eyes reproachfully.

"Dickie has always been afflicted with queer fits. Your Mother died peacefully in her sleep, going to meet her Maker with a smile upon her face. And so I tried to tell him."

"I'm sure Mr. Rees doesn't want to hear this tittle-tattle," Peggy said, meeting Rees's gaze over her brother's head.

"If he is truly interested in Father's killer," Matthew said, pursing his lips and directing a challenging stare at Rees, "then he should pester Dickie Coville."

"I will," Rees promised. He'd intended to visit the Covilles anyway. "Do they live around here?"

"The Covilles do live in Salem," Peggy replied. "But not around here. They're a sailing family, too."

"Whaling," corrected Matthew with a contemptuous snort. "Not at all the same thing as us merchants. They live near Salem Neck. I think you'll find my father's murderer there."

Rees nodded but said nothing. He would speak to the Covilles of course; his investigation was far too young to assume anyone's innocence. But already he did not trust Matthew. Besides his rackety life, the gambling and playacting, which no doubt demanded a great deal of money, he betrayed too much eagerness to pin the crime upon his uncles to suit Rees.

And who better to approach Jacob Boothe in the tunnels than his own son? No doubt Matthew knew them nearly as well as his father. Rees reflected upon Jacob Boothe—a kindly gentleman, he would never suspect his own son of malicious intent.

"Do you know Miss Georgianne Foster's address?" Rees asked abruptly, trying to startle Matthew into an admission. But the young man uttered a braying laugh.

"So, you've gotten on to her already. I admit I'm surprised."

"Mr. Rees comes highly recommended," Peggy said, frowning at her brother. She elected not to mention that it was Twig who had suggested him.

"I daresay it does not take tremendous intelligence to snoop," Matthew said. Rees did not react. "Mrs. Foster lives somewhere near Essex Street. On Turner, I believe. She rents a room to another lady. Her cousin, I think."

"I had no idea you knew so much about her," Peggy said. "How did you uncover all of that?"

"Followed Father, of course. Well, what else was I to do? You girls couldn't do it and William was in Baltimore; I wanted to know in what nonsense Father was involved." He poured himself a cup of coffee.

"And what was that?" Rees asked in a quiet, indifferent tone, afraid if he betrayed too much interest Matthew would stop talking.

"Surely Papa wasn't in love with that woman," Betsy cried, widening her blue eyes in horror. "A lowborn woman of the streets."

"How do you know she is lowborn?" Peggy asked, shooting her sister a mocking grin. "Or of the streets?"

"Of course she is," Betsy said with certainty.

"Father would never have married her," Matthew said. "Not unless he was a bigger fool than I believe."

"Why not?" Rees spoke even more quietly.

"She was a ladybird, of course. Entirely unsuitable. She claims to be a widow but I have my doubts. I daresay she will be looking for another protector, now that Father is gone." Turning his gaze to Rees, he added, "You should speak to her as well. Maybe my father refused to marry her and she killed him."

"I will," Rees said, although he doubted any woman could have overpowered Jacob. And would Mrs. Foster be comfortable talking to him, a solitary man? "I might have to ask for my wife's assistance," he said slowly. Yes—the more he considered that solution, the better he liked it. Lydia could not refuse to join him here if he needed her.

"I'm certain she'll be very comfortable," said Matthew with a leer. Peggy shook her head at her brother but did not speak.

"I do hope this liaison was not one of long standing," Betsy said to her brother. "I would hate to think that this woman will suddenly appear with a child in her arms and a claim upon Father's estate."

"No fear of that," Matthew said. "At least, I don't believe so. I became aware of the relationship just a few months ago, and I don't believe it progressed far enough."

"What do you mean?" Rees asked. "What kind of claim?"

Matthew turned his gaze to Rees. "William inherits the business and all the property, the girls have their dowries, and I have my allowance. After that, all the remaining assets are divided between the children. If that woman can prove she's carrying my father's child, he or she will share . . ."

"Stop!" Peggy cried. "Stop now. How can you both discuss this so . . . so coldly? Father isn't even in his grave." Her face contorted with the effort of controlling her emotions, and tears stood out in her eyes.

"Don't cry, Peggy dear," Betsy pleaded, jumping to her feet and running to her sister's side. She threw her arms around Peggy. "You're right, of course."

"I don't see why," Matthew said. He sipped his coffee. "Of course we miss Father. But we don't want some interloper, some loose woman, to come in and take what belongs to us. Do we?" He seemed to realize at the same moment as his sisters that Rees still stood by the door, watching and listening. "I have the right of it, do I not, Mr. Rees? Even in the worst excesses of grief, we must be practical. And my father's estate belongs to us, his legitimate children."

Rees, who'd seen families fight over farthings, smiled noncommittally.

"You don't have a practical bone in your body," Peggy said, her voice rising with anger. "Please, at least pretend to some grief for your father."

"I do grieve," Matthew said, turning upon his sister with a nasty smile. "But I wasn't his favorite, was I? How fortunate for William that he's the eldest and a son, else you should inherit it all."

Peggy's face went dead white and Rees found himself stepping forward. He wanted to strike Matthew and wipe that malicious smile off his face. But Rees stopped himself; this wasn't his business. He held out a hand to Peggy in case she needed his support. Betsy, bereft of words for once, stared at her siblings in horror, biting her lip.

Peggy did not faint. Instead, she pulled herself erect with a jerk and said to Rees, "Perhaps you would care to see my father's office?" Turning with stiff movements, like a puppet controlled by strings, she walked toward the door.

As Rees followed her, he heard Xenobia say, "You both should be ashamed of your behavior. Your mother and father would be horrified."

"Don't forget you can be sold," Matthew said. "My mother isn't here to protect you any longer."

"Mattie," gasped Betsy.

Peggy glanced over her shoulder, her mouth puckered. "That will not happen," she said under her breath. "Not while I'm here."

She guided Rees to the back of the house. The key to the tunnels dangled on a string outside the office door. Peggy opened it and invited him inside. Rees was interested to see that the door to the office was unlocked. He stepped inside. Windows overlooking the trees and flowers of a private yard lay directly opposite the door, and the chamber was flooded with light. With its fine carpets, marble fireplace, and highly polished furniture, this room appeared more as a sitting room than an office, although a large desk faced the windows. The desktop was absolutely clear of any papers and, to Rees, it appeared almost ornamental.

To the right, behind a wooden screen, was a much smaller room. A window allowed daylight to fall upon the surface of a small desk below it, but the corners of the room remained in shadow. Papers were stacked not only upon the desk but also upon the shelves that ran along one wall, and pens and an inkwell teetered awkwardly upon the desk's corner. Peggy moved aside the screen and pushed the inkwell towards the table's center.

"This is your office, I assume," Rees said, peering in after her. He guessed that all the real work for Mr. Boothe's business took place here.

She nodded. "Well, it was. When William came home he took

it over. And, of course, my father and brother did a significant amount of work at the counting house." Her voice trembled, but Rees could not tell if it was from anger or sorrow.

"What did you do for your father?" he asked.

"Everything." She smiled as she brushed away the moisture in her eyes. "He trusted me. Sometimes I even looked over the books, 'just to insure their accuracy,' he always said."

"And how long have you—did you assist your father?" Rees asked, eyeing her. Many women could not even sign their names, so the fact that Peggy not only handled her father's correspondence but also reviewed the books spoke to an unusual level of education for a woman.

"I began running messages when I was ten or so," Peggy said. "As I learned the business, my father gave me other responsibilities. I kept lists of cargoes and oversaw the ships' manifests. I sent letters to the *banias*—the trading agents in India." She sighed. "My father may have felt awkward about it at first, but Mattie didn't care and William was already in the counting house. I was good at it. And when William took passage as a supercargo on one of my father's ships to learn that part of the business, there was no one here but me to do the rest." She sighed again. "My, I would have loved to sail on one of our vessels. But of course I couldn't, not as a female. And now William," her voice shook with anger, "is taking all of this away from me." Her voice roughened and she sounded as if she might cry.

"He's not going to avail himself of your experience?"

"Do you truly expect that to happen?" She turned to look at Rees, her expression weary. "William would sooner cut off his right leg than 'let a woman interfere in men's business.'" Rees clearly heard the quote. "It doesn't matter that I know most of the details of my father's dealings and that William will surely make many mistakes. The very thought of my help affronts him."

"Then more fool he," Rees said. She smiled at him, looking suddenly girlish and almost attractive. "Maybe you'll marry a ship's captain and travel with him," he suggested. He couldn't see Betsy managing the difficulties of shipboard living, especially surrounded by a crew of crude sailors, but suspected Peggy would do well.

"Maybe," she said, but not as though she believed it. "If you listen to William, I will never marry. I'm too plain. Too awkward. And too unfeminine." With a final glance at the desk that she'd called her own, she stepped away, urging Rees before her.

Rees backed into the larger office. He walked around the room but didn't possess the necessary brashness to open Mr. Boothe's desk drawers. Especially not under the eye of his daughter. "Any problems in business lately?" he asked. "Any conflicts with partners?"

Peggy shook her head. "No, nothing," she replied. "He was well-respected and well-liked. That's why I don't understand . . ." Her throat closed and she couldn't speak.

Rees wondered if that were true; Mr. Boothe would no doubt have sheltered his daughter from the rougher aspects of his profession. But if he had been embroiled in a disagreement, someone would know it. "To whom should I speak among your father's business associates?"

Peggy shook her head at him. "I'm certain you'll find they have nothing but praise for my father. But begin with Mr. Crowninshield, if you wish." Rees also planned to make a circuit of the taverns. A few discreet questions, and then he could sit back and listen. A quiet man sitting in a dark corner with a glass of ale was like a piece of furniture: no one heeded him.

"I will. Maybe Mr. Crowninshield will take you into his business," he suggested.

"I doubt that, Mr. Rees. Most of the businessmen are fond of me, as they would be of a puppy. But they agree with William. My father allowed me too much freedom and now I must be confined to a woman's proper sphere." She bit her lip. "Even my father thought so at the end. But you, you seem unusually accepting of a woman's abilities."

"My wife would not permit me any other opinion," he said with an answering grin. A longing for Lydia assailed him, acutely bittersweet, and he wished she were by his side right now. What would she make of this household?

"I hope I have the good fortune to meet her," Peggy said.

"I think she'd like you," Rees said.

But as he left the Boothe home and began walking west, back to Mrs. Baldwin's, he found himself thinking about his sister. Their father had wanted his daughters to be proper and lady-like. They were not expected to work outside on the farm, as most of their schoolmates did, but were supposed to spend their days spinning and weaving. Phoebe, a much more compliant girl than her sister, had done as her father wished. But Caroline hated it. She wanted to travel, perhaps go to Boston. She wanted more education. Her father refused her. No college would accept a woman, and anyway she'd only marry and have children so why waste any money upon her? Rees remembered scoffing at Caroline's aspirations and telling her she was only a girl. He'd laughed at her attempts to write poetry. He wished now he had not been so heartless, and promised himself he would do better in the future. As he considered this, he realized that Caroline, even more than Lydia, would sympathize with Peggy.

Shaking away these memories, Rees turned his thoughts back to the Boothe family. He stopped, stock still, thinking. Matthew was an unpleasant young man and his behavior was suspicious.

The boy was involved in something—perhaps not the murder of his father, but something—and Rees would wager it was illegal. But he could not be certain of what without further investigation. Betsy? She seemed to be exactly as she appeared, a young woman entirely consumed with her wedding and her future as a wife and mother.

Rees started walking again, very suddenly, attracting a curse from a man hurrying by him. He would visit the Coville family, as Matthew had dared him to do, but a visit to Miss Georgianne Foster was of more importance. Was she the future Mrs. Boothe or a soiled dove as the Boothe children believed?

Finally, Rees considered Peggy. For all he knew, she too could be hiding something. Sometimes even those who asked for Rees's help were guilty. He doubted it, in this case, but then he liked Peggy. And what was the secret he suspected Xenobia was keeping back? Rees tried to pin down his feeling from an elusive sense to something definite. He did not think Xenobia was telling him lies, but she was very carefully not telling him something.

Sighing, he reluctantly concluded that his investigation into Jacob Boothe's death was going to take far longer than he'd first assumed. And this was exactly the kind of situation in which Lydia's assistance could be so valuable: women were more willing to confide in another woman than in a man. He needed a woman's touch; he needed Lydia.

He paused again in the middle of the dusty lane, people shouldering their impatient way past him. He missed Lydia, and not like a silly young girl in love with love. No, this felt as though he were only half there, like his leg or his arm was missing. He was coping, adapting, but the shadow pain and the awful sense of something lacking remained.

He didn't like this dependence, didn't like realizing he would never be able to be far from her for very long. But he missed her too much to dwell on his own womanish feelings. Besides, he needed the assistance her insight would give. He began to figure out how he could bring her to Salem.

Chapter Nine

Twig objected most strenuously when Rees informed him of his intention to leave for Maine the following day. "And what shall I tell Miss Boothe?" Twig demanded. "And Xenobia? That you've abandoned them?"

"I'm not abandoning them," Rees said, for perhaps the third time. He had hoped that meeting Twig in the familiar surroundings of the Moon and Stars tavern would calm him, but that strategy had failed. "I'm fetching my wife. That's all. Since I now expect to stay in Salem longer than I expected, I want my wife beside me. You would be as reluctant to abandon Xenobia for many weeks, wouldn't you?" He sliced the strong yellow cheese and dropped it upon a hunk of bread. This would have to do for today's dinner. "She'll assist me in questioning Miss Foster." As well as Peggy Boothe and Xenobia, Rees thought, but he knew better than to share that with Twig.

"And how long will you be away? A week or more?" Twig's rising voice boomed out, attracting several stares from customers at other tables.

"Two days, if all goes well," Rees said, keeping his tone low with an effort. "I will not stop for anything. And I will return, I promise you that. I'll even ask Mrs. Baldwin to save my room, and pay for it in advance. Will that put your mind at rest?"

Twig stared blankly into space for a moment. "I should do it," he said.

"Do what?" Rees was momentarily confused.

"Fetch your wife. Does she read? You can send her a letter. Yes, this will work much better. I'll travel faster on my horse than you in your wagon."

"And how will she travel to Salem?" Rees asked scornfully. "Riding pillion behind you?"

"Do you own a buggy? We can drive down in the buggy with my nag tied on behind. That may take a little longer, but in the meantime, you can work on identifying Mr. Boothe's killer."

"And what if someone passes away and your services are required?" Rees asked.

"I'll hurry," Twig said. "The body can be put on ice in the shed out back until I return." He paused and added, "Miss Peggy promised to free Xenobia once this problem is resolved."

Rees hesitated for such a long time Twig became restless and began to tap the table. If Rees were honest, he would have to admit he wanted to go home, not just for Lydia but to see the children, too. Even David, although he probably wouldn't speak to his father. Rees missed his whole family.

"And what about Xenobia?" Rees asked at last. "Wouldn't she prefer you stayed home?"

"She'll understand," Twig said with complete certainty. Rees wasn't so sure, although he didn't doubt she'd accept Twig's decision; the double lures of freedom and a position as a married woman must be powerful ones. What was it like, caring for Twig? Probably no different than raising a child. Of course, some women would say most men needed minding.

"What do you say?" Twig broke into Rees's thoughts. "I want to leave at first light tomorrow."

Rees agreed. For the price of a ha'penny, they procured paper, ink, and a quill from the barkeeper and Rees set to writing his note. He was not at all sure Lydia would come, and he could just imagine David's cry: "Are you leaving me with all of these children?" David was well able to care for them; he'd had to mind Caroline's little girls when he lived with his aunt. Rees knew David would treat the children well; if he ignored them at times, at least there'd been no evidence of unkindness. Most of David's ire was directed at his father. And Simon, who David called Squeaker, idolized the older boy. It wasn't fair to David to leave all of the children with him, of course, but Rees tried not to think of that. He told himself that the sooner he discovered the identity of Jacob Boothe's killer, the sooner both he and Lydia would return home.

Once Twig held the letter in his hand, he began twitching and jiggling with nerves and could no longer sit still. Rees, wondering if Twig would even wait until morning light, rose to his feet and accompanied his friend to the street outside. Twig shot off, and Rees made his way back to Mrs. Baldwin's. Spotting her hanging laundry in the tiny yard behind the stone wall, he stopped to tell her of Lydia's likely arrival.

"It will be nice to have another woman in the house," Mrs. Baldwin said. As Rees turned to leave, she added, "Thank you for persuading Billy to stay home."

"I didn't do much," Rees said over his shoulder. "And he will leave eventually. He's growing up, and he wants to see the world and make his fortune."

"But why seafaring?" she wailed as she wiped her chapped hands down her apron. "I lost my husband to the sea. I still don't know exactly what happened to him. I don't think I can bear to lose my only son as well. Why can't he be content with becoming a shopkeeper? Or a sail maker?"

Rees shrugged. Although he didn't want to become a sailor, he understood the pull drawing Billy away from home and family. "He's becoming a man," Rees said gently. "He needs to find out what kind of man he is." He wanted to add that Billy could not stay tied to his mother's apron strings forever, but it seemed unnecessarily cruel. Mrs. Baldwin's eyes filled as she shook her head.

"He's still my baby," she said. "And he's all I have. I wish I'd borne a girl. A girl would stay home."

Fully intending to wait for Lydia's arrival before speaking with Georgianne Foster, Rees obtained directions to George Crowninshield's counting house the next morning from Billy. The counting house was located near the docks, as many of the counting houses were. And a busy place it seemed, too. A constant stream of gentlemen passed in and out of the doors.

He crossed the busy street and entered. A long brass rail with fretwork like a fire screen divided the clerks from the customers. A door in the back wall led into another office. Through the opening, Rees could see a map case and a variety of brass instruments.

The hubbub from the many conversations was almost deafening. "I'd like to speak to Mr. Crowninshield, if I may. It won't take long," Rees said to a young gentleman in the newly fashionable tightly fitted breeches.

The young man, his dark hair combed over his high white forehead, inspected Rees's clothes and replied with a faint air of contempt. "In reference to? Are you an investor? Or a sailor?"

"Neither of those," Rees said. "My name is Will Rees. I'm looking into the death of Jacob Boothe at the request of his son, William. I thought Mr. Crowninshield could offer some insight into Mr. Boothe's business dealings."

"Ah." The disdain did not ease, but at least he considered Rees's request. "I'll inquire," he said at last. "Wait here, please." He disappeared into the back office, reappearing a moment later. "Mr. Rees? Mr. Crowninshield will see you now."

Rees followed him through a gate in the brass railing, across the top corner of the long office, and into the chamber behind it. Besides the map case and a large mahogany desk encircled by several horsehair chairs, there was a large table with a map spread upon it. The gentleman poring over the map looked up. A burly man of about forty with thinning hair and blue eyes, he was dressed in a blue jacket and waistcoat that, although conventional, still managed to suggest a seafaring costume. He came forward with his hand outstretched.

"Mr. Rees? William Boothe told me you might call upon me."

"Thank you for seeing me," Rees said. He suspected William had been complaining.

"Jacob and I were friends and partners for many years. I—and everyone in the industry—was shocked and saddened by his death."

"What do you believe happened?" Rees asked.

"Some sailor down on his luck robbed him," Mr. Crowninshield responded promptly.

"Hmmm. Are common sailors familiar with the tunnels used by the merchants?"

Mr. Crowninshield looked at Rees, startled. "No, of course not. Not generally, anyway. But his business partners, well, even his competitors, none of us have—had—any reason to harm Jacob. How much about this business do you know, Mr. Rees?"

"Nothing at all," Rees admitted. Mr. Crowninshield nodded as though that was just as he expected.

"We are not competitors as you might think, Mr. Rees. Outfitting a ship and sending it to the East is an expensive proposition, and we are all investors in one another's voyages. This is also a dangerous industry. With the best preparation in the world and the most experienced captains, we still lose ships. And dealing with the governments in these countries . . ." He shook his head as though he couldn't believe the strange practices adopted by these exotic places. "You wouldn't believe the amount of bribery necessary. But the rewards are enormous, plentiful enough for us all. Why, the profit for the *Grand Turk,* a Derby vessel that was the first to bring back a cargo of pepper, was 700 percent. And Jacob's captains were successful. We all made money. No, I think you must look elsewhere for his killer than the counting houses."

"Might his death have had something to do with smuggling?" Rees asked. Mr. Crownishield grimaced.

"It goes on," he admitted. "But it is not easy. Our ships stop less than three miles out from the harbor, and the customs inspector is rowed out to inspect the cargo and compare it to the captain's manifest. I suppose a small ship might sail into one of the smaller coves to the north, if the captain knew of a house or warehouse where he could store his cargo. But then, after offloading the smuggled items, he would still need to return to the Salem harbor. And he would have to falsify his records. Or keep two sets of books. Most of us make profit enough without taking on the risks of smuggling. And I am certainly willing to pay the duties. We have a wonderful city here." He smiled at Rees. "But where are my manners? May I offer you some refreshment? Rum from the Caribbean or Madeira from Spain?"

"No, thank you," Rees said. He hesitated, thinking. Finally, rubbing a hand over his jaw, he said, "So, you can think of no one who would want to harm Jacob Boothe?"

"You must not have known him."

"I met him briefly after his wife's funeral, at the averil. He seemed an amiable gentleman."

"He was, he was." Mr. Crowninshield sighed. "I know of no one who did not take pleasure in his company." He looked up at

Rees with sharp blue eyes. "In fact, I'll give you the names of some other gentlemen. You needn't take my opinion as gospel." Dipping his pen in the inkwell, he took a sheet of paper and scratched a few lines upon it.

"Thank you," Rees said, taking it and waving it gently to dry. He wondered if there was any point in speaking to Mr. Crowninshield's fellow businessmen. No doubt they would all tell the same story, true or not. "Do you know how Jacob Boothe accumulated the necessary funds to purchase and outfit his first vessel?"

Mr. Crowninshield, who had returned his attention to his map, looked up with a startled expression, and Rees suspected the other gentleman had already forgotten him. "In the usual manner, I expect. I know he learned sailing at his father's knee, on a shallop fishing for the sacred cod. Tiring of that, he shipped out on a merchant ship as a cabin boy at the age of thirteen. Under the British, of course. That was before the War. That voyage was successful and he returned home with a pocketful of money. He worked his way up to captain and by the time he reached his twenties he'd amassed sufficient funds to send a ship to Russia. For iron, I believe. Really, Jacob had the Devil's own luck. He lost very few ships." Rees, who had wondered if Jacob Boothe might have inherited his money or obtained it illegally, was disappointed.

"Can you think of anyone who disagreed with Mr. Boothe or had some animus toward him?"

"Jacob was an amiable fellow," Mr. Crowninshield said. "I know of no one who quarreled with him." He paused. "Perhaps someone from another part of his life?"

"I know Mr. Boothe argued with his son Matthew," Rees said, frustration sharpening his tone.

Mr. Crowninshield nodded. "Well, he's a boy. And that Derby youth is not a good influence. But Mattie is straightening out as he grows up. I look forward to the play he and his friends are rehearsing."

"I expect William will keep his father's shipping concern going," Rees tried again.

"Indeed he will. But William isn't the man his father was. William doesn't care for risk. He is planning to build ships for the new Navy." His words trailed away and Rees did not think he would speak again. But Mr. Crowninshield added in a burst of candor, "It is truly a pity little Peggy wasn't born a boy. She has the interest and the brains. She would have continued in her father's footsteps. But she's only a woman. And even if she wishes to behave in a manner unbefitting her sex, and assist her brother in running Jacob's shipping operation, William would never allow it."

Rees nodded in reluctant agreement. He had already seen that. "A shame, indeed," he agreed.

"I wish you good fortune, Mr. Rees," said Mr. Crowninshield, extending his hand. "I hope you find the villain who took such an estimable gentleman from us. Jacob Boothe was a good man. Besides, everyone is frightened. I've increased my security force and instructed my wife and daughters not to go abroad without a man accompanying them. Just in case it is someone targeting us merchants." He smiled faintly. "My womenfolk are not used to being so confined and complain loudly about the imposition. Now, Mr. Rees, if there's nothing else?"

Rees bowed. He knew he'd learned everything he could. "Of course. I know you're busy. Thank you for answering my questions." This time he left the office.

Chapter Ten

Rees secured directions to the Coville estate from one of Mr. Crowninshield's clerks and discovered that it was such a distance away he would need to drive. Salem Neck was north and east of the city center. He walked back to Mrs. Baldwin's, buying a pie from one of the street vendors for breakfast, and hitched Bessie to the wagon. She shied and bucked as Rees drove through the crowded streets, and he was hard-pressed to keep the mare moving forward. A buggy would have capsized, but the wagon was heavier and more stable. When they left most of the traffic behind, Bessie settled a bit. But Rees knew if she did not calm down, he would have to find another mare to draw his wagon.

The Covilles lived on a hill overlooking the ocean. From the road Rees could see the granite ledges that edged the shoreline, a sight that reminded him of the coast of Maine. The road sloping up to the house bore witness to the variety of wheeled traffic that had taken this route: narrow buggy wheels, broader carriage wheels, and the deep grooves left by the wagons carrying heavy cargo up to the house. The track was lined with trees but when Rees arrived at the top of the slope, approaching the house from the back, he saw that the trees had been removed from the house's front. Nothing blocked the view of the water.

The Coville house was large with at least two stories, probably three. The Mansard roof disguised the top floor. From ground level, Rees could see the railing of a widow's walk and he suspected that that elevation gave a watcher not only a view of the Atlantic Ocean but of the harbor as well.

Rees tied up Bessie at the back and walked round to the front. It was a point of pride with him; he avoided entering by way of the back door, since he believed he deserved the same respect as those wealthy and important men who were admitted at the front door. He pounded on the door. After a long wait, a young girl opened it. She looked harried; her dark hair was escaping from her cap and a smut darkened her nose.

"I'd like to speak to Mr. Coville," Rees said.

"Mr. Adam is not here and Mr. Edward is busy," she replied and began to close the door. Rees slapped his hand on the wood and held it open.

"Then I'll speak to Mrs. Coville," he said, and before she could ask him which one, he added, "The Dowager Mrs. Coville."

"There's only one," she sniffed, "and she's in mourning."

"Yes, I know," Rees said. "For her daughter. That's what I wanted to speak with her about."

"Who is it, Barbara?" An older woman, gowned in black and with a black ribbon tied around her cap, approached the door. Rees recognized her from the averil in the Boothe home.

"Will Rees," he said, looking over the girl's head. "Both Mr. and Mrs. Boothe died within the past few days and I'm working with the deputy sheriff to investigate the deaths."

"I know nothing of Jacob Boothe's death," Mrs. Coville said, interrupting Rees. "And as for my daughter, well, everyone knows she died from natural causes." He heard an edge to her voice, lending her simple sentence a hidden meaning.

"What do you mean?" Rees asked, meeting the old woman's angry gaze.

She hesitated. "I suppose you'd better come in," she said at last, surprising him. He'd thought she would turn him away but supposed she was so desperate to talk to someone that even he would do.

Barbara reluctantly moved aside, allowing Rees access to the house.

Although the hall and the morning room into which Rees followed Mrs. Coville were nicely furnished, the carpet and the chairs were not the Oriental imports common in the Boothe home. Instead, most of the furnishings appeared to be of English manufacture, and pre-war at that. A Chinese screen before the cold fireplace was the only Eastern import Rees saw. Was it a matter of taste? Or of money? Although not poor, the Covilles did not appear as wealthy as merchantman Jacob Boothe.

Mrs. Coville gestured Rees to a seat upon the sturdy horsehair couch. "We have no idea who might have murdered Jacob," Mrs. Coville said. "We rarely saw him or my daughter these last few years."

"And why is that?" Rees said.

"We are whaling folk. The Boothes are wealthy merchantmen." Mrs. Coville's mouth twisted. "When Anstiss was first married, she was a frequent visitor here, but we saw her less and less as the years went on."

Rees regarded her thoughtfully. She was parsing her words like a scholar—not lying exactly, but carefully masking something. "And what did you think of Jacob Boothe?" he asked her.

"I did not know him well, but by all accounts he was an estimable man. And quite wealthy," she added.

Ah, Rees thought. She didn't like her son-in-law. "How did your daughter meet Jacob Boothe?"

"Oh, we're all sailing folk. He'd begun as a cabin boy, you know. It was a successful trip and he came home with over one thousand dollars. He reinvested most of it in another of Derby's ventures. That was also successful. By the time he was twenty-five, Jacob was rich and was clearly on his way to making a fortune. They met when Jacob was thirty." She sighed. "Anstiss was only sixteen then, but she wanted to wed. And the marriage was a happy one for many years. Jacob certainly supported my daughter and her children very well, despite the War." Rees nodded. The British had captured as many American ships as they could, so many American ship owners had lost both vessels and cargo. "William's birth was a difficult one and she was frail after. But we continued to see her regularly, of course, with William and then with Betsy and Matthew. It was after Peggy's birth six years later that something changed. We saw her less and less. By the time Peggy was two or three, I saw Anstiss only once or twice a year." Her mouth twisted. "I know her increasingly severe illness had nothing to do with the *Grand Turk,* but I connect them in my mind because after that vessel's return from China, Anstiss's health began to decline rapidly."

Rees did not speak, but he did not think Anstiss's experience so unusual. Many women did not recover immediately after child-birth.

"Anstiss was always delicate." Mrs. Coville pressed her lips together but anger prevented her from remaining silent. "Jacob already had three children, two sons among them. Why couldn't he resist his lust? Peggy's birth left Anstiss an invalid, too weak to leave the house. I went as often as I could but she—they were not welcoming."

Rees heard Mrs. Coville's hesitation and wondered if Anstiss had been as close to her mother as Mrs. Coville thought.

"Then Jacob hired that nigra Xenobia to nurse my darling daughter. Then, sometimes when I visited my daughter I didn't even see her. Too ill, Xenobia would say. Why didn't Jacob send her home? I could have cared for her." She extracted a handkerchief from her sleeve and wiped her eyes. "In the last five years, I have seen her barely a handful of times."

"How was she, when you last saw her?" Rees asked. Mrs. Coville's eyes filled once again.

"She was so thin. Emaciated almost, as though she did not eat. Her skin had taken on a yellow cast. And she was so tired. When we visited her, she slept a great deal."

"I'm so sorry," Rees said.

She nodded. "Anstiss was very ill a very long time. And Jacob never asked me to help nurse her," she added bitterly.

"Jacob Boothe murdered my sister," Dickie Coville shouted from the door. Rees jumped, startled.

"Of course he didn't," Mrs. Coville said, rising to her feet and hurrying to her son. "Dickie, stop."

"He did."

"Why do you believe Mr. Boothe murdered your sister?" Rees asked the young man. "She was in poor health for many years." Dickie was older than Rees had first thought, early twenties rather than late teens. Rees wondered if that wiry build disguised enough strength to overpower the bigger Jacob Boothe.

"Because she changed. When she visited with William and Betsy, she would play with us. Sing with us." The longing in his voice was so raw Rees could barely look at him. "But after Peggy was born, she stopped coming. She didn't love me anymore. First he stole her from us, then he murdered her."

"Dickie," Mrs. Coville cried, her voice so loud it echoed. "I'm sorry, Mr. Rees. Dickie was very attached to Anstiss. The age difference was such that she was almost a second mother." She paused and then continued, as though she thought Rees would not understand. "Dickie and William were born within months of one another. Anstiss and I were always visiting, and she cared as much for Dickie as her own son." Rees would have guessed that William was at least a good ten years older than Dickie, and that Dickie was naught but a boy, younger than Peggy. Rees's surprise must have shown on his face because Mrs. Coville added, "Dickie was a child of my old age. When he was born Adam and Edward were already almost men." She wiped her eyes once again. "We were all very shocked by her death, but Dickie most of all." Mrs. Coville went to the door. "Barbara. Barbara, come and fetch Dickie please."

Neither Mrs. Coville nor Rees spoke while the maid collected the sobbing young man. After the door closed behind him, Mrs. Coville said, "I'm sorry for Jacob's death." She did not sound sorry and must have realized it. Offering Rees a lopsided smile, she added, "I can barely think of anything but Anstiss." She stopped, her face working.

Rees hesitated and changed direction. "Where are your older sons?"

Mrs. Coville paused while she composed herself. "Adam is on the docks preparing for another whaling trip to the South Seas. It is a big undertaking, Mr. Rees. Just laying in stores takes days. Edward should be helping his brother but he returned home early. For rehearsal. He is involved in a theater group." She sounded disapproving to Rees's ears and must have heard the tone herself, since she stopped short.

"Will both your sons sail out? Together?" Rees asked.

Mrs. Coville laughed, her expression relaxing for the first time. "No, indeed. Adam and Edward would be at each other's throats before they left Salem Harbor. Brothers, you know. No, Adam runs the operation here. Edward will captain *Anstiss's Dream*, but we own several ships with other captains and once the *Dream* sets sail, Adam will begin preparing the next ship. We've been successful." She looked around her with pride.

"I see that," Rees agreed. "Perhaps I might speak to their wives, then?"

"Oh, neither one is married. They still live here, at home. We're all very close." She smiled in satisfaction, oblivious to Rees's surprise. Two unmarried sons was unexpected and quite unusual.

"One final question," he said. "Have you heard of a Miss Georgianne Foster?"

Mrs. Coville looked at him, mystified. "Why no. Who is she?" And then, as she interpreted Rees's expression, she said, "She isn't Jacob's fancy woman, is she?"

"Well, I don't know . . ." Rees began.

"How could he even look at another woman after knowing Anstiss? How could he?" Anger bathed her cheeks with red. "My dear Lord! I vow, if Jacob wasn't already dead, I would kill him myself."

The words hung in the air. Suddenly realizing what she had said, Mrs. Coville forced a strained laugh. "Oh dear. You must know I didn't mean that. I am just so—so distraught with grief."

"Of course. I'm sorry for your loss," Rees said. He rose to his feet, but as he started for the door something she'd said penetrated, and he turned back. "You said Edward is in rehearsal here?"

Mrs. Coville nodded. "In the ballroom." She sighed. "He is quite passionate about this hobby. I don't think you can speak to him now; he hates being interrupted. But you can look in."

She guided Rees to the other side of the house. The ballroom occupied fully one third of the first floor's space, but the family clearly no longer used this area. The floor in the hall outside was scattered with leaves and spots of mud, and when Rees looked inside he saw spider webs hanging from the chandeliers.

At the far end, on a stage that would usually be occupied by the orchestra, was a crowd of young people. Most were young men, but there were a few young women, all very beautiful. Edward Coville strode back and forth at the front of the stage, declaiming in a loud voice. But Rees paid little attention to him; at the side stood Matthew Boothe, his pale blond hair a beacon.

"Matthew Boothe," Rees said in surprise.

"He's the one who involved Edward."

And she wasn't happy about it, Rees thought.

"Now Edward is always busy with them."

"I see. Thank you." Rees bowed over Mrs. Coville's hand and left the house.

As he drove his wagon back down the rutted slope toward the busy streets of Salem, he felt as though he were returning from a great distance away. Despite its proximity to the docks, the Coville property did not feel as though it was a part of the town. They had separated themselves, and Rees wondered if that was purposeful. Maybe they did not want to rub shoulders with their fellows. If so, they were paying a heavy price for their solitude; now that house had become an island of mourning and loss. As Rees joined the throngs of people hurrying about their lives, he thought the Covilles might be happier in the city. At least they would have the distraction of other people around them.

Chapter Eleven

As the traffic picked up, Bessie began to dance and jump. The trip to Salem Neck had tired her so she was not quite as difficult for Rees to control as usual, but it was still hard enough. Soon his arms and shoulders began to ache from the strain. Finally he climbed down from the seat and tied his handkerchief around her eyes. Then, with a hand on her bridle, he guided her through the crowded streets. Although she had been skittish traveling between the farms and small hamlets, she'd been tolerable. But the congestion in a city terrified her. And she did not appear to be improving.

The road curved west, toward the town center. Rees smelled the faint odor of the tannery and realized he was near Briggs's ropewalk. He passed a sign marking Turner and Essex Streets. Didn't Georgianne Foster live near here? He made up in his mind in an instant to call upon her without waiting for Lydia. He questioned a few individuals, and finally approached one who recognized Miss Foster's name. Soon Rees found himself in front of Number 12. A two-story structure, the wooden siding had been weathered a deep brownish gray by the salt air. But a fence enclosed the property, and the small garden in front bloomed with colorful flowers.

Rees opened the gate and walked up the flagged stone path to the front door. When he knocked upon the door, an unremarkable young woman opened it. Simply dressed in a gray gown, she wore her brown hair braided and coiled around her head. She tilted her head up, looking at him. "Yes?" she said.

"I'm Will Rees. Is Miss Foster at home?" Rees asked, his eyes already rising over her head to search for the mistress of the house.

"It's Mrs.," said the maid, "and she is."

"May I speak with her?" Rees brought his gaze back to her pale angular face. "It's about the death of Jacob Boothe."

She hesitated and Rees thought for a moment that she would not allow him entry. But she finally stepped back and waved him through. Rees followed her into the space on the left, a small drawing room with windows overlooking the flowers in the front yard. It was furnished with two solid chairs, a horsehair couch, and a small harpsichord. A floor cloth, cracked and much worn, covered the scarred floor. It was as different from the Boothe's morning room, with its expensive furniture and Oriental trinkets, as it could be. Rees wondered how it had looked to Jacob Boothe. Simple? Comfortable? Unbearably poor? He began to suspect that the Boothe children misunderstood the relationship. This did not at all look like the home of a woman with a wealthy protector.

"Now, Mr. Rees, perhaps you can tell me why you are involving yourself in this tragic event?" Clasping her hands together, the woman sat down and leaned forward, ready to listen. Rees stared at her, a horrible suspicion creeping into his mind. "Yes," she said, smiling at his expression. "I am Georgianne Foster."

Rees swallowed, cleared his throat, and swallowed again. The knowledge that he'd taken her for the maid sent a surge of embarrassment through him. "Mrs. Foster, I apologize." He stopped. What could he say? Everything that occurred to him would surely insult her.

"I'm not what you were expecting," Mrs. Foster said, her gray eyes dancing. "I don't doubt you've heard no end of stories from

Jacob's children." Rees could think of nothing to say. "Now, please tell me why you're involving yourself in the murder of Mr. Boothe. And murder it was, no one can persuade me it was not." Her voice broke and she shielded her trembling mouth with one hand.

Rees inspected Georgianne Foster's averted face with increased attention. Her plain country mouse appearance was at odds with her forthright and opinionated manner of speaking. Rees would not have expected Jacob Boothe to find a bluestocking attractive. Yet, if the tears in her eyes were any indication, she'd been fond of him and was mourning. "I agree with you," Rees said. "Mr. Boothe was most certainly murdered. In fact, that's why I'm here."

"What do you mean?"

"I'm trying to identify the person who murdered him," Rees said.

Mrs. Foster blinked at him. "You are? And you're here, in my drawing room, because you suspect me?" Her voice rose.

"I hoped you might give me some insight into Mr. Boothe."

"And why would you think I could do that? Because you think me his mistress?" She rose to her feet and circled her chair.

Perspiration popped out upon Rees's brow and began rolling down his spine. He could not help offending Mrs. Foster with every word he spoke. He wished he'd waited for Lydia. "I didn't mean that," he said. "I was told you knew him well." He stammered a little with embarrassment.

"I'm not Mr. Boothe's mistress," she said in an icy voice. Rees could well believe that; she was much too prickly to attract most men.

"But you knew him? And, perhaps, know about those who might have wished him harm?" Rees resisted the urge to wipe his face with his sleeve.

"Of course. He was very active in the committee that offered aid to the widows and children of seamen." She paused and then said, "And what authority do you have to poke into his life?"

"Anyone would think you weren't interested in knowing the truth," Rees said, tiring of her belligerence. "Mr. William Boothe retained me to look into the circumstances surrounding his father's death."

"He did? I wouldn't have expected that. Why would he do that?"

"Because Deputy Swett arrested Xenobia and put her in jail. It is quite clear she could not have harmed Mr. Boothe, she has not the strength, and once I viewed the body . . ." Her cheeks blanched and Rees instantly felt guilty. "Please forgive me."

"No, no, it's all right." She forced a smile. "And what has become of Xenobia now?"

"Freed from jail and home." Rees paused, but Mrs. Foster did not speak. "But someone murdered Mr. Boothe and I mean to find out who. Do you know of anyone who hated Mr. Boothe? A rival businessman, perhaps? Or a disgruntled partner?"

Georgianne Foster shook her head. "No, there's no one like that. Mr. Boothe was an honest man. And a successful businessman. The investors in his merchant ships should have nothing of which to complain. None of them would want to harm him."

"What about one of his children?" The words flew out of Rees's mouth before he could stop them.

She turned a cool assessing stare upon him. "Now, why would you say that? I may have been beneath their regard, but they loved their father. Everyone will tell you the same. Mr. Boothe and his children rubbed along rather well, with little friction. But you must know that yourself."

"Alas, I did not know Mr. Boothe well," Rees said. He doubted he could claim an acquaintanceship with the other man based upon a five-minute conversation. "What about Matthew? Is he in debt? Perhaps his father refused to pay his bills?"

"Well, yes, the boy is in debt, but no more than usual for young men. The Derby boy is a bad influence, at least according to . . ." She bit her lip. "Anyway, I don't believe he owes more than his sister Elizabeth. I've been told her dressmaker's bills are breathtaking." Rees recalled Betsy's appearance; he thought Mrs. Foster was probably correct. But he suspected that Matthew was in much more trouble than Jacob Boothe had let on to Mrs. Foster. Rees eyed the woman before him with interest. Although willing to believe Georgianne was not Mr. Boothe's mistress, Rees could see that she had enjoyed his acquaintance. And now she was doing her utmost to protect his family, answering Rees's questions with minimum information.

"And Peggy?"

"Peggy was always his favorite." She smiled slightly. "I expect you've heard about their recent quarrels? Once William came home from Baltimore, Jacob began transferring all the business responsibilities to him. From Peggy. She didn't like that, but Jacob feared if he continued to allow her to behave inappropriately, she would never marry and dwindle into a spinster."

Rees supposed Peggy might prefer that, but he didn't argue. With his visit to the Coville family fresh in his mind, he changed tack. "Did Mr. Boothe ever speak about his wife?" he asked.

Mrs. Foster's eyebrows rose at Rees's abruptness. "Not often," she said. But her eyelids fluttered and she glanced away. "Just that she was ill and had been so for a very long time."

"Tell the truth, Georgie," said a light female voice from the door behind Rees. He spun around. A woman somewhat younger than Mrs. Foster hesitated in the entrance. She was of slender build and brown-haired like Georgianne, but there the resemblance ended. Her eyes were a velvety chocolate, not gray, and a pink ribbon twined through her short curls. Instead of a high-necked gray gown, her frock was white—no, Rees realized, it was pink, but so light a pink it appeared white. A dark pink sash drew attention to her bosom and the low neckline. Georgianne faded into the background, as dowdy as a peahen.

"My cousin, Isabella Porter," Mrs. Foster said. "When my husband disappeared at sea, I asked her to join me." Her flat tone caused Rees to wonder if Georgianne regretted her generous gesture; certainly she appeared dull and unattractive in comparison to her pretty cousin.

Miss Porter smiled at Rees. "At first I was hesitant to come. After all, isn't Salem known throughout this country as the center of witchcraft and witches?" She shivered with delicious excitement.

"The trials were a hundred years ago," Georgianne said sharply. "Sensible people no longer believe in such things."

"Quite true," Rees said, smiling at Miss Porter. He turned his attention back to Mrs. Foster. "Tell me more about Matthew?"

"Matthew was a trial to his father. He spent every penny of his allowance, mostly upon that theatrical hobby of his," Isabella said.

"Now, Isabella," Georgianne began. Her cousin frowned at her.

"You know Jacob was worried about him, Georgie. And the things missing from the cellar and the warehouse. I would not have allowed the boy to continue."

"Enough," Georgianne said in a severe tone.

So, it was not only William who had noticed the missing items. Rees filed that away for further thought. But at the moment, Matthew interested him far less than the woman taking a seat beside her cousin. Likeliest, Rees thought, gossip had gotten the story only half-right; Jacob Boothe's love interest did reside in this house, but was not Georgianne Foster. "And what did Mr. Boothe say of his wife?" Rees asked again.

"Her illness prevented Anstiss Boothe from behaving as a wife for many years."Isabella Porter pursed her lips in a little moue that left no doubt to what wifely activity she meant. "Everyone knows that. But Jacob was so brave and uncomplaining."

Rees, who could guess to what end Boothe was aiming, felt his lips twist. "I've heard others refer to Mrs. Boothe's illness," he said. "What was it?"

Isabella threw a look at her cousin.

"I'm afraid none of us know that," Georgianne said. "But she kept to her own apartments. It's been years, or so I've heard, since she went out."

"Jacob said she slept a great deal," Isabella contributed helpfully. "Why are you interested, Mr. Rees?"

Again he went through his tale, although he kept it much abbreviated. He was sure Miss Porter was not truly interested in his response, and that her question was simply an effort to keep the conversation going. He saw Georgianne shrink back into her seat as her cousin leaned forward, all sparkle and shine. "How very generous of you to give your time to help solve this terrible mystery," she said. As a young man, Rees might have found the attentions of a pretty woman flattering, but from the vantage of his age, and as a happily married man at that, he was put off. Georgianne must be regretting her generosity to her cousin now.

"Did you know Mr. Boothe well?" Rees asked Isabella.

"Of course." She laughed. "He visited often."

"Did he speak of any business partners with whom he disagreed?" Rees asked.

"Oh no, we never discussed business." She laughed again. "Sometimes he brought exotic gifts, brought for us on his ships from all these countries with strange names. He brought me this necklace." She fingered the thin shining chain with the brownish stone at the end. "It's carved into a rose. 'A rose for a rose,' he said." Her fingers invited Rees to admire her plump white chest.

She exhibited no sign of grieving for the man she claimed to like so much, and Rees recoiled from her callousness. He turned to Georgianne Foster once again.

"We are a household of women, Mr. Rees," she said with a thin smile. "Jacob rarely discussed business with us. And although he spoke of his children once in awhile, he mentioned his wife infrequently." She stopped suddenly, and Rees had the impression she'd planned to say more but had thought better of it.

"It was always so gay when he visited," Miss Porter said wistfully. "Last April Jacob took us to see a strange animal from the Orient. Huge and covered in gray hide, with a long trunk that swung side to side."

"I have never heard of such an animal," Rees said in disbelief.

"Captain Crowninshield brought the elephant from the East, passing through Salem on his way to Boston." Georgianne sounded like a schoolteacher.

"I hope the elephant," Isabella stumbled a little over the word, "is brought back to Salem. I would dearly love to see such an exotic creature again."

"Was the elephant ferocious?" Rees asked. He knew all manner of strange beasts lived in the East. Georgianne shook her head and would have answered, but Isabella jumped in before her.

"The creature was quite tame," she said. "Why, she took the bread from a gentleman's pocket."

"I hope to see such a strange animal some day," Rees said.

For a moment, the three of them sat in silence. Rees looked out the window and saw it was already past noon. His stomach was growling, and before his next stop he would have to eat. He needed to draw this visit to a close if he still intended to stop at the Coville wharf today.

"You puzzle me, Mr. Rees," Georgianne said. "Why are you doing this?" As Rees opened his mouth she held up a hand. "I know, you explained that you are now employed by William Boothe. But I just find it hard to believe that you abandoned your own life to involve yourself in this—this tragedy."

"Stephen Eaton is an old friend," Rees said. "He asked me to help Xenobia. I was already nearby. I am a traveling weaver and I stopped in Salem briefly."

"You have no home? No family waiting for you?"

"I do. And I'm anxious to return to them. But resolving such conundrums is a talent of mine and I owe my friend my life." He paused and added, "You seem reluctant to see this investigation proceed."

Her lips parted, but she held herself still for several seconds. Finally she nodded. "I am. I fear no good will come of this." She leaned forward and clasped her hands together. "I wish you would take care."

"Don't you believe Jacob Boothe deserves justice?" Rees asked. "He was murdered."

"I do. But you are stirring up the mud. You are endangering others." Her eyes met Rees's. "Sometimes it is better to let things lie. Please." Rees stared at her. What did she fear? What secret did she hide? Boothe's children already knew of her existence. Was it Isabella she was trying to protect? Or was it the Boothe children, as a final gift to Jacob?

"I disagree," Rees said. Seeing her alarm, he kept his voice gentle. "If identifying Jacob Boothe's murderer lays bare some secrets, then perhaps they should not be kept hidden."

"Oh, you are both so serious," Isabella Porter trilled. "And we were having such a jolly conversation." She laughed and Rees realized she did so as punctuation. "Well, I hope you'll call upon us again, Mr. Rees. I've so enjoyed your visit."

Rees, who hadn't removed his eyes from Georgianne, saw her mouth twist.

"I will certainly visit once again," Rees said, looking from one woman to the other. "I know my wife will be delighted to meet you." Isabella bit her lip. "I expect her to join me here in Salem soon."

"We'll be happy to meet her," said Georgianne with a smile. The quick look she shot her cousin was not friendly. "Won't we, Bella?"

"Of course," said Isabella.

Rees sensed some vibration between the cousins. Isabella was clearly dismayed by his revelation, and Georgianne seemed almost glad to see her cousin disappointed.

"Let me show you out," Mrs. Foster said, rising to her feet and waving a hand at the door. Rees couldn't ignore the subtle command and also stood up. Silently he followed her into the hall. As he stepped through the front door, she said, "I hope you know what you're doing, Mr. Rees." She hesitated and he guessed she planned to say something further. But she thought better of it and closed the door softly behind him.

Chapter Twelve

After a few moments staring at the closed door, Rees turned and walked back to his horse and wagon. Clearly, Jacob Boothe had been a regular visitor to this household. It was less obvious which cousin he had visited. The fashionable and attractive Isabella seemed the most likely choice, especially considering Georgianne's prickly dowdiness. But it was she who was grieving and frightened. Still, Rees was certain neither woman had murdered Jacob Boothe; like Xenobia, they did not have the strength. But he thought Georgianne knew more than she'd said. How he missed Lydia's insight, especially into the female mind.

Rees struggled to guide Bessie through the narrow Salem streets, busy with carts and wagons, buggies and pedestrians. He began to wish he'd stopped at Mrs. Baldwin's and left his wagon and Bessie there. The traffic became much worse as he approached the wharves. Finally, he pulled over to a livery stable and paid a farthing to leave Bessie and the wagon there for a few hours. He could move much faster on foot. He reckoned by the angle of the sun that it was already approaching four o'clock. Seagulls screamed overhead, more and more of them as Rees approached the docks.

Although it sported a figurehead, the bust of a woman, *Anstiss's Dream* was instantly recognizable as a whaling ship by its differences from the elegant schooners that plied the Cathay trade. Bolted high on the mast was a pair of spectacle-shaped rings. Of course, Rees realized, they were for the lookout, necessary if the crew were to spot the whales. A series of cranes and long slim boats circled the whaler: whaleboats that could be lowered to the water to chase their prey. And a shelf, bloody red in the light of the setting sun, was positioned over the gangplank. Rees couldn't even guess what purpose that filled. All the sails were down, the ropes forming a complex web above the deck.

A sailor in white duck trousers and blue jacket stood by the gangplank, marking off each cask of the parade as it went up into the ship. "Raisins," he muttered under his breath. "Pickles, onions, cheese." Rees neared the man, but paused, waiting until he'd checked off the final cask. Like most of the other sailors Rees had seen, this mate wore a bandanna around his neck. A circular tattoo like a rope decorated his left forearm. Finally, the sailor looked up from his list.

"I'm looking for Adam Coville," Rees said.

"Not sure if he's still here," the mate replied. "Come aboard."

Rees followed the mariner up the gangplank but remained near it. The War for Independence was not so distant that Rees did not remember the impressment of Americans into the British Navy. He was pretty sure the British still followed that custom. For all he knew the American sailors did as well, and he had no wish to go to sea, especially not upon a whaling ship. Underneath the salty tang of the air, he smelled old blood and oil and the stink of men crammed into too small a space. Two deckhands, both dark-skinned, worked on the deck.

"You see the Master?" the mate asked the darker of the two. He was a black man, one of the so-called Black Jacks, and not above twenty, Rees suspected. He shook his head. "Mr. Brewster?" The harpooner kneeling by the metal tools jumped to his feet.

"No, sir."

"Let's search him out, you and I," the first mate said to the black sailor.

As he and the deckhand disappeared belowdecks, Rees turned his gaze to the metal tools spread out upon deck. Blackened with oil and scarred with use, the sharp edges glittered in the sun.

"You been on a whaler before?" asked the harpooner. Rees looked at the man. Although tanned almost as dark as the African, this sailor had eyes of a peculiar light blue-green. Rees shook his head no and turned back to the tools. He recognized harpoons, long and sharp with wicked barbs. Several hooks of different shapes and sizes accompanied the harpoons, and next to them were a variety of long metal implements with leaf shaped ends.

"What are those?" Rees asked, pointing to them.

"Them? Them be lances." The sailor stood up. As tall as Rees, he was broader at the shoulder. Tattoos, almost invisible against his bronzed skin, smudged one calf, his bare back and a bicep. The last, Rees thought, might be a compass. "You push a lance into the whale and twist until it kills the beast." He picked up a long knife with a long square blade and a long handle. "This here be a boarding knife, for cutting up the blubber and bringing it on deck. And this," he picked up another tool with a razor-sharp curved blade, "this be a blubber gaff for taking the blubber."

Rees held up a hand. "Enough." Shuddering, he removed his eyes from the lethal tools, his gaze coming to rest upon the brick stove in the center of the deck. Two enormous iron pots were positioned within the brick shell, over stone slabs blackened by fire.

"That's the tryworks," the harpooner said. "We stoke up the flames and throw the blubber into the try-pot and boil out that oil by the barrelful."

Rees looked at the greasy black film staining the bricks. "Does the ship ever catch fire?"

"Sometimes." The harpooner grinned, his teeth a startling white against his dark skin, and stretched. With the movement of his muscles and under the sheen of perspiration, the pictures on his skin seemed to move. Rees realized he was staring; the effect was curiously mesmerizing.

"You want to sign on to the crew?" asked the man. "You be a big strong man. Good money in whaling. Even for a green deckhand the lay can be a thousand dollars or more."

"No, thanks," Rees said, stepping back a few more steps. "Good money in weaving, too." And he didn't have to kill anything.

"Mister Coville's gone," said the officer, reappearing on deck trailed by the deckhand. "He got a message from home and left. I'm sorry. His sister died," he added helpfully.

"Will he return tomorrow?" Rees asked. He didn't fancy a second journey to the Covilles' house on Salem Neck.

"'Spect so. First thing in the morning. We're getting ready to sail in a few days; a lot of work to be finished before then."

Rees nodded and thanked the man before turning to descend the gangplank to the dock. He wished he could have spoken to at least one of the Coville brothers before they learned of his visit to their house and his conversation with Mother Coville and Dickie. But it couldn't be helped. The mate followed him down. As Rees walked away, he heard the mate take up his list of supplies once again. "Candles. Ship's biscuit."

And now it was time for supper, Rees thought, looking around him. He must find a likely tavern. It would soon be dark, and shopkeepers and sailors alike were heading home. He began walking back to the livery stable, following a rowdy gang of sailors. Bronzed a deep brown by a southern sun, they talked in loud, raucous voices. He followed them to a nearby tavern, the Witch's Cauldron. The walls were weatherbeaten to a grayish brown, but the sounds of laughter and conversation beckoned him inside. It was not a prepossessing establishment. The floors were slick and the tables greasy and he was the only non-sailor in the room. A few of the men, both ragged deckhands with bare feet and officers in their blue jackets and shoes, turned to stare.

Avoiding the most obvious pools of tobacco juice, Rees found a seat in the back, away from the clusters of seamen at the front. After a few moments, a girl with a low-cut blouse and stained apron came to take his order. He watched the slattern fry his cod over the fire. With a mess of fried potatoes and a side of bacon, the fish was hot and filling. When the cook looked at him as though he were strange when he asked for coffee, he made do with ale. It was thin and sour. Since all of the men around Rees were drinking rum, he guessed the tavern did not bother with good beer.

As he ate, he watched the sailors on either side. Many languages contributed to the cacophony: Portuguese, French, even some Indian tongues. It was a well-known fact that some of the local tribes produced the best harpooners.

And there, seated at a table on the other side of the room, was Matthew Boothe. A wide-brimmed straw hat banded with a black ribbon shadowed his eyes, but the sharp nose was unmistakable, and Rees could see the faint shine of the boy's foolish mustache and thin beard. He was talking to a rough-looking fellow with a swarthy complexion and thick wavy black hair. A gold earring glittered in the visible ear. He appeared dangerous, as though he would knife a man as quick as look at him.

The serving girl appeared at Rees's elbow, asking if he wanted anything else. Rees shook his head and handed the girl a few pence. When he looked back, Matthew was gone. Only his companion remained, swigging rum from a jug. Rees stood up and looked all around. No Matthew.

All right, Rees thought, he would just question that swarthy seaman. But as he threaded his way through the tables, a noisy conversation suddenly erupted into a drunken fight. Matthew's companion jumped to his feet and ran for the door. Rees followed, pressing himself against the walls and barely avoiding swinging fists and feet. By the time he fought his way outside, the pirate had disappeared.

Rees went down first one shadowy lane and then another. The pungent odor of strange spices tickled his nose. Rees recognized ginger and cinnamon but not the others. He inhaled, enjoying the suggestion of different food, different customs from the other side of the world. Two young women exited one of the buildings, shrouding their dark hair with filmy colorful scarves. Gold and silver glittered on their arms. Rees sucked in his breath. The fabric that covered their heads swept up from long skirts and over their bodices, but left their midriffs bare. Rees could clearly see the navel of the young woman closest to him. Yet she did not comport herself like a whore. Her eyes were modestly lowered and she kept a firm grip upon the arm of the woman by her side.

He was so captivated by the women that he did not hear the footsteps approaching him from behind. Suddenly an arm went around his throat, cutting off his breath. Rees tried to struggle but the arm tightened. "Get out of Salem," said a husky voice behind him. "You don't belong here." Abruptly the arm released him and Rees fell into the refuse littering the alley floor. Choking and fighting for breath, he turned to stare over his shoulder. But the man was running away, and all Rees saw was the curious rolling gait of a sailor before he disappeared around a corner.

Rees struggled to his feet. He knew he would never catch his attacker now. Cursing under his breath, he headed to the livery for his horse and wagon. Well, he knew now that Matthew Boothe was involved in something. But it had not been the Boothe boy who assaulted him. That man was a sailor, at least as tall as Rees, and probably black. Rees had a confused impression of a dark arm going about his throat. Rees's investigation had upset someone.

Now alert to everything around him, Rees speeded up to a fast walk, pausing only once to purchase a pocketful of Spanish oranges from a fruit seller on his way home. He did not slow down until he was safely inside the stable yard at Mrs. Baldwin's.

By the time he unhitched Bessie from the wagon and moved her into Mrs. Baldwin's stable, the sun had dropped completely below the horizon. Although a few filaments of purple streaked the sky, in the stable it was almost too dark to see. Candlelight spilled out from Mrs. Baldwin's window and Rees could see her and Billy eating dinner at the table. Rees stopped at the trough and washed up, the cool water tingling pleasantly on his sweaty sun-burned skin. Then, too tired even to peel one of his oranges, he went upstairs for bed.

Chapter Thirteen

Rees woke early. His throat hurt where his attacker had grabbed him and his right knee was bruised from his fall. Ignoring these trivial hurts, Rees tossed a few oranges into his jacket pockets for later and went down to the yard. It was just past dawn and Billy was leaving for the docks. Without speaking, the two fell into step together. They tramped in silence down the already crowded lanes, all the traffic heading to the wharves at Salem Harbor. As they neared the harbor, they passed the brothel and when Rees looked up at the second-floor window, he saw Annie again, staring down at them. Billy offered her a tentative wave and Annie smiled in return. Almost without thought, and knowing that the older woman would be summoning the servant girl back to her chores, Rees reached into his pocket for an orange. He whistled and when she looked at him, he held it up and then tossed it at the window. She reached for it but missed and the fruit soared into the room behind her. She disappeared as she ran for it. Oranges were expensive, and she probably ate them rarely, if at all.

Billy looked at Rees in surprise. "She looks hungry," Rees said.

When they reached the waterfront, Billy surged into a run, sprinting away towards the ropewalks. Rees followed at a quick walk but could not keep pace with the boy, who disappeared into the glare from the rising sun.

When Rees arrived at *Anstiss's Dream,* he found the same officer he'd met the previous day standing at the foot of the gangplank. He was still checking off casks as the deckhands rolled them onto the ship. Rees could almost believe he had not moved at all. Stacks of staves for barrels were also carried aboard. Rees assumed they would be used to construct barrels for the oil.

As Rees approached, the officer's pale blue eyes passed over him. Holding up a hand to halt the flow of the goods onto the ship, the sailor turned and shouted to the black crewman. "Get the Masters, will you?"

"Aye, sir," the deckhand responded and moved out of sight.

"The Covilles'll be down soon," the mate said. His blue jacket was worn but the brass buttons were polished to a shine. Rees, from his advanced age of thirty-six, thought the sailor couldn't be more than twenty-five, but his waist-length brown pigtail was already flecked with gray.

Rees withdrew to the side to wait, watching the loading of the *Dream* with interest. He had not realized how much food and water had to be carried, but, of course, it made sense. The sailors could not stop at a little store or barter with a farmer for a chicken in the middle of the ocean.

The two Coville men, both garbed in mourning, hurried down the gangplank. "Where is the gentleman who wished to see us?" asked the taller of the two. The mate tipped his head at Rees, who was waiting a few steps away. The two almost identical faces swiveled toward him.

"You wanted to speak to us?" They stepped off the gangplank and approached. "I am Adam Coville, this is my brother Edward." Lines grooved Adam's forehead, and Rees could see the silver threading his light brown hair.

"How do you do?" Rees offered his hand. "My name is Will Rees. William Boothe hired me to look into his father's murder."

"Ah," said Adam Coville. "And after you spoke to my mother and to Dickie, you thought we might have something to do with it? You must understand that Dickie is . . ." He searched for the right word.

"Delicate," his brother supplied. Unlike Adam, who held himself erect and very still, Edward shifted from foot to foot and seemed ready to bolt. Rees knew Edward must be in his forties, but he gave the appearance of a much younger man. "Dickie was much attached to Anstiss, and her death has devastated him."

Adam nodded. "Indeed, he is mad with grief. I wouldn't take what Dickie said too seriously, if I were you." Rees nodded but decided to reserve judgment.

"Do you know of anyone who might wish Mr. Boothe harm?"

Adam Coville turned to look at his brother. Edward shrugged and shook his head.

"Perhaps one of the investors in his ships?" Rees suggested. Both Covilles grinned and shook their heads.

"Even we are investors," Adam said. "His last journey was a successful one and we turned a handsome profit."

"They lost a few crewmen when the *Hindoo Queen* stopped for fresh water. One of the little islands, you know," Edward said.

"But that happens regularly," Adam said. "Surely no one could be angry at him for that."

"Was Mr. Boothe involved in smuggling?" Rees asked, the image of Matthew in the sailors' tavern fresh in his mind.

Both men burst out laughing. "That old Puritan? You must understand, Jacob Boothe was a careful and rigid man of business. I can no more imagine him smuggling than sailing to the moon." As Adam spoke, his brother Edward nodded in agreement.

"He was an old man," Edward said. "Many years older than Anstiss. Never understood why she married him." His words trailed away when his brother directed a stern look at him. Rees would not have described Jacob Boothe as "an old man," but he didn't argue.

"He gave her a good life," Adam said. "Everything she desired and more." He did not sound approving.

"My mother said you told her Jacob met another woman." Again, words burst from Edward's mouth. Adam frowned at his brother but Edward rushed on. "A Miss Foster. That explains why Anstiss didn't make him happy any more."

"That's just gossip," Adam said, shaking his head. "We don't know if it's true."

"You know, don't you?" Edward demanded of Rees.

Rees recalled Georgianne. That prickly manner of hers seemed unlikely to cause such high passions. "I've met Mrs. Foster," he said, choosing his words with care. "I believe they worked together on some committee that offers aid to indigent widows and orphans. I would describe her as plain and a bluestocking."

"They were seen together," Edward said, his mouth curling. "I asked around. From what I was told, she was clinging to his arm like a barnacle, and it looked as though they were more than acquaintances." Rees thought that sounded more like Isabella than Georgianne, but he did not want to further enrage this man. "I only wonder," Edward added in a soft, angry voice, "why cousin Matthew did not confide in me."

Adam grasped his brother's arm. "Maybe he learned of his father's indiscretion only recently," he said, keeping his eyes fixed upon Rees. "He can't have enjoyed seeing his father become a laughingstock all over town."

"There's no fool like an old fool," Edward said.

Rees did not speak, and for a few seconds the three men stood together in silence. A seagull glided down to the dock and pranced across it, looking for scraps.

"We know nothing and really can't help you," Adam said at

last. "In the last few years we saw Anstiss and her family only once in a great while. And almost never recently. Even our dealings with Jacob went through his supercargo. If Edward and Matthew hadn't both taken on playacting we'd have had no news of Anstiss at all." His voice trailed away.

Rees nodded and gestured to the ship. "You preparing to sail soon?"

"Not me," Adam said. "Edward will captain this voyage."

"I plan to sail with the tide later this week," Edward said, glancing over his shoulder.

"And now, if you have no more questions, we must return to work." Adam turned toward the mate, still busily checking off the casks, although Rees fancied he could see the mate's ears flapping with curiosity.

Rees thanked the brothers and watched them ascend the gangplank. Adam called out to each of his crew, his voice fading as he crossed the deck. Rees began walking away, his feet taking him to the ropewalks at the top of the docks. He thought he might look in on Billy, see what he did. But mostly, Rees planned to wander the jetties looking for the black-haired sailor he'd seen talking to Matthew. Jacob Boothe may not have been involved in smuggling, but Matthew? Probably.

Rees walked back and forth across the docks for the rest of the morning, his frustration increasing with every step. He saw no sign of the sailor with the gold earrings or of Matthew Boothe. Were they hiding from him? Or was Rees looking in the wrong place entirely?

Finally, irritated—a whole morning gone and nothing to show for it—Rees walked back to Mrs. Baldwin's Emporium. As he passed the brothel, Annie, who was shaking rugs out from the back door, offered him a shy little flutter of her fingers. Rees returned the greeting and continued on, feeling a little better. Surely someone would know of that elusive sailor. Why, even Billy might know; Rees could ask him when he came home for dinner. Breaking into a whistle, he hurried down the last lane to the gate into Mrs. Baldwin's yard.

The gate was open and through it he saw a very familiar buggy. Amos was still between the traces. Twig had made much better time traveling to Maine on his horse than Rees would have in a wagon. Rees ran, first to the barn, and then, turning, to the back door leading into the house. As he sprinted across the dirt, Lydia stepped out, smiling. When Rees reached her, he snatched her into his arms and whirled her around. "I am so glad to see you," he cried.

She laughed. "Put me down. Everyone is watching us."

Rees obeyed, realizing as he did so that Mrs. Baldwin and Twig were standing in the open door. Mrs. Baldwin lifted her apron and dabbed at her teary eyes.

"Come in," she said. "Finish your tea, Mrs. Rees. Come in and sit down."

Lydia smiled at Rees. At six months pregnant, her belly swelled within her blue gown. With a twinge of guilt, Rees realized her eyes were shadowed with fatigue. "Are you hungry?" he asked her.

"Very," she said. "I always seem to be, now."

"Nothing for me," said Twig. "I want to see . . ." His eyes sought out Rees's.

Xenobia. Of course. "We'll talk a little later," Rees said to the undertaker. As Twig ran toward his rawboned chestnut, Rees took Lydia's arm and guided her to the house. Mrs. Baldwin had laid out tea and little cakes at the kitchen table. She left the doors into the hall and from the hall into the shop open so that she would hear any customer who entered. Lydia sat down and picked up her teacup. Rees pushed his chair as close as he could to her. Although he accepted a cake that he devoured in two bites, he did not want to sit here, exchanging pleasantries with Lydia and Mrs. Baldwin. He was desperate to spend some time alone with his wife.

"When is the baby due?" asked Mrs. Baldwin, picking up the thread of a previous conversation.

"Some time in the fall; late September, I think," Lydia said, her eyes glancing away from Rees for only a second.

"Let me bring in your valise," Rees said.

Lydia shook her head. "Your friend Mr. Eaton brought it in. My things are already upstairs."

"Were you waiting long?"

"Less than an hour," said Mrs. Baldwin briskly. "I'll ask Billy to unhitch the buggy and put the horse in the barn. Next to the other one," she added with a smile.

"The Moon and Stars is nearby," Rees said, never removing his gaze from Lydia's face. "The food isn't bad; we can eat our dinner there."

She put her cup into its saucer with a little click. "Good." Smiling at Mrs. Baldwin, Lydia added, "Mr. Eaton was so eager to return to Salem we barely stopped. Thank you so much for the tea."

"You're very welcome. It will be nice to have another woman in the house, even if it's only for a little while," Mrs. Baldwin said. She smiled at Lydia and Rees realized with a start that his landlady was only a few years older than his wife, and probably his younger by the same amount. He'd begun thinking of her as an old woman, since she was a widow and had a teenage son, but she wasn't.

He offered his arm to Lydia. She looked at the plates and cups upon the table as though she should gather them up.

"Don't worry about the dishes," said Mrs. Baldwin, correctly interpreting Lydia's expression. "I'll take care of them. You go along with your husband. I'm sure you both have a lot to talk about."

Lydia stood, leaning on Rees's arm. "Thank you, Mrs. Baldwin.

I look forward to visiting with you." Mrs. Baldwin nodded with a smile.

As Rees and Lydia walked arm in arm into the back yard, she reached up and rubbed her hand over his chin. "My goodness, look at these ginger whiskers. You're beginning to grow a beard."

Rees laughed. "Without you, shaving seemed an unnecessary distraction. How are you?" He inspected her face. "You look tired. Are those children . . . ?" He stopped, feeling his face stiffening. He'd thought little of the children. "I left you to care for them alone." Regret silenced him.

"Don't worry," Lydia said. "They were little trouble. Jerusha is quite strict."

"Is David caring for them now?"

She laughed. "No. Sally Potter took Nancy, Joseph, and Judah into her house. Jerusha chose to stay at the farm." Lydia glanced at Rees. "She takes her responsibility as my helper very seriously. And I couldn't separate Simon from David."

Rees nodded. From the first, when eight-year-old Simon had met David and realized he was the one who knew about the farm, Simon had idolized the older boy. Simon had become David's shadow and his adoration had gone some way to easing David's anger. Rees thought David was fond of Simon, nicknaming him Squeaker and allowing him to tag along and help with chores. Relief soothed some of Rees's worry—he'd been more concerned than he'd wanted to admit—and he felt a spurt of cautious optimism about the future of his combined family.

"Suzanne promised to look in on them," Lydia continued. "But Abby won't be there. Her parents refused to allow her to remain while I was absent."

"I daresay David is unhappy about that," Rees said. He suspected that the two young people would wed in a few years. Of course, her parents would hope it was not a forced marriage, and Rees did as well.

"But your sister Caroline haunted me," Lydia's said. "I finally had to ask Constable Caldwell to speak to her and forbid her to visit the farm. You must come home after this, Will, and settle her." A line formed between her brows. "Sam's condition is worse. He has no more sense than a little child and must be watched constantly. If he escapes the house, he wanders and can't remember how to find his way home. I do feel sorry for Caroline, but she is far too demanding. I was happy to leave for a little while."

Rees did not speak. Sam's injury at Rees's hands had made Caroline even more insistent and difficult than before. He didn't know how to fix the issues between them but he promised himself one thing: he would treat Caroline with more respect and not with the condescension he'd witnessed in the behavior of the Boothe brothers toward Peggy.

"But let's not talk about that now," Lydia said. She looked up at him, her eyes beginning to shine with excitement. "Tell me why you wanted me to join you. And about the murder."

Chapter Fourteen

Rees guided Lydia into the Moon and Stars and, once they were seated, he embarked upon the story. He started from the very beginning, when he'd attended the averil after Mrs. Boothe's funeral. Lydia asked a few questions but mostly just listened, eating her way through her lobster pie. Rees ate as he talked, realizing when he scraped his plate that he had eaten it all without tasting it.

"Have you conferred with the men whose names Mr. Crowninshield gave you?" Lydia asked, when Rees finally took a breath.

"Not yet. Anyway," Rees added, "I suspect they will tell me the same tale he did."

Lydia nodded but said, "I would speak to them anyway. Just in case you hear something else, something, perhaps, not to his credit. I would like to meet Georgianne Foster and her cousin. It sounds as though they experienced a different side of Jacob Boothe. He may have confided in them, even if Georgianne elected not to share that with you. Besides, you may be wrong about her relationship with Jacob Boothe. Some men prefer a lively woman." Rees grinned and took her hand in his. "And, of course, I must meet the Boothe family. It certainly sounds, from your description, like Matthew Boothe is involved in something. It might not be smuggling though. He seems entirely too indolent for that kind of profession."

Rees considered Lydia's words. "Yes-s-s," he said slowly. "But I saw him conferring with the sailor."

"Could be other reasons for that," Lydia said.

"And I wonder if that was the same sailor who warned me out of Salem." Although he had purposely minimized the attack upon him, Lydia looked at him in horror. But she had no opportunity to scold him.

"Fire!" A boy suddenly plunged through the tavern door. "Hurry. Fire on Turner Street." He darted out, running to spread the news.

A second's pause, as the tavern customers grasped the boy's warning, and then almost in unison, everyone rose to their feet. In Salem, with its wooden buildings—houses and warehouses both, and all the ships—the threat of fire called everyone to the bucket brigade.

Rees jumped up, a horrible premonition blooming in his mind. He'd taken several steps when he remembered Lydia and turned around. But she was right behind him. She smiled and shooed him forward. Rees took her hand and they joined the crowd running northeast.

A smoky black smudge was immediately visible in the sky, and the smell of burning tainted the air. Rees soon realized that he and Lydia would not be able to get very close to the house, not yet anyway. There were too many people. "Oh no," Rees said as he and Lydia joined the crowd on the other side of the street. Lydia looked up at him. "It's Mrs. Foster's house." A hollow ache formed in his gut. "Oh no."

Rees was tall enough to look over most of the heads, and he could see at least three lines of people sending buckets up to the flames. Two approached the house from Essex, one from Turner. Rees pictured the layout of the rooms; the fire must have begun in the parlor. Every now and then, someone would step out of the waiting throng and replace one of the weary men. Rees pushed his way forward, prepared to do his part. But, by the time he reached the front, the flames were extinguished.

The acrid stench of wet ash filled the air. The brigade began to disperse, although a few men approached the house to inspect the blackened wall. In three long strides, Rees reached the front yard. He grabbed one of the men who'd been passing buckets on the brigade. A long black streak went up the side of his face, and he was flushed and sweating with the recent effort. "What happened?" Rees asked him. The man shrugged.

"Someone saw flames coming out of the window," he said, looking behind him as though that person would appear.

"Two women live inside," Rees said. "Has anyone seen them?" And when the man shrugged again, Rees grabbed the front of his linen shirt and shook him. "Has anyone seen them?"

"No. No one came out." He wiped his sooty hand across his face. "And you'd better not go inside. Deputy Sheriff Swett gets angry if he isn't first."

Releasing the man so abruptly that he staggered, Rees turned and ran up the porch steps, Lydia close behind. "Stay here," he told her. "It's too dangerous for you to go inside." He touched her shoulder gently and hurried into the house. The fire had not reached the front hall, although the air stank of smoke, and when Rees looked left he understood why. Someone had closed the door to the parlor. He thrust it open.

He saw immediately how the fire had begun; a candleholder had fallen off the harpsichord to the floor. Although the candle had guttered out in a pool of melted wax, the flame had caught fire to the carpet. Rees stared at the blistered legs of the harpsichord and the long burnt trail leading from the candlestick to the window. Glowing dots marked live embers. God only knew how long the fire had smoldered in the rug until it reached the window. Once the sparks reached the curtains, the fire had begun in earnest, pouring through the open window and growing into a monster.

Rees saw that in only a few seconds, and then the body lying sprawled upon the floor by the harpsichord bench captured his complete attention. He couldn't see the face, but the soft pale pink gown and the rose necklace identified the woman as Isabella Porter.

"Let's take her outside," Lydia said, a cough punctuating her words.

"Lydia," Rees said reproachfully, as he scooped up the body and followed his wife outside.

He carried her to the edge of the small yard and laid her upon the ground. No attention had been paid to this corner of the yard, and daisies and pokeberries surrounded the body.

"Is it Mrs. Foster?" Lydia asked, her voice shaking.

"I don't think so," Rees said, kneeling by the supine form. He gently turned the body over so that he might stare into the face.

Isabella Porter's eyes were closed. The fire had not touched her and, although her face was bloodless, her expression was peaceful. But she was quite dead.

"Look at her throat," Lydia said, pointing. A broad red welt circled her neck. "Did you see anything that would do that?"

Rees thought back. "No. I saw nothing. The killer must have taken whatever it was with him."

"A scarf, I would suppose," Lydia said. "Or a thin shawl."

"And where is Mrs. Foster now? Is that Mrs. Foster?" Deputy Sheriff Swett's voice grew louder as he approached. Rees stood up and backed away, drawing Lydia with him. Swett ignored them both.

"No," said a boy as he shouldered his way through the men gathering around the deputy. "That's . . ."

"I wasn't talking to you, boy," said Swett. "Go home to your mother." He knelt over the body as though peering into her face. When he rose to his feet, her necklace was no longer around her throat.

Had Swett robbed the body? Rees stared at the deputy in disgust.

"But that's . . ." The dirty youth tried again. At a nod from Swett, one of the men pushed the boy away so hard he fell. Rees took Lydia's arm and pulled her away from the body. But instead of heading for the street, he went to the boy and offered him a hand up. The boy ignored it and scrambled to his feet without help.

"Did you see something?" Rees asked.

"And why should I tell you?" He brushed the dirt from his tattered pants. Rees eyed the child. He couldn't be more than ten. Despite the grime covering his face and hands like a second skin and the shabby clothing, he wore a cheerful red neckerchief.

"Because I'll give you a penny."

"Two," the boy said promptly.

"You would have told that fop Swett for nothing," Lydia said, frowning at him.

"Yeah. And he might have paid me to keep my eyes and ears open in the future. You won't."

"Very well," Rees said. "Two. What's your name?"

"Al."

"I'm Rees. I already know that," he gestured at the still form lying on the ground, "is Miss Porter. What else do you have?"

"I didn't like her much. Now Mrs. Foster, she always gave me something for my trouble. At least a farthing or two for running a message or sweeping her walk."

"Where is Mrs. Foster?"

"Don't know. "The boy answered too quickly.

Rees ruminated for a moment. This child knew something else; Rees was sure of it. "What else did you see?" Al hesitated. "Tell me now, Al."

"She had a caller a bit before the fire started. A woman. Dark gray dress and shawl. And she wore a big hat." Rees and Lydia exchanged a glance.

"How big?" Lydia asked.

His hands opened wide. Rees could not believe any woman, no matter how fashionable, would wear a hat that large unless she intended to hide her identity.

"Of course, you couldn't see her face," Rees said.

"Nah," the boy agreed with a grimace. "Now, that would've been worth some money. Right? If I could've described her. Right?"

"Did you see how long this woman remained inside with Miss Porter?" Lydia asked.

"Not long," Al replied. Rees guessed that that meant anywhere from ten minutes to half an hour.

"But you did see her leave?" he asked.

Al nodded. "She came out in a hurry," he said.

"Walking?'

"Walking," Al confirmed. "But very fast." An expression of surprise crossed his face. "Almost running."

Except for the hat, the woman in question sounded like Georgianne Foster. She was the only woman Rees had seen so far in Salem wearing gray. But surely she would not have wanted to kill her cousin. Besides, why would she approach her own house as though she were a visitor? An answer to his own question immediately popped into Rees's mind: because she wanted any witness to believe her a stranger.

No, he didn't want to believe she had killed her cousin. Surely, it made more sense to assume that Miss Porter's death was connected in some way to the murder of Jacob Boothe. And, in that case, Rees considered another question: was Isabella Porter murdered by someone who thought she was Georgianne Foster? After all, they bore a superficial resemblance to one another. He did not realize he'd spoken aloud until he saw Lydia staring at him.

"If this isn't Mrs. Foster," she said, "then does Mrs. Foster know about this yet?" She looked at the faces in the crowd, as though she might recognize Georgianne Foster from Rees's description.

"I don't know, but it's imperative we find her. If Mrs. Foster was the intended victim, and her cousin was murdered by mistake, then Georgianne Foster is still in danger."

Chapter Fifteen

I t was late afternoon by the time Lydia and Rees reached Mrs. Baldwin's house. The journey home had taken far longer than the earlier mad run, which had appeared to take no time at all, to Turner Street. The events of the day had tired both Rees and Lydia and now, with fatigue dragging at her feet, she walked more and more slowly. Rees offered her an arm, but his shirtsleeves stank of fire. Lydia shook her head in refusal.

Mrs. Baldwin came out of the door as they entered the stable yard. "I've been watching for you," she said, her nose wrinkling as she inhaled the odor of smoke and wet ash. "I heard there was a fire."

"Unfortunately, a woman lost her life," Rees said. He wiped his arm across his forehead and looked at the black streak on his sleeve in dismay.

Mrs. Baldwin grimaced and said in regret, "Oh dear. I'm sorry to hear that." She examined Rees and then Lydia. "I'll put water on to heat, Mr. Rees. You'll want a bath, I think. And you, Mrs. Rees, look as though you could use a rest."

"Yes. And a change of clothing."

"While you're bathing and changing clothes, I'll start supper." Mrs. Baldwin put her arm around Lydia's shoulder and urged her to the house. "You shouldn't be out running around, not in your condition."

"I am a little tired," Lydia admitted. Rees glanced at her in alarm. Usually Lydia refused such offers of assistance. She must be worn out to so graciously accept Mrs. Baldwin's.

"Is Billy home yet?" Rees asked. With Isabella's murder, his enquiry had taken on a desperate pressure. He didn't want to feel guilty about another death.

"In the barn," Mrs. Baldwin said.

"You go on inside," Rees said to Lydia. He pressed her shoulder, trying to convey his love and concern through that one touch. She smiled at him.

"I believe I will lie down for a few minutes," she said. He watched her go to the house, caught within the protective circle of Mrs. Baldwin's arm. Then Rees turned to the barn.

Billy had slipped the bridle over Bessie's head and was preparing to walk her around the yard. Rees's quick glance at the stalls assured him that the boy had already fed and watered both horses. "Thought I'd give her some exercise," he said. "She's been inside all day."

"So have you," Rees said, following the horse and boy outside. Bessie shuddered and jumped with excitement. Rees sighed; Bessie was not settling. Billy began talking to her, his voice low and soothing. "Listen," Rees said, turning his attention to the boy. "I saw someone I want to speak with. I wondered if you knew his name. He looks like a pirate: dark hair, gold earring . . ."

Billy responded immediately. "That sounds like Philippe Benoit."

"What do you know about him?"

Billy paused and Bessie halted as well. "There's some mystery there," he said. "He worked on a whaler for awhile and then switched to a merchantman, one of the Boothe ships, I think.

Hard to know. I heard that most of the crew was Irish, French, and Portuguese."

Of course Benoit worked on a Boothe ship, Rees thought, re-calling his glimpse of Matthew Boothe in the Witch's Cauldron tavern. "But Mr. Benoit is back in Salem?" Rees was beginning to respect the depth of Billy's knowledge. Here was a boy who kept his eyes and ears open.

"I believe so. *The India Princess* returned from the East about two weeks ago." He hesitated briefly, his smooth forehead crinkled with thought.

"What?" Rees demanded.

"Something strange about the ship Benoit captained," Billy said. "What was it? Was it sold to the Boothe family? I can't remember."

"If you do, please let me know," Rees said. Tomorrow he and Lydia would pay a call upon the Boothe family, and Rees would press Matthew. That young man had some explaining to do. "And thank you."

He turned and, pondering the youngest Boothe boy and his secret activities, he went into the house.

Mrs. Baldwin had carried up several buckets of boiling water, which she had emptied into a large metal tub. As Rees bounded up the steps, the woman leaned against the kitchen doorframe panting. "I'll help carry up the last pails," Rees offered.

"Thank you," Mrs. Baldwin said. "I think if we each take a bucket, we can manage the last of the hot water."

Rees accompanied Mrs. Baldwin into her kitchen. Instead of emptying the hot water into the pails, Rees lifted the copper from the fire and carried it up the stairs. Although much of the water had already been lugged to the second floor, the copper was still very heavy and he entered his room blowing hard.

Lydia had bathed in the shallow water already in the tub and then changed into a loose linen shift. The short hair around her face curled damply from the steamy water. As Rees poured the hot water into the large bucket, Lydia lay down upon the bed. Her belly rounded the white linen of her gown into a hill. With a long drawn-out sigh, she rested her hands upon the mound.

Rees shucked his clothing and stepped into the rapidly cooling water. "Tomorrow," he said, soaping his long freckled legs, "we'll call upon the Boothe family. I want you to meet Peggy Boothe and the slave Xenobia. And I must question Matthew." He paused in his ablutions, the sliver of Lydia's fine Castile soap held aloft. "That boy is mixed up in something, I know it." When Lydia did not comment, Rees looked over at her. She was asleep. Rees sighed; it looked as though he would have to make a supper from the last of the oranges.

The following morning Lydia and Rees arose at dawn, both ravenously hungry. Lydia lifted her blue dress from the hanger and sniffed it, making a face. "Smoke," she said. "I'll wash this with your shirt, I suppose." She pulled a clean dress from her valise. Woven of linen, it was dyed pink with madder, and made in the modern loose style with a ruffle at the waist. She shook it but the wrinkles left by its stay in the canvas valise remained.

"Is that new?" Rees asked.

"Yes. Don't you recognize the cloth?" She smiled. "It's some of the dyed linen left you by Nate Bowditch."

"It's pretty." Rees had investigated the murder of his estranged childhood friend a year ago. Sometimes he still dreamed about Nate, an old boyhood friend who'd been murdered the previous summer. Although Rees had found the guilty party, it didn't soothe the estrangement between them, and he thought he would be sorry for it to the end of his days. Getting older seemed to mean an increasing number of regrets.

He dressed quickly and then sat and waited while Lydia dressed and combed her hair. By the time they were ready to go forth and search for breakfast, the sun had been up for an hour. Billy was long gone; Rees had watched the boy leave the house in the dawn gloom and disappear down the street.

They stepped into the early morning sunshine and headed to the Moon and Stars. The proprietress greeted Lydia with a smile. After a hearty breakfast of rabbit pie, fish cakes, and bread they returned to Mrs. Baldwin's, and Rees harnessed Amos to the buggy. He did not trust the skittish Bessie with his pregnant wife. Although he could, and would, walk to the Boothe mansion, he thought Lydia might tire, as she had the day before.

They arrived at the house before nine in the morning. Although most of the working people had been toiling at their jobs for an hour or more, Rees thought it likely that Betsy and Matthew Boothe were still asleep. But Xenobia would almost certainly be awake and busy at her chores, and Rees was cautiously optimistic that Peggy would be up as well.

The servant who opened the door pinched his lips tightly together, but he said nothing as he stood back and permitted them entry.

Rees paused at the door to the inner hall, surprised to find it crowded with young people, mostly men but a few women as well. As he looked around, he realized this was the theater group. Adam Coville hesitated on the fringe, his arms crossed and his expression thunderous as he watched Matthew. Grinning and happy, Matthew seemed to be the center of the activity. Everyone was talking to him at once. Peggy sat on the steps leading up to the second level, watching the scene with an amused smile. When she saw

Rees and Lydia, she jumped to her feet and attempted to force her way through the crowd. Even as tall as she was, she promptly disappeared from sight in the mob.

Edward Coville thrust his way through the throng, heading for his brother. Rees noticed that most of the youths moved out of Edward's path, turning to him with varying expressions of sympathy. Several clapped him on the shoulder as he passed. He pushed by Rees and Lydia without acknowledging them in any way, his face creased by misery. Adam put an arm around his brother's shoulders, and they went through the door together.

"I wonder what happened," Rees said, turning to stare after the brothers.

"He and Mattie competed for the same part," Peggy said, breaking through the mob and hurrying toward them. The skirt of her dark blue gown was streaked with black. "Edward won, but he just withdrew from the play." She paused for breath.

"What play are they performing?" Lydia asked. As Peggy gestured them toward the morning room, Matthew began trotting toward them.

"*As You Like It* by William Shakespeare," Peggy said.

"I have the lead now," Matthew said. His pale hair was tousled and his face flushed with pride and excitement.

"I cannot imagine how you have managed to fund this little pastime," Peggy said. "The rental of the Assembly House alone must be very dear."

"We were given a discount," Matthew said, his words clipped. "But of course, you, a woman unconnected to the world of the theater, would not know how these things work."

"Hmmm," said Peggy, not noticeably crushed by her brother's remark. "I think you'd better pray William continues giving you the generous allowance Father did. Otherwise, this company may be searching for another lead."

"He must," Matthew said. But he frowned. Rees would have wagered William was not so supportive of the young man's hobby.

"You've chosen a wonderful play," Lydia said. Matthew broke into a wide smile.

"Yes. I thought for our first production we should choose a comedy. And one by Will Shakespeare," as though he and the playwright were on close speaking terms, "would do nicely."

"Well, you can't rehearse in the front hall from now on," Peggy said in an unsympathetic tone. "The rest of us still live here."

"Don't worry," her brother replied shortly. "We're looking for another space now. And anyway, we'll soon move to the Assembly Hall to practice on location."

"I have a few questions for you," Rees said.

"Later. I am far too busy at present."

"Matt," one of the young men called, "are you coming? We want to begin."

"Immediately," Matthew said over his shoulder. Turning back to his sister, he added, "And you can't use the morning room. We need it for the rehearsal."

With a pained sigh, Peggy said to her guests, "In that case, please come into the breakfast room." She shot her brother an angry glance, promising retribution, but he had already directed his attention to the acting troupe. "Honestly," she said in annoyance, "my brother is a man obsessed since he returned home from Harvard."

"You have no interest in theatricals?" Lydia asked.

"It does look like fun," Peggy admitted, "but my father would never permit his daughter to participate in something so unladylike. And William doesn't even want Matthew involved. I think my older brother wishes the theater was still banned, as it was a few years ago."

She guided them to a door at the back and threw it open. This space was located behind the other chamber and looked to be furnished with castoffs from the other more public rooms. A used plate and half-drunk cup of coffee sat alone with an open account ledger beside them. An inkwell was positioned at the top of the place setting, and black drops speckled the white tablecloth around it.

"Now," Peggy said, "we can talk." She fixed her gaze upon Lydia. "You must be Mrs. Rees. I am very happy to meet you."

"I apologize for arriving so unexpectedly and unannounced," Lydia said.

"Please, don't. As you can see," said Peggy, gesturing at the noisy hall outside, "we are not so formal here. Please, sit down. Would you like breakfast? May I offer you some tea or coffee?"

"You seem busy," Rees murmured, eyeing the ledger.

"Yesterday William found me at my desk in Father's office and was quite appalled. So unfeminine, you know." She made a moue of disgust. "The long and short of it is, he locked the room. I can no longer get to my desk. Fortunately I had already—" She stopped talking abruptly, as though afraid to say too much.

"Surely *he* doesn't bother with the household accounts," Lydia said in a sympathetic tone.

Peggy threw her a grateful glance. "No, although now he wants to see every entry. My father was always content to allow me to handle it. But I know you didn't come here to discuss such domestic issues."

"My husband has told me of your recent loss," Lydia murmured. "I'm so sorry."

"Thank you." Peggy looked at Rees. "That loutish deputy has been sniffing around Xenobia again. I hope you have better news."

"Nothing definite," Rees said. "I did speak with the Covilles, though."

"You see there is something wrong with Dickie," she said with a shake of her head.

Rees avoided replying to Peggy's comment. "I also spoke to Adam and Edward."

"I daresay they were preparing one of their ships for a whaling run?"

"Yes."

"Anyone would think the whales were put in the ocean for their exclusive use," Peggy said tartly. "Their ships are constantly on the hunt."

"Edward will be serving as captain on this one," Rees said.

Peggy's eyebrows rose. "So, that is why he withdrew from the play. He said he had to work. I thought he meant in the counting house with his brother. Why is he going out to sea? Bit old for it, I should think."

"Peggy! Surely you aren't entertaining Mr. Rees and his wife standing over a dirty breakfast table!" Betsy paused in the door, glaring at her sister. "What is wrong with you? I vow, you have no more sense than a goose." She wore a Chinese shawl of scarlet silk embroidered with all manner of exotic scenes over a plain white dress. Her fair hair lay loose upon her shoulders, breathtaking in its beauty. Rees realized he was staring and quickly shifted his gaze to Peggy. She was smiling at her sister, her lips twisted.

"You aren't even completely dressed," Peggy said. "Don't lecture me."

"I am not wearing a dirty old gown," Betsy said. "Look at it. What have you gotten on it? Ink? Oh my, you know how difficult ink is to wash out of linen."

"I didn't want to chance splattering ink upon my mourning clothes," Peggy said. "I only have the two gowns made thus far."

"But people have seen you out of mourning, and dirty besides."

"Enough, Bets." Peggy's voice took on a snap.

"Your shawl is quite lovely," Lydia said in an admiring tone, breaking into the brewing quarrel.

"Yes, thank you," Betsy said, looking down at it. "My father brought it back from the East. He brought three; one for me, one for my sister, and one for Mama."

"But Mama gave hers to Grandmamma," Peggy said.

"Yes." Betsy looked down at the embroidered silk around her shoulders in satisfaction. "And I've never seen you wear yours, Peggy."

"I have not found the proper occasion," she said. "Certainly it is not appropriate to wear a silk shawl to breakfast."

"And why aren't you meeting with our guests in the morning room?"

"It's being used for the rehearsal," Peggy said.

"I certainly hope those—those mountebanks do not continue using our hall," she said. "My fiancé would be horrified."

"Matthew promised they would find another place."

"Good." Betsy turned to Lydia, who was regarding the sisterly scene before her with a smile. "I am so eager to make your acquaintance," Betsy said, clasping Lydia's hands in hers. "Although I can't support meeting guests in this room," she glanced around her shabby surroundings with a grimace, "at least I shall have an opportunity to talk to you." With a nod promising nothing, Lydia withdrew her hands from Betsy's.

"I wonder if Xenobia is available as well," Rees said.

"My goodness," Betsy said, "we shall have everyone in here before you know it."

"I'll see if I can find her," Peggy said. "She's probably in my mother's bedchamber, sorting her clothing and so on." Tears suddenly flooded her eyes. "And now . . . my father's things will have to be looked at as well."

Lydia stretched out a hand and clasped Peggy's. "I'm so sorry."

"I wonder," Rees said, diffident because he knew he was being very forward, "if I could take a quick look at the bedchamber?"

"My mother's?" Peggy asked in surprise. "There is nothing to see. She was ill a long time."

"Your mother and father slept separately then?" Rees said. It was Jacob's quarters he'd been hoping to inspect.

"Their rooms connected," Peggy explained. "But my father wasn't in his chamber when he was so foully struck down." Tears bloomed in her eyes and Rees knew that, despite her melodramatic speech, she was sincerely grieving.

"Sometimes seeing the surroundings of the poor victim prompts a sudden inspiration," Lydia said.

"Yes," Rees agreed, nodding his thanks at his wife. "Frequently the dead man leaves behind some indication of the reason for the murder. A letter or something like it. So it is important that I examine your father's living quarters." Peggy shook her head as though trying to understand Rees's request.

"My father's bedchamber? I assure you, you'll find nothing there."

"I know my husband," Lydia said, jumping to Rees's aid again. "If he doesn't see these rooms, no matter how innocent they may be, the omission will nag at him. Better to allow him to peek in at them now than listen to him complain for the next few days."

"Oh, let him see Father's room," Betsy said, biting into a piece of bread with her sharp white teeth. "It will take longer to argue over it than for him to peek inside."

"Very well," Peggy said reluctantly. "But I don't want you touching anything." Rees nodded to show he understood, although he knew he might not necessarily be able to keep to that rule. "Follow me, please."

They threaded their way through the rehearsal to the central staircase. The wall of the first landing was dominated by an enormous painting of a military scene. Rees took an instant dislike to the bright reds and yellows, especially when seen from this close perspective. A bit too red and angry in his opinion. The stairway divided, with six steps rising to the second floor on the right, and six on the left. Rees and Lydia followed Peggy up the right. The hall went around the stairs, with a series of doors leading into bedrooms. Most of the doors were closed, but there were two that stood open. One clearly led into Betsy's room; the faint scent of her perfume emanated into the hall and clothing covered the floor, the chair, and the bed. The second open door, opposite the painting, led into a larger room. Light streamed through the interior windows and out into the hall beyond. Xenobia's humming, which resolved into a dirge with incomprehensible words as Peggy and her visitors approached, drew them forward, into Anstiss Boothe's bedchamber.

Chapter Sixteen

Xenobia looked up from the froth of brightly colored dresses covering every surface except the bed, which had been stripped to the mattress. Rees realized as he caught the subtle sheen of the gowns that most were made of silk. To one side was a whalebone hoop.

"Why, Mr. Rees, what are you doing here?" Xenobia asked, her voice lilting over the words.

"I wanted to introduce you to my wife," Rees said, gesturing to Lydia.

Dropping her handful of bright blue, Xenobia stepped forward and grasped Lydia's hands in her own. "How happy I am to meet you. You have a good man here, Mrs. Rees."

Rees looked around. Although the front windows and the door were open, allowing the fresh salt-scented air to sweep in, the room smelled fusty, the air stale from Anstiss's long illness. Rees looked at the bedside table. Dust coated the top, except for the rings left by teacups, and a lace of cobwebs decorating a book of poetry. The room bore every hallmark of occupation by an invalid.

"My father's room is just through here," Peggy said, throwing open the connecting door between the two chambers.

"Thank you," Rees said, stepping inside. This chamber, much smaller than the one joined to it, was so spare and so clean it resembled a monk's cell. Besides the bed, made with almost military precision, there was a chair and a clothespress. No desk. The front windows were closed, although the curtains were drawn back, and the air smelled faintly of leather and some kind of pomade. On a whim, Rees opened the door of the clothespress. Mr. Boothe had favored brown and black jackets and breeches to accompany his white shirts.

"My father slept in here," Peggy said, "but all of his papers are located downstairs in his office." She scowled and looked as though she might burst into angry sobs. "And now one must apply to my brother to read them."

"I may do that," Rees said. "It's possible your father's murderer is a business associate."

Peggy immediately contradicted his suggestion. "I will never believe one of his partners killed him." She wiped her wet eyes with impatient fingers.

Rees planned to speak to some of the partners, just in case, but he also expected little success from it. "And you know of no one who was quarreling with your father?" Rees asked, trying hard to be diplomatic. He meant Matthew. But Peggy shook her head. "What about your brother? Matthew?" Rees abandoned tact.

"Nothing's changed there," Peggy said, pursing her lips. "My father reprimanded Matt on a regular basis. Without effect, I might add."

"What if your father discovered Matthew was smuggling? Or involved in something illegal?"

"Matt?" Peggy laughed. "That isn't possible. What time my brother does not employ in playacting, he spends attending parties with his friends. He has no time or energy remaining for smuggling, or anything else that seems like work." Her disapproval hung in the air.

Rees didn't argue, but he didn't agree. Matthew's occupations were costly ones. Perhaps Jacob had cut off Matthew's income? In any event, Rees certainly couldn't believe William Boothe would gladly support his brother's pastimes.

"Have you seen enough?" Peggy asked, rather pointedly, Rees thought. He nodded and Peggy opened the door into the hall. When he stepped out, he could hear the low murmur of the conversation between Xenobia and Lydia. Peggy poked her head into her mother's room and, a few seconds later, Lydia came out. She was frowning and she cast Rees an indecipherable glance. But she did not speak as they descended the stairs.

As they stepped into the chaotic scene below, one of the actors was arguing fiercely with another, and Matthew detached himself from a crowd of thespians and approached. "Mr. Rees," he said. "Are you leaving now?"

"Perhaps," Rees said, unwilling to promise anything.

"I just heard about the fire at Georgianne Foster's. Is that true?"

From behind Rees, Peggy made a small sound of dismay. Rees turned. "I hadn't heard," she said. "What happened? What fire?"

"I think it was accidental," Rees said. Peggy was biting her lip in distress.

"My sister and I were out driving with Mr. Morris. We passed near the fire. I had no idea it was someone we knew."

"Well, one of my fellow actors told me that Georgianne Foster was shot and her house set on fire," Matthew said, his voice shaking with excitement.

"Shot?" Peggy went pale and collapsed upon a stair. "Matthew?" She stopped, her gaze going to Rees and Lydia. "Was she badly hurt?"

"A woman was found dead inside the house," Rees said, fixing his angry eyes upon the young man. "But it wasn't Georgianne Foster; it was her cousin Isabella Porter."

"Her cousin?" Matthew looked at Rees in consternation. "The pretty one?"

"You knew what Miss Porter looked like?" Rees asked.

"Of course," Peggy said. "We all saw the two women together at one time or another." Her trembling hands were clenched together between her skirt-covered knees.

"Isabella wasn't . . ." Lydia began. Rees grabbed her wrist warningly. Let the wider world believe Miss Porter was shot. Her killer knew the truth.

"I didn't know she was dead." Matthew looked from his horrified sister to Rees and the blood drained from his cheeks. "You don't think I had anything to do with this? I couldn't. I didn't."

"I know you were worried about your inheritance," Rees said, stepping down the final few stairs. Matthew shrank back, shaking his head. "I know you're involved in something," Rees went on. "Something illegal. My bet is on smuggling. I saw you at the Witch's Cauldron, sitting with Philippe Benoit."

Peggy pressed her hand to her chest and closed her eyes.

"Who?" Matthew shook his head, a crease forming in his forehead. "I don't know what you're talking about. I've never heard of anyone named Philippe Benoit. And I've certainly never been in the Witch's Cauldron." Turning to his sister, he said hopefully, "You believe me, don't you, Peg? I swear, I had nothing to do with the shooting or the fire or anyone named Philippe Benoit."

"I saw you with him," Rees repeated.

Matthew sniffed and when he spoke again he sounded more like his usual self. "That's a low-class establishment, frequented by sailors. I wouldn't be caught dead there." He spoke so vehemently Rees could almost believe him. "I think you're desperate, Mr. Rees. You've decided I am the guilty party. Well, you can't prove it. It's time you leave my house." His voice trembled and broke on the final word.

Rees nodded. "Very well," he said. "For now. But I won't stop asking questions." Turning, he took Lydia's arm. They cut through the throng of actors, most of whom remained oblivious to the drama that had unfolded so suddenly nearby.

In silence, Rees and Lydia walked to the buggy. He handed her into the seat and then climbed in himself. "That didn't go very well," he said.

"No. Although Matthew Boothe seemed more insulted that you would suggest he would visit the Witch's Cauldron than engage in smuggling," Lydia said. "He didn't know Miss Porter was strangled. And it sounded as though he didn't know Mr. Benoit."

"Matthew is an actor," Rees said, adding, "A better one than I would have suspected."

"Clearly he feels he is a man of consequence," Lydia said. "What will you do now?"

"Speak to some of Jacob Boothe's business partners. And look for Benoit. We'll ask him if he knows Mr. Boothe." He paused, thinking, and then added with a sigh, "I may have to request the deputy sheriff's help in that."

"Why don't you ask your friend Twig? He seems to know everyone."

"Of course. Good idea."

After a short silence Lydia began speaking again. "Mrs. Boothe was seriously ill, Will. Those gowns Xenobia was preparing to give away? Fashionable ten years ago and more. I saw hoops and panniers, for Heaven's sake. And, from what I understand, Mrs. Boothe stayed in that room with the shades drawn, in unrelenting pain, for many years. Only the finest opium straw tea offered her relief."

Rees thought of Jacob Boothe's monastic bedchamber and nodded. He must have been a very lonely man; no wonder he'd sought solace with another woman.

"Xenobia also told me that during the last few years, Mr. Boothe almost never visited his wife. In fact, no one did but Peggy, and that infrequently. She always left her mother's room sobbing. Anstiss's illness was terrible for everyone."

Noon and dinnertime were rapidly approaching. Rees's stomach was beginning to grumble and he suspected that Lydia, who always seemed hungry now, would also be ready for dinner. But he took the long way back to Mrs. Baldwin's, stopping in front of Georgianne Foster's house. Except for the charred stain around the window, the dwelling looked peaceful. Sunlight dappled the front yard through the leaves of the maple tree. The house already radiated the unmistakable air of abandonment. No one had broken the windows, and the front door still seemed securely locked, at least from Rees's view from the buggy seat in the street, but that would surely not continue. This part of town, a short distance from the fine large houses of the well-to-do, was still genteel, but it was shabby and the rougher, poorer areas lay only a street or two away. This house wouldn't be safe for much longer.

"And where is Georgianne Foster?" Rees muttered.

"She must have women friends we could speak to and find out," Lydia said in reply, even though Rees hadn't been asking her. "Did she mention anyone to you?"

"No. Only the Widows and Orphans committee . . ." Rees's voice trailed off.

Lydia pondered a moment. "Mrs. Baldwin will probably know who I might approach on that committee. I daresay the wives of Salem's influential men serve on it, and they'll know if Mrs. Foster has any special friends among them. And yes," she added as Rees turned to look at her, "I'll be the one to ask them. They'll be much more likely to confide in Mrs. Foster's relative, just recently arrived in Salem, and looking to visit her cousin."

Rees considered her suggestion and finally inclined his head in assent. "Yes," he agreed. "They'll be more comfortable speaking with a relative. And also with another woman. And so will Georgianne, when we find her," he added. "She's probably terrified."

"I would imagine so," Lydia agreed. "I'm very interested in her opinion of Mr. Boothe."

Rees grunted. He knew Mrs. Foster's opinion would be wholeheartedly positive. But perhaps Lydia could tease out a more nuanced estimation; Georgianne would at least be honest.

Chapter Seventeen

Rees drove home and deposited horse and buggy in the stable. Then he and Lydia walked down to the Moon and Stars. She seemed unusually silent and, as they sat down to partake of boiled goose, shoat, and spoon bread, he said, "Is something the matter?"

"Just thinking. The murder of Georgianne's cousin and the fire," she paused and took a breath. "Let me go back. You spoke about the tunnels under Salem."

"Yes," Rees said, startled by the rapid change of subject.

"Someone who knows the tunnels well stabbed Mr. Boothe. The killer knew exactly which tunnel led to Mr. Boothe's door. And I'll wager the merchants know those tunnels as well as their own names."

"Yes," agreed Rees with a nod. "That's why I began looking at Jacob's business partners."

"But the murder of Isabella Porter is something different. Unless you believe in coincidence—a second murderer who just happens to kill someone connected to Jacob Boothe—Isabella's death must be connected to his. And why would Jacob's business partners care about Georgianne Foster or her cousin? And then there's that urchin's description of a woman entering the house." She stared at Rees intently, willing him to understand.

"Isabella's murder was personal," he breathed.

"Yes. I asked myself, why would Georgianne kill her cousin now? She knows you and the deputy sheriff are looking into Jacob's murder. So, unless she is a very stupid woman . . ."

"Which she is not," Rees said.

"Exactly. And that led me to the two women who have a personal interest in this case: Betsy and Peggy Boothe."

Rees regarded his wife in an appalled silence for a moment. Although he knew women were as capable of murder as men—he'd had too much experience to believe otherwise—he struggled to accept Lydia's assessment. "But they are not strong enough to overpower a healthy man," he objected after a few seconds.

"Perhaps not. But if Betsy had the help of her brother . . ."

"Matthew," Rees said involuntarily.

"Yes. Although I don't think we should focus upon him exclusively," Lydia said.

"But Matthew knows the tunnels," Rees said, his thoughts moving rapidly ahead. "And he has some association with common sailors, who might help him for a shilling or two." He paused. "Perhaps you may enjoy a stroll upon the docks."

"Where I might spot Philippe Benoit or Matthew Boothe?" she asked. "Two pair of eyes being better than one?"

"Yes, exactly," Rees agreed with a grin, covering her hand with his. "I also want to see what ships are docked at the Boothe wharf."

"Very well." She smiled. "I will enjoy assisting."

They left the tavern well after two and walked down the alley toward the wharves. Rees had forgotten they would pass by the brothel until they were actually outside the wall. A soft whistle attracted his attention. When he glanced up, he saw Annie leaning out of one of the upstairs windows and waving shyly. Rees saluted her.

"Who is that?" Lydia asked in a peculiar tone.

"I think her name is Annie. She's one of the servants here. Sort of a friend of Billy Baldwin's."

"You do know this is a seraglio?" Lydia said in a chilly voice. Rees turned to look at her. Her brows were drawn together over her eyes and the corners of her mouth drooped down. "Or would you prefer I pretend not to know?" she added.

"Of course not," Rees said, regarding her in surprise. "I haven't visited the place. I offered that girl an orange." And then, fully understanding her reaction, he said emphatically, "She's just a child, not one of the soiled doves inside. And they're working her to death," he added. "I'm sure she's hungry."

Lydia muttered something about a three-legged pig, but Rees elected not to ask her to repeat it.

Then they stepped onto the dock, bright in the blazing sun with the glittering water beside it. Sailors, all ages, from boys to grizzled veterans, swarmed the boards, shouting at one another in a variety of languages. All were burnt as dark as Arabs. Lydia stared at the neckerchiefs tied about their necks and at the tattoos on arms and calves. Rees watched her with pleasure as she began to smile.

Rees took her arm and propelled her to the Boothe wharf. Although the *Hindoo Queen* had sailed, another ship was now docked in its place. "*The India Princess,*" Lydia read aloud. As with the *Anstiss's Dream,* a sailor stood at the foot of the gangplank, tracking all the barrels and bundles going into the ship. This mate was African, a short skinny fellow with scarified dots on his forehead. He wore the duck trousers and blouse as though it were a costume, put on for the benefit of an audience, although, for cosmopolitan Salem, he was barely exotic.

The sailors sang lustily as they rolled barrels up the gangplank, coiled ropes, and stacked bales, but this wharf was subdued in comparison to the frenzied activity on the others.

"Why did you want to see this?" Lydia asked.

"Curiosity mostly," Rees said. "This is Billy's dream, to sail on a merchant ship."

Lydia nodded. "Mrs. Baldwin told me you persuaded the boy not to sign on to one." Her head turned from side to side as her fascinated gaze was caught by one astonishing sight after another.

"That was a whaler. He doesn't really want to work as a whale man. I suggested he wait until an opportunity to sign on to a merchant vessel presented itself." Rees looked at his wife. "I hope Mrs. Baldwin realizes it's only a matter of time before he leaves home." Lydia did not reply, but her forehead under the straw bonnet wrinkled.

"I understand how she feels," Lydia said, putting one hand protectively upon her belly.

"This ship is smaller and older than the *Hindoo Queen,*" Rees said. "For all it seems well maintained." As they approached the ship, he turned his gaze upon each of the crew in turn, wondering if Philippe Benoit was among them. He could be, couldn't he, since he had some connection to Matthew Boothe? But Rees didn't see the Frenchman. And these sailors appeared little different from the other men working on the docks, a polyglot mix of varied backgrounds.

"Do you see Monsieur Benoit?" Lydia asked.

Rees shook his head. "No." He took a few steps closer to the gangplank. "Is Captain Benoit around?"

The mate turned. He was easily more than a foot shorter than Rees, but despite his scrawny build, his arms were corded with muscle. "No, sir. He not here." His accent was so thick Rees could barely understand him. Like his fellows, he wore a bandanna at his neck, and pictures of ships and a compass decorated his arms.

"Thank you." Rees returned to Lydia's side. "He's not here. I thought it was worth a chance."

"I would have liked to see him," Lydia said. "Just fancy; a real smuggler." Rees looked at her. Her face was turned away from him, half-hidden by her bonnet, and what he could see of her cheek was in shadow. He could not read her expression but suspected she did not believe his smuggling theory. Her next words confirmed his suspicion. "Matthew Boothe seems too lazy to be a smuggler."

"But not too lazy to be a killer. Maybe Jacob discovered his son's activities."

Lydia turned to look at her husband. "Possibly." She sounded doubtful. "I don't want to concentrate on Matthew and ignore all others. In my estimation, neither his sisters nor the slave Xenobia have been entirely truthful with us."

"Surely you don't see Betsy as a smuggler," Rees scoffed.

"Of course not. I don't see any of them as smugglers. But . . ." She hesitated again. "There's something . . ." Abandoning her efforts to explain, she said, "Let's inspect the Coville wharf. I'd like to see their whaling ship."

Rees looked at his wife and the belly that swelled her gown. "It's a little distant," he said, unprepared for the protectiveness that surged into his chest. "I don't want you to tire yourself."

"Don't fuss, Will. I'm sure I can manage," she said.

They walked north. *Anstiss's Dream* was still docked and supplies continued to roll up the gangplank onto the vessel as though there would never be an end. Rees could not imagine how the hold could take any more; it must be full to bursting by now. When he looked up to the deck, he saw Edward Coville staring down at him. Rees waved.

"There's Edward Coville now," he told Lydia. She tipped her bonneted head back, shielding her eyes from the sun, and looked at the captain. He flung a rag to one side and hurried down the gangplank to greet them.

"Mr. Rees. And this must be your wife." Casting her belly a quick glance, he bowed over Lydia's fingers. "What brought you to this end of the docks."

"My wife wanted to see your ship," Rees said. And then, deciding that a little flattery wouldn't hurt, he added, "I told her yours was an especially fine example of a whaler."

"One of the best," Edward Coville agreed, his chest puffing out just a little. "You won't see a better ship anywhere, whether it be in Boston or New Bedford."

"How long will you be at sea?" Lydia asked.

"Can't tell. Could be three months to a year or more. That depends upon the whales." He glanced over his shoulder at the ship, his expression full of pride. "She's a beauty all right. And, God willing, she'll be as successful as most of our ships."

"Who is your ship named after?" Lydia asked, affecting innocence. "Your wife, perhaps?"

Edward Coville's expression darkened. "No. My sister. She passed away less than a week ago."

"Oh dear, I am sorry," Lydia said with genuine sympathy. "You must miss her."

"Captain?" The first mate peered over the ship's side.

"Yes?" Edward glanced over his shoulder, his expression irritated.

"Problem, sir," said the mate with a jerk of his head.

Edward nodded. "Forgive me, but I must return to the ship." With an abrupt bow over Lydia's hand, Edward spun around and hurried away. The sound of his boots clattering up the gangplank echoed down the wharf.

"My word," Lydia said, looking at her husband. "Mr. Coville's departure was so hasty I could almost be offended."

"Indeed," Rees said, his gaze following Edward. "I wonder why. And where is Adam?"

———

Although Rees thought about his investigation all through the afternoon, he did not mention it to Lydia. He wanted her to remember these few hours as solely pleasurable. So they spent a pleasant time returning from the docks to Mrs. Baldwin's Emporium. Lydia exclaimed over the different fabrics and touched the silks gently but, although Rees watched her closely, she exhibited no partiality to anything. When they returned to their room, Rees showed her what he'd already purchased for the family. She was pleased by it all. "I had thought to purchase some silk for you to make into a dress," he said, putting his arms around her. "But it is so very dear."

Shaking her head with finality, she said, "Please don't worry. I prefer simple clothing, and besides, I can use this to freshen up one of my older gowns." Leaning forward, she kissed him on his cheek. "I am content."

They retired early to bed, but Rees awoke only a few hours later. Although the sky was dark, he could hear the sounds of conversation and the clinking of glasses coming from the brothel on the corner. The room's windows overlooked the back yard and the barn but, by leaning out and turning his face to the right, Rees could see down to the docks. Although the wooden vessels themselves were invisible, the masts of the ships formed a forest of black spears pointed at the rising moon.

But it was the brothel that filled most of Rees's field of vision: every window ablaze with candles and conversation and raucous laughter shattering the nighttime peace. He could see movement too, as the women and their clients walked past the windows. He hoped Annie was not among them. She was just a child and, from his few glimpses of her, she still seemed innocent and fresh.

Did that house contain a tunnel that connected to Salem's underground labyrinth? For that matter, did the Witch's Cauldron, the tavern from which both Matthew Boothe and Philippe Benoit had disappeared? A nearby tunnel would certainly explain their vanishing acts.

"Will? What are you doing?" Lydia sat up in bed, yawning. "Did something happen?"

Rees pulled his head inside. "No. Just thinking about Benoit."

"Perhaps he's already left Salem?"

"Possibly, but I doubt it. I think he realizes someone—me—is looking for him, and he's hiding. And that means he must feel guilty about something, otherwise why not present himself to me? Tomorrow I'm going to speak to Twig."

"No doubt he knows Monsieur Benoit. Twig seems to know everyone."

"Indeed. And maybe he can suggest a few places to search."

"I thought I would go to the Customs House tomorrow and talk to Inspector Oliver," Lydia said. She yawned again and added, "I'm certain he can direct me to the women on the committee charged with aiding widows and orphans, and probably to the most important ladies at that. But tomorrow is another day." She patted the sheets next to her. "Come back to bed, Will dear. There's nothing we can do now."

Rees directed one final glance at the brightly lit house near the harbor and pulled his head inside. He closed the window against the cool night air and rejoined Lydia between Mrs. Baldwin's lavender-scented sheets.

Chapter Eighteen

ꙮ

After breakfast the following morning, Rees hitched Bessie to the buggy. He was concerned about the mare's steadiness, but he'd taken Amos out the day before and thought he would give the gelding a day's rest. He assisted his wife into the buggy seat, and they set out for the docks and the Customs House. Although still early, the lanes were crowded with pedestrians. Bessie trembled with nerves but moved at a good pace, and Rees began to hope they would experience this outing without incident.

"When are you planning to speak to your friend Mr. Eaton?" Lydia asked, turning to look at her husband.

"After we visit the Customs House," Rees said. "We'll look for him then. Finding him may take some time." His peripatetic friend seemed to roam around Salem as his whims took him. "He may even be visiting the Boothe residence. If so, we don't want to just drop in on them."

"Not after Matthew asked us to leave," Lydia agreed.

"And not unless we have some new information." Rees also didn't want to run into William, who might take it into his head to fire his investigator, especially now that he was asking pointed questions about Matthew. Not that that would stop Rees. Now that he was involved and knew the players personally—neither Jacob Boothe nor Isabella Porter had deserved such deaths—he would see this through to the end no matter what anyone said. But he enjoyed more clout among the denizens of Salem with the Boothe family behind him. "I wish I could find that Philippe Benoit."

"I doubt William Boothe will take the word of a sailor over that of his brother," Lydia said, her tone dry.

"I know. I doubt the deputy sheriff will either. And I think it unlikely they'll listen to me. But at least I will have another account to add to my own."

"Where do you think the Frenchman is hiding?"

Rees shrugged. "I don't know. But there are thousands of people here in Salem; it is almost as big a city as Boston. If Benoit wants to stay hidden, he can surely do so. I've tried the docks." His voice trailed away. He had already decided to return to the Witch's Cauldron that night, and as many nights as it might take, to wait for Benoit to appear. Matthew knew now that Rees was aware of Benoit, and he would want to warn his partner that they were under observation. Then Rees would follow the sailor back to his room. He wasn't sure whether to involve Deputy Swett or not.

He did not intend to confide his plan to Lydia. She would be alarmed and try her best to persuade him against taking such risks.

With a horse and buggy, Rees couldn't follow his usual route down the lane. Instead, he followed one of the wider thoroughfares. Although jittery, Bessie was manageable.

They arrived somewhere in the middle of the docks, the current Customs House visible at the south end. The Inspector, who rented his office, had had to move more than once. Rees had been assured that plans for a permanent customs building were being prepared.

The strip of land running past the wharves bustled with activity. All the warehouses were open and dockworkers trundled barrels of goods offloaded from the ships into, them. Another wagon, drawn by two rangy farm horses, trotted by, the wagon bed full of cabbages. Seagulls drifted down to the ground and squabbled over scraps. Rees breathed through his mouth; the smell of salt and tide and rotting food was overwhelming.

A large barrel, escaping from the dockworker, hurtled toward the water, rumbling loudly over the ground as it headed straight for the buggy. Bessie jumped in the traces and burst into a run. Rees felt as though his arms were being torn from their sockets. He began shouting, trying to soothe her as he held her back from bursting into a wild, terrified gallop. Controlling her took all of his strength, but she finally slowed to a trot. She shuddered and twitched away from every pedestrian, every seagull who approached her. Still, they were moving in the right direction and finally arrived at the broad steps of the Customs House. "You go in," Rees panted, leaning back against the reins. He didn't dare release them, not even to tie Bessie to the rail. Lydia struggled down from the high seat, arriving on the ground flustered and disheveled. She straightened her skirts and walked up the broad steps. Rees began crooning to the mare, watching her gradually calm down. Then he slowly and carefully descended from the buggy. Still keeping a tight grip upon the reins, he moved to her head and began stroking her nose. She settled but she was trembling, and every sudden noise brought on a fresh bout of shudders.

Rees was just preparing to tie the reins to the rail when Lydia came down the steps. "I have a name," she said. "Mrs. Weymouth is at home afternoons from three to five. She lives on Chestnut Street. I'll call upon her later. The poor Inspector seemed harried. He didn't even ask why I wanted to know. So I didn't have to lie," she added. Rees understood; Lydia prized honesty and she hated lying, even in the aid of some greater purpose. Lydia tipped her head at Bessie. "How is she?"

"Still frightened." He sighed. "She's too high strung for my purposes. I hope David can use her on the farm; I must find another more placid animal to pull my wagon." He put the reins in his right hand and assisted Lydia with his left into the buggy seat. "We'll walk from now on."

"We can use Amos," Lydia suggested as Rees went around Bessie and climbed into the seat.

"As long as we use the buggy. He's an old horse and the wagon is heavy." Rees turned the horse around and as quickly as he could, he directed her into a lane heading away from the docks and back to Mrs. Baldwin's yard.

By the time the mare was unhitched, cooled down, brushed, and backed into her stall, noon and dinnertime was fast approaching. Since the Moon and Stars was Twig's favorite tavern, Rees hoped his old friend would be there. But when he asked the woman proprietor, Rees was told Twig had been and gone. Rees turned to look at Lydia. Under her straw bonnet, her eyes were shadowed with fatigue. "Do you have any idea where Twig—ah, Mr. Eaton went from here?"

"He didn't say," the publican said, peering around Rees at a customer who was waving his hand to attract attention.

"All right," Rees said, pondering. "We'll have dinner then, and look for him later."

Since this establishment was busy, Rees and Lydia were shown to a table right next to the fireplace. The serving girl, her cap askew and her apron dirty, hastened over with ale for both. Lydia pushed the beaker aside and asked for tea but by then the girl had already darted away. "I hope she heard me," Lydia said. Turning her eyes to Rees, she said, "What do we do now?"

Rees did not want to run all over Salem with his pregnant wife in tow as he searched for Twig. "After dinner, we'll check his house. It's not far from here. If he isn't there, I'll return you to

Mrs. Baldwin's. Then I'll look for Deputy Sheriff Swett." Rees would prefer speaking to Twig rather than the deputy but wasn't sure he would have a choice.

"Will Xenobia be at the house?" Lydia asked.

"Perhaps. Why?"

"No reason," Lydia said vaguely. Rees directed a suspicious look at her, but at that moment the girl arrived with Lydia's pot of tea. When she bent over to put the pot and the bowl of sugar chunks upon the table, the smell of sweat and onions billowed over Rees. He choked. But the bread that came out next was fresh baked and the roast turkey flavorful. Rees piled the white meat onto the bread and covered it all with gravy. He ate it in a few big bites. He followed it up with artichokes and half a chicken and a thick wedge of strawberry pie. Lydia, a daintier eater, had cut her meat into smaller bites and conveyed each morsel carefully to her mouth on the point of her knife. Rees was forced to wait, curbing his impatience with difficulty.

Within the hour they were back outside. Taking Lydia's arm, Rees turned west, toward Twig's little house.

A twenty-minute walk brought them to it. Rees could see Twig's glossy brown gelding in the stable at the back. Although the presence of the horse did not confirm that Twig would be here, Rees felt cautiously optimistic. He pounded on the door.

A minute of silence passed. Rees turned to Lydia in dismay. But suddenly the door was flung open. "Oh, Will. I was in the kitchen. Come in." He stepped back. Rees stood aside so Lydia could precede him into the empty hall. "Xenobia should be here soon."

Twig's long legs took him far ahead of his guests. He paused at the kitchen door, looking back impatiently. As they neared him, Twig disappeared inside. Rees and Lydia followed. She did not wait for an invitation to sit before finding a chair. She knew as well as Rees that Twig would not think to offer.

"So," Twig said to Rees, "do you know who murdered Jacob Boothe yet?"

"Not yet," Rees said. He paused, but after all, there was no point to dancing around the subject with Twig. "Do you know a sailor named Philippe Benoit?"

"Never heard of him," Twig replied. He leaned his arm against the fireplace mantel. Since the fire was burning, although banked, Rees wondered if that position wasn't uncomfortably hot. Twig gave no sign he noticed. "But then I probably wouldn't. I usually meet people only when they're dead," he said with an unexpected flash of humor. "Or when they know someone dead. Does he have something to do with Mr. Boothe's death?"

"Maybe." Rees hesitated. He wasn't sure how much he should confide to Twig. "I wonder if . . ." Twig's gaze went over Rees and his expression suddenly changed, transforming into one of joy. Rees looked over his shoulder. Xenobia had come up the back steps and through the door. She halted just inside, her gaze going from Rees to Lydia. Her straw bonnet was tied around her chin with a black band and she carried a basket of fish just bought at market. Twig hurried to her side. Xenobia smiled and put her hand out to take his, but she turned a wary glance upon Rees.

"I'm trying to find someone who knows of a sailor named Philippe Benoit," Rees said. Her eyebrows climbed up her forehead. Whatever she'd been expecting, it wasn't that.

"I've never heard the name," she said. "Why?"

"I saw Matthew speaking with him in a tavern on the docks," Rees replied.

"On the docks? A common sailor? Not Matthew. He's too important for that."

"I know," Rees agreed. "But Monsieur Benoit is a ship captain. I think they might be involved in smuggling or something."

Xenobia sighed. "Matthew likes money, that's true. But

smuggling? How would he know anything about it?" She smiled at the thought.

"Perhaps he has nothing to do with any actual smuggling," Lydia suggested. "Suppose he buys some of the contraband and sells it at a profit."

Xenobia nodded. "That is possible." She added abruptly, "You've upset the Boothe children. Matthew and Betsy talked about you for an hour after you left yesterday morning."

Rees exchanged a glance with Lydia. "I asked about Georgianne Foster," Rees said, returning his attention to Xenobia. "Her cousin was murdered."

"I know. Peggy can't talk of anything else."

Rees recalled his visit to Georgianne Foster and her pretty, charming cousin. "Matthew knew about Isabella Porter," Rees said. "Did the other Boothe children also?"

"No. Well, Miss Peggy did. But the rest of us have just heard about her," said Xenobia, unconsciously allying herself with the Boothe family. "She joined Mrs. Foster only within the last few months."

"Was the connection between Miss Porter and Mrs. Foster and Jacob Boothe commonly known?" Rees said.

Xenobia shrugged. "I don't know."

Something about that situation, Rees thought, did not sound right. Jacob Boothe had behaved with no discretion at all. And Georgianne, well, she was as far from a ladybird with a low-cut bodice and shapely ankle as Rees could imagine.

"How did the Boothe children first learn of Mrs. Foster?" Lydia asked from her seat at the table. Rees nodded at her, pleased to see her thoughts were traveling the same road as his own. "Neither Mrs. Foster nor her cousin move in the same social circles as Jacob Boothe. I would think he could keep any connection secret."

"Matthew followed his father."

Of course he did, Rees thought. "And how did they learn of Isabella Porter?"

"Miss Peggy saw the three of them together once or twice, while she was running errands. In fact," Xenobia admitted in a burst of candor, "Matthew thought his father preferred the cousin. Maybe Georgianne killed her, out of jealousy."

"Did Jacob's children quarrel with their father over his—his attachment?" Rees asked. Xenobia tensed. It was so subtle Rees would have missed it if he had not been watching her.

"What do you mean?" Xenobia was stalling.

"Matthew told me he feared for his inheritance," Rees said.

"Of course." Xenobia's shoulders relaxed slightly. "William will inherit the house and business. The girls have their dowries. What's left for Matthew? He isn't a worker."

Rees nodded in agreement. Matthew would view any kind of genuine labor as beneath him. "I know Peggy quarreled with her father," Rees said. Xenobia's shoulders tightened.

"Because he gave her jobs to William," she said quickly. "But he was right to do it. She's a woman."

"And William and Betsy, did they ever quarrel with their father?"

"Of course not," Xenobia said. "Betsy had her father wrapped around her finger."

"What form of illness did Mrs. Boothe have?" Lydia asked, inserting herself into the conversation.

"Anstiss was delicate before William's birth," Xenobia said. "She was cursed with terrible pain. But she managed until she delivered Peggy. Anstiss never recovered from her daughter's birth. And she became much worse this past year."

"Nineteen years?" Lydia said. "She's been an invalid for nineteen years?" Xenobia nodded. Rees stared at her. Certain questions caused her to tense and parse her words with great care; Xenobia was not telling them everything. As he prepared to question her further, Lydia leaned over and took Xenobia's hand. "Yet she bore four children who all survived."

"She was cursed," Xenobia repeated. She paused, and then the words spilled from her. "I told Master Jacob he should take her away from Salem and the woman who put that affliction upon her. He laughed at me." Her eyes darted to Rees who could not suppress his smile. "You are a fool, Mr. Rees, if you do not believe in witches."

Neither Rees nor Lydia knew what to say. Xenobia pulled her hand from Lydia's grasp and said, her eyes darting to Twig. "I must return to the Boothe house soon. I want some time with Stephen."

"I haven't seen Obie since yesterday," Twig said. "Go away."

"Of course," Lydia said, rising to her feet. A line crept between her brows and she seemed puzzled. "I'm sorry if we offended you." Rees was more annoyed than puzzled. And if he'd been alone, he would not have been so compliant. He fixed his eyes upon Xenobia, willing her to confess what she knew. But she kept her head lowered and her gaze trained upon her hands.

Lydia did not protest as Rees offered her his arm.

"Tossed ignominiously into the street," Rees said as they walked back to Mrs. Baldwin's.

"And why?" Lydia asked. "Mrs. Boothe's illness is not a secret. Why blame it on witchcraft?"

"I don't doubt Xenobia believes the source of Mrs. Boothe's illness was a curse. But she knows something else, something shameful, judging by the way she is trying to hide it. It might not even have anything to do with Anstiss's illness." Rees paused. He would have to reflect upon the conversation later, in quiet. "Yes, Xenobia knows something, and she doesn't want us to discover it. She couldn't wait to push us out of there."

Chapter Nineteen

They took twenty minutes to walk back to Mrs. Baldwin's. Rees hitched Amos to the buggy. Although Lydia suggested walking to Chestnut Street to call upon Mrs. Weymouth, Rees knew she wasn't serious. Ladies making social calls did not arrive on foot. Also, although Lydia claimed she felt quite well enough to walk that distance, her face was pale and she was breathing fast. Rees worried that she would overtire herself and refused to consider allowing her to walk. And Lydia did not argue. So it was almost four by the time they arrived at the large white house with pillars flanking the door. Rees pulled the buggy into the line of vehicles—fancy carriages as well as buggies and even a coach or two—and jumped down. He planned to question one or two of the coachmen and see if they'd heard anything.

He avoided the uniformed drivers. They clustered together, ignoring the other men, clearly of the opinion that they were a cut above. After a moment of consideration, Rees chose a portly middle-aged man in a suit of fustic yellow to question. Although his breeches and jacket were worn, his thinning hair was pulled neatly back into a queue, his stock was clean, and his cheeks had been recently scraped clear of whiskers. No doubt a gentleman with aspirations to gentility. Rees approached him. After making a few neutral comments, Rees inserted a few discreet questions about the Boothe family into the conversation. The fustic-garbed gentleman was not the only one of the drivers with an opinion. Mr. Boothe was universally described as a generous and honest man, and everyone seemed to know of Mrs. Boothe's illness. Matthew, though, came in for a lot of criticism.

Finally the coachman, who identified himself as a Mr. Bumble, drew Rees aside. "You're not from Salem," he said. Rees allowed as how that was so. "Otherwise, you'd know about Matthew Boothe. He doesn't pay his bills, and his tailor had to apply to Mr. Boothe Senior several times to get the account settled."

"What will happen now that Mr. Boothe is dead?"

"Well, young Matthew will not have so much success having his debts discharged, that's for certain," Mr. Bumble said. "I've seen his brother William and he, I assure you, will not be so generous."

"He's a dull gentleman," said one of the other drivers, a skinny fellow with rotting teeth.

"Honest, maybe," agreed the coachman, drawing Rees even further down the lane, "but without his father's sense of humor. Now Miss Peggy, well, she has her father's common touch. Comfortable with sailors as well as society ladies. All of us have seen her since she was a child, running errands for her father. He permitted her an unusual freedom, for a female."

"So I've heard," Rees said, not interested in hearing about Peggy. "About Matthew . . ."

But the gentleman was following his own train of thought. "Miss Elizabeth, what a beautiful lady. All the young men courted her, including Mr. Russell Morris. Quite an achievement, for the daughter of one of the upstart Republicans to attract a son from an old Salem family. A'course, I heard there's trouble between them now."

"What kind of trouble?" Rees asked, interested.

"I don't know exactly. But there's rumors he might break the engagement. I'd guess," said the driver, spitting into the street for emphasis, "he don't like the murder. Don't look good, you know?"

"But if Mr. Morris's affections are genuine, the murder of Betsy's father should not discourage him," Rees objected. "Quite the opposite, in fact. He should want to support her during this terrible time."

"The rich are different than you and me." He gave a sharp nod. "Mr. Morris wants to marry a woman whose family is unexceptional. No scandals!" He stopped abruptly, his gaze flying to a woman in a white gown tripping down the stairs. Over the flowing frock, she wore a short jacket of a blue that exactly matched the blue ribbon on her bonnet. Abandoning Rees without a backward glance, the driver trotted to his carriage and opened the door.

"What about Matthew Boothe?" Rees called, but the driver did not turn around. And a moment later Lydia came down the steps. Rees went forward to greet her, his mouth tugging into a wide smile. But he did not speak until Lydia was installed in the buggy. As they pulled away from the walk, he said, "Did you learn anything?"

"I should not wear pink," Lydia said.

"What? Why not? I think you look beautiful," Rees said, turning to regard her.

"Pink clashes with my red hair, or so Mrs. Weymouth and her set believe." Lydia chuckled. "Instructing me in the finer points of fashion encouraged the ladies to feel comfortable with me, and they were frank in their discussion of both Georgianne and her cousin. The ladies liked Georgianne," Lydia continued. "She was described as a bluestocking, rather too outspoken for her own good, but a pleasant woman nonetheless."

"And Isabella?"

"Although they phrased their comments about her in flowery language, none of the ladies liked her. They thought she was common. Mrs. Weymouth did remark that Jacob Boothe visited Georgianne more frequently once her cousin came to stay. But I am not convinced he was visiting Isabella. Georgianne sounds much more appealing, more intelligent and lively than her shallow cousin."

"And was any lady identified as an especial friend of Georgianne's?"

"No one claimed that privilege," Lydia said. She bit her lip, her expression pensive. "I wonder . . . I suspect one or two of the younger ladies are closer to Georgianne than they admitted. I'll find out. Mrs. Weymouth invited me to call upon her again, and I'll give my particular attention to those women." She leaned back against the buggy seat. "I'd forgotten how tiring it is to attend one of these social afternoons and make polite conversation."

Rees nodded without really listening, his thoughts a jumble of names and snippets of conversation. He hoped that his visit to the Witch's Cauldron tonight would bring some clarity to this very muddled situation.

Rees and Lydia ate an early dinner. Lydia settled down with her knitting; she was making a baby blanket for the new arrival. But Rees was too restless to settle. He knew what he was planning for that night, and the effort of keeping his intentions from Lydia inspired a certain furtive energy in him. Finally, he unfolded his loom and examined the warp remaining upon it. There were at least five yards wrapped around the beam, and he thought he could weave something with the scraps of yarn he always carried.

"Can you weave diaper?" Lydia asked, speaking for the first time. "We'll soon need clouts." Rees knelt and examined the tie-ups on the treadles. Although the current setup was not changeable to diaper, not without re-threading, he thought he could weave a thick twill that would serve. He dragged out the bag of leftover yarns and began winding his bobbins.

He settled down to weaving until the sun began to set and the shadows made seeing too difficult.

Lydia began to prepare for bed. Rees took up a position by the window, watching the purple shadows lengthen. Candles sprang to life in the windows around them. Billy came home and the sound of Mrs. Baldwin's voice floated up and into the window. Rees, who'd heard nothing from Lydia for the past twenty minutes of so, turned around. His wife was already sound asleep.

Moving as quickly and quietly as he could, Rees slipped out of the room. Within a few minutes, he was out of the house and hurrying northeast toward the docks. He hoped Matthew hadn't already found Benoit and warned him that Rees was looking for him.

Candlelight flickered behind the grimy windows of the Witch's Cauldron and raucous laughter poured through the open door into the street. Rees expected the tavern to be so busy that all the seats would be occupied. But the rowdy merriment was due to one small group of drunken sailors. Rees recognized some of the men from *Anstiss's Dream*. As Rees squeezed past, sidestepping so as to avoid a stream of tobacco juice coming his way, he heard someone say, "I came into unexpected good fortune."

Rees settled himself at a shadowed table at the back and ordered a jug of ale. He inspected the men around him. Mostly sailors and dockworkers, but there was Matthew Boothe, seated in the thick shadows on one side, stroking his mustache with thin, nervous fingers. Of Philippe Benoit there was no sign.

Two hours passed. The Coville brothers came in. They regarded the table of sailors, their crew, but did not call out to them or attract their attention in any way. Instead, they sat together at a table, their heads close as they talked over plates of stew. They left again as soon as they were finished. Rees wondered if the brothers did everything together.

Some of the customers staggered out of the tavern, but men identical to them in every way, at least to Rees's eyes, replaced them. He was beginning to consider leaving himself, going home to bed and returning the next night, when Philippe Benoit swaggered through the door. He paused in the doorway, the gold in his ears glittering in the candlelight.

He was taller than Rees had realized, and as he strode through the tavern he kept his hand upon the pommel of a long knife. Rees's gaze fastened upon the weapon. Could that be the instrument of Jacob Boothe's death? Was it long enough? From here, the blade looked too narrow.

Benoit nodded around, recognizing some of the other sailors, but he made a beeline for Matthew. He sat down. The young man leaned forward, his hat casting a long dark shadow across the scarred wooden table, and said something in a low voice. Benoit shook his head, glancing around him before leaning forward to whisper in a vehement hissing tone. The conversation rapidly grew heated and soon took on the appearance of an argument. It went on for some time. Rees wished he could hear what was being said. Whatever it was, it did not please Benoit. He slapped his hand upon the table and leaned forward, expostulating, but Matthew shook his head and rose to his feet. Benoit grasped Matthew's coat to hold him back and said something, his words clearly audible. That's when Rees realized Benoit was speaking French.

Matthew shook off the Frenchman's hand and strode from the tavern. Rees gathered himself to follow, but Benoit did not leave immediately. Instead he drank his rum, his gaze fixed blindly upon the ceiling. He called for bread and cheese and devoured the lot. Only then did he finally rise to his feet and start for the door.

Rees was instantly upright and on the move. He followed Benoit out and into the shadowy alley next to the tavern. Although Rees was watching the sailor carefully, determined not to lose him in the darkness, he almost missed the door set into the wall around the corner. It seemed that Benoit just disappeared. Rees retraced his steps and caught the faint gleam of a metal handle. He pulled it open. The odor of damp soil billowed out. Steep stairs dropped into blackness so deep it seemed solid. Rees hesitated. He wouldn't be able to see anything. What if he lost his way in the darkness? With one hand holding open the door—compared to the blackness in the tunnel the alley seemed well illuminated, and Rees was reluctant to leave it behind—he went down the steps. In the distance he spotted the bright dancing light of a torch.

Rees closed the door behind him and hurried after the flame.

His haste made him careless. He realized only when he heard the soft scrape of a shoe behind him that Benoit had known he was being followed. Had Matthew seen Rees and recognized him?

The torch began moving back, toward Rees, rapidly nearing him. He tried to sidestep, thinking he might hide in the darkness, but he wasn't fast enough. To the man behind him, Rees was visible, limned against the flickering light. Something came whistling out of the darkness and smashed into his head. The velvety arms of the darkness wrapped themselves around him and he fell to the ground, unconscious.

Chapter Twenty

❧

H e awoke in a strange room. The bed curtains were blue silk, matching the curtains on the windows. Positioned by the head of the bed was an upholstered chair, as though someone had been sitting by Rees and just gotten up. A flowery perfume scented the air. Groaning, he touched the bandage around his head.

A woman came into the room. Although gowned in white, her costume was so low cut it left nothing to the imagination. The flowing draperies clung to her body and Rees, even distracted by pain, was certain she wore nothing underneath. Her dark hair was expertly cut and curled and she was quite beautiful, despite the black patch hiding her left eye. "Ah, Mr. Rees, you are awake," she said.

"Where am I?"

"In the Black Cat." She paused. Rees must have looked blank. "One of the bawdy houses on the docks. Annie found you in the tunnel nearby."

"But I was nowhere near here," Rees said, trying to understand what had happened. His attackers hadn't killed him; that was the first surprising thing. And although he felt muzzy and confused, he was pretty sure he hadn't been this far south when he'd been attacked. As the rest of her statement penetrated, he fumbled with the covers. "I have to go home. My wife will kill me."

"I may kill you anyway." Lydia, speaking as she entered the room, did not sound as though she were joking. "What possessed you to behave so foolishly? You could have died." Her voice failed her and tears overflowed her red-rimmed eyes and spilled down her cheeks.

"I was following Philippe Benoit," Rees protested, sounding guilty in spite of himself. "I thought I could find his bolt-hole." Lydia dashed away her tears.

"You waited until I was asleep and sneaked out without telling me," she cried angrily. "What possessed you to go into the tunnels? If Annie hadn't found you, you could have been lost for days. And you were unconscious when she found you."

Rees digested this. "Where did Annie find me?" he asked at last. There was so much he didn't understand, he focused on the one point that made sense. Lydia turned and gestured to someone waiting in the hall. The young girl stepped hesitantly into the room.

She was dressed in a shabby dark-blue dress with a dirty apron over it and a kerchief tied upon her head. She smiled shyly at Rees, her eyes shifting away from his. If she was older than twelve, Rees was a three-legged sailor.

"I see I must offer you my gratitude," Rees said. "Thank you." Annie's cheeks went scarlet.

"Answer the gentleman," commanded the Madame.

"You're welcome," squeaked the child.

"How did you happen to find me?" Rees asked her.

"I— Sometimes I go into the tunnel and sit. It's quiet there."

"And roundly scolded she is for doing so," said Annie's employer. "She's not supposed to leave the house." Hearing a burst of conversation floating up the stairs, she turned and listened. Then she said, "I must go downstairs. I'm working."

"I'd like to ask Annie some more questions," Rees said. "Can she stay?"

Annie's mouth opened in a little 'O' and she began pleating her grubby apron.

"I'll be here as well," Lydia assured her, coming around the bed to sit in the chair. "I'm sure my husband wants to know how you happened to find him."

"Very well," said the Madame. Whirling in a flurry of translucent skirts, she hastened from the room and started down the stairs.

For a moment no one spoke. Then Lydia extended her arm and drew the child closer to the bed. "Tell Mr. Rees where you found him."

"First," Rees interjected, "please describe the location of the tunnel underneath this house."

"It's," Annie cleared her throat. "The door goes from the kitchen. There's a skylight in the garden. I usually sit under it." She paused. When she didn't begin speaking again, Rees nodded at her encouragingly, the motion sending a wave of pain through his head. "I heard you, groaning," she said. "So I went to the kitchen and took a lantern and went back to find you. You were lying where a couple of tunnels joined."

"How far was that from the door into this house?" Rees asked.

"Not far. Sometimes men come down from Essex and Chestnut streets and enter the house through the kitchen, so no one knows," Annie said. Rees didn't know which horrified him more: that Annie witnessed such carryings on or that she found them perfectly normal.

He tried to visualize the location of the Black Cat in relation to the Witch's Cauldron. The brothel was far to the south. So his attackers, rather than killing him, had carried him a good distance. And why hadn't they just left him where he lay?

"Then what happened?" Lydia asked when neither Rees nor Annie spoke.

"I went back home and fetched Mustafa. You know, our door-man?" For the first time she looked directly at Rees. "He had to come back and get some help. You were too heavy for him. They brought you here and Mama—One-Eyed Mary—said you could stay, and they brought you up to this room."

"I see," Rees said. "And you went for Lydia?"

Annie nodded. "I saw you with Billy." A faint rose tinted her cheeks. "So I knew you were staying with Mrs. Baldwin."

"Thank you," Rees said. "I owe you a debt." She smiled slightly and turned to go. As she passed through the door, Lydia rose to her feet and closed it behind her.

"I'm sorry, Lydia," Rees said. "I didn't mean to worry you. I thought I could find out where Benoit lived and be home before you knew I was gone."

"You should be sorry," Lydia said, two scarlet circles forming on her cheeks. "I could strike you, I'm so angry. I woke up alone and no one knew what had happened. I was out of my wits with worry. No one had seen you, not even your friend Mr. Eaton. Then that child arrived to tell me you were in a bordello, that she'd found you lying half-dead in the tunnels."

"I'm sorry," Rees said again. "I never thought, when I followed Benoit, that he would have a partner." Had Matthew been the man behind him in the tunnels?

Lydia heaved a sigh. "The earlier attack didn't warn you to be careful? Sometimes you count too much on your strength to save you. You forget you are just a man."

"I was lucky Annie happened along," he admitted. Lydia smiled and Rees saw she was calming down.

"Not entirely lucky," she said. "You gave her an orange?" He nodded, mystified. "You asked for nothing in return. She hasn't gotten many gifts; most offerings come with an expectation." Her voice trailed off.

As Rees grasped her meaning, anger flooded him in a fiery wave. "She's just a child. Barely older than Jerusha."

"Fortunately," Lydia said on a sigh, "this isn't a house that caters to that particular appetite. Still, she has been approached several times. And she told me she has two years before she must decide whether to enter this . . . profession, or find another way to support herself." She paused and added, "I suspect she has that grace period only until some gentleman offers enough money to turn One-Eyed Mary's head."

Rees thought of Annie, the soft childlike curve of her cheek, the unformed skinny body, and choked. He wished he could fold the child in his arms and tell her everything would be all right. "I hope our children are safe. . . ." He looked at Lydia, wishing he could assure himself of their continued health.

"I know." She sniffed and took a moment to compose herself. "I miss them so much. We must finish this investigation as soon as possible so we can go home."

Rees nodded. "We will." He paused. "I suppose Annie is an orphan," he said in a grim tone. Lydia directed a humorless smile at him.

"She says One-Eyed Mary is her mother," Lydia said. "Otherwise I suspect Annie would not enjoy even this scant protection." Rees shuddered. "But I have a thought."

"Another adoption?" he asked, unable to keep the reluctance from his voice. "The house is full and bound to become even more crowded." He put his hand gently upon her belly and felt the child—his child—kick. The water that flooded his eyes embarrassed him and he quickly wiped it away on his sleeve. "Maybe Annie and Jerusha can share a bed. If we move the little kids to the trundle?"

"No adoption." Lydia smiled at him and covered his hand with her own. "I thought maybe the Shakers? The community at Zion might offer her a refuge."

"What a good idea." Relief swept over him. "Will she agree?"

"She must," Lydia said. ""She has few other choices."

Rees nodded and for a moment they were both silent.

"And now we should see about taking you home," Lydia said. "I know they're eager to take back this room."

"What time is it?" Rees asked.

She crossed to the window and twitched aside the heavy silk draperies. He looked through the glass to the sun setting over the ship masts docked at the Salem wharves.

"How long was I unconscious?" he asked, turning to his wife in astonishment.

"Almost a full day. Annie found you last night." She paused. Rees realized he had missed all of Sunday. Lydia added with a mixture of remembered fear and tartness, "I suppose we should both be glad you have an exceptionally hard head."

Rees didn't speak. He was ashamed of his carelessness. He pushed the soft silken cover down and swung his legs to the side of the bed. Someone had removed his breeches and stockings; well, the inhabitants of this house were no doubt used to seeing a man in nothing but his body linen. Sitting upright left him dizzy and sick to his stomach. He paused, waiting for the nausea to pass. Then, with Lydia's assistance, he dressed. He could not bend over to put on his stockings; the room spun. She had to kneel beside him and slip the hose over his toes and up his calves. The shoes, into which he could slide his feet, were easy. Carefully he stood up.

The room tilted. He was very glad his stomach was empty, else he should have deposited its contents upon the fine French carpet. Lydia slid her hand under his elbow. They stood without moving until the walls of the room righted themselves.

Descending the first flight of stairs was horrible; Rees truly doubted he would be able to proceed. But, as he continued moving, he began to feel better. The second flight was easier to navigate, and by the time he reached the grand staircase that swept to the ground floor, he was able to descend under his own power. They did not pause but walked straight across the hall to the front door and out to the street.

By the time they let themselves into Mrs. Baldwin's yard, the sky over Salem had darkened to purple and the lanes lay in deep shadow. Billy hurried out of the house to greet them. "My mother has been worrying," he said, his gaze drawn to Rees and the white bandage around his head. He supposed he must look seriously injured. "What happened?"

"I was hit by something," Rees said, making up his mind in an instant to say nothing about the tunnels or following a sailor.

"He was attacked," Lydia said.

"But I don't know by whom," he added very quickly.

"Probably by some old tar down on his luck," Billy said wisely, hurrying to the older man's side and putting his strong young shoulder under Rees's left arm. He did not really need the support, although he appreciated it when climbing up the stairs. Lydia helped him into a chair by the window while Billy went down to speak to his mother about supper.

Lydia found her sewing scissors and began snipping at the linen strip binding Rees's head. "I never had a chance to see the wound," she said. "By the time Annie found me, someone had already bound your injury. I believe it was still bleeding." Her voice broke and her busy fingers stilled. "Annie said she found you lying in a pool of blood." Rees turned to look at her. She turned away from his gaze, wiping the tears from her eyes with her apron.

"I'm sorry," he said, reaching out to take her hand. He did not like apologizing, but her tears, so unusual for his feisty wife, inspired in him a surge of guilt. "I could have been more careful."

"Indeed," she said. "You might have left me to care for all those children by myself. Turn around. Let me finish with the bandage."

It took her several minutes to snip away the linen strip and as the bloodstained pieces dropped to the floor Rees no longer wondered that everyone had feared for his life. "Of course," he said aloud, comforting himself as well as Lydia, "head wounds do bleed."

Lydia said nothing, but she pulled the last piece of linen away with unnecessary force. "Oh my," she said involuntarily.

"What?"

"There is a long cut. And a bump. It looks as though you were hit by a board. Or something like it."

"Whoever hit me brought that instrument into the tunnels then," Rees said. "There were no stray pieces of wood lying around."

"Of course he did," Lydia said. "He followed you." For a moment neither spoke. Lydia was wholly occupied with separating the hairs that were glued into a mass by clotted blood. And Rees, who found the tugging on his hair almost as painful as the cut, was trying not to cry out. "Have you thought . . . do you realize that Benoit was traveling west? If he were following a tunnel familiar to him, well, was he aiming for the Boothe home?"

Rees tried to visualize the alley outside the tavern, and the tunnel that went at right angles to it. "You're right," he said. "And that makes sense if he's in league with Matthew Boothe."

"I'm not wholly certain of that," Lydia said.

"You're pulling too hard."

"Sorry." But she didn't sound sorry.

"You may be right. I mean, I'm sure Matthew Boothe and Philippe Benoit are partners. I just can't see Matthew at the other end of that board."

"I agree. But does he know other men who might be willing—for a few pence?" Lydia wondered, as she found Rees's comb and began tugging it gently through his red hair.

"He does. And I suspect Matthew saw me and told Benoit to lead me into the tunnels."

A soft knock upon the door interrupted him. Mrs. Baldwin, carrying a tray shrouded in a linen napkin, tiptoed in as though she thought Rees was on his deathbed. Lydia stepped away from Rees to take the tray. "It's just soup," Mrs. Baldwin said, "but the bread was fresh yesterday. And I added a wedge of cheddar. I bought it at the market. And a fresh roll of linen, as you requested."

"How kind of you," Lydia said. "It will do very well. I am grateful; I don't believe we could manage a tavern just now."

"No," agreed Mrs. Baldwin, her gaze resting upon Rees's wounded head. "Dear me, I don't know what the world is coming to. But this is exactly why I rarely venture abroad after nightfall."

"I'm sure my husband will be more cautious in future," Lydia murmured, urging Mrs. Baldwin toward the door. Once they were alone again, Lydia said to Rees, "The wound is still oozing a little, but I believe I've cleaned it as much as possible without washing your head." She took up the roll of linen and began wrapping it around her husband's head, her fingers quick. Then they sat down at the small table by the window. Rees picked up a piece of cheese, realizing as he regarded it that he was almost too tired to eat.

Chapter Twenty-one

Billy's farewell to his mother at dawn awakened Rees from slumber. He climbed out of bed and staggered to the window. Dawn streaked the sky with rose. The alley outside the yard was choked with people hurrying about their business. Rees felt much better, although he was ravenously hungry. He folded a leftover piece of cheese into a slice of stale bread and ate it. Without coffee to wash it down, the dry bread settled in his throat. He looked at Lydia, who was still sleeping peacefully. He didn't want to disturb her. He dressed quietly and departed in search of something for breakfast.

Despite the early hour the sun was already hot on his shoulders. He walked to the Moon and Stars. Once he'd eaten, he would enclose something for Lydia in Mrs. Baldwin's napkin and bring it back.

Twig was there, seated at a back table with the local paper lying before him. Rees threaded his way through the chairs and tables to join his friend. Twig looked up at him in surprise. "Where have you been? Your wife was looking for you."

"She found me," Rees said. He turned to the waitress to order coffee and beef.

"She came to the house."

"I was looking for that sailor Monsieur Benoit," Rees said. "She didn't know where I'd gone."

Twig nodded without curiosity. "Did you find him?"

"I found him. But there was no opportunity to talk to him." Rees's voice trailed away and he scowled. How frustrating to lose his chance to pry some information from that sailor.

"After your wife left me," Twig said, "I went and spoke to Deputy Sheriff Swett. He said he would look for the Frenchman." He sounded quite pleased with himself.

Rees regarded Twig in annoyance. "I wish you'd asked me first," Rees said, trying not to sound accusatory. "And I hope Mr. Swett does not assume Benoit is Mr. Boothe's killer. I'm not convinced he's guilty."

Twig's mouth twitched in surprise; he hadn't considered the possible consequences. But he did not speak as the serving girl brought Rees's plate and a cup of coffee. Rees eyed the food and asked for bacon and fried bread; Lydia would need something. When the girl left, Twig changed to a topic of more importance to himself. "Did you know Mrs. Coville and Adam visited the Boothes yesterday?"

"I thought they were estranged," Rees said.

"Why would you think that?" Twig said with a shake of his head. "Xenobia told me Master William invited them to visit, so they might take some memento to remember Anstiss by. She was quite upset."

"Who was?" Rees was confused.

"Xenobia, of course. Mrs. Coville wept so uncontrollably she had to be taken to the kitchen and plied with whiskey."

"What did Xenobia say?"

"That, after years of devotedly nursing Anstiss, Mrs. Coville accused Xenobia of contributing to her daughter's death."

"Surely not," Rees blurted in spite of himself.

"Well, as good as," Twig said. "All this blather about preventing Mrs. Boothe from visiting her family. As though Xenobia was a jailor instead of a nurse. If I'd been there," he went on, his voice rising with anger, "I would have put a flea into Mrs. Coville's ear. I swear it."

"And Adam? Didn't he speak?"

Twig shrugged. "I guess not. Xenobia didn't say." And of course Twig would not think to ask.

Rees pondered Twig's statements. Although he discounted Mrs. Coville's accusations, made in the heat of grief and loss, he knew Xenobia was keeping something back. And Lydia agreed. He needed to question Xenobia more forcefully.

"Will Xenobia be at your house this evening? Maybe Lydia can speak with her," he suggested. "Another woman . . . Xenobia may be comforted."

Twig's eyes widened and he grinned. "Yes. What a capital idea! Please come. She should be home by seven."

Rees wrapped up the fried bread and the bacon. "Lydia will be wondering where I am. Again. We'll see you later this evening." He went to reach for his purse but Twig waved his hand away.

"Let me."

Rees stared at his old friend in surprise. Twig was not usually so sensitive to social niceties; maybe Xenobia's attentions were having an effect. "Thank you. We'll see you tonight."

When he reached Mrs. Baldwin's house, he found Lydia seated in the kitchen. An empty cup and plate on the table before her indicated she'd eaten some breakfast. When Rees knocked on the door, she stood so hurriedly her chair toppled over. "Where have you been?" she demanded. "I've been worried sick."

"I brought you some food," Rees said, holding out the napkin-wrapped bundle. "I went to find some breakfast and ran into

Twig." Lydia took the packet and opened it. She stared at the bread with its white coating of congealed fat and gagged.

"I can warm that up," Mrs. Baldwin said, breaking the uncomfortable quiet. Lydia handed it over, keeping her face turned away from Rees. "Sit down," Mrs. Baldwin said to him. He righted Lydia's chair and sat in the seat beside it. From his chair he could see through the open door and into Mrs. Baldwin's shop. After several seconds of silence Lydia sat down. She had bitten her lip in her fury and a drop of red blood stained her chin.

A faint hissing pop sounded from the pan by the fire. Mrs. Baldwin bent and carefully turned the bread over. "Where did you buy this?" she asked.

"The Moon and Stars," Rees said, fixing his gaze upon Lydia's averted face.

The soft sound of a closing door interrupted the tense moment. A woman in a plain gown but wearing a large straw hat that dipped to hide most of her face stood uncertainly by the front door. "A customer," said Mrs. Baldwin. "Watch the bread." She hurried to the shop, directing the instruction over her shoulder to Lydia.

"How could you leave without a word again?" Lydia hissed at Rees as she rose to her feet. "Barely a day after you were attacked and left for dead."

"I just went to the tavern," Rees protested, his attention focused upon the woman in the big hat. Could she be the woman seen outside Georgianne's house?

"I didn't know that, did I? For all I knew, you could have been lying dead in an alley. Why didn't you tell me?"

"But you were sleeping peacefully," Rees protested. He didn't understand why she was so angry. "I thought you needed your rest."

Lydia turned and glared at him. "You should have found some way of alerting me," she said. "A note. A message to Mrs. Baldwin.

Something so I didn't wake up to find you gone and no one knowing where." An involuntary sob interrupted the flow of words.

"I'm sorry. I didn't mean to worry you." Rees rose to his feet and went to her, holding out his arms. She stepped away from his embrace.

"You are too used to considering only yourself," Lydia said in a trembling voice.

"Excuse me," Mrs. Baldwin said from the door. "But this visitor is for you."

The woman in front of Mrs. Baldwin raised her head. She held back the broad floppy brim of the hat so that Rees could recognize her: Georgianne Foster.

After a few seconds of shocked silence, Rees said, "Where have you been?"

"I'll be in the shop," Mrs. Baldwin said, looking curiously at Mrs. Foster's back. She paused, but neither Mrs. Foster nor Rees or Lydia acknowledged her. She closed the connecting door quietly behind her.

"I've been worried about you," Rees said. Mrs. Foster nodded as she untied the broad ribbons beneath her chin and tossed the hat aside.

"This must be your wife," she said, glancing at Lydia.

Rees automatically introduced them, adding, "We were at your house, when . . ."

Tears flooded into Mrs. Foster's eyes. "Did you see Isabella?"

"We did," Rees admitted. "I am so sorry."

"I wish you hadn't meddled," Georgianne cried out, taking several steps toward him.

"Mrs. Foster, please," Lydia said. She moved forward to intercept the other woman. "Sit down, I beg of you." Taking Georgianne's arm, Lydia pressed her into a chair. "Did you expect someone to assault your cousin?" She sat down beside the other woman.

"Jacob—Mr. Boothe warned us his children would not be made happy by his visits."

"Warned you?" Lydia glanced quickly at Rees.

"Warned you that someone might come after you?" Rees asked.

"I don't think he expected murder. But he talked about not understanding people as well as he thought." Mrs. Foster's brow crinkled as she struggled to bring the memory forward. "That even those most loved could grow into strangers."

"Sounds like he was speaking about one or more of his children," Rees said, wondering what exactly Jacob Boothe had suspected.

"Becoming a second wife, especially when there are grown children, is always difficult," Lydia said, throwing a quick look at her husband. Rees, startled, wondered if Lydia had felt David's initial reserve as dislike. But he couldn't pursue that inquiry now.

"But there . . . I mean he . . ." Georgianne stopped talking and took in a deep breath. "He never talked of marriage, either before or after Anstiss's death. Jacob loved his wife and he never behaved improperly. I know Isabella believed he would turn to her, once he was widowed. She hoped so anyway."

And so did you, Rees thought, regarding Mrs. Foster's downcast eyes in growing sympathy.

"I am not so sure it would ever have happened. He loved his wife so much."

"How did you know him?" Lydia asked.

"Through the Widows and Orphans committee. That's how we became friends. But we were never anything more."

"But even his children believe . . ." Rees stopped. He couldn't find a way to suggest what they thought without offense.

"Yes," Georgianne said. "I know. A friendship between Jacob and me sounds unlikely, doesn't it? It's just that, well, we were alike on some level. We discussed many serious topics and almost always agreed. When Isabella came to live with me, Jacob liked her, too. She was so gay and lively. But somewhat," she searched for the right word. "Shallow." Raising her eyes to Rees, Georgianne added, "But Isabella always believed he called on us to visit her. And that someday they would be married." Rees, whose opinions had undergone several rapid shifts during the conversation, thought now that Isabella had probably never had a chance. It was more likely Boothe would have married Georgianne, just as Lydia thought.

"May I offer you tea?" Lydia asked her, standing up and moving quickly to the fireplace. A swift shake confirmed that the teakettle was full of water. She put it on the hook and swung it over the fire.

"And where were you the day Isabella was . . ." Recollecting the tender feelings of the woman before him, Rees stopped abruptly.

"Murdered?" Georgianne said on a sob. "I say that word over and over to myself. I suppose I'm trying to believe it really happened." She sighed. "I was at a meeting with some of the ladies from the Widows and Orphans committee."

Lydia nodded. "Mrs. Weymouth confirmed that."

"When I came home," Georgianne continued, "the street was crowded with people. One of the women told me there'd been a fire."

"I think that was accidental," Rees said. "It looked to me as though the candle had been knocked to the floor."

"I approached the house as closely as I dared. I overheard Mr. Swett saying he wanted to question me." She shuddered. "I didn't know Isabella had been found dead until several hours later, when I was told by the people I'd fled to."

"She didn't suffer," Lydia said as she poured the boiling water over the tea leaves. Georgianne nodded and wiped her eyes upon her handkerchief.

"You didn't go in?" Rees asked, recalling the street urchin's description of a woman in a big hat. She shook her head. "You're sure?"

"There were too many people. And I was so frightened. It never occurred to me then that Isabella had been killed." She gulped. "I feared for my own life, you see." Her voice broke and she paused. Neither Lydia nor Rees spoke while she struggled for composure. "What happened?" Georgianne asked at last. "No one seems to know. Was it the smoke? Or was she shot, as Captain Wey— as someone else heard?"

Lydia poured tea into a cup and placed it before Mrs. Foster. But she did not drink. Instead, she turned the cup around and around, her eyes fixed blindly upon it.

Finally, as the silence grew uncomfortable, Rees said, "She was strangled. I believe she was already dead before the fire took hold." Mrs. Foster nodded slowly, horrified but not surprised.

"The two people I care most for in the whole world," she said in an exhausted voice. "Murdered." She wiped away her tears with a sodden handkerchief. Lydia offered her a fresh linen square. "How could this happen?" she asked. Lydia patted Georgianne's hand. When she was calm enough to take a few sips of tea, Rees continued.

"The question is this: was Isabella murdered in your stead, because someone thought she was you? Or did the murderer know who she was? And if so, why kill her? Did he believe she was Jacob Boothe's mistress?"

"I can't imagine," Georgianne said. "Certainly, Isabella and I went out together frequently." She paused and added slowly, "And when Jacob accompanied us, an onlooker might be forgiven for assuming she was his interest. She was such an affectionate person. She clung to him."

Rees imagined the scene. The more reserved widow standing aside while her cousin took Mr. Boothe's arm.

Suddenly Georgianne's face crumpled. "I asked Isabella to accompany me that afternoon, but she refused. She said it would be tedious." She looked up at Rees and Lydia. "I should have insisted. She would still be alive."

"That isn't your fault," Lydia said warmly. "Her death is attributable to the villain who murdered her, not to you or anyone else." Mrs. Foster gulped and tried to nod. She forced herself to take a small sip from her cup.

"Where are you staying?" Rees asked. "It's probably better that you don't return to your house, not immediately anyway."

"With friends," Georgianne said. She attempted a smile. "I know; the murderer could come after me next. I've been advised to write the deputy sheriff."

"No," Rees said forcefully. Mrs. Foster looked at him in shock. "I am sure he wishes to speak with you," Rees said, tempering his vehement tone. "But I would hate to see you put in jail. He's a lazy investigator. Give me a few days to unravel this knot. If you're safe where you are, that is."

"Yes, I think . . ."

The smell of burning, of which Rees had only barely been aware, suddenly intensified, and a stream of oily black smoke began pouring into the room from the fireplace. The door to the shop opened very abruptly. "Oh my," Mrs. Baldwin gasped, hurrying to the fireplace.

"I have it, Mrs. Baldwin," Lydia said, using a folded towel to push the spider away from the hearth. The fried bread and bacon that Rees had brought from the tavern, unnoticed during the conversation, had begun to char. Now a blackened mess, it filled the kitchen with an acrid stink. Mrs. Baldwin grabbed the towel from Lydia and, picking up the pan, quickly rushed the carbonized food to the back yard. Lydia and Rees followed her, watching as she tossed the mess into the yard. Unappealing as it appeared to Rees, the food became a battleground between a band of chickens and a flock of seagulls that screamed down from the sky.

"I'm so sorry," Lydia said as Mrs. Baldwin returned to the house. The three of them returned to the kitchen, the air still pungent with the stink of burning.

"I reminded you to watch the bread," Mrs. Baldwin said, turning her reproachful gaze upon Lydia.

"I know you did. But we— I lost track of it."

"I'm afraid we were all rather intent upon our conversation," Georgianne said to Mrs. Baldwin. "I am happy to see your shop doing well. And how is that son of yours? He must be quite grown up by now."

"I wondered if that was you," Mrs. Baldwin said, stretching out her hands. Georgianne clasped them. Turning to Rees and Lydia, Mrs. Baldwin explained. "I know Mrs. Foster. She was with the group of ladies that helped me." She looked around at the kitchen. "I owned this house. When my husband was lost at sea, they gathered the necessary funds so I could convert the front rooms into the shop." She bowed her head in Mrs. Foster's direction. "I'm happy to be able to repay your kindness, even in some small way."

Georgianne nodded and dropped the shopkeeper's hands. Directing her gaze to Rees, she said, "I should not have been so quick to blame you. It's just that Jacob was worried and I thought, if no one knew about our friendship . . . but of course people saw us. Of course they did. The villain who murdered Isabella would have found us eventually, with or without you. Poor Isabella. She harmed no one. And I don't think she should be blamed for dreaming of marriage and a family of her own." She looked around for her hat.

"Where are you staying?" Lydia asked. "In case we have more questions for you."

"Apply to Mrs. Weymouth. She'll send word to me." Georgianne tied the ribbons under her chin and after bidding everyone farewell, turned to leave. Mrs. Baldwin escorted her out of the kitchen.

As they disappeared through the door and into the shop, Rees asked Lydia in a quiet voice, "Do you believe her?"

Lydia smiled. "About what? She was clearly in love with Mr. Boothe. Still is." Rees nodded. "I don't think she much enjoyed having her cousin visiting either. But, with that said, I doubt Georgianne Foster is responsible for Isabella's death. I think she told the truth when she denied any romantic connection with Jacob." She hesitated, frowning as she tried to find the most appropriate words. "Georgianne would have looked and sounded different if they were intimate. Mr. Boothe is that unique specimen: a faithful husband."

"Faithful husbands are more common than you believe," Rees said, smiling at her.

In another, less ladylike woman, Rees would have described Lydia's reaction as a snort.

Rees volunteered to take on the dirty and tedious job of scouring the pan. He felt guilty about forgetting the bread and bacon on the fire, and anyway he wanted to think in peace. The women agreed with alacrity and left him to it. So he threw a handful of sand onto the bottom and took it outside to scrub away the burned black crust.

He agreed with Lydia; he thought Georgianne had indeed been in love with Jacob Boothe. What's more, Rees suspected the merchant had had feelings for the young widow as well. He must have known what people would think of their friendship, even if it were as innocent as Mrs. Foster claimed, and yet he visited her frequently anyway.

And then there was Isabella. Intended victim or murdered in mistake for her cousin? If the latter, then the murderer had to be someone who did not know either Georgianne or Isabella. In which case, none of the Boothe children would be guilty—they knew the difference between the ladies. But if Isabella were the intended victim . . .

"Will?" Lydia's voice broke into his thoughts. She came through the door carrying a towel. "Maybe you should allow me to finish that." She handed him the linen and took the pan from his hands. He examined his fingertips with dismay. The sand had abraded his skin. He hoped the rough bits did not catch on his yarn when he was weaving. "You got most of it," she said, inspecting the pan's bottom. "The rest will come out with hot soapy water." She looked up at her husband. "Did your friend Mr. Eaton say anything of interest at breakfast this morning?" Rees smiled at her, glad she had recovered her good temper.

"Twig said, well his interpretation is . . ." He stopped and took a moment to entirely switch his thoughts from Georgianne Foster. "Apparently Mrs. Coville accused Xenobia of conspiring in the imprisonment of her daughter." He went to the trough and plunged his hands into the water, pleasantly warm from the hot sun.

"Imprisonment?" Lydia repeated with a frown. "Xenobia must be distraught."

"Yes," Rees agreed. "I promised Twig we'd call on them tonight. I thought Xenobia might appreciate talking to another woman." He grinned at his wife, feeling quite pleased with himself.

Lydia nodded but said, "I feel sorriest for Mrs. Coville. Anstiss was her only daughter. I don't wonder that she finds Anstiss's death difficult to accept."

Rees hesitated before speaking. He dried his hands on the towel and examined his fingers as he considered his words. "Yes," he said slowly. "But death is common. Anstiss might have died from any number of causes. "

"She almost did, with Peggy, didn't she?" Lydia said.

"Yes. So why is Mrs. Coville so certain Jacob Boothe and Xenobia are to blame?"

"Here's Mr. Eaton," Lydia said in a totally different voice.

Rees turned and looked over the fence to the street outside. Twig's tall lanky body was bobbing up the lane toward them. He was not looking ahead of him. His eyes looked down as though focused upon his feet. Then, as the ground dipped, he disappeared from view and a moment later Rees heard a scrabbling at the gate. Rees tossed the towel to Lydia and went to greet his old friend.

"Smells like something burned up," Twig said.

"Yes. Lydia's breakfast," Rees said. But Twig was not really interested.

"Listen," he said. "I just heard. The constable found Philippe Benoit. He's in jail now."

"What?" Rees scowled at Twig. "This is why I didn't want you to involve Deputy Swett. I didn't want him to arrest Benoit. I told you, I'm not sure the sailor is guilty. I just wanted to question him." Twig, abashed, fixed his gaze upon the ground. Turning to Lydia, Rees said, "I've got to talk to Benoit. I've got to go now."

She nodded and flapped the towel at him. "Tell me everything when you return."

Rees ran from the yard.

Chapter Twenty-two

❧

There was no sign of Deputy Sheriff Swett at the jail; he was in his favorite tavern, no doubt boasting about his capture of this dangerous criminal. When Rees peered through the grate on the door all he could see was wavy black hair and a lean body huddled on the bench.

"Monsieur Benoit," Rees said. "May I speak with you?" The prisoner looked up. "My name is Will Rees."

"I know who you are." Benoit stood up. "I didn't kill Jacob Boothe." His accent was so faint it was almost undetectable.

"I'm not accusing you of murder," Rees said. "I'm more interested right now in your sailing career. I saw you meet with Matthew Boothe in the Witch's Cauldron." He looked around to see if Twig had heard that, but he had vanished. Rees cursed in frustration. He would have liked Twig to serve as a witness to his interview with Benoit.

"Who? I know no man by that name," the Frenchman said now.

"Of course you do," Rees said impatiently. "I saw you talking to him." Benoit approached the grate. His eyebrow was split and bleeding and a bruise the color of a plum marked his cheek. "The deputy sheriff do that?"

Benoit tossed his head. "He accused me of murder and when I

denied it, he and his friends," Rees didn't miss the contemptuous tone, "hit me."

"But you did meet Matthew Boothe," Rees repeated.

Benoit tipped his head back and peered through the bars. "What's wrong with you? I do not know a Jacob Boothe or a Matthew Boothe."

"That can't be true. They are well known in this town."

"Maybe I've heard of them." Benoit sounded like a sulky ten-year-old. "But I don't know them."

"So, if not Matthew Boothe, who have you been meeting in the Witch's Cauldron tavern?" Rees asked, his voice heavy with skepticism.

"John Hull. I serve as captain on his ship, the *India Princess*."

Rees caught the pride in Benoit's voice and guessed his captaincy was recent. "I see. You worked your way up from cabin boy?"

"No. I was a whaler first. Worked my way up to first mate. Then Mr. Hull approached me and asked if I wanted to captain a merchant ship east. I've sailed twice so far."

"To Cathay?"

"Not yet. From the Ile de France to Turkey and India."

"I followed you into the tunnels," Rees said. "You beat me up." Benoit looked away. When he did not say anything, Rees continued his questioning. "Does Mr. Hull own a house that connects to the tunnels?" Another pause.

"That was my first time in the tunnels," Benoit said finally. "Hull knew you were watching him; he gave me directions. He doesn't live in Salem, but further up the coast." He suddenly bit off his words as though fearing he had said too much.

"If Hull doesn't live in Salem, how does he know about the tunnels?" Rees asked. He thought of how he'd been transported via tunnel to the intersection outside the Black Cat. "And he knows them well." Benoit shrugged, a motion that engaged both shoulders and managed to convey complete disinterest. If John Hull was Matthew Boothe in disguise, as Rees suspected he was, then the answer to Rees's question was obvious. "Describe Mr. Hull then, if you please."

"You said you've seen him; you know what he looks like," Benoit said in a sullen tone.

"I want to hear your description," Rees said.

"Fair hair, blue eyes, mustache, and beard." His hand gestured to his chin but paused. Rees could see Benoit was remembering something. "He speaks in a peculiar manner, as though his upper lip is frozen."

"Are you sure?" Rees demanded. That certainly did not sound like Matthew, who spoke well and, like his sister Betsy, barely ever shut up.

"Mr. Rees." The shout drew Rees's attention. The deputy sheriff, flanked on either side by rough-looking flunkies, was hurrying up the lane toward the jail. "What are you doing with my prisoner?"

"Talking to him," Rees said, turning a scowl upon him.

"The last time you spoke to one of my prisoners, she walked free," Deputy Sheriff Swett said. "I don't want to see that happen with Benoit here. He's the villain who murdered Mr. Boothe."

"I only wanted to speak with him about sailing," Rees lied. "I didn't know you arrested him for murder. Anyway, what proof do you have that he is the killer?"

"You were looking for him," said the deputy, grinning nastily. Rees looked away from the man's brown teeth. "I figured, if you wanted him, he must be important. And who's going to care about a common sailor?"

"I'm not a common sailor," Benoit protested. "I'm the captain of the *India Princess*."

"Yes, I know. You told me. Who really owns that vessel? And don't tell me John Hull. No one named John Hull lives in Salem."

"You sure?" Rees asked, darting the deputy sheriff a look.

"Of course. I know everyone in Salem. Everyone that matters, anyway. There is a Hull family but they live a bit farther north. Whaling family. I asked Adam Coville about them. The Hulls have never owned a merchant ship, and none of the sons are named John."

So why, Rees wondered, did Matthew choose to disguise himself as a member of a family that lived in the area? Any search of the name would surely betray his deception. He could have made up any alias he wished without discovery.

And did Matthew even know his confederate had been arrested and jailed? Rees looked up at the sky. It was coming on noon; that lazy boy would surely be awake by now. Rees decided he should pay a call upon Matthew and tell him what had happened. Glancing first at Benoit and then at Swett, Rees said, "I see. I'd like a chance to question the captain here. Please, don't hang him until I have a chance to do so." Although he'd asked most of his questions, he didn't want the deputy sheriff to know that. And he certainly didn't want Swett to execute an innocent man.

"Once he has his turn with judge and jury," said Swett, expectorating bloody sputum into the dirt, "I'll do the necessary, whether you've talked to him or not."

Rees nodded and sauntered away. But once out of sight, he broke into a run. After picking up Lydia he would go directly to the Boothe house.

Lydia, swathed in an apron and cleaning Mrs. Baldwin's kitchen, was only too glad to abandon her domestic tasks and join Rees. While she finished scrubbing the table and hung her apron on its hook, Rees went outside and harnessed Amos to the buggy. Although Lydia assured him she was well able to walk that distance, sounding exasperated as she did so, it was a longer walk than Rees felt comfortable permitting. "I'm not ill, you know," Lydia said tartly, yielding to him only to prevent an argument.

Once they'd climbed into the buggy, the drive to the Boothe home took less than twenty minutes. They found the household in an uproar. Shown to the morning room, Rees and Lydia joined Peggy, William, and Matthew. "Mr. Morris will be arriving shortly," Peggy explained. "He invited Betsy out for dinner at his home. With his parents."

"I understood they were already engaged," Lydia said, sounding as puzzled as Rees felt.

"They are." Throwing a quick glance at her brothers, Peggy lowered her voice. "Mr. Morris has not been very attentive of late. Betsy was worried that he would break the engagement. But now it seems as though the wedding will go forward."

Rees exchanged a glance with Lydia. He thought Betsy might be overly optimistic; Mr. Morris could have chosen this outing to communicate different news.

"Where is she now?" Lydia asked.

"Upstairs dressing," Peggy said.

"She's been dressing all morning," Matthew said, his tone tart.

Peggy smiled. "She wants to look perfect so she's been putting on and then discarding every gown she owns. Ah, I hear her now."

Rees too heard the soft step on the floor outside and turned just as Betsy entered. She was clad in dark gray, almost black, silk, cut low to expose her chest, with a white silk shawl draped across her shoulders. Her bonnet, a feminized version of a tall riding hat, was decorated with a spray of artificial flowers and a large gray bow. "You look divine, Bets," Matthew said, stepping forward and kissing his sister upon the cheek. She switched her black gloves from one hand to another.

"Perhaps I should wear the black? To acknowledge our recent tragedies."

"Definitely not," Peggy said. "Mr. Morris knows about the deaths. You want him to think of your future together."

Betsy looked at her sister. "You aren't going to wear that, are you?" she gasped.

Peggy looked down at her simple sprigged cotton. She spread out the skirt and looked at it. "What's wrong with this? I'm not planning to go out, so no one will see I'm not in mourning."

"Don't let Mr. Morris see you." The sound of the front door opening and the low mutter of conversation in the front hall distracted her.

"It's too late for Peggy to change," William said. And a moment later, Mr. Morris appeared at the morning room door.

At first glance, Rees thought the gentleman unprepossessing. A short slender fellow, with a long narrow face and thinning hair, he appeared to be a number of years older than his future bride. Rees guessed Mr. Morris was closer to his own age than to Betsy's. He greeted her siblings, but his gaze passed over Rees and Lydia as though they were invisible. Neither William nor Matthew made any attempt to introduce them.

Mr. Morris extended his hand to William; he shook and with a few general comments the two men and Betsy passed into the hall. Rees focused his gaze upon Peggy, who collapsed into a chair with an exhalation of relief, and Matthew. "Thank God that's over," he said.

Peggy nodded. "I believe she tried on all of her dresses and some of mine. Even the inappropriate ones."

"I find that hard to believe," Matthew said, throwing a critical glance at his sister's clothing. "Betsy knows how to dress. You don't."

Peggy brushed away his criticism with one bony hand. "Just because I don't often wear my nice gowns doesn't mean I don't own them," she said. "I wore my black gown with the ruffles when we went driving with Mr. Morris, didn't I? The day of that fire at Mrs. Foster's." Moving her eyes from her brother to Rees, she asked, "Do you have news?"

Rees looked at Matthew. "Deputy Sheriff Swett has jailed a certain Philippe Benoit and charged him with your father's murder."

Peggy gasped audibly.

"Who is that?" Matthew asked. "And why did he murder my father?"

"I don't believe he did," Rees began.

"I see we didn't need your help at all," Matthew interrupted "The deputy sheriff succeeded in discovering the murderer without you."

Rees stared at the young man. "What do you mean? You don't want to speak to the deputy and free your confederate? I tell you, Swett is planning to hang Benoit."

"Why should I care?" Matthew retorted. "My confederate? He is nothing to me."

"He knows you as John Hull. He claims to captain the merchant ship *India Princess* for you." Rees, who was beginning to wonder if Matthew was completely heartless, watched the young man's eyes widen.

"A merchant ship? I don't own a ship," Matthew cried. "What are you saying? And I've never heard of either John Hull or Philippe Benoit." He glared at Rees. "I wouldn't tell you if I did. You'll have no joy of accusing *me*. And now, I have a rehearsal to attend." He turned on his heel and stalked from the room.

Peggy sagged in a flutter of skirts onto the couch. When Rees looked at her, he realized her face was as white as chalk.

"Are you all right?" he asked.

She forced a smile. "I am so shocked. I hardly know what to say. Do you really believe my brother is a ship owner? And a merchant?"

Lydia hurried to Peggy's side. "Will saw someone he thought was your brother talking to Captain Benoit in the Witch's Cauldron," she said. Peggy, her eyes wide and staring, turned to look at Rees. He had the impression she wished to say something, but she did not speak.

"I did," he said gently. "But I don't believe Matthew murdered your father."

"Are you accusing the captain then?" Peggy asked, forcing the words through trembling lips.

"Of course not," Lydia said promptly. Rees knew he could not speak with such certainty. Peggy did not remove her wide-eyed gaze from Rees.

"Are you?" she demanded of him.

"No," Rees said. "Not yet anyway. Benoit as good as admitted that he and Hull—that's Matthew—attacked me in the tunnels. But murder?" Rees shook his head. "I'm just not sure. The deputy is convinced Benoit is guilty. I hoped Matthew would step up and defend his captain."

Peggy nodded. The color was beginning to return to her cheeks. "Yes, I see. But he won't. Matthew is . . ."

"Selfish," Rees supplied, when Peggy seemed incapable of finding the right word.

Her lips twitched, "Indeed. Let me talk to him. Maybe I can persuade him to behave with character, as a gentleman should. Or," she looked up in concern, "is Mr. Swett going to hang Captain Benoit immediately?"

"No. He promised to go before the magistrate first," Rees said. "We have a little time. Of course, Benoit will be imprisoned until he appears before the judge."

Peggy nodded, her expression going blank. She folded her hands together in her lap, clenching them so tightly together the knuckles went white. "Of course." Looking up at him with a polite smile, she added, "This has all been quite a shock. I hope you don't believe me unmannerly if I retire to my room."

"Of course not," Lydia said, rising to her feet.

"I'll call on you again," Rees said, eyeing the girl in surprise. He wouldn't have thought her susceptible to the vapors. "See if you're able to persuade Matthew to behave as a gentleman should. In the interim, I'll talk to Captain Benoit."

Peggy slanted a quick look at Rees from under her lashes but said nothing.

Rees took Lydia's arm and they stepped out of the morning room into the hall. Peggy followed on their heels. As the serving man opened the front door, Rees glanced back over his shoulder. He was startled to see Peggy, skirt hiked almost to her knees, running up the stairs two at a time.

Chapter Twenty-three

A s Rees helped Lydia into the buggy, Lydia said, "Are we going to have dinner? I'm hungry. Again."

"Of course. You are eating for two," Rees said, smiling down
at her. "But then I want to visit the docks once more."

Since Amos and the wagon had to be returned to the barn
behind Mrs. Baldwin's house anyway, Rees drove straight there.
After unhitching the horse and cooling him down, Rees put him
in the stall next to Bessie. Then he and Lydia walked the few short
blocks to the Moon and Stars. As they had eaten here many times
now, the proprietress had unbent sufficiently to nod and smile in
a friendly way. Lydia chose turkey and fish. Rees preferred steak pie.
While they dedicated themselves to their dinners neither spoke.
He finished first. Pushing away the beaker of ale, he called for
coffee.

"Why do you want to go back to the docks?" Lydia asked.

"I want to visit the gentlemen whose names Mr. Crowninshield gave me," Rees said. "And then I'll stop at the *India Princess*."
He began turning his mug around and around in his freckled
hands.

"Why? We already saw that vessel," Lydia said. "Remember?"

"Do you think the crew has been told their captain is in jail?"
Rees mused.

"I wouldn't be surprised," Lydia said. "I'll wager someone saw him and ran to the ship as fast as he could to spread the news. What about Mr. Hull? Or whoever is playing at Mr. Hull. Do you think he knows?"

"Probably. Especially if Hull is Matthew Boothe."

"Young Mr. Boothe seemed genuinely shocked when you accused him." Lydia eyed her husband doubtfully. "I know you dislike him, but I think you are too focused upon him. Maybe it's William. Or . . ."

"Matthew is an actor," Rees interrupted with a shake of his head. "He's experienced at pretending to be someone else. I swear it was he whom I saw speaking with Benoit. Not William. And not just once." Lydia chased a fragment of meat around and around on her plate. Rees sensed that she did not agree.

"I suppose none of the Coville brothers resemble their Boothe cousins," Lydia said at last.

"Not in the slightest," Rees replied. "You've met Adam and Edward. And Dickie, although fairer than his brothers, does not have that pale blond hair."

"I wonder, did Jacob Boothe have brothers and sisters?" Lydia persisted. "Perhaps it is one of the cousins from the paternal line."

Rees frowned. "Then why," he wondered aloud, "haven't we heard about them?"

"We didn't ask," Lydia said.

They lapsed into silence while the serving girl collected the plates. Lydia, whose appetite seemed to be increasing daily along with her waistline, accepted the offer of a slab of pie. Rees, not to be outdone, followed suit, pouring cream upon his.

Afterward they strolled toward the docks and the counting houses nearby. Some of the blank walls already boasted signs advertising the upcoming play. Edward Coville's name had been scratched out and replaced with Matthew Boothe's.

Obtaining directions from a passing gentleman, Rees found the counting houses belonging to the first two names on Mr. Crowninshield's list. In both cases, they described Jacob Boothe in exactly the same terms as Mr. Crowninshield had: amiable, generous, and honest. They had never heard the name Hull. And the last businessman, to whom Rees put a question about Georgianne Foster, replied in a crisp voice, "I do not engage in gossip. I leave that to my wife. And anyway, no one would blame him if there were anything there. Not after coping with an ill wife for near twenty years."

"I'm not going to visit the remaining names," Rees said as he rejoined Lydia. "If there is anything discreditable in Jacob's past, none of these men will tell me." And he was beginning to believe there was nothing there.

A few minutes walk brought them to the docks. Rees stood on the pier and inspected the *India Princess*. Provisions as well as trade goods—beaver furs, twine, and leather—were still rolling up the gangplank. This time the mate checking the manifest was a white man.

"Wait here," Rees told Lydia before approaching the Jack Tar. He knew sailors were superstitious about women and ships.

The mate turned, blue eyes staring at Rees from a tanned face. A bright yellow calico neckerchief circled his neck and both forearms bore familiar tattoos. "What do you want?" he asked in lilting Irish-accented English.

"Where's the other fellow? The African?" Rees asked.

"Run off." The sailor paused, eyebrow raised questioningly.

"I expect you're waiting for Captain Benoit," Rees said. "I spoke with him earlier. I fear he will not be returning to the ship today."

"You saw him? And where was that?" The sailor leaned forward slightly, his posture a mix of eagerness and wariness.

"At the jail. When are you supposed to sail?"

"With the tide on Thursday morning."

Only two days away. They would certainly miss that. "I wonder if you know the owner of this vessel, John Hull?"

"No. Even the captain don't know him well. Seen him maybe five or so times. At the most."

"So, you couldn't give me a description of the man?"

The mate shook his head. Rees looked up at the faces staring down at him from the deck. Like the man to whom Rees was speaking, almost all were tanned dark. Several Indians and some black men with kinky hair were mixed in. The few pale faces among the bronze belonged to boys, young boys too, early teens at most. One or two of the sailors were grizzled veterans, men Rees's age, old for the grueling life of a sailor.

"How did you come to work on the *India Princess*?" Rees asked.

"Captain Benoit picked every man jack of us." The sailor looked away. "Not many'd serve under the captain. He was a whaling man before, and the *Princess* ain't backed by the rich merchantmen like the Derbys and the Crowninshields. Well, they might invest now. We've got two voyages under our belts. Successful voyages," he added emphatically. "I seen more money than I ever dreamed of making."

"Have you sailed to Cathay?" Rees was genuinely curious.

"Not yet. Generally sail to St. Petersburg for iron. We stop at Turkey for opium, then on to the Ile de France, Bombay, and Sumatra." The sailor sighed. "This was supposed to be our first voyage to China."

"I see," Rees said and prepared to turn away. But a thought struck him and he asked the sailor, "Do you know Mr. Matthew Boothe?"

"Matthew Boothe? No. Maybe the captain does. But the

Boothes allow us to tie up here, at their wharf. And this ship," he gestured to the *India Princess,* "used to belong to the Boothe family. Under another name, of course. They sold it to the owner."

"John Hull," Rees said, finishing the mate's sentence. He nodded. Rees hesitated a moment, thinking. "Do you know where this Mr. Hull resides?"

"A'course not. If I never met the man, I wouldn't know where he lives, now would I?" But something changed in the man's expression, as though shutters had come down over his eyes. Rees suddenly felt sure the mate was lying. He knew something.

"Ahoy. Man overboard." The cry was faint at first, but it grew louder as it traveled across the docks, passing from one sailor to another. The crew that had been intent upon Rees's conversation with the first mate abandoned the bales and casks they'd been ferrying across the deck and rushed to the side of the merchant ship. Rees turned around, staring north across the wharves that jutted into the harbor, to the men clustering together on one of the northernmost quays. Although Rees couldn't hear the conversations, he could see them pointing at something in the water.

The crew from the *Princess* made a united move for the gangplank. "And where do you think you're going?" cried the mate. "None of you gobshites can swim."

"You can't either, you damn sheeny," someone yelled.

"But I got a piece of the caul that covered me at my birth from my mam," the mate retorted. "So I know I'll never drown. I'll go." He hurried away in a rapid but peculiar rolling walk.

Rees was not confident the man in the water would be rescued; sailors who could swim were bad luck, and none of the watchers had jumped off the dock. "Wait here," he told Lydia and ran after the mate.

Arriving on the wharf a few minutes later, Rees and the officer from the *Princess* joined the throng staring into the dark water below. At first Rees could see nothing. The mate turned to one of the other men. "Where is he?"

"By the pilings." The man spit through the toothless center of his mouth. "Dead." Rees peered into the gloom. Although the brassy rays of the late afternoon sun poured down upon the wharf, the sea below was in shadow, the object just a darker blot in dark water. It moved with the swells, bumping into the pilings with subdued thumps. It was hard to tell what that was: dead man or something else. Rees looked at the men around him.

"What happened?" he asked.

A young man with a shock of dirty blond hair shrugged. "Saw it about an hour ago. Stupid tar drowned."

"You're sure it's a body?" Rees hoped it was not. He couldn't explain his fear that this was more than a simple drowning.

"Yes."

"Any idea how long he's been there?" Rees asked.

Shrugs all around. "Could've been days before the tide washed him in."

Rees sighed and stared down at the almost invisible mound moving with the tide. He didn't *know* that that man hadn't drowned—after all, what could be more common this close to the sea—but an ominous premonition had stolen over him. What better way to dispose of a corpse than to drop it over the side of a ship? He needed to examine that body. Perhaps, he hoped, this was some awful coincidence. "He has to be pulled out. Anyone have nets? A hook?" Rees looked around. Everyone shook his head.

Turning and narrowing his eyes against the glare, Rees looked both ways on the wharf, searching for something, anything he could use to pull the body from the water. And there, a short distance away, with the Customs House as a backdrop, was a rowboat drawn up against the rail. "Let's get that boat into the water," Rees said. "Anybody willing to help me?"

"You, sheeny," said an old man to the mate from the *India Princess*. "You help him. You got the caul."

The mate sighed. "I'll do it."

"But we'll have to put the boat back where it is," said a boy with dusty colored hair, "put it back exactly or else old man Jenkins . . ." He rolled his eyes.

"Of course." Rees cut him off. "Let's get it now."

By the time they carried the rowboat to the plank ramp and slid it into the water, the sun had dropped to the horizon. They would have to work quickly if they were to reach the body and bring it to shore before dark. Rees settled himself into the bow and watched the mate, Rees's younger by fifteen years, put the oars into the oarlocks and begin rowing, smoothly and almost effortlessly, with the ease of much practice. He rowed out into the harbor, where the water was more turbulent, guiding the boat around the moored whalers.

"We're fortunate the corpse fetched up at this end of the dock," the mate said suddenly. "If he'd floated into shore at the other end, why, it would take us an hour or more, and be much more difficult to boot, to row around those long Derby and Crowninshield wharves." Rees nodded and tried to look over his shoulder as the sailor spun one oar in the oarlock to guide the boat toward land.

No ships were docked near the body—*Anstiss's Dream* had sailed—and the rowboat slid easily up to the pilings. The movement of the water did not appear so gentle here; the waves rose up and splashed against the wood in foot-high swells. And the body, for it was a body, though Rees had been hoping it was something else, crashed into the posts with every motion. Rees looked at the mate.

"I'm as close as I can get," he said, his face glistening with sweat and saltwater. "I don't want to crash against those pilings."

Rees waited for the lull between waves and then reached across the water to grasp the back of the victim's shirt. The body, in clothes weighted with water, moved toward the rowboat slowly, oh, so slowly. The next wave almost tore the burden from Rees's hand. He quickly released the side of the boat and stretched across the filthy, slimy water to grab the corpse with both hands. He held on although his hands, so cold from the water, began to cramp. And in the next pause between rollers, Rees dragged the body to the side of the rowboat and tried to pull it in. Even as strong as he was, he could not do it. The sailor, with an impatient epithet, threw the oars into the boat and, kneeling, lent his strength to Rees's. And the sea reluctantly released its prize. The body flopped into the boat. The mate spared Rees one triumphant glance before grabbing up the oars once again, fitting them into the oarlocks, and bending into them to row away from the pier. Rees could see the strain in the man's shoulders and arms; the cords in his neck stood out like cables. Slowly the boat crept away from the pilings and into open water. It seemed almost calm after the breakers by the dock. Rees, who hadn't realized he'd been holding his breath, exhaled in a great gust of relief.

"I knew I could do it," the mate said with cocky confidence. Rees tried to smile in return but his lips were trembling too much. The skin of his face wore a mask of salt and his mouth tasted of brine.

When they pulled the boat up on shore, the mate helped Rees tumble the body facedown onto the planks. The sailor took one glance and retched. "S'a sailor," he said, his words labored as he tried not to vomit again. "I'll take the boat back." Rees put his handkerchief across his nose and mouth and bent to inspect the corpse.

Although he gagged at his first look, that feeling passed. As always when he examined a body, he did not allow physical discomfort to deter him.

The body's rough clothing did suggest a sailor, maybe a common deckhand. But, Rees reminded himself, the shoes that could indicate an officer might have been washed away. Through the tattered shirt, he saw the darker markings of a tattoo on the man's swollen back. The man's hair, spread out upon the dock, lay long and lank like seaweed.

The shirt, cut through, hung in rags around the man's slashed back, and the wound riveted Rees's attention. Although the sea had washed the laceration clean of blood and the fish had nibbled at it so that the lips of the cut were ragged, Rees saw that the gash was almost identical to the one upon Jacob Boothe's side.

Rees struggled to turn the heavy body, finally succeeding as the corpse flopped over with a thud. His eyes went first to the belly. But this time, although the wound on the cadaver's back was deep, the blade had not gone all the way through. The dark skin on the man's front was uncut, although he was bloated and an odd greenish color overlay his brown skin. Rees examined the corpse's face. The swelling that had lifted the body from the deep had also distended his features. Or what was left of them. Fish had eaten the eyes and the lips, and repeated blows as the tide had washed the corpse up against the pilings had battered him until Rees thought the man's own mother wouldn't recognize him. Still, a sense of familiarity nagged at Rees. He had an unhappy suspicion that this cadaver was the remains of the African mate from the *India Princess*.

Rees straightened up with a sigh. As he'd feared, this sailor had not drowned. He'd been murdered—and probably by the same hand that had killed Jacob Boothe.

Chapter Twenty-four

During his examination of the body, Rees had collected a small crowd of onlookers, although no one wanted to approach too closely. "Does anyone know this man?" Heads shook no. No one was willing to admit to it, anyway.

"He looks familiar," one grizzled old veteran said finally. "But I don't know 'im." Rees glanced from face to face. No one stepped forward. Rees gestured at the *India Princess*'s first mate.

"You said you thought he was a sailor?"

The man nodded. He still looked pasty under his tan. "He's got a tattoo. At least one. And if he wasn't a sailor, what's he doing in the water?"

"But you didn't know him? Could he be the man missing from the *India Princess*?" The mate's eyes shifted over to the corpse and quickly flicked away.

"Maybe." He gagged. "I'll go fetch the undertaker," he said and fled. Several other men took the opportunity to quit the wharf as well. Rees invited the old man to approach. He carried himself with the air of someone who had seen everything and had lost the ability to experience surprise.

"The fish have been at this fellow," Rees said, pointing at the damaged face. "How long do you think the body might have been in the water?"

The veteran looked at the victim's face, a quick fleeting glance, and grimaced. "Hard to say. The water is warm. Corruption goes quick in the warm. And all of his face would have been completely devoured in a couple of days. So I'd guess two or so days. Most likely happened at night. He was probably drunk, missed a step, and got washed overboard."

Rees nodded his thanks and stepped away from the corpse. Now that the excitement was over, most of the spectators were departing. The sun was almost touching the horizon; work would soon be over for the day and the men were eager to leave. Rees turned around and looked for Lydia. Despite his command, she'd followed him along the docks and he'd seen her standing in the crowd watching him. Now he'd lost her. He swept his gaze up and down the length of the wharf. Finally he spotted her, talking to a street vendor. As he watched, she turned from the man and began walking down the wharf toward Rees. In one hand she carried a small cake. The other clutched a corner of her apron. As she approached him, he smelled ginger, sweet and spicy. "I bought you a ginger cake," she said when she was still several yards away. "I thought you might need it to settle your stomach."

"I'm fine," Rees said. "What do you have there?" He nodded to the lumps tied up in her apron.

"Lemons. I thought I might make a pie." Her voice trailed away as her gaze fastened upon the body lying on the wharf. "Who is it?"

"I don't know. But the mate went for Twig."

"I'm here," he said as he came striding up the dock. Grinning at Rees, he added, "I should have guessed you'd be here, and involved in some way."

"Not involved," Rees said. "I just helped bring the poor soul out of the water."

Twig shook his head as though he knew Rees were lying and

turned to look at the body. "You might almost have left him. I think he'd have preferred it to Potter's Field outside of town."

"And the Negro side of Potter's Field at that," Rees said. He did not mention the wound. He knew Twig would see it, but did not want to discuss this or Boothe's murder on the dock in earshot of the spectators. Twig motioned to the wagon waiting several yards away. Painted lamp black, the death cart was driven by a scruffy fellow who swayed in the seat with each step the horse took. His partner, even dirtier than the driver, sat in the wagon bed. Rees eyed them and decided they were too drunk to care they were handling a dead man.

"Don't bury him," Rees told Twig, tipping his head at the corpse lying at his feet. "I want to take another look first thing tomorrow."

"I knew you were investigating this," Twig crowed.

"This is not the time to congratulate yourself on your intelligence," Rees said softly, leaning forward. "I want this kept private for now."

Twig made an elaborate pantomime of laying his finger over his lips. "Of course. You can rely on me to keep this a secret. I'll put him on a block of ice."

Rees sighed in exasperation. Every man on the dock would be curious now, after Twig's playacting.

The body went into the wagon and the swaybacked old nag started back to Twig's home. The steady motion of the wagon caused the corpse's hands to twitch and its head to move; Rees shuddered at the macabre sight and turned away.

By now, the sun was almost hidden behind the horizon. Rees rolled his neck from side to side. He would pay for his good deed tomorrow with sore shoulders and a stiff neck. With the excitement done, his energy had drained away and left a haze of fatigue behind.

"I wish I had not promised to call upon Twig and Xenobia tonight," he said.

Lydia nodded. "But we did."

With dusk fast approaching, the lanes were growing dark. Here and there, a candle flame made a spot of light. Rees and Lydia turned up the alley that ran by the Black Cat. Thrifty housewives might light a candle or two now, but they would wait until darkness was fully advanced before illuminating every room. The Black Cat, however, glowed like a beacon: candles in every window, and more shining in the rooms behind. Beeswax candles at that. Rees automatically glanced up at the window where he'd seen Annie. But instead of the girl, a woman in a filmy dress sat gazing over the sill. She waved provocatively at Rees. He looked quickly away, his face burning. Lydia, without demonstrating any sign that she'd seen the woman, grasped Rees's arm tightly.

Mrs. Baldwin's shop was closed for the night. In unspoken agreement, Rees and Lydia went past the shop and headed north, to Twig's house. Rees knew if he retired to his room and sat down, he would not want to rise again.

Xenobia was already at Twig's house when Rees and Lydia arrived. She seemed surprised to see them, and Rees guessed Twig had not told her they were coming. Coffee perked on the hob. Xenobia swung the teakettle over the fire and brought down cups from the cabinet built in by the fireplace. Lydia sat down at the table but Rees, although he planned to participate in the discussion with Xenobia, was drawn to one side of the room by Twig.

"Do you want to take a look at the body?" he asked Rees in an elaborately private whisper.

"What, now?" Rees looked around the kitchen. Despite the fire burning in the hearth and the candles upon the table, shadows lurked in the corner. He couldn't imagine what he would be able to see in the shed.

"Certainly," Twig said.

Rees looked at the other man. He knew from past experience that Twig wouldn't take no for an answer. "Very well," he said with a sigh. Twig took the lantern hanging on a hook by the back door and lit it with a candle. By the flickering golden light, they descended the back stairs.

"The talk in the taverns is that Captain Benoit killed Mr. Boothe," Twig said.

"No one knows that. And I believe if he's guilty of that deed, he did so at the behest of someone else." Rees heard the sharpness in his voice and took in a deep breath. It wasn't Twig's fault gossip had already tried and convicted Benoit.

"Was it robbery? A sailor down on his luck?" Twig put down the lantern and began fumbling at the shed's latched door by the pale silvery light of the crescent moon.

Rees thought of Mr. Boothe's gold pocket watch and the gold earrings in Benoit's ears. "I don't think robbery was the motive," he said.

Twig swung back the door, and the faint smell of decay rushed out. Rees gagged and swallowed. He put his handkerchief over his nose and mouth. Twig seemed unaffected. He flipped the canvas covering aside, disclosing the body lying upon a table scattered with sawdust and shattered ice. It was melting fast; water pattered steadily upon the ground. "You owe me for the ice," Twig said. Rees stared down at the dark form. He could barely see it. Twig collected the lantern and held it aloft. The corpse sprang into view, but details were not visible in that uncertain light.

"I can't even see the color of his skin," Rees said. "This will not do."

"But corruption will advance rapidly in the heat," Twig objected.

"I'll return first thing tomorrow," Rees said, adding recklessly, "I'll pay for the ice. But I need light to thoroughly examine him."

Twig said nothing but he flipped the canvas over the cadaver with a sharp, angry motion. Rees left the shed and started back to the house, leaving Twig to close up by himself.

". . . ill since before Peggy's birth," Xenobia was saying when Rees reentered the house. "But Anstiss seemed to grow so much worse in the weeks before her death."

"Did anything unusual happen?" Lydia asked.

Xenobia rose to her feet and took the kettle from the fire. She poured hot water into the pot. "Your coffee will be ready in another minute, Mr. Rees," she said.

"Thank you," he said, taking a step toward the table.

"Do you want tea or coffee?" Xenobia asked Twig as he lumbered noisily into the kitchen.

"Ale," he said. Xenobia shot him a look. "Please," he added.

Into the sudden silence, Lydia said, "So, Mrs. Boothe eased her pain with regular infusions of opium tea. Is that right?" Rees, realizing that Lydia had repeated this for his benefit, turned to look at Xenobia,

"Yes. And, oh, without the tea Anstiss was in such pain." Xenobia shook her head, her eyes filling with tears. "She was writhing and screaming like an animal. None of us could bear it."

"Everyone is saying that prisoner will hang," Twig said to Rees, talking over Xenobia. "And I heard Deputy Swett is planning to ask William Boothe to pay him instead of you, as he was the one to find the sailor and jail him." Now Twig had gained Rees's full attention.

"But there's no proof that Benoit is guilty," Rees said, his voice rising. "And he hasn't gone before the magistrate."

Twig nodded. "I know. The deputy always threatens to hang his prisoners. Sometimes the families come forth with a gift, money usually, to rescue the accused."

Rees stared at Twig. "He takes bribes?" He heard the outrage in his voice. But then, why should he be surprised? It was of a piece with Mr. Swett's character, and he had to pay for his fancy clothing somehow.

"Mr. Rees? Your coffee." Xenobia put a large mug upon the table with a sugar bowl full of chunks and a pitcher of cream beside it. She added a plate of lemon chess tarts.

Twig gave Rees a push toward the table. "Let's eat."

Suddenly realizing he was very hungry, Rees sat down across from Lydia and helped himself to several of the yellow squares.

"So," Twig continued in Rees's ear, "if you're sure the Frenchman is innocent, you may be able to free him. But if he is, who murdered Jacob Boothe?"

Rees turned his attention back to Twig. "I think the owner of the *India Princess* may have something to do with it," he said, more to himself than to his companion. His thoughts were in turmoil.

"Who?" Twig asked. But Rees shrugged. He didn't want to offer Twig any more information. Rees feared his friend, whose judgment varied, would broadcast it at the tavern.

"And how are you feeling?" Xenobia asked Lydia, with a wave at her belly.

"Hungry," Lydia admitted. "I could barely eat at all for the first few months. But now I can't stop eating."

"I understand the Covilles visited the Boothes," Rees said, interrupting the ongoing conversation almost without realizing it. His spinning thoughts had brought him back to Anstiss and her birth family. Lydia frowned at him.

Xenobia turned a startled glance upon him but she nodded.

"Yes. Master William offered them the opportunity to choose a memento of Anstiss's to keep. As I told Miss Lydia."

"And?"

Xenobia sighed and darted a resigned glance at Twig. "Mrs. Coville accused the entire Boothe family in general, and me in particular, of imprisoning her daughter and keeping her from her mother and brothers."

"You?"

"Yes. Because I nursed Anstiss. Because I spent all my time with the poor lady. Because I protected her. Mrs. Coville admitted to me that she knew Anstiss was ill, seriously ill, but she still doesn't want to accept the death as a natural one."

"I feel sorry for her," Lydia said. "She's half-mad with grief."

"They all are," Xenobia said. "Anstiss was the only girl in the family, and a beautiful and loving daughter and sister." She spoke with compassion and understanding, but Rees heard the hurt underneath, that she should be accused of harming her charge. Lydia reached out and clasped Xenobia's hand, her pale skin looking even whiter next to Xenobia's caramel.

"The grief is fresh now," Lydia said. "When it fades, Mrs. Coville will regret the accusation she made against you." Xenobia nodded, but her face worked.

"Is there any reason Mrs. Coville might have for believing . . ." Rees began.

Xenobia burst into angry speech. "I cared for Anstiss for more than nineteen years," she said. "How could anyone believe I would ever hurt her?"

"Don't cry," Twig said, his eyes moistening as though he might weep in sympathy. "It will be all right."

Rees ate his second tart, trying to see his way through the thicket of emotion. He knew very well that most murder victims met their ends at the hands of their nearest and dearest: husbands, wives, children. His thoughts turned again to Jacob Boothe. Rees could think of any number of reasons for believing someone close to Boothe had murdered him, not the least of which were the location in the tunnels where his body had been found, and the fact he had not been robbed. "Is there anything else you know," he said, interrupting Xenobia's conversation once again, "that might help identify Jacob Boothe's murder? Something you haven't told me?"

"Nothing to do with the murder," she declared furiously. Rees believed her.

"You should go," Twig told Rees. "I thought you would comfort her, not accuse her."

"I didn't mean to offend you or your lady," Rees said.

"I have to return to the Boothes tonight," Xenobia said, polite but stiff. "William expects to see me working around the house." She rose and began putting on her bonnet. Lydia threw Rees a reproachful glance as she stood up. They found their own way to the front door and descended the steps in silence.

As they walked down the dark street, Rees said to Lydia, "Did you learn anything?" He wished Twig had not pulled him away.

"No. Nothing new, anyway. Xenobia really cared about Anstiss."

"She knows something," Rees said. "Something she is keeping back."

"It may have nothing to do with the murders," Lydia said.

Rees shook his head. He knew he was missing something, but right now his thoughts were in a jumble. If only he weren't so tired.

Chapter Twenty-five

By the time Rees and Lydia arrived at Mrs. Baldwin's back gate, only the stars and the thin quarter moon illuminated the sky. The alley was black and Rees fumbled at the latch, opening it by feel. Fortunately, they could see Mrs. Baldwin through her kitchen window sitting at the table, head bent, with a candle before her. The reddish glow of the banked fire glimmered behind her. As they started for that friendly beacon, Rees thought he caught a flash of light in the barn, but when he turned to look he saw nothing. He could hear Amos and Bessie moving in their stalls, but otherwise all was dark and silent. He rejoined Lydia, and they went through the back gate, through the garden, and into the house.

Lydia washed her face and hands in the basin and undressed in the dark. She lay down with a tired sigh. Rees, whose hands and clothing smelled of saltwater, followed suit. But, although he lay down, he couldn't find a comfortable spot. His shoulders hurt and the events of the day whirled through his brain in a maddening loop. He couldn't make sense of the clamor. Finally, he pulled himself out of bed and sat by the window.

Most good folk had retired for the night; only a few candles were visible through the windows. And down by the docks, a haze of light marked the location of the Black Cat. A sudden movement in the back yard caught his eye. Billy peered through the barn door, a shrouded lantern in one hand. Seeing nothing, he turned back inside. A moment later he and a smaller form exited the barn and hurried through the yard to the gate. As Billy held the lantern aloft, the dim light fell upon the features of his companion: Annie. Rees whistled softly. Well, this was an interesting development. Annie slipped through the door into the alley and Billy extinguished his light. Rees heard the sound of the boy's footsteps—very faint as Billy took care not to be heard—through the yard and the creak of the garden gate. Seconds later, he tiptoed up the stairs, and Rees heard the muffled click of the bedroom door closing across the hall.

How long had those children been meeting? And should Rees inform Mrs. Baldwin? He spent a minute or two considering his responsibility to another parent. What would he want another adult to do if this was David? He couldn't decide. Finally, he pushed a decision forward to morning and returned to his consideration of the murders.

What was he missing? Someone had told him something important, and he couldn't place it. Rees tried to remember what it was but couldn't identify either the speaker or the stray fact. Perhaps Philippe Benoit was hiding something. Rees nodded to himself. That would make sense. The Frenchman must know more than he'd confessed, despite his denial. Maybe he knew more about John Hull? And who was John Hull? Matthew Boothe, or someone else? Well, Rees thought, he would press Benoit tomorrow. If that Frenchman knew anything, Rees would squeeze it out of him.

Then there was Deputy Swett. Twig was sure that the man accepted bribes. Swett might be persuaded to release Benoit for the proper remuneration. But who would do that? Not Rees; he didn't have the necessary funds, even if he wanted to free Benoit. John

Hull? Well, not if Hull was a pseudonym for Matthew Boothe, who had already denied any knowledge of or interest in the sailor.

And I'm back to John Hull, Rees thought.

"Will?" Rees heard the rustle of the bed linens as Lydia sat up. "What are you doing out of bed?" She paused, and in the silence he heard the faint sound of a yawn. "I thought you were tired."

"Thinking," Rees grunted. "About John Hull, mostly." Should he tell her about Billy and Annie? He couldn't decide. Rising to his feet, he crossed to the bed and sat on the edge. "Who is Hull? Matthew Boothe? William Boothe? Someone else? I don't know."

"You know he owns the *India Princess*," Lydia said. "The mate said Mr. Hull bought the vessel from Jacob Boothe."

"Yes," Rees said. "So?"

"Well, there's got to be a record of that sale. Right? The Elders and Eldresses in Zion kept track of everything. Would Jacob Boothe be less careful?"

"No," Rees agreed, excitement flaring in his chest. "He wouldn't. I'll wager the record of this transaction is in one of the ledgers in Boothe's office." Reaching over, he grasped Lydia's hand in his. "First thing this morning, before William Boothe leaves for the day, I'll call upon him and apply for the key to his father's office. Perhaps the ledger will include Mr. Hull's address."

"Perhaps," Lydia agreed. "Now, try to go back to sleep. Dawn will arrive early enough."

Rees awoke very suddenly. The morning sun was already up and shining through the windows into the room. The spot beside him in the bed was empty.

He leaped to his feet and began throwing on his breeches and his vest over his linen shirt. Most mornings he changed his shirt, washed, and sometimes shaved, but he had no time today. He hurried downstairs. The door to Mrs. Baldwin's apartment was open, and when he looked through he saw Lydia and the landlady sitting together at the table. A teapot and two cups between the two women told Rees they'd already drunk their morning beverage and probably consumed some breakfast as well.

Mrs. Baldwin waved to him, and Lydia turned to look at her husband over her shoulder. "I'll put the coffee pot on," Mrs. Baldwin said, struggling to her feet.

"I can't stop," Rees said. Directing an accusatory glance at Lydia, he added, "I overslept. Why didn't you wake me?"

"It is not so late as all that," she said, raising her eyebrows at him. "You were tired."

"William Boothe leaves home early," he said, hearing the annoyance in his voice. "I told you last night I wanted to leave first thing."

"I offered your wife some leftover egg pie," Mrs. Baldwin said, attempting to diffuse the tension between husband and wife. "Would you like some?"

"I don't have time," Rees said. Lydia frowned at him. "I don't want to miss William Boothe—and my chance to check his father's office. That John Hull is the key to Jacob Boothe's murder. I'm certain of it." Rees was overwhelmed with the sense of evaporating time, and he didn't want to waste any precious minutes. He hesitated, eyeing his wife, not sure he wanted her with him just now. He didn't want to take the time to harness Amos to the buggy. That meant traveling on foot, and Rees planned to run. Lydia would only slow him down. "Do you want to come?" he asked. A line furrowed the delicate skin between her brows, and he suspected she'd heard the reluctance in his voice.

"Not this time," she said. "I believe I'll remain here and, if Mrs. Baldwin doesn't mind, I'll make the lemon pie."

Mrs. Baldwin nodded. "Mind? I look forward to it. I'll enjoy eating something cooked by someone else," she said.

So Rees, offering the ladies a scant nod, hurried out the back door. As he passed through, he heard Lydia say, "He must think he's close to identifying Mr. Boothe's murderer. He gets like a dog chasing a squirrel when he's nearing the end." Rees, burning with embarrassment at hearing himself discussed, almost turned back. But he heard both affection and pride in his wife's voice, along with the exasperation, and anyway Lydia added, "He has a gift for unraveling his mysteries and finding the truth at the center."

"I still miss my husband and grieve for him, even after these five years," Mrs. Baldwin said, her voice fading as Rees went through the yard to the gate.

Rees broke into a fast walk that was almost a run. He was desperately afraid he would miss William Boothe.

But when he was shown into the breakfast room at the Boothe home, he found William just finishing his breakfast over the paper. The room smelled pungently of cigar smoke and flecks of tobacco spotted his white neck cloth. "Why Mr. Rees," William said. "So early. Even Peggy is still abed, and as for Betsy and Matthew, they won't rise for another few hours."

"It was you to whom I wished to speak," Rees said. William, looking surprised, folded the paper and put it aside.

"But I know nothing. I only just arrived from Baltimore a short while before my mother's death."

"Several years ago," Rees interrupted, too impatient to be polite, "I believe your father sold one of his older ships." William looked at Rees with no comprehension. "The merchant vessel was rechristened the *India Princess.*"

William's expression did not change. "I told you, I was not in Salem then." William spoke in a sharp tone. "I lived in Baltimore taking instruction in shipbuilding for several years."

"Yes. I know. But I'm certain your father kept records of all his transactions. I thought if I applied to you for the key to your father's office?" Rees paused and looked at William hopefully.

"It's true," the young man said, "that my father kept very few of his records at the counting house."

"I need to know the details of that sale," Rees said. "The name of the man who bought the ship and, if possible, his address." William did not speak. "I believe Mr. Hull was involved in your father's death," Rees continued. William abruptly rose to his feet.

"I suppose you won't leave until I give you what you want. Come with me. That transaction shouldn't be difficult to find; my father organized his ledgers by date and, under that, ship name and cargo. Do you know exactly when this sale took place?"

"No." Rees recalled Benoit mentioning two previous trips to the East and added, "I would guess at least two or three years ago, but it could have been four or five."

"Very well. We'll begin with 1795 and work backward." William started for the door. Rees followed him from the breakfast room, across the hall, and toward the office.

"No rehearsals today?" Rees asked, joking and trying to prompt a smile from the dour William.

"No." He looked even more severe. "I quickly put an end to that. Such foolery. I believe they are rehearsing at the Assembly House now." He sighed. "After this upset is finished, I shall have a talk with my brother. He isn't a boy anymore; he needs to work. One more year at Harvard and then into the counting house."

Rees could just imagine how furiously Matthew would react to that plan.

William paused in front of the door to his father's office and hunted for the key on his ring. "I apologize for all the security," he said. "I doubt my father had anything to hide; a more honest gentleman never lived, but my sister is so lost to the proper behavior for her sex I felt I must take this extreme step. At the last, even my father quarreled with her." Rees, who liked Peggy very much, said nothing as he followed William into the chamber. "Sit in that chair, there," said William, pointing to a chair covered in scarlet silk embroidered with dragons. "I'll search."

Rees sat where directed and looked through the windows to the back garden. A gardener was clipping the roses, blooming in enthusiastic profusion. William disappeared into the smaller room to the side of this larger and grander one. Rees heard the impatient banging of several large books hitting the desk and the soft rustle of turning pages.

Peggy, Rees thought uncharitably, would probably have been able to lay her hands upon the information in a few seconds.

Another series of thuds. Rees felt his mind beginning to drift. Philippe Benoit must know more about John Hull than he confessed; Rees's next stop would be the jail.

"Found it," William said, exiting the small room with a large ledger in his hands. "At least, I think this is probably the sale in which you are interested. In 1793 my father sold a small merchant vessel named *Jacob's Queen* to a Mr. John Hull."

"That's it," Rees said, jumping to his feet. "The ship was renamed *India Princess*." He paused, examining William's strange expression with interest. "What's wrong?"

"It's just that, well, Hull is my grandmother's maiden name. I wonder if my father sold the ship to one of my cousins. I guess that would make sense. But I thought he was estranged from his family, and anyway there aren't very many of them left. The farm in Hulls Cove was abandoned years ago. That's what I heard anyway. But Hulls Cove is listed as the address."

"Hulls Cove?" Rees repeated, excitement burning along his veins. "How far away is it? How long would it take someone to ride from there to Salem?"

"Oh, a few hours, I expect. I haven't been there since I was a boy. My brother and sisters, in fact, have never been there."

It was close enough for the *India Princess* to dock and offload cargo that could then be brought into Salem by wagon. "May I see the ledger?" Rees said, holding out his hand. William handed over the book. Rees looked at the entries for *Jacob's Queen*. The vessel had made only a few voyages, and had not gotten farther east than Calcutta before the sale. But the profits listed in the final column, even after all the expenses had been paid, made Rees's eyebrows shoot up. The share for a common sailor was more than Rees made in several years of weaving. No wonder this profession attracted a steady stream of men wishing to make their fortunes.

The final entry listed the sale date and price and the name of John Hull. Rees looked at the price listed. "Is this a typical amount?" he asked. Although he knew nothing about the sailing industry, the price, close to that of a good carriage and a matched set of four, seemed remarkably low.

"No," said William with a shake of his head. "It's more than reasonable. But we don't know what condition the vessel was in. It may have needed significant repairs. And of course, John Hull was family, so my father may have offered him a discount." His words trailed off in doubt. Rees thought that Jacob Boothe was too much a canny businessman to give a ship away for so little, especially to a part of the family from which he was alienated, but he said none of this to William. Instead he examined the page one final time, noting a tiny MB in the lower right-hand corner, before slamming the ledger shut and returning it to William. If Matthew Boothe had accomplished this transaction, the low price was easily explained; Matthew probably knew only marginally more about the business than Rees himself. And if Matthew were masquerading as John Hull, he would have been selling the ship to himself.

"Thank you," Rees said, extending his hand to William. "Thank you very much. I think I'm finally unraveling this mystery."

"How did you find out about this?" William asked. "Was this unimportant sale discussed in the local tavern?"

"No," Rees said with a shake of his head. "I spoke with the first mate on the *India Queen*. He told me the vessel had special permission to dock at the Boothe wharf."

"What?" William's voice rose. "At my wharf? They should be berthed at the Union wharf. Who gave them that permission?"

Rees shrugged.

"I'll have to have a talk with the captain."

"The captain of the *India Princess* is in jail," Rees said. "I doubt he knows; the owner—this John Hull—seems to keep all information to himself."

"In jail? Does that mean he murdered my father? Of course, he's French. We all know what they're like."

"I'm not certain Benoit is the killer. I suspect John Hull." And then Rees paused, eying William with surprise. "You didn't know? Didn't Peggy tell you?"

William's mouth arched down, and he shook his head. "I haven't seen my sister since breakfast yesterday."

Rees said a hurried good-bye, and a few minutes later he was running toward the jail.

Chapter Twenty-six

M onsieur Benoit," Rees called through the small grate in the door. "I have a few more questions." No reply. Rees peered into the shadows, trying to see a body curled upon the bench, but it was too dark. Nothing moved. Rees realized he couldn't hear the sound of breathing. Standing on his toes so his shadow fell across the door and equalized the light, Rees peered through the bars. His suspicion was correct; the jail was empty.

A shiver of anger, touched by fear, trembled through him. Had Swett already hauled Benoit off to be hung? Or had he simply accepted a bribe and allowed the French captain to go free?

Rees spun around and trotted, his feet thudding furiously into the dust, to the nearby tavern favored by the deputy.

Swett was sitting at the same table as before. His table, no doubt. The one at which he held court, being such an important official, of course. Rees consciously arranged his features in what he hoped was a pleasant expression, instead of the angry one that more accurately reflected his feelings, and moved forward.

The group was laughing and the number of empty beakers on the table in front of them betrayed their current occupation. As Rees stepped into the outer ring of the group, one of the men turned a bleary-eyed glance upon him. "Want a drink?" he asked Rees in a slurred voice. "He's paying."

From the shelter of the rowdy throng, Rees inspected the deputy. His waistcoat looked new and his jacket had been recently cleaned and brushed. He was clean shaven and freshly bathed as well, and that, combined with his largess in the tavern, told Rees as clearly as if Swett had shouted that he'd come into money. Rees's heart sank. As he'd feared, Swett had been bribed to free the captain. And who would have done that? Had Matthew come through? But then, as he realized that Benoit must still be alive and there was still had a chance to find him, his spirits rose. Rees pushed his way forward. He examined the man seated before him. That new waistcoat was silk; the payment must have been significant.

When the deputy looked up and saw Rees, his eyes narrowed. "What are you doing here?"

"Captain Benoit is not in the jail," Rees said.

"He's not? By the Great Horn Spoon, what a shock!" Swett put his hand over his heart. "He must have escaped." The lackeys surrounding him laughed uproariously at the jest.

Rees's rising anger sent a flush of heat throughout his body. "Tell me, did Matthew Boothe offer you money to free Benoit?"

The laughter died into a few snickers, and eyes avid for a fight turned to the deputy, waiting for his response.

"Are you accusing *me* of a crime?" Swett demanded, sounding as outraged as only a guilty man can. "Perhaps I deemed Benoit innocent?"

"Huh," said Rees. "You'd believe Satan himself innocent if there was money in it."

"You go too far," Swett hissed, stung to anger.

"Really. Well, I daresay bribery is not a crime in Salem," Rees said. "You sicken me." Shaking his head in disgust, he stepped back as though he planned to withdraw. But he remained alert and when the deputy hurled the whiskey jug at him, Rees was ready. He ducked and the glass bottle smashed into the head of one of the other men. The man's smile instantly disappeared and he dropped to the floor with blood pouring from his scalp.

As Rees expected, since anything could trigger a tavern brawl, several meaty fists came at him. He felled the closest fellow and, using a chair as a shield and battering ram, made his way to the door. Some of the punches coming Rees's way landed; blood from a cut above his eyebrow streamed into his eye and down his cheek, and a kick to his leg made him grunt in pain. But the chair—and the drunken state of his adversaries—enabled Rees to keep most of them at bay until he could take to his heels and run as fast as he could. Even he, big and strong and a scrapper, could not defeat eight or ten men at the same time.

Shouting curses, a few of the men pursued Rees into the street. He headed for the docks. He couldn't remember telling the deputy where he was staying and didn't want to lead these ruffians home. His thigh hurt with every step, and he knew he wouldn't be able to outdistance all of the men chasing him. As he ran down the alley, he made an instantaneous decision; he darted up the walk to the Black Cat and onto the front porch.

Gasping, he crouched down, his bruised thigh wringing an involuntary groan from him. The porch provided very little cover. He hoped that the roses perfuming the air with their scent would screen him. The door behind him opened. When Rees turned, he saw Annie, staring at him. He put a finger across his lips. She nodded. When the men—only two of the six or so remained— paused at the front gate, she pointed north. They thundered onto the docks and away.

"Thank you," Rees whispered. She nodded and opened her mouth, looking as though she might speak.

"Annie. Annie. Annie!" Someone called the child, their voice growing ever more impatient with each repetition. Very quietly, she closed the door.

Rees pulled out the tail of his shirt and wiped his face. The cut over his eyebrow had bled copiously; the linen was soon sodden with blood, and still the wound oozed. He pulled the other tail free. Briefly he considered tearing a strip and binding the wound, but that would instant draw attention to him. He gingerly tucked the bloody linen into his breeches and started for home.

Despite his efforts, passersby stared at him, looking quickly away when he tried to catch their eyes. The wound, and the blood oozing from it, must be fearsome. But the cut above his eyebrow barely stung. It was his thigh that hurt, a sharp pain that ran up to his groin and down to his ankle. Now that the first fury had left him, he found himself limping.

With frequent glances over his shoulder, and the spot between his shoulder blades tingling with nerves, he hurried home as fast as he could. Lydia was still in the kitchen, a plate of bread and cheese before her. "Oh, my dear," she gasped when she saw him. "What happened?"

"Philippe Benoit is gone from the jail. Swett as good as admitted he took a bribe from Matthew Boothe." Rees collapsed into a chair at the table with a groan.

Lydia frowned. "And you, no doubt, accused him to his face," she said in exasperation. She leaned over him and tipped up his face to better see the cut over his eyebrow.

"I lost my temper," he admitted in a low voice. "Him sitting there in a new silk waistcoat, buying drinks for all the tavern rats."

"This isn't too serious. The wound is already beginning to close."

"It bled like a fury," Rees said. "I need to change my shirt."

Lydia sighed audibly. "Very well. I'll bring up a basin of cold water." Rees struggled to his feet, gasping with the pain. "Why are you limping?" Lydia asked.

"One of the dirty dogs kicked me," Rees said. He went out

into the hall and started up the stairs. He had to take one step at a time, like a child, and he groaned every time his injured thigh took his weight. Lydia followed with the basin of water. Once inside their room, Rees carefully lowered his breeches and took out the shirt-tails. Lydia inhaled. "It's from the cut over my eye," Rees said, striving to make light of the blood. "Head wounds always bleed."

"No, it's your leg." Lydia fixed her gaze upon Rees's exposed thigh. He looked down. A huge purple and red bruise was spreading across Rees's freckled skin. No wonder it hurt. "I suppose I'll spend the rest of my life bandaging you up and worrying that the next injury will be your last," Lydia said, lowering herself to the foot of the bed.

"Now, now, Lydia Jane, it's not that bad," Rees said, sitting beside her and putting his arm around her shoulders. She burst into tears. "Really," Rees said, not understanding this sudden emotional outburst, "the scrapes don't hurt that much." Lydia wept harder. Rees pulled her to his chest and patted her back. Her sobs did not diminish for several minutes. Finally, using a corner of her apron to wipe her face, and holding her breath, she brought her tears under control.

"It's just that," she said, her voice hoarse and shaking, "I don't want to be a widow. Now you've been both threatened and badly hurt within the space of a few days. Maybe you should stop. Captain Benoit is gone. Let this investigation end here."

Rees hesitated for several seconds. He could offer her some soothing lie, but he wouldn't treat Lydia with such contempt. He told the truth. "I can't. Maybe Benoit murdered Jacob Boothe, but if he did, it was at the command of someone else. Probably John Hull. And I need to know who Hull really is. Matthew Boothe? Maybe. Did he also murder Isabella Porter? I would suspect yes, but I don't know for sure." He'd known that at some point, Lydia would object to something he chose to do. He'd thought it would be the constant traveling for his weaving, not this, not the investigation into murders. This was something she'd participated in, several times. "Remember, in Zion?" he went on. "The murderer of Charles and Sister Chastity would never have been found without us. My friend Nate Bowditch would not have had justice, and Maggie Whitney's killer would have gone free. And there are so many more." He paused, thinking back to other investigations. "This is what I do."

"But what if you're killed? Or what if they come after me? We're going to have a baby now." She put her hands protectively upon her belly.

Rees shivered. He had not thought of the peril in which he had placed his wife. A truly good husband would cease his dangerous work. But Rees knew he couldn't. Once he'd started something, he did not stop. In fact, the more resistance he met, the harder he tried. And in this case, he was working to find justice for two people that, although he had not known them well, had not deserved their deaths.

"I'll try to be careful," he said. "That's all I can pledge. Lydia, you know me. I could promise I'd stop involving myself in these kinds of adventures. But I'd be lying. And you know I'd be lying."

She raised her head and looked at him, her blue eyes smeared with tears. Finally she nodded. "Yes. And you do good and necessary work, along with the weaving that helps us keep body and soul together. I know that. I can't imagine what I was thinking."

"You're thinking you love me," Rees said, dropping a kiss upon her forehead. "But you, you must take care as well. I don't want anything to happen to you."

She pushed him away. "Change your clothes so I can wash these. And then we'll continue this investigation. Both of us. Let's get it over with. And let the end be soon," she added in a much lower voice. "I want to go home."

Rees did as he was told, stripping off the bloody shirt. Lydia insisted he add the breeches: blood from the shirttails had stiffened the waistband with brownish smudges. Lydia added them to the basin while Rees changed into his last clean pair, blue dyed linen so old it was soft. "I know where Benoit has gone," he said.

"Where?"

"To the ship. The *India Princess*. I'm going to go to the docks, see if she's sailed already."

"Oh, and how are you going to get there?" Lydia asked. She gestured to his thigh. "Walk? On that?" Rees did not reply. "I suspect the ship is long gone. Probably out in the middle of the Atlantic by now."

"I'll harness Amos to . . ." Rees began.

A light tap sounded upon the door. Lydia crossed the room to open it. "Someone is here to see you," Mrs. Baldwin said, frowning. "Downstairs. By the kitchen."

Lydia and Rees exchanged glances. Mrs. Baldwin's manner was odd. "Twig?" Rees said.

"Not Mr. Eaton," she replied with a shake of her head. "And not Mrs. Foster either. Someone else."

Lydia hurried down the steps, Rees following more slowly and cursing the pain that hobbled him. Mrs. Baldwin motioned to the door into the garden. She had not invited their guest inside. Lydia opened the door. Xenobia stood outside. She was breathless, as though she'd run all the way from the Boothe residence, and her face was wet with tears.

"What happened?" Lydia asked.

"Miss Peggy is missing."

Chapter Twenty-seven

"Missing?" Mrs. Baldwin's shrill question cut through the sudden quiet.

"You mean she ran off?" Rees suggested. For the first time, he wondered if she knew Captain Benoit, a man handsome enough to set any maiden's heart to beating. "Was her bed slept in? Did she leave last night?"

"She ate—well, cook says Peggy ate breakfast very early," Xenobia replied. "I searched her room but didn't find a letter or anything. Master William wants you to come and look. Maybe you can find something that will tell us where she went."

"Exactly when did you notice she was missing?" Rees asked.

"She didn't eat dinner," Xenobia said. "Cook asked if Miss Peggy would be out again for supper. So, I looked for her."

Lydia turned a significant glance upon her husband but said, "Perhaps it is a social engagement? Or maybe she is visiting with a friend?"

"She has no friends," Xenobia said sharply. "Not lady friends, anyway. And someone in the family would know if she had plans." When both Rees and Lydia stared at her, startled by her tone, Xenobia inhaled a deep breath. "I'm sorry. But you must understand, Miss Peggy's whole world was her father's business, especially the ships. She didn't have time for social engagements or lady friends."

"Perhaps a man then," Lydia said. Rees looked at her. What did she suspect?

"A man?" Xenobia barked a laugh. "And where would she meet a man? In her father's office? Yes, she ran to the counting houses every day, but her father wouldn't allow her to marry any of his employees. And that's if she'd had a chance to talk to those young men. Besides, how many men would want to wed a girl who behaves like a boy in skirts?"

Lydia did not reply, but Rees could see from her pursed lips that she did not agree with everything Xenobia was saying.

"Run and tell Master William we are on our way," Rees said. "We'll arrive directly." Xenobia opened her mouth but decided not to speak. With a nod, she turned and hurried away. When she had disappeared through the outside gate, Rees looked at his wife.

"All right. Tell me."

"Tell you what?" She did not look at him.

"Whatever it is you were thinking while Xenobia was speaking."

Lydia sighed. "Philippe Benoit is missing as well, is he not?"

"Perhaps that is a coincidence," Rees said, sounding unsure. "As far as we know, they've never met."

Lydia shook her head at him. "Don't tell me you haven't already thought of a possible connection between Peggy and Captain Benoit. Especially if Matthew is involved. What could be more natural than Matthew introducing his sister to one of his captains?"

"Why then did Philippe Benoit not mention her?" Rees asked.

"Perhaps he is a gentleman," she retorted. Leaning forward, she put her hand upon Rees's arm. "I tell you, Will, when you spoke to Matthew and told him Captain Benoit was in jail, Peggy looked horrified and frightened and determined all at once. She did not look like a woman worried about her brother, for all of her assertions. She looked like a woman in love and hearing for the first time that her man was in danger. Peggy is more involved in this affair than you believe."

Rees hesitated. He'd learned to trust Lydia's intuition, and Peggy had been acting strangely. But in love with Philippe Benoit, a foreigner, and a man so far out of her social class as to be virtually invisible? He did not see how she would have gotten to know him well enough to fall in love, even if Matthew had introduced them. "Perhaps," he said cautiously. "I don't want to make any assumptions now."

"We'd better leave," she said briskly. "The Boothes will be expecting us."

Rees harnessed Amos to the buggy and helped Lydia over the high wheel. They drove to the harbor, Rees keeping a sharp eye out for the deputy and his lackeys. It was possible that they'd lost interest in him, but he couldn't be sure.

He could see, from the dock end of the Boothe wharf, that the *India Princess* was gone. "Blast," he muttered, disappointment welling up inside him. The ship had sailed a day early, just as he'd feared.

Now he just needed to know *when* the *India Princess* had sailed. He looked around the busy wharf, busier now after noon than during the morning, as everyone hurried to complete the day's work. A street vendor hawking pies caught Rees's attention, reminding him he'd eaten nothing since breakfast. "Wait here," he told Lydia. He jumped down and approached the man. Grizzled and tanned dark, he looked to Rees's eyes like a sailor, too old to go to sea and yet wanting to live out his final years around the ships. "I'll take a pie," Rees said, handing over a penny. As the man wrapped the pie in a bit of brown paper and handed it over, Rees asked, "How early do you get here?" His first mouthful demolished almost a quarter of the pie.

"Dawn, most days."

"Did you see the *India Princess* leave?"

"Aye. She sailed with the tide, first thing this morning. Light enough so I could see the wooden eagle at her bow." Rees gave him another ha'penny in thanks for the information and returned to Lydia.

"The *Princess* sailed at dawn this morning," Rees said. "Peggy Boothe could not have been on her because the cook saw her at breakfast. But I'll wager Benoit was." He offered Lydia the pie. "Care for a bite?"

She eyed it with doubt. "No, thank you."

"It's good." He took another big bite. Although Rees couldn't identify the meat, the gravy was savory with sage and full of fresh vegetables.

"The Boothes are expecting us," she reminded him. Rees nodded and quickly ate the remainder of the pie. Then he wiped his fingers on the greasy paper and took up the reins.

Rees parked the buggy in the yard behind the Boothes' house. He'd planned to leave it with the grooms while he and Lydia walked to the front of the house. But as they alighted, Xenobia came out to the steps behind the kitchen and gestured frantically to them. Rees, who resisted entering any house through the back door, stopped and shook his head. But Lydia had no such hesitations. She put on a burst of speed, traveling up the drive at such a pace she left Rees behind her. He hurried after her so they reached the steps together.

"Where have you been?" Xenobia asked, holding the door open. "Master William has been waiting a good hour."

Rees, who felt sure less time had elapsed, grunted.

"He's waiting in the morning room." She ran ahead of them, pattering across the black and white marble floor. But William

Boothe did not wait for them to reach the morning room. He popped out of the door and darted across the hall to meet them. His neck cloth had come untied, but he didn't seem to notice.

"Xenobia came to the counting house to tell me my sister was missing," he said. "To the counting house!"

"Are you sure she is missing?" Rees asked. "Xenobia told us she ate breakfast early."

"No one's seen her, and we have only cook's word that she ate breakfast," William said. "I left after I saw you this morning," he said with a nod in Rees's direction. "I assumed she was still asleep."

"Did you see her last night?" Rees asked.

William nodded.

"How did she seem?" Rees asked. "Worried or upset?"

"Of course not," William said, biting off each word. "What does she have to be worried about? Besides, Peggy doesn't engage in drama, not like Betsy. She is always cheerful."

Rees knew that was not true; he'd seen Peggy weeping, angry, and both worried and upset. But then William had never shown much understanding of his sister.

"Did she seem happier than usual?" Lydia asked.

William hesitated. "Yes," he said, drawing out the word. "Now that I recall her manner, she did. She was . . . humming." Lydia threw a triumphant smile at Rees.

"Humming?" Rees repeated.

"Yes. One of those shanties sung by the sailors on the merchant ships."

"You recognized it as such?" Rees asked. William nodded.

"I've heard it before, and it is not something a gently bred young lady should know." He frowned. "I reprimanded her, of course." He sighed. "She laughed at me."

"You didn't see her this morning?" Rees asked, turning to Xenobia.

"When I went upstairs to continue my work in Anstiss's room, Peggy's door was closed. I was surprised; she is usually an early riser, but I didn't think anything was wrong. I went to her room just before dinner to remind her William would be home soon. When there was no answer, I went inside. She wasn't there."

"Maybe she slipped out on an errand," Rees suggested. But he didn't believe it, and he saw from the scornful look Xenobia shot him that she didn't either.

"Maybe. But she told no one where she was going. Clothes are missing." Xenobia paused and tears sprang into her eyes.

"Please look at her room," William said to her. "When Betsy comes home—well, she'll know exactly what Peggy has taken. He looked at Rees. "This is your fault. You should have left well enough alone."

"We're happy to help you," Lydia said, directing a challenging stare at William. "It's important to discover the truth, not just assign blame."

"Indeed," Rees said. "We should endeavor not to accuse someone simply because she is convenient."

"Perhaps we should look at her room?" Xenobia said, taking a few steps toward the stairs.

"Of course," Lydia said. She turned and followed Xenobia. Rees hurriedly trotted after them.

Peggy's room was next door to Betsy's and they shared a connecting door. But the two chambers could not be more different. While clothing lay across every surface in Betsy's, and cosmetic powders and such covered every inch of her dressing table, Peggy's bedchamber more closely resembled military quarters. Her bed was carefully made. Instead of perfumes, the strong odor of starch filled the air. But several frocks lay across the bed's foot, and garments covered the floor around the clothespress.

While Lydia went to the bed and began examining the gowns, Rees's attention focused upon the windows facing the side yard. He crossed the room. Both sashes were up and a cool breeze blew off the ocean. Rees poked his head through the opening. A large maple tree grew just outside, and from the other window a limber person could stretch across to a thick branch and climb down. A fence screened the yard from the drive; Rees could imagine Peggy climbing down to the garden below and sauntering through the gate to the street outside with no one the wiser. But navigating the climb down in skirts would be difficult. And a solitary woman carrying a valise would cause comment. Where would she go? He considered Peggy's disappearance and the sailing of the *India Princess*. Had the two events happened at the same time by coincidence, or were they connected, as Lydia believed?

"Will, come and look at this." Lydia's voice broke into Rees's musing. He crossed from the window to the bed. Lydia had shifted the gowns to the blanket chest at the bottom of the bed, uncovering a letter. She offered it to Rees. He quickly perused the document, realizing immediately that he held a Letter of Manumission for Xenobia. Without surrendering any particulars as to her plans, Peggy freed the slave from servitude, effective at once. "Does she have the authority to do so?" Lydia asked Rees in a low voice. "William may own Xenobia." Rees nodded in agreement but did not comment. Xenobia, in her aimless wanderings about the chamber, had come within earshot.

Lydia began sorting through the gowns, shaking out each one in the event another letter had gotten tangled in the fabric. Rees peered through the door into Betsy's room. He wondered if the young woman had dressed hurriedly or whether her room always looked so chaotic. Xenobia, coming to stand behind Rees, said, "I'll have to mention this untidiness to Peggy. She'll speak to the maids—" Remembering Peggy's disappearance, she threw an anguished glance at Rees.

"We'll find her," he said, trying to comfort her. "How often do the maids clean this room?" Rees asked. He thought maybe a week or so had passed.

"Every day, of course." Xenobia flashed him a glance. "But Betsy, well, she likes to see all of her gowns spread out around her."

"Her room looks like this every day?"

"Yes. As soon as the maids finish, Miss Betsy brings her dresses back out. And then she scolds the maids if something can't be found." Rees gazed around him, appalled at the lack of consideration a person must have to cause this mess and then leave it for someone else to clean up—and not once but over and over. "And there is her shawl." Xenobia suddenly darted under Rees's arm and into the room to wrest a ball of silk from behind the dressing table. When she shook it out, it transformed into a large rectangle of red silk, now quite wrinkled, embroidered in bright blues and greens.

Rees, who remembered it, reached out to take the garment from Xenobia. He wondered why Betsy had thrust this beautiful shawl out of sight behind her dressing table. When he said as much, Xenobia shook her head. "It must have fallen behind. This is one of her favorites. Her father brought it back from China."

Rees took it from Xenobia, marveling at the weight of it and the smooth silky weave. This shawl must have been very expensive, worth more than a year's salary for the average working man. "Where is Peggy's?" he asked.

"Gone." Xenobia looked at Rees, her face stiff with fright. "She must have taken it."

"Xenobia," Lydia said from behind them, "can you identify the gowns Peggy took with her?"

"Some of them," Xenobia said, quickly squeezing past Rees to return to Peggy's bedchamber. "Her pink lawn is missing, of that I am sure. But Betsy will be able to tell you more."

"More about what?" Betsy hurried up the stairs, appearing at the door to Peggy's room. Although she'd untied her bonnet, she hadn't removed it from her head, and the long black ties hung down her chest. Her glowing pink cheeks and the sparkle in her eyes hinted at a pleasurable outing—and told Rees that William had not shared his anxiety about Peggy with Betsy yet.

"It is possible," Lydia said, "that Peggy has . . ." she hesitated, struggling to find the best word.

"Run off," Rees said.

Throwing him a stern glance, Lydia said quickly, "Eloped."

"Eloped?" Betsy repeated. She laughed. "Impossible. She knows few men and none of them, at least as far as I've seen, are interested."

"He may be a ship captain," Lydia began.

"Or a sailor," Rees interrupted her.

"Eloping with a sailor? Surely not. She wouldn't be so cruel to me. Mr. Morris is such a stickler, and we've already had the scandal of my father's murder in this family. Likeliest, she's gone to some counting house or on some other errand for William."

"I think not," Rees said curtly. "William called us in to look at her room."

"And we found this," Lydia said, holding up the Letter of Manumission.

Betsy snatched it from Lydia's grasp and quickly read it. "Oh, she can't do this to me." She glanced at the frocks lying on the blanket chest and then threw open the door to the clothespress. "Her blue sarsenet is missing. And her cashmere shawl." She pushed past Lydia and Xenobia into her own room. Rees couldn't see how Betsy could detect the absence of anything in the welter of gowns and shawls and ribbons strewn about the room, but she returned a few moments later. Her face was scarlet with fury. "My best white lawn is gone, along with a wool pelisse. Oh, I swear I'll kill her for this."

Chapter Twenty-eight

B etsy paced the room ranting, her fury silencing Rees and Lydia. "How could she do this to me? She steals one of my favorite gowns and then runs off with a seaman? And I'll wager that Jack Tar is naught but a common deckhand; that would be just like Peggy. I tried to introduce her to appropriate young men but she wouldn't even look at them."

Rees could not decide what angered Betsy more: the loss of her gown or what she perceived as the loss of her family's honor.

"We don't know Peggy ran off with a sailor," Lydia said now, her tone stiff. "In fact, we don't know that she ran off to marry anyone at all. We were just proposing that as a likely reason for her disappearance."

"You've got to find her," Betsy said, whirling to face them. "Bring her back, if she isn't completely ruined, that is. Maybe we can hush up this entire affair. Mr. Morris will simply *not* accept another disgrace in this family."

"Please find her," William said from outside the door. "Peggy doesn't know what the world is like. I blame my father. He allowed her such freedom."

Since William seemed disposed to jump on his hobbyhorse once again, Rees cut him off. "I can't promise to bring Peggy back home; I don't know where she went."

"You must have some ideas," William said in a sharp voice. "After all, it was Peggy who brought you into this house."

"Yes, to discover your father's murderer."

"At which you have failed miserably," William replied, his tone even more unpleasant.

Rees leaned forward, his mouth opening. Lydia grasped his arm in a tight grip. "Will," she murmured. "William is upset."

Rees took a deep breath. "Very well," he said. "Do you have any idea where Peggy might have gone?"

"If I did, I would have already fetched her back," William said angrily, his cheeks flushing a dark red.

Before he could explode, Lydia pulled Rees away, into the hall and down the stairs. Xenobia followed them quickly, not speaking until they were outside the back door. "You must forgive William," she said. "He's very worried about Peggy." Rees turned to look at her, but he did not speak. "We all are," she said with a suppressed sob.

Lydia put a sympathetic hand on Xenobia's shoulder before joining her husband. "What are you going to do?" she asked as they started to the stables.

"I think I know where the *India Princess* might have gone: to Hulls Cove. We know that Philippe Benoit has an association with John Hull. It makes sense that at least some of the ship's cargo is stored there. And if she's making another voyage, the crew will need to load the ship."

"And Peggy could be on her way to meet Captain Benoit."

"I'm going to follow them. But I need a map."

"I should go," Lydia began. Rees shook his head.

"Not in your condition. I'll be moving fast and sleeping rough. Besides, it might be dangerous."

"William Boothe must have a map," Lydia said. "But I guess you don't want to ask for it."

"No." Rees managed a smile at Lydia. "And not just because I want to punch him. I don't want to show my hand. At this point, I don't trust any member of that family. But Mrs. Baldwin may have a map, or know where I can find one. Since her husband was a sailor."

"Of course," Lydia breathed in agreement.

Rees did not unhitch Amos from the buggy when they pulled into the yard behind Mrs. Baldwin's Emporium. Instead, he tied the gelding to the bar and helped Lydia down. Mrs. Baldwin, wiping her hands upon a towel, came to the back door. "Do you know where Hulls Cove is? Or do you have a map?" Rees asked her.

Mrs. Baldwin blinked. "North, I think. I used to have one. It belonged to my husband. It's a sailor's map, with the soundings along the coast." She paused and considered. "I don't know what happened to it, I confess."

"Maybe Billy will know," Lydia said. Both Rees and Mrs. Baldwin looked at her in surprise. She shrugged. "It's something of his father's. And both of you told me Billy wants to become a sailor."

"I've cleaned Billy's room every week for years," Mrs. Baldwin said, but not as though she was objecting, "and I've never seen it."

"We'll have to ask Billy," Rees said. "I'll walk up to the ropewalk and find him."

"I'd like to eat some supper," Lydia said. Mrs. Baldwin smiled and brought out a fresh baked pie. She cut a thick wedge, poured cream over all, and gestured Lydia to the table.

"Mr. Rees?" She held the knife over the pie. He looked at it uncertainly. "You don't have time to drive to Hulls Cove today anyway," Mrs. Baldwin said. "If memory serves, it is at least four hours northwest by road. Maybe more. You wouldn't reach Hulls Cove before dark, and you would still need to return to Salem. Unless you travel by ship. Then it would be a much shorter journey."

"Peggy Boothe has already left for Hulls Cove," Rees said. "I must catch up to her, if I can." Anyway, it would be advisable to give Deputy Swett and his crew a day or two to forget about him. "And I need to question a certain John Hull, who seems very involved in the activities of this vessel."

Mrs. Baldwin rose to her feet and put her plate in the dishpan. She took the steaming kettle from over the fire and poured the hot water over the dishes inside. "Well, Mr. Rees, unless you can fly, you can't reach Hulls Cove any faster than four hours. Not even on a galloping horse. And I would guess neither of those cobs in the barn are fast, even if they are broken to the saddle."

"Peggy can't travel any faster than you," Lydia murmured, "and they still have to load the ship."

Rees hesitated and then accepted the pie Lydia handed him. He sat down and began eating hurriedly.

"You'll want to find an inn for the night," Mrs. Baldwin suggested.

Rees involuntarily shook his head. He needed to be in Salem, where the Boothes were. He always found this point of an investigation difficult, when time was short and he needed to press his sources for final answers and everything took too long. "I'll walk up to the ropewalk," he said, "and speak to Billy. If he doesn't have the map, maybe someone there will be able to offer me some directions." He scraped his plate clean and left.

He half-walked, half-trotted in a kind of jumping limp northeast to the ropewalk. His thigh hurt but he couldn't baby himself, not now with so much at stake. In Dugard, his hometown, his speedy and uneven gait would have occasioned comment, but here, in busy Salem, few paid Rees any attention. He reached the ropewalk in less than twenty minutes and poked his head inside. Billy was turning the wheel that took up the hemp cables for all he was worth. Rees stepped inside and sidled up the building wall toward Billy.

"Hey, you," one of the older men called to Rees. "What are you doing in here?"

"Sorry," Rees said. "But I need to speak to Billy. It's urgent."

"You can wait until he takes his dinner?"

Rees hurriedly crossed the floor, cursing the man for wasting these precious minutes. "I told you," he said impatiently, "this is important. It has to do with Jacob Boothe's murder." The man's brown eyebrows, as thick and fuzzy as caterpillars, crawled up his forehead. Although younger than Rees, the gentleman's brown hair was retreating backward across his head. In the warm close air of the ropewalk, his bald pate was spangled with perspiration. "I need one minute only with Billy," Rees promised. "Unless you can offer me a map of the Salem Harbor and surrounding coves." The man's eyebrows climbed even higher, and he threw a look behind him as though expecting a map to spring up by magic.

"All right. Ask your question of Mr. Baldwin. But one minute only."

Rees turned and hastened across the floor to Billy. The boy eyed Rees in trepidation. "It's not my mother, is it?"

"No. She told me she gave your father's map to you. Do you still have it?"

"Of course. It's one of the few things I have from him."

"Where is it? I desperately need to examine a map."

"In my room. Nailed to one side of the clothespress." Billy, his eyes widening in sudden excitement, lowered his voice. "Is this to do with Mr. Boothe's murder?"

"Yes, it is," Rees said, also in a whisper.

"Take it then," Billy said. "But you must promise you'll tell me the entire tale when it's done."

Rees nodded his promise. He turned and, shouting a thank-you to Billy's supervisor, he left.

The salty breeze from the water felt cool and refreshing after the few minutes inside and quickly dried the perspiration on Rees's face and back. He paused for a few seconds to look at the far end of the ropewalk, on a wharf that protruded far into the cove. Rees could see the bluish smudges of land on the other side of Collins Cove and wondered if one of those spits of land shielded Hulls Cove. With a ship, the coast to the north would be easily accessed.

Rees turned and, with a rapid limp, hurried back home.

Mrs. Baldwin and Lydia were waiting for him. "What did he say?" Mrs. Baldwin said.

"Does he have the map?" Lydia asked at the same moment.

"In his room," Rees replied. Mrs. Baldwin cast a wary eye upon the shop in the front, but led the way up the stairs. Billy's room was across the hall from Rees's and overlooked the street out front. She threw open the door.

They found the map, old and stained and ripped in several places, nailed to the clothespress as Billy had promised. Rees peered at it. Now he understood why the journey would take so long by road: a rider must first travel west, then north, to avoid the coves and inlets that gave the coast its ragged appearance. He carefully detached the map, producing two additional tears in the corners, and rolled it up. He was already thinking ahead to the supplies he would need for the journey.

It was after four before Rees got on the road, but Amos was fresh and willing to travel at a smart pace; Rees hoped to reach Hulls Cove before dark. The first leg out of Salem did not go as rapidly as he expected. Traffic, mainly farmers on their way home, choked the road. But once Rees turned north, the number of fellow travelers diminished rapidly and he was able to increase his speed. Amos adopted a steady trot that ate up the miles.

Rees lost some time twice. He had to stop by the side of the road and, in the long rays of sun slanting over his shoulder from the west, study the map. Although Hulls Cove was clearly marked, none of the roads were, and he had to guess what would be the most rapid route.

By about seven the small farms through which he had been traveling gave way to a hamlet of about fifteen cottages. He could smell the sea and when he began descending the ridge he saw the inlet. Shallops and other fishing vessels dotted the harbor. The one wharf held a building Rees suspected was devoted to the processing of cod, although no one was working there now.

Rees stopped an old man and asked him the way to Hulls Cove and, if he knew, to the Hull farm. "Keep going," the old man said, using his thumb to mark the direction. Rees's heart sank. His back hurt and his hands were stiff and cramped from his clutch upon the reins. "You can see the house from the road. Old white house with a widow's walk." Rees wondered if this man with the grizzled beard could tell him more, but Rees didn't have the time to question him. The sun would set in a little more than an hour.

The distance to the house proved much longer than Rees expected, and the sun was rapidly dropping to the horizon when he finally spotted the square white box with the widow's walk on the roof. Even from the road, the building looked in poor shape, almost derelict. Rees turned Amos down the dirt lane, the green ground marked by wagon wheels, and smacked the reins down upon the horse's flanks. But Amos was tired. Although he jumped ahead, his gait soon slowed to a walk.

The road bent left, approaching the house. There were no lights and no activity, although Rees spotted a horse in the stable. A rough path led away from the house, down the slope toward the water. Rees jumped out of the buggy and groaned. He was stiff, and besides, his bruised thigh still ached. He hid both horse and buggy behind the stable, where the shadow made them invisible.

From the top of the cliff Rees could see the *India Princess* anchored out in the deeper water. Two dories were approaching the ship; a third had just left the beach below. The first two rode low in the water, laden heavy with cargo, but the third was filled with men. Rees broke into a rough trot upon the path but, as it wound down the steep cliff to the rocky beach below, he had to slow down. The surface was weak, the dirt slid away beneath him, and he half fell. Scrambling to his feet, he ran across the short beach shouting. He wasn't sure the occupants of the final boat could even see him; the beach was dark in the shadow of the cliff. But Rees could clearly see the occupants of the boats, outlined against the sun-streaked water.

Philippe Benoit was identifiable by the gold earrings glittering through his long wavy black hair. Rees ran forward, yelling. "Captain Benoit." The boat was already too far out in the water for Rees to reach, even if he were an accomplished swimmer. Benoit lifted a small glittering object—Rees thought it was a pistol, but the man next to him put a restraining hand upon his arm. Was that John Hull? Rees focused upon that figure. Lydia's hints came together in his head. He shouted tentatively, "Peggy?" She turned her head, and her long blond braid blew in the wind. Rees stared through the twilight. It was definitely Peggy, dressed in a man's jacket and neck cloth, and presumably breeches, although Rees couldn't see them. She must have been John Hull all along. She was barely recognizable. Now he understood why her room smelled of starch and why Benoit had described a speech impediment. She'd applied a fake beard and mustache, sticking them on with starch, to disguise her gender. She waved an arm. And, although Rees couldn't see her expression, he imagined she was smiling.

Chapter Twenty-nine

Rees came to a halt on the pebbled beach. For some reason he did not understand, all he could think about just now was his sister Caroline. Her hair was brown instead of blond, and she was already married with children, so Rees could not picture her joining the crew of a merchant ship. But just like Peggy, Caroline had always been headstrong. Rees wished he'd been kinder to her, and promised himself he would be in the future.

The first two boats reached the *India Princess* and, shortly after, the third. Rees watched the men swarm on board. Peggy was indistinguishable from the rest. Soon both Benoit and Peggy would disappear. Depending on where they chose to sail, they might not return home for three or four years. Or more.

Rees swallowed. He did not relish returning to Salem and informing William that his sister had not only run away, but that she was in the company of the man suspected of murdering her father. And that maybe Peggy herself might have had something to do with her father's death.

Rees turned and retraced his steps back to the cliff. Although there were two clefts side by side in the wall, a quick examination revealed that both were too shallow for long-term storage of goods. A few steps into the damp and Rees could touch the back walls. He didn't fancy climbing the path back to the top either, and anyway, if cargo had to be carried to the beach, it would surely have had to come down via another route. Besides, by now the beach was deep in shadow. Rees followed the curve of the wall north, guessing that any other descent would be located on that side. And sure enough, within a minute or two, he found a set of stone steps, cut into an indentation in the rock, and concealed by the granite swells on either side. He began to climb, using his hands as well as his feet for the sake of speed, until he reached the top.

A pale gray light shot with pink still illuminated the top of the cliff and even that would not last much longer. The *India Princess* was just a black dot against the purple sky. Rees turned and looked behind him. A candle burned in one of the house windows. Rees trotted up to the glass and peered through it. A solitary woman was bent over some sewing at a table. He was just about to bang upon the window when a tall and heavyset man came into the room. He did not speak. Instead he tapped the woman on her shoulder and, when she looked up, made several gestures. She rose instantly to her feet and disappeared from view. So, she was deaf.

Rees cast another look at the ruffian who, catching the movement, stared fixedly at the window. Surely, Rees thought, the man couldn't see him. And yet the black-eyed gaze seemed to lock onto Rees, eye to eye. As the man began to shout, his hand fumbled at his waistband. Rees figured it was time to leave; no telling how many others remained in the house. He sprinted for the barn, and for Amos and the buggy, still hidden out of sight behind the wall. As he jumped into his vehicle and snapped the whip across Amos's withers, the man Rees had seen through the window hurtled through the door. He moved with a rapid but peculiar lurching gait; a wooden peg formed the bottom of his left leg. Two more forms burst from the door, but Rees did not linger to see if these three were the only crew left to guard the house. He whipped

Amos into a gallop and they tore down the lane toward the road in a cloud of dust.

Rees set a stiff pace upon the road, but only for a short time. Amos wheezed with effort. Besides, Rees could barely see; the light dust of the road was a slightly lighter strip of gray in a dark world. As soon as he could, he turned off in an unused pasture, the weeds already almost knee high. There he set up camp and by the light of a tiny fire he ate the bread, cheese, and bacon that Lydia had packed for him. Tomorrow he would stop somewhere for a proper meal. And then back to Salem with his unhappy news.

And he would hurry. Although he was not looking forward to seeing William Boothe, Rees was eager to discuss this new development with Lydia.

By daybreak the following morning, he was on the road, but he was not traveling as quickly as he wished. Amos, although well used to pulling the buggy, was old and not accustomed to the pace Rees had set yesterday. So Rees restrained himself from pushing the gelding.

He could do nothing but think. It was clear to him—finally—that it was Peggy who had been operating her own shipping operation under the name John Hull. Not Matthew. And probably, he thought ruefully, Lydia had seen it before he did. He'd been blinded by Peggy's gender, but now, in retrospect, her masquerade made sense. With the merchants she'd met running errands for her father, her ability to purchase excess vessels from the business at a vastly reduced rate, as well as the use of the Boothe wharf, and all the insider knowledge she'd gained, Peggy would enjoy a tremendous advantage over her competitors. But only if she were a man.

Rees wondered how she'd met Philippe Benoit, since it was now obvious that Matthew had not introduced them. Benoit came from the whaling world, not from the merchants and the counting houses. Was it possible one of the Coville brothers had introduced Peggy to Benoit? Unconsciously Rees nodded. That made sense, since the Covilles were whalemen, too.

Rees had been told Peggy quarreled with her father when he began giving her jobs to William. Had Jacob taken that step when he discovered Peggy's secret?

Perhaps Peggy was smuggling? No, Rees didn't want to even consider that, and he cast around for an alternative explanation for the house at Hulls Cove. She must have required some place to store her cargo. She couldn't use her father's warehouses, especially not since William's arrival home. He would have noticed and asked inconvenient questions, as he had done when he noticed valuables missing from the cellar. And maybe some of those items belonged to Peggy. Until William's arrival, no one had looked at them or paid them any attention. She would have transported them via the tunnels. Rees sighed. This looked bad for her.

And how could it be that no one noticed the oddities in Peggy's behavior? She must have given herself away every day. Well, her siblings were blind to her; that was true. But surely Xenobia must have seen something. Of course she had. That explained the secret she wouldn't tell.

None of this meant Peggy was the murderer. He liked her and didn't want to believe that. But as he recalled the grief she'd displayed in the tunnel, he now saw it could be guilt. The woman the street boy had seen in front of Georgianne's house before the fire—that could have been Peggy. But what about the black sailor who'd been stabbed and dropped in the harbor? Although Rees could easily imagine a motive for murdering him—perhaps the mate had recognized John Hull as a woman and tried a spot of blackmail—Rees couldn't imagine Peggy killing him. She might have approached her father and Isabella without causing suspicion, but surely the sailor would have been wary of anyone carry-ing a sword. And Peggy would not have had the strength to run the blade through either man. It was not possible. Rees must as-sume she had the help of Benoit. Three people would be even more likely. Perhaps the dead sailor was the third man, murdered when his usefulness was done. Rees nodded. That hung together. Peggy would have wanted to warn Rees away. When he didn't listen, he'd been attacked in the tunnel.

But Peggy could have killed Rees and didn't. Knocked uncon-scious, he would have been easy prey. Instead, they had carried him to a junction in the tunnels where he would surely be found.

He rolled into Mrs. Baldwin's yard just after dinnertime, his thoughts still running in circles. Lydia appeared almost instantly at the back door, and Rees knew she'd been watching for him. Oh, he was glad to see her. She looked astonishingly pregnant and very beautiful. He hurried forward to put his arms around her. She returned his hug but looked over his shoulder. "Peggy?"

"Have I story for you," he said. "Let me put away Amos and the buggy. Or come into the stables and I'll tell you as I unhitch him." He did not want to be parted from her so soon, even for a few seconds.

She nodded, a crease forming in her forehead. "I have news for you as well."

"I wonder what you'll think about this," Rees said, drawing her toward Amos. She made herself comfortable on the bench by the yard wall. As Rees unhitched the gelding, he told her about his arrival on the beach of Hulls Cove and the boat speeding away to-ward the *India Princess*. She inhaled sharply when he described Peggy but did not display great surprise. "Did you guess that Peggy was John Hull?" he asked her.

"I wondered." She shook her head. "She acted for her father for such a long time. And she didn't like the constraints put upon her by William. But it seemed so incredible." Lydia looked up at Rees, adding with a frown, "I refuse to believe she had anything to do with her father's death. Of all Jacob's children, Peggy was the closest to him, despite the quarrels. I think you're not seeing something."

"Oh, how I've missed you," Rees said with a grin. "You'll never allow me to take the easy way, will you?"

She offered him a slight smile. "No. And I'm glad you realize it."

In two steps, Rees reached the bench upon which she was sitting. He pulled her into his arms. "I'll always travel. But you should know that I carry you with me wherever I go. I carry you in my mind. You are always a part of me, like—like my legs."

Uttering a soft laugh, she returned his embrace. But then she pulled herself free. "Legs, indeed. What will Mrs. Baldwin think?" But she regarded him with shining eyes as she carefully lowered herself to the bench once again.

Rees returned to Amos and pulled the bridle free. "Perhaps Benoit served as Peggy's accomplice, not just because of the *India Princess,* but because Jacob Boothe objected to the marriage of his youngest daughter to a Frenchman." Lydia ran her forefinger down her nose, staring over Rees's head for a few seconds. When he began to pull Amos toward the stable, she rose and followed him. "Perhaps. But, from your description, I'm inclined to believe Benoit did not realize that John Hull was a woman. Or was connected to the Boothe family in any way. Peggy took a big risk when she ran away to meet him. She couldn't know when she revealed herself whether he'd even be interested in her." She sat upon a haycock, compressed by the weight of other bodies into a misshapen seat.

Rees nodded. "She has courage, I'll grant her that."

"Indeed. Running a merchant company in the guise of a man." Lydia shook her head in mingled incredulity and admiration. "And no one knew."

"Maybe someone did," Rees said. They exchanged glances.

"Xenobia," Lydia said.

Rees backed Amos into the stall next to Bessie. When he turned around, he saw that Lydia, still seated on the hay, was pleating her skirt with nervous fingers. He watched her twitching fingers for a moment.

"All right," he said. To his own ears, he sounded resigned. "What happened?"

Lydia's eyes slid rightward. "Annie is upstairs."

"Annie? Annie who?"

"Annie, the girl who found you in the tunnels." Lydia shook her head at him.

"The little girl?"

"Not so little, apparently. One of the customers of the Black Cat expressed interest in her and One-Eye Mary said yes." Lydia's voice faded away and she looked up at Rees with angry tears filling her eyes. "Annie ran away. Of course, I took her in."

"She must have been glad of that," Rees said, his thoughts flying to Billy. Now their meetings would be easier. And then, "Where will we put her?" Rees's thoughts turned to their little house in Maine.

"I know. But Annie wants to join the Shakers."

"She does?"

"Why not?" Lydia nodded in satisfaction. "I told her we could bring her to Zion. We have to visit anyway, to sell the farm." Lydia had inherited a farm from her first husband, a property that had been the cause of several deaths. Considering it cursed, she had wanted to rid herself of it ever since she'd discovered her husband had left it to her. When Rees did not immediately speak, she filled the uncomfortable silence. "I couldn't leave her there, in that horrible place, where anything might happen to her." Her restless hands came together in a tight clasp that left her knuckles white.

Rees considered the profession Annie had escaped.

"Of course, you did the right thing," he said and was gratified to see those anxious hands relax. "But you should know I saw her with Billy."

"Saw her how?" Lydia asked in quick concern.

"They were together in the barn." He looked at the haycock. "Probably right where you're sitting."

Lydia paled and looked up to meet Rees's eyes. "Then we will have to speak with them both," she said. "And soon."

Mrs. Baldwin gaped in surprise to find Rees and Lydia outside her kitchen door asking to speak with her and Billy. And the boy's expression took on a guilty look when Lydia announced she would fetch Annie from upstairs. Mrs. Baldwin motioned Rees to a seat at the table, her eyes never leaving her son. Rees sat down. Billy, who'd been eating his stew with a good appetite, pushed away his bowl. Mrs. Baldwin offered Rees a plate but he shook his head. He did not think Mrs. Baldwin was going to like his news.

Lydia and Annie could be heard descending the stairs and in a few moments they appeared at the door. Mrs. Baldwin's gaze fastened upon the girl, who flushed under the older woman's regard. Rising to his feet, Rees gestured Lydia into his vacated seat and dragged over one of the chairs by the wall for himself.

Everyone looked at him. "I saw you two together," he said, staring at Billy and Annie in turn. "A few days ago, in the barn."

"We didn't do nothing," Billy cried, a tide of red sweeping into his cheeks. "Just talked." Rees looked at Annie.

"That's true," she said, meeting his eyes. Her mouth was trembling and her eyes shone with tears but she sounded determined. "We only talked."

"How long has this been going on?" Mrs. Baldwin cried. "In my barn." Words failed her.

"We've only met a few times," her son replied.

"Is that why you ran away from that—that house?" Mrs. Baldwin demanded angrily. "To be closer to my son?"

"No, I told the truth." Annie turned a beseeching look upon Lydia. "I was afraid that Miss Mary would turn me over."

"You can't stay here," Mrs. Baldwin said. She looked at Lydia. "She can't stay here."

"But that's why I ran away," Annie cried, her tears beginning to fall. "I don't want people to think I . . . that I'm . . . and I don't want to be."

"What do you want?" Lydia asked, her voice low and quiet.

"I want to marry Billy."

Rees's eyes involuntarily twitched toward Billy. The boy's mouth dropped open but no sound came out.

"I know he wants to go to sea," Annie said. "I thought I could live with the Shakers in Maine until he returned . . ." Her voice trailed away.

"That was our plan," Billy said. "I'd go to sea and make my fortune, and then I'd collect her from them and we'd marry and return to Salem."

Rees, who suspected Annie's dream was as much a surprise to Billy as it was to the adults, shot an approving glance at the boy. He'd quickly recovered from his astonishment and spoken up in support of Annie.

"You're both too young," Mrs. Baldwin said.

"I think it is a good plan," Lydia said.

"What?" Mrs. Baldwin said.

"Annie will be safe with the Shakers," Lydia said. "And Billy will be free to pursue his dream, whatever it is." She stared at Mrs. Baldwin, trying to communicate some message with her intent gaze.

Rees understood. "In a few years, when they're older, if they still feel the same, they can marry."

Mrs. Baldwin's mouth puckered. Although she did not speak, she clearly did not approve of Annie as a wife for her son.

"You will not spend any time alone together," Lydia went on. "Not without one of us," she gestured at the adults, "with you." Annie nodded with relief.

"I'm not a child," Billy argued.

"Of course—" Mrs. Baldwin began. But Lydia talked over her.

"Of course not. That's the point, isn't it? If you were a child, we could comfortably leave the two of you alone together without worry." As the meaning of her words penetrated, Billy jumped to his feet. He glared at Lydia but didn't dare blurt out his angry thoughts. "I have to go back to work," he said and fled the kitchen. Annie, her face and neck scarlet, began to cry. Rees couldn't tell if she wept from rage or humiliation—probably both.

"Go to the room," Lydia said gently. Annie stumbled to her feet and, sobbing wildly, she ran up the stairs.

Chapter Thirty

⟋

Most of the afternoon still remained, enough time to speak with Xenobia once again. But first, Rees required a good dinner. So, although he was a little nervous about meeting either the deputy or one of his tavern rat lackeys, he and Lydia walked over to the Moon and Stars. Walking into the tavern felt like coming home.

He ate quickly. Although he didn't anticipate questioning Xenobia again with any pleasure, he was eager to see the end of this investigation. He wanted to go home. He missed his children and he couldn't help wondering how David was faring. Lydia wrapped some bits of cheese, some bread, and a corner of her pie in her napkin for Annie. "Mrs. Baldwin is helping feed her," she said. "Or was. She might not want to now. But Annie is afraid to leave the room, and I know she must be hungry."

And Rees, who knew how famished Lydia had been lately and how much it cost her to give away some of her dinner, patted her hand. "You are a kind and generous woman, Mrs. Rees," he told her.

They brought the food back to Mrs. Baldwin's house, and Lydia brought it up the stairs. Rees waited on the bench in the yard, pondering his questions for Xenobia. Since he didn't look forward to visiting the Boothes, and possibly running into William or Betsy—what was he was going to say to them?—he decided to walk up to Twig's, on the chance that Xenobia would be there.

As soon as Lydia came downstairs, they set off. It was a pleasant day. The stiff breeze off the water kept the air from growing too hot. But Rees noticed that Lydia began to pant after a few minutes of brisk walking. He slowed his long-legged stride. Lydia offered him an apologetic smile. "Sorry," she said. Rees smiled and took her arm, slowing even further. He should have taken the buggy, but his thoughts were so full of this case that he hadn't even thought of it. The memory of his first wife's pregnancy with David was blurred after fifteen years.

Twenty minutes later, they reached Twig's little house and knocked upon the door. After a long pause, it opened a crack. Xenobia peered through the narrow opening. "Come in, come in," she whispered.

Wondering at this secrecy, Rees followed Lydia into the bare front room. Xenobia led the way to the kitchen at the back. She pressed Lydia into a seat, throwing Rees a look in which he read accusation.

"She wanted to come," he said.

Without replying, Xenobia fetched Lydia a glass of cold tea. Rees waved away her offer of ale. "What are you doing here?" he asked her.

"Master William doesn't quite know what to do with me," she replied with the ghost of a grin. "His father's will left everything to him, but I was always Peggy's, and now that she prepared a Letter of Manumission . . ." Her usual smile faded. "Any news of Peggy?"

"I saw her," Rees said. Lydia glanced at him in surprise and he realized he'd sounded angry. Taking a deep breath, he went on. "She was dressed in men's clothing. Do you know anything about that? And she was in the company of Philippe Benoit." He hesitated, wondering if he should question her about John Hull. Xenobia spoke into the silence.

"Miss Peggy kept her own secrets."

"But?" Lydia encouraged her. "Tell us the truth, Xenobia."

"She didn't want to remain her father's secretary forever," the servant blurted. "A curiosity. You know?"

Lydia nodded. "I do."

Rees looked at his wife in wonder.

"Especially since, in the last few years, she ran her father's company. Kept the books, paid the crews, arranged for cargo, everything. But it was all under her father's name." Xenobia looked at Lydia, who nodded again in understanding.

"She did all the work but her father took the credit. And Peggy owned none of it. And I'll guess she earned no money from her labors either."

"Of course not. And Peggy wanted something of her own."

"Then, when William returned, he began stepping into the realm that had once been solely hers," Rees said.

Xenobia nodded. "She'd already begun her own company when her brother came home. I guessed what she was up to when I found breeches in her room, and a blond mustache and the starch for putting it on."

"Did you know about the house in Hulls Cove?" Rees asked.

Xenobia's eyes widened and she shook her head. "No. But it makes sense. Especially after William returned. He began checking all the bills and making a list of everything in the cellar. Peggy is clever. She must have known she couldn't run her business out of their house forever. Besides, things kept going missing—not just those items she took because they belonged to her—and she didn't want to be accused of theft."

"No one noticed until William came home?" Lydia asked, sounding surprised.

"Well, Jacob Boothe began to notice," Xenobia said. "A lot of little things disappeared. Peggy was worried, too."

"And Philippe Benoit? How did she meet him?" Rees asked.

Xenobia lifted one shoulder in a shrug. "She met many sailors and ship captains through her father. That Mr. Benoit never came to the Boothes's house, though, so I don't know."

"So, Peggy knew the tunnels well," Rees said. "As John Hull, she would have traveled them often. She knew sailors, and probably a number of ruffians among them." Rees sighed. Xenobia stared at him.

"You think she murdered her father? No, that can't be true. No. Peggy loved her father." Her eyes blinked convulsively. "No, I won't believe it."

"She would have been very angry with him when he transferred her tasks to William," Rees said. "She knew the tunnels. She knew many sailors and I'm sure some of them would take a man's life without a pause."

"No," Xenobia repeated, shaking her head. "I won't believe it. I won't."

Rees thought Xenobia must have believed it; she was trembling all over.

"What do you know that inspires such fear in you?" Lydia asked, her voice soothing and gentle. "What do you know about Peggy? Or is it one of the others, William or Matthew?" Xenobia shook her head again. "What did Peggy and her father argue about? The whole truth." An involuntary shudder rippled through Xenobia's body. Rees turned his gaze upon Lydia. All of her attention was wholly focused upon Xenobia. "Did Mr. Boothe find out about Peggy's activities?" Xenobia offered the merest shake of her head.

"He didn't know about the—the men's clothing or her business as a ship owner," Xenobia said. "And he wouldn't believe it, if anyone had told him."

"So, what was the argument about? Philippe Benoit?"

"No. None of us ever heard about him. The argument was something personal. Nothing to do with anything else."

Lydia nodded as though she understood everything now. "Not about Peggy's inappropriate behavior then. Not entirely anyway. What was the argument about?"

Xenobia's eyes rounded and her brown irises moved rapidly from side to side but she pressed her lips together as though afraid to say anything.

Now we are to the crux of it, Rees thought, eyeing Xenobia's hunted expression with interest. "Come on, Xenobia," he said in a low voice, "if the quarrel had nothing to do with Mr. Boothe's death, you have no reason to keep the secret." She stared at her dark hands, clenched tightly together in her lap. Dear Lord, Rees thought, she does think Peggy had something to do with her father's murder.

"Xenobia," Lydia said in a soft and understanding tone, "Jacob Boothe is dead. Murdered. And we've already discovered Peggy's secrets. Maybe the reason for that quarrel is something that should be told now."

No one spoke. The silence was becoming unbearable even for Rees when Xenobia burst into speech. "Miss Anstiss was in such pain, always such pain. She drank straw tea every day. All times of the day. It was the only thing that gave her relief. Poor lady. Well, Master Jacob decided she should have no more tea. She should overcome her pain without help. He took away the opium. Miss Peggy didn't agree. She argued with him but his mind was made up. He wouldn't listen. Oh my, how Miss Anstiss suffered. Tossing in her bed and screaming, diarrhea so terrible she was soon too weak to stand." She paused, shaking her head at the memory.

"And Peggy didn't agree?" Lydia murmured.

"No. I— Sometimes I got some straw and made her a little tea. Just to ease the pain for a little while. But Peggy, well, one day she slipped into her mother's room with a sack. The best opium from Turkey, she said. But her mother had to keep it secret."

"And were they able to keep Jacob Boothe from knowing about it?" Rees asked.

A furrow appeared in Xenobia's brow. "I'm not sure. Certainly my lady's pain eased and she spent a more restful night. But two days later she died in her sleep."

Rees, who hadn't expected such an abrupt and tragic end to the story, started. Raising his eyes, he met Lydia's gaze. He saw his own confusion mirrored in her expression. "But why did you feel this needed to be kept a secret?" he asked Xenobia. "The poor lady died."

She heaved a sigh. "Perhaps because that was the first time I knew Peggy was into something she shouldn't be. She had so little money of her own and yet she appeared in her mother's bedroom with an expensive amount of that medicine. And, when I put that together with the starch and the breeches in her room . . . well, I knew Miss Peggy was consorting with the devil."

"You thought she was planning to kill her mother?" Lydia's voice rose and broke with surprise.

"I know, I know." Xenobia nodded. "It seems silly now. But I wondered if Peggy had decided to end her mother's suffering with a pillow."

"Not very likely," Lydia said. "Not after acquiring the opium. If she were going to murder her mother, Peggy would have done so before supplying the medicine that relieved her mother's pain. Purchasing a large quantity of medicine and then murdering the patient doesn't make sense."

"I think you should put your mind at rest," Rees said.

"But you should have heard Miss Peggy and her father," Xenobia said, the line between her brows deepening. "Screaming at one another. The two people who loved each other best in all the world. It was terrible. Why, Mr. Boothe told Peggy she would never marry if she didn't study to become more womanly, like her sister."

"You were afraid the murderer was Peggy," Lydia murmured. "All along that's what you suspected."

"But Peggy actively encouraged her brother to employ me," objected Rees, although he knew sometimes the people most eager for his services were the guiltiest. He hoped Xenobia would lose that frightened expression.

"She is fond of me," said Xenobia. "She didn't want me to hang."

"And you of her. So you were afraid that, because Peggy and her father quarreled," said Lydia briskly, "she must have killed her father." Xenobia turned anguished eyes to Lydia and nodded.

"If she murdered her mother and he guessed, well, she would have had to. Yes?"

"But if she did not murder her mother, she had no reason to kill her father," Rees said, wishing he had more comfort to offer her. For a moment they sat in an unhappy silence. Then Xenobia jumped to her feet.

"But I am forgetting my manners." She pulled a crock from the back of the cupboard and put a number of small biscuits upon a plate. She made coffee for Rees, and, while it perked cheerfully over the fire, she sat down beside Lydia. Rees sat in silence at the table, his thoughts entirely occupied with Xenobia's disclosure. He did not listen to the women and could not have said what they discussed. The memory that kept recurring to him concerned his first visit to the Boothe home, for the averil, after Mrs. Boothe's funeral and interment. After Dickie's little scene, Jacob had approached his daughter. Surely, if he'd known Peggy's secret, he would have been angry and upset. But she had been the angry one, not her father. Maybe Peggy blamed her father for her mother's death.

Rees knew he was still missing something, and it nagged at him like a sore tooth.

When they left the house an hour later, Lydia said, "I saw that look on your face. Despite what you said to reassure Xenobia, you really do suspect Peggy. Don't you?"

Rees hesitated but admitted the truth. "This looks bad for her," he said. "She had reason, or thought she had anyway, and opportunity. I still don't know what she might have used for a weapon, but she knows the tunnels as well as any man. And then there is Isabella Porter. We know none of the Boothe children wanted to see their father with another woman."

"But Georgianne assured us that neither she nor her cousin served as Jacob Boothe's mistress," Lydia objected.

"Yes," Rees agreed, looking down at his wife with affection. "But none of the Boothes heard that assurance. And they probably wouldn't believe it anyway. You remember, I told you Matthew and Betsy were terrified that their father's liaison would bring shame upon the family. And might cost them their inheritance besides. And that urchin Al said he saw a woman entering the house not too long before the fire began."

"I don't want to believe it of Peggy," Lydia said in a small voice. "She always seemed so honest, so straight."

"Yes," Rees agreed. He felt his mouth twist. "I don't like even considering such a possibility. But she has the passion and the strength of will. Certainly more than Matthew," he added. "That boy came near to fainting at the sight of blood. But Peggy, well, she didn't like seeing it, but she did not weaken. And she brought me down into the tunnel and watched me examine the floor. She could give Matthew lessons in character." Despite himself, he admired her.

"I hope you're wrong," Lydia said. Rees heard the grief and regret in her voice, as well as the fear that he wasn't. "But if you're right, well, Peggy is beyond the reach of Salem's law now. Any punishment meted out to her must come from God and her own conscience."

"She'll never be able to come home now," Rees said regretfully. Maybe she would prefer that, but he doubted it.

When they approached Mrs. Baldwin's Emporium, Rees saw an unusual number of people, mostly men but with a few women scattered among them, congregating around the front of the store. "Something's happened," he said, increasing his pace. Panting, Lydia tried to keep up. As they neared the store, they saw that the front door was closed. Rees tried the knob. The door was locked. Realizing that the crowd was even thicker in the lane, by the back fence, although some of the onlookers were beginning to drift away, Rees broke into a run.

He pushed his way through the throng, right up to the back gate. This too was locked. "Mrs. Baldwin," he shouted at the top of his lungs. "Mrs. Baldwin." In the pause that followed, he turned around and bellowed at the people behind him. "Go away. Nothing to see here. Get out of here, now." Folding his arms, he stood sentinel right in front of the gate.

Lydia panted up to stand by his side.

Rees heard the bar across the inside of the gate being removed. He turned and pushed the gate open, urging Lydia inside before he whipped in after her. He shut the gate behind him and, taking the bar from Mrs. Baldwin, threw it across the hooks.

Then he inspected Mrs. Baldwin. She was weeping. "What happened?" Lydia asked, putting a hand upon the other woman's arm.

"I tried to stop them," Mrs. Baldwin said. "I really did. But they took Annie."

Chapter Thirty-one

The clamor of the crowd outside the gate, almost unnoticed before, suddenly seemed very loud. Rees stared at Mrs. Baldwin.

"Who took Annie?" he asked. "Who?"

Lydia shook her head at him. "Let's get you into the kitchen," she said to Mrs. Baldwin.

"You've got to go after them," Mrs. Baldwin cried. Putting an arm around the woman's shoulders, Lydia drew her toward the house.

"You must tell us the whole story first."

They crossed the yard and went in through the back door. While Lydia pressed Mrs. Baldwin into a chair, Rees, who could not sit still, filled the teakettle with water from the jug and put it over the fire.

"Who took Annie?" Lydia asked.

"That harlot from the Black Cat. The one with one eye missing. Claims she's Annie's mother. You know what she said?" She lifted tear-filled eyes first to Lydia and then to Rees. "That it was time for Annie to earn her bread. Annie didn't want to go. She ran away screaming but that big black man caught her and threw her over his shoulder like a sack of grain. He carried her out of here, screaming and wailing. She drew a crowd, I'll say that, and some of the men were willing to help Annie. But that black slave drew his sword and took Annie out of here. And then some of the people wanted to come in and look around, so I shut the gate and locked it." She stopped abruptly and wiped her eyes with the back of her hand.

Lydia turned to look at Rees with frightened eyes. But her voice, when she spoke to Mrs. Baldwin, was soothing. "My goodness, you have had an exciting morning."

What if Annie had been his daughter? What if Jerusha had been taken? Rees began to shake with anger. "I'm going to get her back," he said, wheeling around and heading for the door.

"I'm going with you," Lydia said.

"You can't go," Mrs. Baldwin argued, fixing her gaze upon Lydia's belly. "You might get hurt." Rees saw a moment's consideration speed across Lydia's face, but then she shook her head.

"I must. I'll appeal to One-Eyed Mary, mother to mother, and maybe I can persuade her to release Annie."

Rees did not want to waste any more time in pointless talk. He spun around and marched toward the door. Lydia pushed herself to her feet and hurried to join him.

Only a few people remained outside the gate, and most of those were trying to discover the cause of all the excitement. Rees and Lydia thrust their way through them and trotted down the lane toward the harbor. "I pray Annie is safe," Lydia said.

"They don't have a long head start," Rees said. "With any luck, we'll reach the house before anything happens."

It was still too early for much custom, and the man who usually guarded the door was not there. Rees tried the knob; the door wasn't locked. Raising his eyebrows at Lydia, he cautiously opened the door. The hall was empty as well. But they both could hear Annie's screams coming from somewhere on the first floor. Without a second's thought, Rees raced to the back, Lydia panting at his heels.

Annie's cries drew them to a solid door tucked under the stairs. Rees opened it and saw the girl, tied to a chair in front of a desk, her face scarlet with her screams. "You are being foolish," One-Eyed Mary was saying, her tone calm but unyielding. She was garbed in an ice blue gown of the finest muslin that molded itself to the body underneath. "What will you do to support yourself in the streets? Same thing you'll do here. So you might as well stay here where you are safe, well-treated, and protected." Her eye widened when she saw Rees appear in the open door. The bodyguard began to turn but Rees, the beast raging within him, hit the man with all his strength and saw him fall. Shaking his stinging hand, Rees turned to Mary.

"Let Annie go."

"Mr. Rees," Annie cried in relief, struggling against the restraints.

The Madame smiled without humor. "Well, well, another applicant for my daughter's favors. It will cost you to become her protector."

"That's not how it is," Rees began, crossing the floor and kneeling beside Annie's chair. He took out his pocketknife and began sawing at the silk ties binding her ankles and wrists.

"We'll take Annie someplace safe," Lydia said from the doorway. "She'll be educated and trained in all the housewifely arts. And she will not have to sell herself."

One-Eyed Mary's laugh expressed a lifetime of broken promises. "I don't believe you. And don't tell me you're acting from good Christian charity; I've seen too many pastors in here."

With a gasp, Rees cut through the final strand and watched the restraints fall from Annie's torso. She leaped to her feet and hurled herself into Rees's arms.

"I wasn't sure you'd come."

"Of course, we would," Rees said. The feel of her baby fine hair against his chin reminded him of Jerusha and her younger siblings. And what if Lydia bore a girl, his daughter? The intensity of his rage and loathing made him tremble, and when he turned to stare at Mary she took an involuntary step back.

"So," she said with a toss of her head, "which of you is interested in my Annie?"

"She's just a child," Rees bellowed. He'd never struck a woman, but the urge to hit Mary was almost overwhelming.

"We are parents," Lydia said at the same time. "I know a place where Annie can go. They are celibate there. She'll work and work hard, I don't deny that, but it is good, honest work." And then, to Rees's astonished admiration, Lydia stepped forward and put her hand on the woman's wrist. "Do you truly want to see your daughter live this life? Especially when she doesn't want to? She has a chance."

To Rees's disbelief, tears rushed into the Madame's eye and begin rolling down her cheek. "But it's not such a bad life," she protested. "Not here, anyway. I could protect her."

"From the streets, yes. But we'll bring her to a place where she will be as safe and much happier. If she isn't, why, she can return to you. No one will stop her."

Mary hesitated. The bodyguard rose to his feet rubbing his jaw. Rees put Annie aside and moved around so he could keep an eye on the man. He was not black, as Mrs. Baldwin had said, but a dark brown. His head covering had come off. Although the bands that made up the turban were beginning to unwind, he put it back on. Scowling at Rees, he said, "I can kill this man for you, Miss Mary."

"No, Mustafa, I think not." She eyed Rees and Lydia with her good eye. "Bring chairs for our guests, please, and see about refreshments." Another humorless smile. "It seems some negotiation is in order." Mary walked to the desk, every step an invitation. "Annie seems to like you, but she is young and naïve. Tell me about this paradise you plan to bring her to." Lydia began describing Zion, the Shaker community in which she had lived before meeting Rees. Mary listened without comment for several minutes. "It sounds too good to be true," she said finally, when Lydia paused for breath.

"They are good people," Lydia said. "And they won't force her to sign the Covenant and stay, if she doesn't wish to." She stopped. Rees noticed she said nothing about Billy.

With a clatter of crockery, Mustafa carried in a large silver tray, polished to a high gloss, and put it on the desk. Mary inspected the cups and pitchers. "Besides tea, Mr. Rees, I have Madeira. Would you prefer ale? Or whiskey? Or rum?"

"I'd prefer coffee," Rees said. "But ale is fine as well."

Mary nodded at Mustafa. "And tell cook some of those little cakes," she said. When Mustafa left the room and closed the door behind him, Mary turned her eye upon Annie. "What do you say, Annie?"

"I want to go with them," she said, lifting her chin. "I don't want to work in this house. I don't want to stay in Salem."

"Where everyone knows you're One-Eyed Mary's daughter," Mary finished. She paused, but although she said nothing Rees saw the struggle in her face. She loved her daughter, and Rees was surprised by a sudden flash of pity. "Very well," she said at last. She looked at Rees. "And how much are you willing to pay?"

As Rees, his sympathy evaporating, emptied his pockets upon the desk, Annie said, "You're selling me?"

"Of course. I'm losing not only a maid but also a future whore." She stopped when Annie burst into tears.

"You never loved me."

"Of course I did. I do." Mary paused again. This time her struggle lasted several seconds longer. "Oh, very well." She eyed the coins upon the dark mahogany. Besides the English farthings and pence, the tiny heap included a few new United States' copper pennies, a shilling, and two French sous. "It's not enough anyway. You might as well be a gift." Rees quickly scooped up the coins, before Mary changed her mind. William Boothe's deposit was almost gone, and if he did not pay the second installment Rees would need this money to settle his bills. "Gather up your things." Mary's voice caught and she cleared her throat. Annie hesitated, her mouth curved in a smile of joy although tears ran down her cheeks. Now that she knew she was definitely going, she was hesitating. "Go on now," Mary said. Annie looked at her mother once more and then bounded from the room.

Mary turned and regarded Rees and Lydia. "Please, sit," she said. Lydia collapsed gratefully into the horsehair chair positioned across the desk from Mary. Rees picked up the chair to which Annie had been tied and carried it to the front of the desk next to his wife. For a few seconds no one spoke. Rees took this opportunity to look around him. He thought that, despite the fine desk, the couch in its cover of Chinese brocade, and the beautiful Turkish carpet underneath, this room was as much a business office as Jacob Boothe's counting house. "This is my private chamber," Mary said, watching Rees's eyes wander. "I allow few inside that door."

"It is lovely," Lydia said. Rees nodded. Mary was a skilled businesswoman, but he couldn't find a way to say so without sounding offensive.

"All of this could be Annie's," Mary said.

"She can choose to return," Rees said, although he did not believe she would.

"I'm trusting Annie to you."

"Zion is as I told you," Lydia said, her tone sharpening. "Annie will be safe there."

A discreet tap upon the door signaled the arrival of Mustafa with another tray. Rees smelled coffee and cinnamon. No one spoke as Mustafa placed the plate of cakes upon the desktop and a tiny cup in front of Rees. He stared at it in dismay. He could easily drink four or five times that amount. Mustafa poured the coffee from a small flagon into the cup, put a small bowl of sugar chunks and a pitcher of cream in front of Rees, and then withdrew.

"You will find the coffee stronger than you are used to," Mary warned as she watched Rees add sugar and cream to the inky brew. Rees took a gulp. He gasped. The coffee was hot, but more than that he could feel it sizzling through his body. Like lightning, energy and fire both. He wondered if he would be able to finish this cup. "Mustafa brews coffee as he learned in his homeland," Mary said. Although she didn't smile, Rees knew she was laughing at him. She poured tea for herself and Lydia and took a cake. "And now, how is your investigation into Mr. Boothe's murder faring?"

"You know about that?" Rees said in surprise.

"Of course. Deputy Sheriff Swett is a regular patron." She showed her teeth to Rees in something that was not quite a smile and added, "He's not very happy with you. Anyway, there is very little that happens in Salem that I do not know of. I number most of the leading citizens among my patrons."

Rees wondered if she knew that Peggy had been accustomed to going about disguised as a man. He'd wager this was information Mary did not know.

"Did Mr. Boothe—um," Lydia stopped, her cheeks coloring. She didn't have the courage to ask if he'd been a customer.

Mary shook her head. "No, I'm sorry to say. He didn't frequent this establishment. Or any establishment, as far as I'm aware. But then, I believe he had a mistress. Not that that prevents a gentleman from availing himself of the services I provide."

"Matthew Boothe," Rees said, already certain of the answer. "Was he a patron?"

"Oh yes. A very generous man. He always brought little gifts for the girls. We haven't seen much of him, though, since he took on his new hobby—playacting." Her mouth quirked up as though she found the very idea of acting amusing. "Yet we saw more of Edward Coville, Matthew's cousin you know, until he sailed." She shook her head as though amused by the vagaries of men.

"What kind of gifts did Matthew Boothe bring?" Rees asked, bringing the conversation back to the topic. This Matthew sounded like a different person from the man Rees knew.

"Silk and cashmere shawls, jewelry and other trinkets. What you might expect from a young man engaged in the shipping business." She added with a trace of genuine warmth, "Yes, Matthew is popular with the girls. Pleasant, funny, and generous."

"He didn't have a favorite?" Rees asked. Mary shook his head.

"Not so far. He loved them all. I sometimes think his goal was to try out every girl in my house. Unlike his cousin; only Lottie would do for Edward."

A sharp rap sounded, and before Mary could invite the visitor in, the door opened. Annie hurried in, almost running. "Annie, please," Mary said. "You wait to be invited. And no lady gallops into a room like a colt." But Rees heard the tears under the reproof. Annie dropped the small canvas valise and went to her mother.

Lydia put her hand on Rees's and motioned to the door. They stepped outside the office so that mother and daughter could say their good-byes.

With the onset of dusk, the house was coming alive. Rees could hear masculine laughter and the clink of glasses from the parlor across the hall. Beautifully dressed young women were descending the stairs and disappearing into the parlor. Mustafa's fellow servant had taken up his post at the front door and as Rees watched, a gentleman entered. He handed his hat and stick to the doorman and disappeared into the parlor without looking around. A regular patron, Rees guessed. He couldn't help wondering if that man was married, had a family.

"May we help you?" A soft feminine voice drew Rees's attention and he looked down at two young women. The girl who had spoken was the taller of the two, brown-haired, with sultry half-closed blue eyes. But Rees's gaze was drawn to her companion, a small blond with full succulent lips. Although he knew he had never seen her before, she looked familiar.

"We're waiting for Annie," Lydia said, grasping Rees's arm in a possessive clutch.

Both girls examined her, particularly noting her belly and, without acknowledging her any further, turned their attention back to Rees. "Are you sure you don't want to visit for a while?" asked the brown-haired girl.

"No," Rees said firmly. He glanced at the blond again. "What are your names?"

"I'm Ruby. She's Lottie."

Rees's gaze sharpened. Was this Edward Coville's Lottie? "Do either of you know Matthew Boothe?" he asked.

"We both do," Ruby said. She smiled like a cat drinking cream. "He gave me this hair ornament." She turned her head so that Rees could see the gold pin, a blue stone flashing at the end, which protruded from the knot on her crown. "I also have a bracelet and ear bobs."

"I'm ready." Annie plunged into the hall. Her face was smeared with tears but she held her head high. Rees took the canvas sack from her and they turned to the door, Annie hurrying as though she couldn't wait to quit the place.

Chapter Thirty-Two

❧

By the time Rees and Lydia reached the gate, Annie was already through and hurrying up the alley toward the house. Light still streaked the sky, but in the lanes it was almost too dark to see. "Annie," Rees called. "Stay with us." He could hear the sharpness in his tone; the shadowy streets around the docks were no place for a young girl. But she increased her speed and soon disappeared into the gloom.

"The wages of sin are not death, but wealth, I guess," Lydia said. Rees looked at her, surprised by the sourness in her tone.

"Would you wear a gown like One-Eye Mary's?" Rees asked. He thought of the silk he'd been tempted to buy for her.

She laughed. "Of course not. That gown—well, she might as well have been naked. But it was beautifully cut and no doubt cost more than your yearly income."

Rees nodded involuntarily. That fine muslin alone was expensive. "But we have her daughter," he said and watched Lydia's expression soften.

"Yes, we do," she said. "I'd rather have my child than any number of gowns." She put her hand protectively upon her belly. Rees stopped and covered her hand with his. For a moment they stood together in silent communion.

"What I'm wondering," Rees said, when they continued walking, "is how Matthew could afford his expensive tastes. A gift like that hairpin . . ."

"That stone was a sapphire, if I'm not mistaken," Lydia said. Rees turned to look at her. He might have guessed the stone was a sapphire, but he did not know. Lydia sounded certain. Her wealthy background occasionally manifested itself in situations such as this, surprising him. He wondered with a little ache if she missed sapphire hair ornaments and silk gowns, luxuries he would never be able to provide for her. "It would have been expensive, for us anyway," Lydia said, unaware of Rees's sudden worry. He felt a little better that she had said "us." "Maybe it is just a token for Matthew."

"Perhaps," Rees said. In his view, Matthew was living beyond his allowance. Where was he acquiring the extra money? Although the boy had not proven to be John Hull, Rees wondered if Matthew had known about his sister, if perhaps she'd paid him for his silence. Maybe blackmail was the connection with the murdered sailor. Rees suddenly thought of Twig. Oh no! "Twig," he said aloud. With all the other crises surrounding him, he'd forgotten about the body in Twig's shed. Rees hoped the undertaker hadn't buried the body before Rees had a chance to inspect it. Tomorrow, he promised himself, first thing, he would call on Twig.

Annie refused to set foot outside the house, even to visit a tavern for supper. She ate a bowl of bread and milk at Mrs. Baldwin's kitchen table and then went upstairs. Rees and Lydia each ate a slice of Mrs. Baldwin's pie before following their charge to the room. Annie was already asleep in the bed. She did not stir when Lydia lit a candle and undressed. Rees pulled the chair up to the window and rested his feet upon the sill. In that uncomfortable position, he fell asleep.

He awoke suddenly during the night, something teasing at his brain. But the sudden jolt awake shook it out of his mind. All he could recall was that it had something to do with a painting, but of what, and where it hung, he could not remember. Although he tried to drag it back into his conscious mind, the thought resisted and finally he closed his eyes and tried to find sleep again.

Uncomfortable in the chair, he awoke at dawn. He put a handful of coins upon the table for Lydia and Annie's breakfast and set out for Twig's. Xenobia opened the door for him. "He's been waiting for you," she said, unsurprised to see him this early. "He's already in that barn, talking to the dead," she added with a grimace.

She allowed him to pass through the house to the back door. He crossed the yard, his shoes darkening as the dew saturated the leather. When he entered the shed, he passed three coffins, of varying sizes, ready made for some future inhabitant. The fragrance of the wood shavings did not disguise the stink of corruption.

The corpse lay upon a wide plank of wood with a canvas sheet as a shroud. Twig was stroking a coffin with a plane and the long curls of white wood dropped soundlessly to the dirt floor. "Came to see what you thought of the body," Rees said, dropping down to a stool. It did not sit quite right—one of the legs was shorter than the other two—and Rees suspected this was one of Twig's earlier creations. "Hope you haven't buried him yet."

"You said not to," Twig said, just as though he always obeyed Rees. "Come and look at this." He walked to the swaddled shape and, with a soft scratching sound, folded the cover all the way back to the body's ankles. Rees rose reluctantly to his feet. By now that greenish tone was spreading over the skin and the smell was ferocious. He took one look at the chewed eye sockets with their missing eyes and quickly looked away. "You're right," Twig said. "He was murdered with a sharp blade. Not a sword. Something square-shaped, about two inches in width. Must have been razor sharp."

"The same weapon that killed Jacob Boothe?" Rees asked.

"Probably. If not, as similar as don't matter." Rees nodded. He wasn't surprised. It was almost as though he'd guessed, right from the moment he'd heard about the body in the water, that it was connected somehow to Jacob Boothe. "The wound looks a little different," Twig added.

Rees bent over the gash, the edges a bloodless white and crenellated with bite marks. But the slash wasn't straight, a clean stroke. Instead, regular tears marked the edges. Rees suddenly recalled an episode from the War: a young British soldier in his fine red coat, stabbed by a bayonet as he fled from Twig, struggling to break free. Blood quickly soaked his coat and began pattering upon the ground. "Remember, Twig," he said. "That boy. The one you bayonetted. We tried to save him."

Twig nodded. "We took him behind the lines and removed his coat," he said. "We thought we could patch him up. But he died anyway, a few minutes later. How old do you think he was? Fourteen?" Rees nodded. So Twig remembered that incident too, although the memory seemed to rest more lightly upon him than upon Rees. Twenty years later, and the memory of that boy still haunted him. More now in fact, especially when he thought of David, now the same age as that boy.

"What made you think of him?" Twig asked, looking curiously at Rees with bright blue eyes.

"This wound exhibits the same signs of tearing." Rees stopped abruptly. After a pause in which he swallowed several times, he continued. "That explains the differences in the wounds between this sailor and Boothe. Boothe was surprised. He didn't have time to struggle or resist. Just in and out from the front, that was the sword thrust. His murder was carefully planned and cleverly executed. But this sailor, well, it looks almost impulsive. He was on guard, wary. When he tried to run away, the killer struck."

"He was stabbed from the back," Twig agreed with a nod.

"Boothe was pinned to the wall," Rees muttered. "This poor tar tried to break free and run."

"But he was caught like a fish on a hook," said Twig. Then he blinked, his mouth twisting, and looked sorry he'd drawn that particular analogy. Rees nodded. Both men were silent, the image of the sailor struggling against the weapon thrust that killed him hanging in the air between them. After a pause, Twig continued. "But why? That's what I wonder. What could this seaman have in common with Jacob Boothe?"

"I suspect he sailed upon the *India Princess,*" Rees said, staring at the body. "He probably saw something he shouldn't have, and when he tried to earn a few coins with his knowledge, he was killed in his turn. Can you tell if he was thrown from the docks or overboard from a ship?" Rees asked.

Twig shook his head. "But he was clearly a sailor, a longtime sailor. Look at the tattoos."

Rees glanced at the meaty biceps, each decorated with a blurry picture, and the tattooed rope around the sailors left wrist. Against the dark skin, the tattoos were almost invisible. Rees realized he had seen the compass on the right arm when he'd taken the body from the ocean but hadn't marked it. "He was stabbed and then his body was dumped into the ocean," Twig continued. "It was a lucky stroke for you that the tide swept this sailor into shore instead of out to sea." Rees didn't think it was a stroke of fortune. More like a murder committed in a hurry, and the body thrown into the harbor to dispose of it before anyone could see it. "Oh, and one more thing," Twig said.

Rees looked at him.

"He isn't African."

"What? Then why is he black?"

"Corruption turns the body that greenish black. Besides, he's been burnt dark by the sun. Very dark. Look at the hair." Trying to avoid looking at the ruined face, Rees obeyed. The corpse's hair lay long and straight upon the board. Rees stared at it for several seconds, trying to understand what he was seeing. He'd been so sure this was the mate from the *India Princess*. Finally he spoke.

"If he's not an African, then who the Hell is he?"

Rees started back to Mrs. Baldwin's with his mind churning. The identical weapon used in the murders of Jacob Boothe and the nameless sailor could not be coincidence. Were either William or Matthew familiar enough with the common sailors to be blackmailed? That seemed unlikely. And what about the killing of Isabella Porter? She certainly was not connected to the sailor.

But Peggy could be. And if Twig was correct about the time of death, Peggy could have been involved.

As Rees blundered down the street back toward Mrs. Baldwin's, oblivious to all around him, two men came up behind him and grasped his arms, one on each side. "The deputy sheriff wants to see you," one said. Rees realized that Mr. Swett had not forgotten Rees's humiliating comments in the tavern.

The men frog-marched Rees to the tavern for sentencing by the deputy. Swett looked Rees over and a smile curled the corners of his mouth. "Well, well," he said, "so we found you at last. I think a visit to the jail will teach you manners."

Rees considered offering the man money, but he had little of it, and anyway he didn't know if it would work. The deputy might accept Rees's few coins and still keep him in jail. And no one knew where he was. Rees had mentioned his plan to seek out Twig to Lydia, but she wouldn't know he'd been captured by Deputy Swett.

The deputy and his lackeys wrestled Rees to the jail and pushed him in. Laughing uproariously, they sauntered away down the hill.

At first Rees tried to attract someone's attention. But most of the good folk lowered their eyes and scurried away. Only a gang of boys looked at him, and they hurled clods of mud and other filth until he was forced to take shelter in a rear corner of the jail until they'd gone.

Then he spent several long hours leaning against the door waiting for someone, anyone, who he might know to appear. And at last he saw Mustafa coming up the hill.

"Mustafa," Rees cried out. The man looked all around. "Mustafa. Over here." Finally identifying the direction of Rees's cries, Mustafa warily approached the jail. "I want you to find William Boothe and tell him where I am."

"Oh, and he'll hurry over and get you out, will he?" Mustafa asked, eyeing Rees doubtfully.

"He will if he wants to find out what happened to his sister," Rees said. "Tell him I know about Peggy. He's probably in the counting house." Mustafa hesitated. "Well, go on. You wouldn't want me to tell your Mistress you could have assisted me, but didn't." Mustafa hesitated and Rees watched emotions play across the brown face. Mustafa had no love for Rees, in fact quite the opposite, but clearly feared his Mistress's wrath. And she had released her daughter into Rees's care.

"Very well," he said at last.

Rees settled down to wait. Now that he had done what he could to save himself, his thoughts returned to the body in Twig's shed. What thread linked the common seaman to Isabella Porter? Jacob Boothe? But what linked the merchant to this unknown sailor? Rees couldn't make sense of it. Round and round the questions spun until he was dizzy.

"Mr. Rees." The sudden shout jolted Rees awake. Rubbing his

eyes, he sat up on the hard bench. Questions with no answers had put him to sleep. William Boothe glared at him through the small barred opening in the door. "Wake up. What do you know about Peggy?"

Rees lurched upright and almost fell over; his left leg had fallen asleep and now it tingled and swayed beneath him. He must have slept a few hours for the sun was high in the sky. His stomach grumbled. "Find the deputy. I've done nothing wrong. He's angry because I accused him of accepting bribes." William's eyebrows rose. "He does so regularly," Rees said. "I believe your sister bribed Mr. Swett to free Philippe Benoit."

"Why would she do that?" William asked in disbelief. "She could not possibly have known him."

"She did know him," Rees said. It felt odd to realize that all of the investigation, all of the speculation in which Rees had been immersed these last two days, was still unknown to William Boothe. "You sister had a life outside your home," Rees said. "A secret life. And I'll be glad to tell you about that life, but not here and not now. Swett will not deny *you* when you instruct him to release me, not the William Boothe of the merchant Boothes. And if you want the identity of your father's murderer revealed, you will do as I ask." William hesitated.

"But why has it taken so long?"

"Too many secrets," Rees said. "And too many lies. It takes time to unravel that kind of knot." He paused and added with more sharpness than he intended, "I'll tell you everything, but not now."

William eyed Rees, the furrow between his brows deepening. "Do you know who murdered my father?" he asked.

Rees wanted to lie and assure William that yes, indeed he did know, but couldn't. "No, not yet," he admitted. "But I do know what happened to your sister Peggy."

"Whatever it is, I am sure it will bring dishonor to the family," William said in a frosty tone. He turned and marched away. Rees watched him go in consternation. Now what?

"Is he going to free you?" Mustafa asked.

"I don't know," Rees admitted. "Would you tell my wife?" He had not even a scrap of a piece of paper in his pockets.

"I am not your servant," Mustafa snapped.

"I know," Rees said, bowing his head. "But she doesn't know where I am."

"Very well," Mustafa grumbled. "This and no more." He disappeared into the crowd.

A passing street vendor provided a pasty, charging twice its worth. But Rees paid the sum requested; he was too hungry to argue. And although the pie was cold, the fat congealed, and the crust soggy, it was filling and Rees ate it gladly. Then he settled himself to wait.

Chapter Thirty-three

❦

"W ill?" Lydia appeared suddenly at the small grated window in the door. "Are you there?"

Rees leaped to his feet. "Lydia." It had to be at least noon, he thought.

"What happened?"

"I was set upon by the deputy and his lackeys. Mr. Swett has not forgiven me for accusing him of taking bribes." Rees looked at Lydia's shadowed eyes and her trembling lips. "I didn't mean to worry you."

"I wasn't worried," she said. "I knew you were planning to visit Twig, but I didn't realize it would be first thing this morning. And this . . ." She swept her hand over the jail's grille.

"I'm sorry." Guilt swept over Rees. "Swett's men grabbed me as I was coming home."

"Annie is distraught. She was afraid you'd abandoned us. And left nothing but a few coins on the table."

Rees reflected for a few seconds on Annie's experiences. She must think every man came and went, unreliable as the wind.

"I won't share Annie's fears with you," Lydia continued, pressing her face closer to the bars. "But she was inconsolable and I couldn't reassure her. Although I guessed where you'd gone, I didn't know for sure. And, instead of being in jail, you might have been floating in the sea. Or dead in the tunnels. I wish you would tell me where you're going instead of just disappearing." She paused and then added in a low voice, "What would you think if you awoke and I was gone?"

Rees jerked, his head snapping back as though he'd been slapped. "I'm sorry. You're right. I should have woken you. Or left a note at least."

Lydia nodded. "Good. Of course I know it wouldn't have changed this outcome." She clutched at the grille.

"Move along, mistress." At the man's command, Lydia glanced back over her shoulder and reluctantly released her grip. The deputy, his expression set in sulky lines, came forward with the large key and unlocked the door. William Boothe stood behind him. He glowered at Rees.

"I must return to the counting house for another hour or so," he said. "I've wasted too much time on this affair as it is. Tomorrow is Thursday. I'll work only half a day. Attend upon me at two-thirty in the afternoon and we'll see if you're able to make good upon your promise." He turned his gaze to Mr. Swett. "I don't want to hear of you putting him back in jail either."

The deputy nodded, Rees thought with some reluctance, and cleared his throat. "I'd like to hear his explanation, if you would permit it," he said.

William inclined his head in curt assent. "Very well." He bowed to Lydia and, turning, strode away.

"I look forward to seeing your show tomorrow," Swett said to Rees, adding with a smirk, "I daresay we shall all see what manner of fraud you are."

Rees did not respond to the gibe. Instead, he took Lydia's arm and walked stiffly away, his head held high. Lydia stepped away from him but did not release his arm. "You'll have to bathe," she said. "You stink." Rees sniffed his sleeve. He smelled nothing un-usual but thought he'd probably gotten used to the pungent stench that marked jails.

"Have you unraveled this puzzle?" she asked as soon as they were out of earshot.

"No," Rees admitted grimly. "I haven't. The connections bet-ween the deaths continue to elude me."

Annie must have been watching for them. As soon as Rees and Lydia entered Mrs. Baldwin's yard, the girl raced out of the house. "I thought you were gone," she wept, hurling herself at Rees. "I thought you'd left us."

"I would never do that," Rees said, awkwardly patting Annie's back. He looked at Lydia in dismay. "Help me," he mouthed at her. Smiling, Lydia moved forward and detached the girl from Rees.

"Everything is fine now," she said.

"We'll be going home in a few days," Rees said, catching Lydia's gaze. "I miss the children."

She nodded. "I do, too."

Annie wiped her streaming nose upon her sleeve. "I was so scared."

"There's nothing to worry about anymore," Lydia said sooth-ingly. "You'll begin your new life soon."

Annie hiccoughed. "He smells," she announced, looking at Rees.

"He does indeed," Lydia agreed.

"I'll take a basin of water into the barn and wash up," he said. "Then we'll go to supper. I'm famished."

He borrowed a kettle and a few rags from Mrs. Baldwin, whose nose wrinkled at his approach. Rees decided he would change his clothes as well, after his bath. He filled the basin with water from the trough. Warmed by the sun, it would be pleasanter to wash with this rather than the icy cold water from the well. He set it up on a mound of hay and stripped to his waist.

The water felt cool and refreshing on his hot skin. He scrubbed away the sweat and dirt from his face and had started on his neck and chest when Billy came into the barn. He dropped into a pile of straw. "Annie told me what you did," he said. "Thank you."

"It was very little," Rees said, his voice muffled by the rag over his face. "But you're welcome."

"And the map, it helped you?"

"Yes. I couldn't have reached Hulls Cove without it." There was a silence but Billy did not leave. Rees realized the boy was hoping to hear some details from Rees's investigation. He didn't intend to oblige.

"I heard you helped pull a drowned sailor out of the harbor," Billy said, grasping for another topic.

"You heard about that, then?" Rees said.

Billy nodded. "At the ropewalk." He paused. "Why did you risk your life for a drowned man?"

He wasn't drowned. But Rees didn't say that aloud. No one on the dock had noticed the sword wound, and neither Twig nor Rees had told anyone, so the news hadn't gotten out to the wider world. Until it did, Rees preferred to keep that piece of information a secret. Maybe the killer was still ashore and would make a mistake. "I'm assuming he's a sailor," Rees said now. "Because of the tattoos."

"What were they?" Billy asked. "Some of them have meanings."

Rees paused, trying to recall what he'd seen. "He had a rope tattooed around his right wrist and what I think was a compass on his right bicep."

"The compass rose," said Billy in a knowledgeable tone. "Many sailors have the compass rose. It's to help the sailor find his way home again. Did he have anything on his left arm?"

Rees hadn't looked specifically. He tried to picture the body lying on the board in Twig's shed. "Yes," he said, "I think so. And on his back was a ship, fully rigged."

"Then he went around the cape," Billy said. "Many whaling men have that; it shows they hunted whales in the Pacific."

"Billy." Mrs. Baldwin's voice floated into the barn.

Billy sighed. "I have to go in for supper now. But if you need any more help," he put a little bit of swagger into his voice, "just ask me."

Rees suppressed his chuckle. "I'll do that," he said.

But he sobered at he finished his wash and threw the water out into the yard. He had less than a day left to solve the puzzle.

When Rees entered the room to collect the two females, Annie greeted him with a fresh bout of weeping. He looked at Lydia in surprise. "Annie is glad to see you, aren't you, Annie?" Lydia said. She shot a quick warning frown at Rees. He nodded. Despite having sisters and having been married twice, the female heart was frequently too mysterious for him to understand. "Let's go to supper," he said.

"But what if my mother changes her mind?" Annie protested, still frightened.

"I don't think she'll bother you," Lydia said in a no-nonsense voice.

"We'll keep a sharp lookout," Rees promised. "Is she really your mother?"

Annie shrugged. "She says so. But who knows? I could be the child of one of her whores. I don't remember anything else but the house."

Through the gathering dusk, they walked to the Moon and

Stars. Rees nodded at the proprietress and the man behind the bar in greeting. The young serving girl looked at Annie, who was scarcely five years younger, and then looked around the crowded establishment before finally motioning the little family to a table close to the kitchen. "At last," Rees said as they sat down, "a decent meal." He had to pitch his voice loud and even then, with the roar of conversations all around him, could hardly hear himself. He leaned forward and said to Lydia, "What I can't work out is a connection between a common sailor and the wealthy owner of a merchant company."

"I saw Mr. Boothe sometimes in the tunnels," Annie said, her child's high voice piercing the bass growl of male voices like a knife. "He used the tunnels to go to the docks." Lydia shook her head warningly at Rees—it was time to choose another topic of conversation—but he ignored her.

"Did you see anyone else in the tunnels?" And then, realizing he had to be more specific, he added, "Going to the Boothe door, I mean. For instance, a man with wavy dark hair and gold earrings."

"I saw him once or twice," Annie said. "And twins. Brown hair. But usually I saw a blond man. I saw him many times."

Twins? Rees hadn't met or heard anything about twins. But a blond man—now, that could be Peggy Boothe in disguise or Matthew Boothe. Or both. Matthew might have used the tunnels to hide his visits to the Black Cat.

"Of course," Annie continued, "other men went to other doors."

"How did you see all this?" Lydia asked. "It's dark in the tunnels."

"Not everywhere," Annie said. "Some places there are glass panels, into gardens and such. And most of the men who travel though the tunnels carry a lantern."

"And you followed them?" Rees guessed.

Annie dropped her eyes to her hands. "Sometimes," she confessed. "I was curious. Especially about the men who came into the Black Cat."

Rees and Lydia exchanged a glance over the girl's head. "Tell me more about the tunnels," Lydia said.

"The wealthy shipping captains built them, mostly," Annie said. "Not sure why. All the warehouses are on the docks. Someone in the house was talking about plans to extend the tunnels."

Rees could think of several reasons, smuggling being only one of them. The tunnels allowed easy movement from place to place in secret. Something floated tantalizingly into his mind, but before he could grab hold of it, Lydia began speaking about the Shakers at Zion and the moment passed.

Sitting in a chair with his feet resting upon the windowsill did not promote the necessary comfort and serenity for sleep. That night, once again, after trying and failing to find a relaxing position, Rees gave up. He lit a candle and went to his loom. This was just plain weaving, with scraps, so if he made mistakes it wouldn't matter. The rhythmic strokes helped him to think—and he desperately needed to work though this knot. Who was the unknown seaman? What had Billy called the tattoo on the sailor's arm? The compass rose. Rees knew he had noticed that tattoo on someone else before he'd seen it upon the body, but he couldn't remember where. Just that he'd met this sailor on one of the ships tied up at the Salem docks; Rees recalled the hot sun blazing down upon his shoulders. But he couldn't remember which wharf, and when he tried to drag out the memory, it was the Boothe jetty and the *India Princess* he thought of. Everything brought him back to Peggy.

Rees's thoughts began to drift and scatter. Annie turned over in the bed and muttered something and he started, rising to partial wakefulness, and lifting his head from the warp. Time for bed. He blew out the candle and settled down in the chair by the window, his head resting upon his arms on the sill. Tattoos: they were the key. And Billy had said something else . . .

He awoke to Lydia's hand upon his shoulder. "You were mumbling in your sleep," she said. She held a hairbrush in one hand. Annie sat on the bed, one side of her head with combed hair, the other still bushy and tangled. Slowly, painfully stiff, Rees sat up. Both arms were numb. He stretched and tried to shake off the dream—the black sailor, sharp knives in either hand, had been pursuing Rees across the docks.

"It's this investigation," he said. He yawned. Last night's poor sleep had left him feeling light headed. "I've got some of it. But not all. And I don't understand the whys."

"Start at the beginning," Lydia suggested. She returned to Annie and started brushing the other side. "That's helped you in the past."

"I'm not sure what the beginning is," Rees said. "That's the problem." For a moment no one spoke. Rees splashed cool water from the basin over his cheeks. Lydia quickly plaited Annie's hair into a braid and tied a ribbon tightly around the end. "Let's go to breakfast," she said. "We can talk about it there."

He did not speak as they started down the stairs. Instead, he thought about Lydia's advice and his facile answer. Maybe, as so often had been the case, Lydia had identified the very strategy he needed to employ.

Rees walked to the Moon and Stars without speaking and ate his steak in silence while Lydia and Annie talked about the Shakers and Zion. He considered Jacob Boothe. Frequently, when he began investigating an important man like Boothe, Rees discovered a whited sepulcher with feet of clay. But not in this case. Rees had found nothing to contradict Jacob Boothe as the good and honest man everyone described.

But still, someone had killed him in a particularly brutal manner.

Murder for gain? That might explain the murder of a good man. But, although the youngest three children would inherit something, only William as the eldest would truly benefit from his death. Was William the murderer? Try as he might, Rees couldn't believe it. Both Betsy and Peggy had generous dowries already, and Betsy would wed a man equally as wealthy as her father. Peggy, well, she'd left her dowry behind, apparently without a second thought. That left Matthew, a young man clearly living beyond his means. Rees thought of Ruby's sapphire hairpin. Matthew had not been concerned enough to halt his freehanded generosity. Up until his death, Jacob had paid his son's bills. But now? Matthew must have found another source of income. Was Matthew involved in smuggling after all? Or perhaps he knew of Peggy's secret life and blackmailed her. Yet none of those explanations explained the carefully planned murder of Jacob Boothe.

Then there was Isabella Porter. Perhaps that was a crime of passion? Rees tried to imagine either Georgianne Foster or Isabella Porter inciting a violent passion in a man's breast. He couldn't. And anyway, a woman was identified as Isabella's last visitor.

And finally, Rees pondered the sailor, murdered in the exact same way as Jacob Boothe.

Lydia suddenly put her hand over his. "Will," she said. He looked down. He had finished his breakfast without conscious awareness and, in the fury of his cogitation, was clenching his napkin so tightly the linen was now a crumpled ball. "Are you all right, Will?"

"Just thinking," he said.

"I've spoken to you several times." She turned her eyes toward Annie. "You were frightening her."

"Sorry," Rees said. He smiled at Annie. "I lose all awareness of my surroundings sometimes when I'm thinking." He looked at Lydia. "I'd like to take a walk along the docks." Maybe that would help shake some inspiration loose.

Lydia turned to Annie and a silent communication passed between them. "I'll walk with you," Lydia said. "Annie will go back to Mrs. Baldwin's."

Rees nodded although he wasn't best pleased. Lydia would slow him down. But he couldn't refuse her.

They headed due east, cutting through the lanes and crossing the larger more important streets like Essex, straight to the harbor. As they passed near Georgianne Foster's home, Rees and Lydia paused to stare down the street at it. The front door gaped open and the path was unswept.

"It looks abandoned," Lydia remarked. Turning to her husband, she added, "We must ask Mrs. Baldwin to communicate with Mrs. Foster. She'll want to hear your resolution of the puzzle this afternoon."

Rees nodded without speaking. He wasn't sure he had a resolution yet. He would never have agreed to William's demand for a solution this afternoon if there had been any other way of escaping the jail.

They headed south, finally passing through the alley that ran by the Black Cat. He looked up at the windows, almost expecting to see Annie, abandoning her cleaning to stare longingly over the street below.

When they arrived on the docks, Rees turned directly toward the Boothe wharf. No ships were tied up there this morning. He stood by the water, picturing his conversation with the crew on the *India Princess*. Rees did not recall the tattoos on the African. And anyway, he was not the victim.

They walked north along the quay, Rees stopping from time to time to close his eyes and rummage through his memories of the place. But no recollection of the dead Jack Tar surfaced. At least, not until he left the merchant wharves behind and approached the Coville jetty. *Anstiss's Dream* had sailed a few days ago, but as Rees walked the empty pier the memories of his visits to the whaler popped into his head, as bright and fresh as if the vessel was still before him. He remembered the two sailors. The harpooner had been stripped to the waist as he cleaned the lethal tools spread out before him. And on his bronzed upper arm and calf, there had been the same tattoos Rees had just seen on the body in Twig's shed.

"You've remembered something," Lydia said, looking at Rees.

"The drowned sailor served on a whaling ship. On *Anstiss's Dream,* in fact." Rees turned to stare down into Lydia's blue eyes. "And Philippe Benoit told me he served on a whaler before John Hull hired him as captain of the *India Princess*. What do you guess that Peggy Boothe met Benoit through her cousins? Met him as Peggy Boothe, and hired him on in her masculine disguise as John Hull. What's more, and I'll speak to Adam Coville to confirm this, I'll bet my very soul that Benoit served on *that* ship, *Anstiss's Dream*."

"Benoit and the sailor you pulled out of the water would have known one another," Lydia said in agreement.

"Yes. And," Rees continued, his thoughts moving forward at lightning speed, "I wonder if they were partners. I was seen at the Witch's Cauldron. Peggy, as John Hull, set a little trap for me. I followed Benoit but there was another man I didn't see who came behind me. He was the one who hit me. And he must have been very strong. After all, they carried me away from the Boothe door to the tunnels nearer the Black Cat."

Lydia did not respond immediately, but her mouth drooped into a downward curve. "Oh dear," she said. "I think you may be right. Peggy's played a dominant part all the way through, from the very beginning, even though she had to do it disguised as a man."

"I'm just having a hard time imagining her killing her father. And not just because she couldn't, physically. I don't see her as a killer." He sighed. But with Philippe Benoit? Maybe. "And why Isabella Porter? Peggy never cared about her inheritance. I mean, she was always more interested in the shipping business, and that went to William." When Lydia looked at him with her eyebrows raised, he added, "It doesn't feel right. The timeline is off, for one thing. Jacob was murdered first. And. No, I'm missing something."

They walked in silence for a few minutes.

"I am beginning to tire," Lydia said, casting a glance around the busy dock. "Is there anywhere to sit down?" Rees looked down into her pale face. Shadows stained the delicate skin under her eyes and she was panting, one hand pressed to her side. Quickly he grabbed a small cask and upended it. He helped her lower herself upon it. While she sat and caught her breath, Rees hurried to one of the vendors plying his trade upon the dock and bought Lydia an orange. As he carried it back to her, tossing it up into the air and catching it on the way down, he remembered buying the handful of oranges during one of his first days here in Salem. Rees hadn't known Annie then, although he'd pitied the child. And Billy—Mrs. Baldwin had been so afraid then that Billy would ship out.

Rees squeezed his orange in frustration. Much of what he had as a solution to the deaths was nothing more than guesses, flimsy ones at that. But he had run out of time.

Chapter Thirty-four

Rees spent the remainder of Thursday morning arranging matters for his presentation to William Boothe. Mrs. Baldwin was dispatched to invite Georgianne Foster. Rees invited both Billy and the street boy Al to his explanation and then made his way to the Boothe counting house where he informed William that several interested parties would join them. William did not look happy, but he grudgingly assented. Rees had left him little choice to do otherwise. Deputy Sheriff Swett would also be in attendance, and Rees looked forward to a certain amount of gloating.

A messenger was sent to the Coville family. Although Rees was not sure they would attend, because of their estrangement from the Boothes, he thought they might be interested. The Covilles were connected, after all, through Anstiss.

At two, by Mrs. Baldwin's clock, Rees, Lydia, and Annie, who had refused to stay behind, left for the Boothe home. Rees had wondered if William Boothe would confine his unwelcome guests to the front hall where Jacob Boothe had held the averil for his wife. But no, the servant directed them to the morning room, where additional chairs had been brought in for the occasion. Betsy and Matthew already waited there. They had chosen to sit in the wooden seats set up before the fireplace. Matthew's expression shifted from a cocky grin to a frown of assumed seriousness when he saw Rees. Betsy's eyes were red-rimmed and she looked flushed and upset.

Rees's gaze went to the portrait of Anstiss on the wall by the fireplace and just above Betsy's head. How odd that Anstiss Boothe had been such a force in the lives of her husband and children and brothers, Rees reflected. A woman who had lived as an invalid for almost twenty years and whom he had never met had nonetheless been a presence in his investigation. Rees stared at the portrait for several seconds, trying to identify the nagging sense of familiarity. Of course, Anstiss had passed her blond beauty down to Betsy.

Rees just stopped himself from looking for Peggy. Her absence felt strange. He looked again at the portrait. Peggy had inherited her mother's coloring, but not the soft feminine chin or rounded cheeks. No, Peggy's sharp features were her father's contribution.

"She was such a lovely girl," Mrs. Coville said from behind Rees. He turned. Mrs. Coville was dabbing at her cheeks with a lacy handkerchief.

"I can't stand to look at it," Adam said gruffly, moisture shining in his eyes. He turned his chair so his back was to the portrait.

They hadn't brought Dickie, and for that Rees was very grateful. He'd been worrying about the boy's emotional reaction to the proceedings.

Xenobia and Twig sat together at the other side of the room, separated from the others. A young serving girl was handing round cups of tea for the ladies and whiskey for the men. She eyed Xenobia and Twig several times, uncertain of the proper behavior in this unusual circumstance. Xenobia was black, and a servant, possibly still a slave to the house. Twig took matters into his own hands. He stood up and took saucer and cup from the servant, and handed them to Xenobia. She stared at the floor, looking as though she longed to be anywhere but here. Twig glared around, daring the others to protest.

Rees refused the refreshments. His belly felt like it was on fire. He didn't think he had ever been so unprepared to discuss an investigation as he was now. He hoped that as he talked about the murders and began laying out the pieces of his solution, the reactions of the others invited to this gathering would fill the gaps and dispel any lingering uncertainties.

A light footstep outside the door and a faint gasp of hesitation heralded the arrival of Georgianne Foster. As she paused in the opening, Betsy jumped to her feet. "What is *she* doing here?" she demanded. "She has no right. She's nothing but my father's fancy woman." Her lips twisted.

"I'm not . . . I never . . ." Georgianne reddened and then went white to the lips. "I'll go then." Both Rees and his wife rose to their feet, Lydia several beats behind her husband.

"Stay," said Rees.

"Of course, you must stay," Lydia said, taking a few steps across the carpet to lay her hand upon Georgianne's wrist. Lydia turned a defiant and angry frown in Betsy's direction.

"She's here at my invitation," Rees said.

"But this is my house," Matthew proclaimed, jumping up to support his sister. "How dare you invite a woman like her into my house?"

"Like what?" Rees asked, his voice very quiet but so furious Matthew stepped back and fell into the chair. "You know nothing about her. I promise you, everything will become clear."

William came through the door and cleared his throat. Matthew removed his offended gaze from Rees and shifted it to William. "He brought Father's mistress," Matthew said, aggrieved.

"I agreed to allow Mr. Rees full authority in this matter,"

William said, "so he was able to invite anyone he chose." But he turned to look at Rees with his mouth pursed. With that expression, and dressed entirely in black, even to his waistcoat, he looked the very picture of a disapproving old Puritan.

"She was not your father's mistress," Rees said. "She simply knew him."

"Then she lived with my father's mistress," Matthew shouted, his loud aggressive tone causing the others in the room to shift and look away from him uncomfortably.

Rees looked at William. "I'll explain everything." He could only pray that was true.

"I look forward to witnessing that," said Mr. Swett, appearing behind William's shoulder. The deputy's coat was of as fine a manufacture as William's but dyed a bright blue. His breeches were tightly fitted, and as Swett came further into the room, Rees noted the bright jonquil silk waistcoat and the silver buttons sparkling at his knees.

"Please, sit," Rees said, gesturing around the room just as though he owned the house. William threw him a frown but said nothing as he crossed the carpet to join his siblings. The deputy found himself without a chair, unless he joined Xenobia and Twig. After a few seconds of indecision, he dragged that chair closer to Georgianne Foster and sat down.

Mrs. Baldwin and Billy arrived next, with the street urchin Al close behind them. He had made some effort to clean himself up. His face had been recently washed, although a ring of dirt framed his scrubbed cheeks and darkened his neck. William turned to look at Rees with his eyebrows raised.

"I think we need more chairs," Rees said, meeting William's eyes and daring him to protest. After a moment's pause, William signaled the servant and asked that he bring in some chairs from the breakfast room. An awkward silence ensued. When the chairs arrived, Mrs. Baldwin sat near Georgianne Foster—both ladies seemed glad of a friendly face—with the boys behind them. Al kept his gaze trained upon Rees.

"So," William said, "who murdered my father? Well?" His tone sharpened with impatience when Rees did not immediately answer.

"First of all," Rees said, "Jacob Boothe was not the only murder victim. Isabella Porter was also slain." Georgianne made a slight sound. "And a sailor was stabbed to death with the same weapon as your father." Rees's gaze went to the portrait of Anstiss on the wall. "A case might also be made, in fact, that your mother was killed."

"I knew it!" Adam Coville exclaimed, his right fist connecting with his left palm with an angry smack. "And no doubt that crazy sister of yours had something to do with it." He glared at William.

"Are you referring to my sister Margaret?" William asked, his tone icy.

"You know I am," Adam said. He shook off his mother's restraining hand.

"Cousin Peggy never behaved as a proper woman should, running all over town with messages given her by your father. And where is she now? Why isn't she here?"

Al stared at them, his eyes and mouth rounding. He turned to Billy and said in an audible whisper, "These are our betters?"

"My cousin Isabella behaved with the demure circumspection of a proper lady," Georgianne interjected, leaning forward, "and someone murdered her, too. I don't believe you can accuse Miss Boothe of anything on those flimsy grounds." Both William and Adam turned to stare at her. Some of the angry tightness around William's eyes eased, and he regarded Georgianne with surprised approval.

"Who is this female?" Adam asked, gesturing at her with disdain.

"My father's mistress," Betsy Boothe said. Darting a scornful look at Georgianne, Betsy added, "I would have thought he had better taste. She's nothing but a bluestocking."

"Maybe I am a bluestocking," Georgianne said. Her voice was low and calm, but Rees, turning to look at her, noticed the clenched knuckles bleaching white. "But I was not your father's mistress. And neither was my cousin, Isabella." She paused and added, looking from Betsy to William, "He loved your mother very much. He wanted her to recover her health more than anything else in the world."

Betsy sniffed audibly and Matthew leaped to his feet.

"Enough!" Rees's shout silenced everyone. Blows would be struck if he didn't intervene. "Shall we continue or do you prefer to quarrel? Matthew, sit down." With a defiant sneer, Matthew remained standing. "Fine. Let's talk about Peggy, shall we?"

"I refuse to believe she murdered my father," William said instantly. Rees acknowledged the comment with a jerk of his head.

"Peggy served as Jacob Boothe's secretary from her early teens." When Adam seemed poised to interrupt, Rees added, "Improper for a female or no. Doing so introduced her to shipping vessel owners, captains, and crew, and also instructed her in the workings of the shipping business. She kept his books and, in fact, she ran the daily operations. And she knew the tunnels, probably as well as her father."

"No, that's not true. She ran messages and handled his correspondence," William protested.

"But she was always his favorite." Matthew sounded sulky. "Who knew what she got up to?"

Rees ignored them both. "Yet father and daughter were estranged by the time of Anstiss Boothe's funeral."

"Surely you are not suggesting *she* stabbed him?" William was so white Rees feared he might faint.

"Whiskey," he ordered Xenobia. She jumped to her feet and hastened to obey.

"I don't know when Peggy set up her own shipping company, but it was in full operation by the time of her mother's funeral. She operated under the name John Hull. Since she was still assisting your father then, she was able to buy at least one merchant ship from the Boothe company, without her father's knowledge, I suspect, and give herself permission to use the Boothe wharf."

"You're wrong. She was only a woman. She couldn't . . ."

"But she did," Rees said. "This is not conjecture. It is fact."

"But why? My father gave her everything. And she has—had a substantial dowry."

"I believe she was trying to prove herself to your father, hoping he would leave his firm to her. But when she quarreled with him over your mother's care, he called you home to take over her responsibilities as well as learn the business. Fortunately for her, she already had her own fledgling company established."

Throughout Rees's explanation, William's mouth gradually tightened, and by the conclusion he was bereft of speech.

Adam Coville, however, stood up and shook his finger in Rees's face. "Her own company? You mean she was arranging cargo and buying and selling? Impossible."

"Mr. Coville, please," Rees said, motioning the other man back to his seat.

"She must have had help," William said. "Probably that Frenchman she ran away with. My sister was nothing but a pawn."

"Captain Benoit worked for her," Rees said in a dry voice. Thinking back to Benoit's manner when questioned about John Hull, Rees added, "I doubt he even suspected the ship owner was a woman. Peggy was careful to meet with him in disguise and only at night, in a dimly lit corner of a tavern. In fact," he admitted, "I didn't guess either. Not for certain anyway, not until I saw her in the boat."

"Was Peggy smuggling?" William gasped.

"Maybe," Rees said. William covered his face with his hands. "But I suspect she was using the house in Hulls Cove to store her cargoes—especially after you came home and began listing everything."

"It was Peggy who took the jewelry and the other things from the cellar," William said. Rees thought he heard relief in the other man's voice.

"Some of it, I think. It was, after all, her cargo. But not all of it." He moved his gaze to Matthew. The boy was smiling. "Where did you get all of your money, Matt?"

"Wh-what do you mean?" Matthew's smile vanished and his voice came out in a croak. "I don't know what you're talking about."

"I thought you might have been a smuggler," Rees said. "But you were just a petty thief."

William fixed his horrified gaze upon his brother. "You stole from me? You did. Don't even try to lie. I know when you're lying."

Matthew's expression changed from anxiety to resentment. "Father gave me only a tiny allowance, not anywhere near enough to cover my expenses," he said in a pained voice. "And when I asked for an increase, he said I should learn to live within my means."

"But he paid your gambling debts and tailor's bills." William sounded as though he couldn't believe what he was hearing. "As well as giving you an allowance."

"There were costs associated with the plays," Matthew said angrily.

"And gifts for the girls at the Black Cat as well," Rees interjected. He stopped, his gaze flashing involuntarily to the portrait on the wall as he recalled Ruby and Lottie. He began thinking furiously.

"Did Peggy murder Isabella, too?" Georgianne asked in a hushed voice, shaking with grief. "I know a woman was seen entering the house." Tears trembled upon her lashes and fell slowly to her cheeks.

Rees turned to Xenobia. "Would you fetch Betsy's shawl, please?"

"My shawl?" Betsy repeated.

"The one brought back by her father from China," Rees clarified. Looking puzzled, Xenobia darted from the room. "I was distracted by Peggy and her secrets," Rees said. "But it wasn't her secrets that mattered. Not entirely anyway. I heard about Peggy's quarrels with her father." He moved his gaze to William. "The quarrels that precipitated William's return. I thought that Jacob Boothe knew, or suspected at least, that Peggy was disguising herself as a man and running her own shipping company. But that wasn't the case. Peggy and her father argued over Anstiss and her care. That was important." Mrs. Coville suppressed a sob and Rees glanced at her. "Anstiss had been ill since before Peggy's birth. In constant pain, so I've been told, pain she treated with regular infusions of opium tea. Jacob wanted his wife back and denied her the medicine. Peggy couldn't bear her mother's suffering and fought with her father. He refused to yield, so Peggy brought the medicine to her mother. That disagreement, and Peggy's flagrant disobedience of Jacob's wishes, caused him to bring William home. Isn't this true, Xenobia?" He turned to the woman hesitating in the doorway. She swallowed and took a step back, clutching the scarlet bundle in her arms to her chest.

"Be careful with that," Betsy said sharply.

"Xenobia?" Rees said.

She nodded. "How my mistress suffered," she said. Something went dead in William's eyes.

"So, Peggy did murder Father," he said. "In revenge."

Instead of answering, Rees turned to Adam Coville. "You knew Captain Benoit, didn't you?" Rees said. "After all, he worked on a whaling ship first. One of your whaling ships, I believe. Probably *Anstiss's Dream*. Why, you or your brother might have introduced him to Peggy on one of her many trips to the warehouses on the docks."

Adam Coville seemed unmoved by these questions, but his mother's face was bone white, her hands clenched. Rees thought that only Adam's arm was keeping his mother upright.

"I employ a hundred and more men," Coville said shortly. "I can't be expected to remember every common deckhand."

"I think you know exactly who Philippe Benoit is. He told me he was a mate, not a common deckhand. He was experienced enough to sign on to the *India Princess* as the captain. And that day I met you on the wharf, you knew the names of every crewman I encountered." Adam pressed his lips together. "In any event, Peggy did meet Monsieur Benoit and, in her guise as John Hull, hired him as captain for her vessel."

"No doubt Peggy's emotions overwhelmed any sense or caution," Adam said, not troubling to hide his scorn. "She was attracted to him and so chose Benoit over the more appropriate men introduced to her by her father."

"So, you do remember Captain Benoit," Rees said. "He is a handsome devil, isn't he?" He thought that although Peggy's emotions were clearly engaged, her behavior had been both practical and logical. "He is also a skilled captain. The *India Princess* accomplished at least two successful voyages to the East."

"And I had Benoit in jail," remarked the deputy smugly.

Adam Coville rose to his feet and stretched out a hand to his mother. "Congratulations," he said to Rees. "You've solved the murder. Now my mother and I shall be on our way."

Rees held out a hand to stop them. "It makes a tidy story," Rees said, "and I've no doubt most of it is true. But neither Peggy nor Benoit murdered Jacob Boothe."

"But you just said . . ." William gaped at Rees.

Adam stilled, a vein beginning to throb in his forehead. "You're playing with us," he said.

"I am trying to lay out my investigation so that everyone understands. You see, I pulled a sailor from the harbor. He was a whaling man, and he was murdered in the exact same manner as Jacob Boothe, with a whaling tool. And he was from *Anstiss's Dream*." Rees pinned Adam Coville to the floor with his stare. "Where is your brother Edward?"

"At sea. On a whaling run, of course. You knew that."

"And when did *Anstiss's Dream* sail?" Rees could hear the coldness in his voice. William shifted slightly in his chair but no one else moved. "I'll tell you. *Anstiss's Dream* sailed on the tide within days after the murdered sailor was dumped into the harbor. The ship was seen leaving the dock."

"Of what are you accusing my brother?" A faint sheen of perspiration dotted Adam's hairline. "Of murder?" He dabbed at his face with a linen handkerchief. "That's ridiculous."

"I am accusing you both. It would have taken two to hold him. But he was strong enough to run. One of you stabbed him in the back. He realized, didn't he, that you'd used one of his whaling knives to kill Jacob Boothe, and tried to squeeze some money from you. I thought at first you might have used a harpoon to murder Jacob Boothe and the sailor, but the harpoon heads were the wrong shape. The wounds I saw were square, and the weapon had to be sharp enough to pierce a man front to back. But I saw that sailor cleaning his tools, and there was one in particular, a square one with a long handle, that looked to be the right shape and size. A strong man accustomed to handling such a weapon could easily run a man through."

Adam shrugged. "Let's say you've guessed correctly," he said. "I have no sympathy for a blackmailer."

"Was it you who stabbed Jacob Boothe?" Despite the gasps of protest, Rees continued inexorably. "No. I don't think you have the stomach for it. I think it was Edward. But you were there."

"You used a boarding knife?" William asked, sounding numb. "A knife used to cut blubber and bring it on deck? That's how you killed my father?"

Betsy cried out, and when Rees looked at her, he saw her sway and hold her hand to her mouth. Matthew, his cheeks as sallow as his sister's, said, "Please, stop."

Rees ignored them, his gaze fixed upon Adam.

"This is mere speculation," Adam said, his voice quavering as though he were trying not to laugh. "Why would we murder Jacob Boothe?" His eyes danced with mockery. "You have nothing against us." William slowly rose to his feet. His face was white.

"Because of your sister, of course," Rees said. "Anstiss. She's the one who mattered. Young girls marry and bear families of their own. But you blamed Jacob Boothe for taking her from you. Since you saw her infrequently, you persuaded yourselves Jacob was her jailor. That Anstiss was unhappy. And when she died, although she died from her illness, you were convinced Jacob Boothe had murdered her."

"She wasn't happy; she was never happy," said Mrs. Coville in a trembling voice. "She should have been home, with her family."

"*We* were her family," William said, staring at his grandmother in disbelief. "She was our mother. She belonged with us."

Rees kept his gaze upon Adam Coville. "Why did you send your brother Edward out to sea?" Rees asked. "Peggy told me how unusual that was, that Edward should go out to sea at his age. He'd already served upon a whaling ship, just as you had. Did you think he had to be gotten away? Were you afraid he would speak? Or were you afraid he would murder again?"

Adam, the slight smile never leaving his face, shook his head at Rees. "You are a wonderful storyteller," he said. "But you can prove nothing. Besides, wasn't my uncle murdered in the tunnels? Those are used only by the merchants, not by whaling men. I don't know them."

"But I saw you." Annie's clear soprano suddenly sliced through his baritone. Rees, who'd forgotten she was there, jumped. "You and your twin."

Adam laughed, a strained sound that persuaded no one. "Be quiet, you silly child. I have no twin."

"But Edward resembles you very strongly," Rees said. "I remember noting the similarity when I first met you both. At a distance, in the dark, you might be taken for twins, especially by someone who didn't know you."

"Did you kill my father?" William demanded of his cousin.

Adam shrugged. "Of course not."

"And my cousin?" Georgianne demanded in a trembling voice.

"Why would I bother with a soiled ladybird?" Adam sneered at her. "Even my uncle would not be so desperate as to choose you or your cousin, not after Anstiss." For the first time he sounded completely honest, his casual brutality bare and unforced. Georgianne went white. Rees's gaze went to Mrs. Coville. She was staring at the young woman with hatred. Georgianne pulled herself back into her upholstered seat, clutching the arms to tightly the skin on her knuckles looked ready to split. Mrs. Baldwin reached over and laid her hand soothingly upon Georgianne's.

"Jacob had already chosen his second wife." Mrs. Coville's lips were trembling. "He killed my darling to make way for *her*." The pronoun sounded like an epithet, it was hurled at Georgianne with such force.

"That's not true," Georgianne protested. "He loved Anstiss very much."

"Why else would he spend so much time with you? He did not appreciate my daughter." Mrs. Coville broke down into sobbing, harsh guttural cries that sounded as though they were ripped from her. Adam put an arm about his mother. Xenobia, without being asked, quickly poured a cup of tea and pressed it into the older woman's hands. She took a couple of shaky sips and fought for control. As Rees regarded the old woman, the last pieces of the puzzle fell into place: click, click, click.

"The motivation behind Isabella's death was the most difficult to unravel," he said. "After all, her connection to the Boothe family was tenuous at best: she was a cousin to Jacob's friend." He nodded at Georgianne. "She wasn't killed with a boarding knife, but strangled with a scarf. Xenobia, would you hold up the shawl." As she did so, Al leaned forward. "Did the woman you saw enter the house wear a wrap such as this?" Rees asked the boy.

"Yes. Except it was gray. But it had all those . . ." His hand made a motion in the air. ". . . things on it."

"Wasn't that Peggy?" Georgianne asked, her forehead furrowing. "I thought she—you said . . ."

"No," Rees replied. "The more I considered Peggy, the more I realized that of all the Boothe children, she had the least reason to fear her father's remarriage. She and William." He bowed at the other man. William did not return the acknowledgement. He seemed stunned into paralysis by the revelations. "Both Matthew

and Betsy expressed concern that they would lose their inheri-
tances. One of the first things Matthew told me was that after
William's share, which was the bulk of the estate, and the dowries
for the daughters, the remaining percent was divided equally
among the children. If Jacob had fathered a child with another
woman, that child would—or could," Rees amended, "demand a
portion. Peggy didn't care about that. She was earning a substantial income of her own from her shipping business. Betsy and
Matthew, however, would be made poorer."

"Another heir would beggar us," Matthew said with feeling.
He did not realize the implications of his careless words until all
eyes turned first to him and then to Betsy. She gulped. All the
bright vivacity fled from her face, leaving it pale and frightened.

"But I didn't . . . I would never . . ."

"I agree. The lady seen entering into Mrs. Foster's house was
dowdy," Rees said, adding with some asperity, "I couldn't imagine you ever appearing less than fashionable. In any event, you
and Peggy both had been out driving with Mr. Morris during
the time in question. So I concluded that neither you nor Peggy
were guilty, and that Isabella was strangled by someone else."

"Was it you?" Georgianne accused Mrs. Coville. "Did you
murder my cousin, an innocent woman?" Her voice rose with
mingled grief and fury. "She could be silly, but there was not an
ounce of harm in her."

"My father gave my mother a shawl exactly like mine, except
it was gray," Betsy said in a strange, hard voice. "And she gave
it to her mother. You." Mrs. Coville gasped and raised a trembling hand to her mouth. She looked every bit of her sixty or so
years.

"It was not Mrs. Coville," Rees said. "She rarely visited Salem.
I doubt she would have the strength anyway. And although I

blame myself for telling the Coville family of your and Isabella's existence, I never mentioned an address."

"It would have been an easy thing to obtain," Georgianne said, tears streaming down her cheeks. "Who else would think to murder Isabella? There are no other females involved in this sad tale."

"No," Rees agreed. "But there are men involved in amateur theatricals who would think nothing of dressing as women."

With a soft rustle, everyone in the room turned to stare at Matthew. Blood flooded into his face and then fled, leaving his cheeks a pasty white. "I didn't do it," he cried in mingled fear and outrage. "I admit I took a few things from the cellar, but that's all." Adam laughed. Rees wanted to punch that arrogant amusement from his face.

"I did consider you," Rees said to Matthew. "You were furious at the prospect of losing even a penny of what you believed you deserved. And you knew where Mrs. Foster lived. You'd followed her. But you aren't a killer. And," Rees looked around at the group, "both Matthew and Betsy knew of Isabella Porter's existence. They'd seen Georgianne and Isabella together and knew the difference between the two women. The person who killed Isabella thought *she* was Georgianne Foster." Rees's gaze fastened upon Adam Coville. He was still wearing his smile and staring at Rees as though none of this concerned him. "You wouldn't know, would you?"

"Me?" Adam chuckled. "Have you run mad, Mr. Rees? I told you. I don't care about Jacob's ladybird."

"But Edward did, didn't he? He felt as your mother does, that Jacob had chosen another woman over his sister, and had in fact murdered Anstiss so he could marry again. And he participates in amateur theatricals as well, doesn't he?" Rees glanced at Matthew.

"He—" Matthew cleared his throat, "He does. Did."

"It would be an easy thing to borrow a silk wrap from his mother, as well as a hat."

Adam flung a glance at his mother, mingled horror and disbelief chasing away his supercilious sneer. "You're accusing my brother of strangling a woman?" His tone and his desperate pleading stare at his mother begged her to refute Rees's accusation. But she did not look up from her clenched hands. "Mother?" Adam's voice broke. Rees saw Adam's face change when he realized she'd known all along. "You knew?" She did not reply.

"An innocent woman," Rees said. "She wasn't even Jacob Boothe's friend, not really. Georgianne Foster was out that day." Adam tried to say something but could not force the words out. "You see, Mr. Coville," Rees added in a soft voice, "murder can become a habit. And it's easier with practice. You might see a difference between the executions of Jacob Boothe and the sailor and the cold-blooded murder of a woman, but to your brother, they were all the same."

"But a woman . . . a woman we didn't even know." Adam closed his eyes and took in a deep breath. Rees could see Adam building up his defenses, brick by brick. "Of course, you have no proof," he said at last. "No eyewitness of the actual crime. And certainly no confession. You have nothing." He turned to his mother. "We are leaving." But he made no effort to help her from her chair and did not offer her his arm. Everyone in the room remained silent as they watched the Covilles depart. Even Swett seemed stunned.

Rees fixed his gaze upon William. He looked as though he'd aged twenty years, his shoulders rounded with the weight that had descended upon them. He raised his eyes and met Rees's. William believed the explanation—and Adam's reaction was as good as a confession. And Rees, staring at the anger beginning to break through William's shocked numbness, decided he would not want to be in either Adam or Edward Coville's shoes.

"So," William said, "Edward is the murderer?" His voice was empty, as though all his emotions were used up.

"Well," Rees temporized, "he strangled Isabella Porter, we can be certain of that. And he killed the mate, who had the temerity to ask for money. I didn't realize it at the time, but I saw the mate in the Witch's Cauldron buying drinks for all the crew. He said he had come into money—I should have guessed he was talking about blackmail money. I think Edward held the knife that stabbed your father. But it was Adam who planned it and helped. Someone would have had to hold Jacob." He stopped abruptly, hearing a gasp behind him. "It wasn't only Dickie who thought Anstiss had been stolen away. The entire family thought so. And when she died . . ."

"They blamed my father," William said.

Rees nodded.

William looked at Mr. Swett. "I will need your help. They can't be allowed to get away with this."

Swett's mouth curved down unhappily but he did not protest.

As Matthew and Betsy joined William, Rees backed up until he felt the chair at the back of his knees. He sat down, suddenly very tired. He had done what he had contracted to do; it was time to go home.

Rees turned to Lydia and Annie, but before he could speak, Twig called to him. "Will?" His voice sounded unusually tentative. Rees looked at his old friend questioningly. "We are getting married." Twig gestured to Xenobia. "Will you come for the wedding?"

"You and your wife, of course," Xenobia said quickly.

"Of course," Rees said. "But what about . . . ?" He motioned to William. "I mean, are you free?"

"I will let Peggy's Letter of Manumission stand," William said, raising his voice over Betsy's sobbing. Matthew was patting her shoulder and looking as though he wished he were elsewhere.

"They're free to marry." He regarded Rees with a direct and steady look. "I owe you more than any sum of money I could pay."

"For what?" Betsy wailed. "No one will ever want to marry me now."

"Mr. Morris broke the engagement," Xenobia explained in a low voice. "He said there was entirely too much scandal in this family."

"But I saw him escorting one of the Derby daughters," Twig said, "so I think he decided to marry in his own class."

Rees eyed Betsy. He did not doubt she would marry soon and marry well; she was so beautiful. But he could not imagine living with someone so self-absorbed. It would be like marrying ice: hard, inflexible, and always cold. A sudden shiver overtook him. Benoit had won the better of the two sisters, and Rees hoped he appreciated it.

"There's one more thing," Rees said, turning his attention back to William. "These lads, Billy Baldwin and Al . . ." He gestured at the street urchin.

"White," Al put in helpfully. "Alfred White."

"They want to go to sea. Can you make a place for them on one of your merchant vessels?"

"Of course," William said, bobbing a little bow. "You have solved three murders. It is a small thing to hire cabin boys." He looked first at Billy and then at Al. "Come to me at my place of business on Monday."

"He's only fifteen," Mrs. Baldwin said.

"Not a baby," Billy said with a scowl.

"Don't worry," William said, looking at the boy's mother. "I'll make sure he's well looked after."

"Thank you," Rees said. With a satisfied sigh, and feeling that everything had been resolved, Rees turned to Lydia.

"Is it finally time to go home?" she asked with a smile.

"Yes," Rees said, nodding. "Funny. After meeting Peggy, I've been thinking a lot about Caroline. They have much in common." He sighed. "It's time to deal with my sister. And I can hardly wait to see the children again. I missed them."

Nodding, Lydia took his arm and gestured at Annie. "Let's go home then."

6/15